The Cycle Unbroken

Aspen Ireland

Published by Aspen Ireland, 2022.

THE CYCLE UNBROKEN

First edition. February 2, 2022.

Copyright © 2022 Aspen Ireland.

ISBN: 979-8201667641

Written by Aspen Ireland.

This one's for all the

people who encouraged me

to keep on writing.

I - In Which a Goddess is Freed

THE NIGHT WAS DEEP and moonless, clouds masked the stars, and the bare branches of hundreds of gnarled trees stretched into the air like thousands of bony claws.

A shadow flitted through the woods, his shape feline and dark one moment before Shifting into the form of a man, over and over again as he traversed the rough terrain. The trees seemed to reach for him as he ran, and there were many times where he had to stop to unhook his heavy cloak from the reaching branches.

Most of his face was obscured by the cloak's hood, but one detail, a scar that cut across the corner of his mouth, pulling it into a terrible mockery of a smile, glowed pale in the dark. He was wearing armour of hardened leather, simple, but strong, and cut into squares held together by tiny loops of metal, for the sake of freedom of movement. Despite the autumn chill, his clothing was thin linen, and he had a broadsword hanging by his hip.

He was ready.

His form rippled as he Shifted again, his panther taking control, the great, black cat springing over a tangle of roots before bleeding back into his human form again.

The bushes blocked him from sight for a moment, but in a second he stood again, pulling up short before his destination, his breath hitching, his heart pounding.

A monstrous tangle of golden wire wrapped into a fortress-like cluster of metal and roots rose before him, like a nightmare in the dark.

The man smiled, his face twisting, and he knelt before the tangle. His voice was rough, metal dragging over stone.

"My Lady. Finally, I have found you." he murmured, and an unearthly, screaming laugh echoed from the twisted metal cage as a form slipped up to the bars.

The woman who appeared from the depths, her skin made of dark, writhing shadows, her eyes as black and bottomless as her shifting skin, her hair a stark white that hung in a long, smooth sheet around her face, laughed.

"You *chose* to find *me*?" she asked, her voice no more than a rasping whisper, but carrying much further than it should have been able to. "As if that could possibly be true. And which of my brothers and sisters sent you?" she asked him, a bitterness and a bite creeping into her otherwise emotionless voice.

The man smiled again. "None of them, Lady Chaos." he told her, and the woman, the goddess, smirked back. "You are a fool, then." she hissed.

A fool to whom I believe that I will soon owe a great debt.

"Remove your hood and let me see your face."

The man complied, and she laughed. His skin was a dark brown, hair long and inky black. And his eyes - His eyes had slitted pupils, the irises a strange shifting hazel-green. His ears were oddly pointed at the tips, lendinding him an elvish look, but his teeth offset the image. His canines were too sharp to be human, tapering into wicked points.

"A werecat?" the woman murmured, her head tilting to the side in an eerily bird-like gesture. And then she laughed again, the noise sending a chill down the man's spine. "And your name is...?"

The man's gaze flickered down to the ground before drifting up to meet the woman's steely eyes. "Kir." he said, raising his chin a bit. "Of the Southern Clan. Second in line for the title of Chieftain."

Lady Chaos's eyes burned with a fierce intensity. Her hands gripped the golden bars a little tighter. "Second in line... You must have a fine life then, little werecat. What could have compelled you to seek me out?"

Kir of the South swallowed hard, then dared to smile. "Perhaps not as fine as one would imagine. You see, Rane, the South's Chieftain, is younger than me. They took the title at the will of my mother, the Chieftain before them. She did not trust me, nor my father, with the power."

His face twisted with rage and pain at the memories that accompanied the statement. "I came to you because I have heard of what you did to the West. An unknown conquest. I discovered it when one of I went to them, as an ambassador, for a meeting. I saw the death, the destruction, and I heard of what you were offering. I heard that you would spare me and *my* people if I came to you, and offered my clan to you, if only you would let us live when you take Erathien as your own. I heard that you would reward those who followed you. So I came. For the good of Erathien."

Chaos smiled. "You are brave, Kir of the South. You are wise, to come to me. I can save you. I can give you the power that your mother stole out from under you. You must only do one thing for me."

Kir nodded eagerly, and the goddess noted the look or reverence, fear, and the lust for power shining in his eyes. She would use all of his weaknesses against him.

But for now, he would make the best of pawns.

"Come closer, little werecat, and free me from my prison."

II - Dreams

Four Moons After the Escape

EVERYTHING STILLED around him. Everything spun to a stop. For a moment, every detail of that second was suspended in time around the werecat boy.

The way that the warm blood felt, dripping down his blade and onto his fingers, dark trails attesting to all that he had done that day... Everyone he had killed.

The way the stars looked, glinting down at him as if in spite.

I am so sorry.

The way that the black-eyed, shadow-skinned woman stared down at the boy, her booted foot planted on his chest, her long, thin fingers clasped around the hilt of her sword, the tip of it planted directly over his heart.

The way the silver wire, twisted around the slim braids that framed her angular face, glinted in the moonlight.

The way that a dark smile curved the corners of her lips.

The hungry light that shone in her eyes.

The words that she said, in a sweet-as-honey tone. Honey, mixed with shards of glass.

"My daughter will be glad to have your soul, boy..." She said, her cold smile broadening with every word. "And she will have it in time... But first, you belong to me."

And he knew then that this was all over.

The boy wasn't going to survive the night.

He waited for the blade to drive home, for Death's face to loom above him, for everything to end.

Instead, a dense fog swept in, blanketing everything, until he could no longer see the weapon hovering above him, inches away from ending his life. It was blinding.

A dark form moved in the fog, and it slowly cleared away to reveal the vague form of a woman standing before him in the mist. It was not the shadow-woman, but a new figure. She wore a gown, and her arms were outstretched, but that was all that he could see.

He stood, facing her, and stepped forwards, but with every step he took, she receded equal distance back into the fog. She planned to stay indistinct.

Coren! *The voice echoed loud in his ears, and he tried to muffle the noise, but to no avail. It was not coming from the woman, but rather inside of his head.*

"What..." he started, his voice weak, as if he had not spoken for years. "Who are you?"

The only response was the whistling of the wind that swirled the fog before him, obscuring the woman even further.

He blinked in disbelief. When he opened his eyes he was... Home. But a twisted version of home.

The surroundings were grey and cold, and werecat screams echoed through the air. The fog had thinned to mist - no - smoke, and the lady was gone, replaced by his band. Their howls of pain, fear and bloodlust rang out crisp and clear, despite the fact that their figures were blurred around the edges. Flames flickered around their dancing, frantic feet.

Find her! Protect your people.

Lin cried out, "Coren! No! You'll be killed!"

"Our people are being killed! I need to be here!" He screamed back.

"What are you doing? Cor-" Sioch's voice morphed into a scream as a shadowy creature lunged for him, it's black form wisping in the air. Lin was there in an instant, her blade slicing into the creature, inky blood spraying everywhere.

"I need to be here for you!" he yelled again, and he ran, trying to find the person he'd been sent to protect. "MYR!"

THE BOY'S EYES SNAPPED open. He was sweating, and breathing hard, his chest heaving. The nightmares. They were coming more often now.

The dream was always the same. The starry night. The eerie woman. The blood.

Calm down. You are perfectly alright. It is always just a dream. Just a dream.

He shivered, closed his eyes, laughed softly to himself, his sharp canines grazing his bottom lip. Always the same dream, and always the same thoughts running through his head afterwards. *Maybe just a dream. Maybe not.*

Looking around, he sighed, sat up and stretched, his fingertips brushing the tentpole above his head. Letting himself relax, he slumped a bit, replaying the nightmare over and over in his head. It was so realistic, felt so real, and yet he was sure that he had never seen the woman before. If he had never seen her before, then where was that image coming from? There was no rhyme or reason to it all. It just seemed like one big elaborate joke.

Perhaps there was a *malefica*, a witch, out there, who had decided that it seemed like fun to be messing with the mind of an eighteen-winters-old boy.

Maybe, if there were any witches left...

Snorting at himself, he snatched up his quiver from the floor, stringing the bow, and then strapping them to his back. Then came his twin knives. He clipped the sheaths to his belt, one to his left and one to his right, and checked to make sure that his leather armour was buckled on correctly.

One could never be too certain, after all, especially since the Guard had reported seeing a Southern patrol on their side of the border.

It had been six golden autumns since the Twenty-Years-War with the Southern Clan, which had taken his father, and many more, and yet the South still acted as if they were the ones who had won, as if they owned the North.

He shook his head, and then pushed his way outside, the tent flap creaking gently, the stiff fabric bending, and the frost covering it cracking and falling away.

The air was crisp and cold and wonderful, and the boy smiled, taking in the world. Everything was dusted with a thin layer of snow that would surely melt within the hour, but that hinted at the oncoming winter.

Looking away, towards the woods, the boy smiled to himself. Then he looked back at his tent, and the sea of identical ones that stretched out around it.

A sudden, unexpected pang went through him, one that made him press a hand to his heart, and inhale sharply, coughing on the icy air.

There was an uncomfortable feeling that something was off. That he shouldn't be there. That something was very wrong.

He shifted from foot to foot, hesitant to make a move, and cast a quick gaze over everything, trying to make sense of the wrongness.

At first glance, everything seemed in order.

The central tent rose, bloodred, above the sea of smaller ones, and the boy let out a breath, the warm air steaming around him. He looked just to the side of the red tent, and shook his head, thinking of his Aunt Myr, and her wife, Lana, surely still asleep in their little white one.

His gaze wandered across to his cousin's respective tents. Lindara and Sioch, the twins.

Lin was a deep sleeper, and never awake until later in the morning. Sioch was the early riser, preferring to get a fire started early, but even he didn't seem to be awake.

And then on to one last tent - his Aunt Khara's. Lin and See's mother. The woman who had taken care of the boy since his mother had died and left him alone. Her tent, at first glance, seemed in order -

Until his gaze snagged on a small detail.

A pang went through his entire body. The front tent flap was hanging open. In this chill, so early in the morning. His entire body tensed, and his catlike eyes widened. Khara was a sweet woman, gentle, but paranoid. She would never have left her tent open like that, even if she was simply getting something from inside.

For a moment, he could have sworn that he had seen a shadow flitting across the heavy canvas of the structure, and the pang and the chill intensified. Something *was* wrong, it was not just his thoughts wandering away from him.

Khara.

Something had happened to Khara. The woman who had cared for him, held him as he sobbed after he had been told that he was an orphan, that his mother, the storyteller, all vibrant life and grace, was dead.

He looked to the woods again, just for the briefest of moments, wishing himself away from the situation, before a memory hit him hard.

"Remember, darling, to always do the right thing, even if that could mean placing you in harm's way. Remember that these people are the only family that you will ever have. Love them, care for them, long after I am gone, Coren."

The boy's grip on the pommel of his knife tightened as he remembered his mother's last words to him, before the plague that had swept through the camp not long after the war had killed her. *Always do the right thing, love.* How many times had she said that to him?

He gritted his teeth, and shook his head, and then began to run.

Something was wrong. Something had happened to his aunt, a person he loved. He couldn't just walk away from that. His gaze fastened on that tent, he Shifted, his form rippling as he let the lion wash away his human form, and his massive paws pounded the frozen ground, a frenzied heartbeat breaking the silence.

THE BOY SHIFTED BACK to his human form as he approached the tent, padding down the row of canvas structures on silent feet, the air prickling on his skin. That sense of pure *wrongness* was stronger now, and the boy shivered again, drawing his knife and tensing his body, ready for something to strike him from any direction. He would be ready.

Slowly, he crept past his cousin's tents, and for a moment he considered waking them. After all, this was about their mother, and his aunt. But as soon as the thought crossed his mind, he shook it off.

They should sleep for as long as they could.

And then Khara's tent was in front of him, the flap disappearing into the darkness inside. The boy bit his lip, lightly, so that he wouldn't cut himself with his sharp teeth, but the pressure was enough to get him to move, his knife drawn, towards the tent. He stopped before entering, scanning the outside, and his eyes widened for a moment.

The knots. They had been cut, right next to the tangle of fiber, on the left side, all the way down. Cut, not untied. Someone *had* been in Khara's tent. He took a deep breath, and looked around one last time.

If he had not been so unnerved he would have seen the dark red, perfect oval prints on the inside of the canvas, where someone had left a mark when they gently pulled the canvas aside.

He would have seen a figure, seemingly made out of shadows, insubstantial as smoke, with burning coals for eyes, peer at him curiously before smiling darkly and melting away into the grey of the woods.

He would have seen the single, scuffed footprint, toes outlined in the frost outside of his aunt's tent.

He would have expected what was coming.

This was not a simple robbery.

This was murder.

III - A Story, Part One

IN THE BEGINNING, BEFORE *the world, there were nine gods and goddesses. Siblings who held the power to create, and destroy, in their hands. Soon, they would have a beautiful, terrible legacy: Our world. But before Erathien, there were just the nine. Nine beautiful immortals.*

The eldest was the most powerful, all dark eyes, and the bite of steel. She was like a drawn weapon. Never resting, always ready. Vengeful, cruel, and sharp. Nothing escaped her. Every wrong, however small, was remembered, held against the others. They called her the Nameless One. The Forgotten Goddess. The Fallen One. She was Lady Chaos.

And while Chaos brings many things - plague, wars, vices - she bears but one fruit: Death.

The dark goddess had one child, a deity like herself, and this child was called Illira. She ruled the place beyond our world. She was the empress of the Void. She was Death.

Death and Chaos are not alone, of course. There must be balance in our world, and so came the other gods.

They say that they held court, once, before they left our world.

To Chaos's right was Death. To her left was Life:

Lord Micha, god of the earth, of living things, patron of our Southern neighbors. He is everything we see around us. The earth we stand upon is his gift to us.

Beside Earth sits Water, a beautiful woman as fickle as the seas. Lady Nyx, giver of the water that quenches our thirst.

Then Air, the skies, the winds, the storms, patron of the West. Lady Ria, provider of the air we breathe in each passing moment.

The last god to Chaos's left hand is Lord Duman. God of the seasons, of change and rebirth. Lord of the cycle, the never-ending, spinning wheel.

The final three sit beside Death. They are named: Varien, god of time, Titor, lord of peace and family, and lastly, our Lady of the Stars, the night and the light, dark and the day, and all the in-betweens.

Lady Kinaar. Our patron.

That is all. Those nine. They created our world, and then... They disappeared.

"What happened to them, Mammah?" The little boy's voice broke the spell that the words had woven. His mother stroked his head, soothingly, running her fingers through his sandy hair.

"Oh, child of mine. A long, long time ago, there was imbalance in our world. It rocked Erathien to its very foundations, and the gods? They vanished. Some say they died that day. Some say they sleep. Some say that the gods still walk with us. No one truly knows, and if anyone once did, they would have passed on many, many years ago."

The woman smiled to herself, softly, and then patted the boy's shoulders, sighing.

"But those stories are for another night, Coren, my dear. Sleep tight, now. I'll see you in the morrow. I love you."

The little boy was too tired to protest her leaving. He just allowed himself to be tucked in, and kissed on the cheek.

"Love you too, Mammah. Til the morrow..."

IV - In Which A Murder is Discovered

THE BOY STEPPED INSIDE the tent, slowly, stepping lightly, his boots crunching on - Ice? No. His heart stuttered.

Broken glass.

The boy hesitantly took a match from the pouch at his hip. It took him three tries, fingers trembling, but in the end he managed to light the lamp hanging from the tentpole, nerves and adrenaline humming through his body...

The blackened match fell from his numb fingers.

The remains of another lamp were scattered across the floor, mixed with the blood of a woman he loved like a mother.

A simple knife, much like his own, was dripping obsidian-black blood into the earth, speared point down into the dust at the edge of the raggedy carpet.

And, in the pale, flickering lamplight, lying on the bed, was the corpse of a woman.

The boy screamed, the sound tearing at his throat, and collapsed to his knees, broken glass digging into his knees, through the layers of fabric and thin leather pads.

"Aunt?" he whispered into the dark. "Aunt?"

Not again. Not his mother, and his father, and now his aunt? The people that he had dared to love, taken, one by one. Who was next - Myr? The twins?

Again, and again, and again. Bad news.

Khara was lying on her pile of furs and blankets. Her eyes were wide, glazed but scared and *furious*, her mouth gaping open grotesquely, as if frozen in a tortured scream.

The boy shook his head.

No. Nonono. He swallowed hard, and bit his lip again, a fang sliding through skin this time, the pain bringing him back to himself.

No. This couldn't be happening.

He reached out a shaking hand, to pull back the covers, revealing a bloodied mess. A knife, not that of anyone he knew, all silver and gold, was driven through the breastplate of her slept-in armour, having slid through the hard leather as if it were air.

Blood had spilled out around the wound, soaking the woollen clothing she wore, and staining the leather, already drying to a dull, macabre brown in the chilled dawn air.

It was impossible to tell how long his aunt, his mother's sister, the mother of his cousins, the people he loved most in the world; his caretaker and almost-mother had been dead. Her skin was cold to the touch as he gently closed Khara's eyes.

Tears spilled down his cheeks, and he only vaguely heard his name being called, through the fog in his mind.

DEATH WAS THERE. SHE was always there. She had curled her tiny, child's fingers around the dying woman's, she had pressed a kiss to her cheek, convincing the woman to come with her.

And now she sat in the dark corner of the tent, deep in the Veil, the gauzy, magickal in-between betwixt life, and the Void.

She knew what had truly happened to Khara of the North. She knew who had commited the crime. She had seen everything.

And now the goddess watched the boy crumple with cold eyes, chillingly used to the rawness and pain the end of a human life brought.

Why, mother? She asked no one, knowing that the goddess who had sent the assassin, aiming for a different target, couldn't hear her.

This death, a death that had come so long before it's time, became just another tally to add to the list of wrongs.

V - A Story, Part Two

ONCE, THERE WAS NOTHING. And then, from that nothing, came the gods. And they created a world, lonely, underneath a bright sun, and twin moons.

That world is ours. It is called Erathien.

Seven gods shaped it, lovingly. They gave it all it needed, and more. Light, dark, water, air, earth, change, time.

One goddess sat forgotten, watching, clutching her baby girl close. Her younger siblings forgot her. They left her, alone in the dark, and she watched for hundreds of years, raising a girl who did not seem to grow.

They had completely forgotten about her. And she watched. She watched and something dark writhed inside of her, gnawing at her, and hatred blazed in her dark eyes.

The girl, her daughter, Death, was raised by this hate, and the two, oh, they were fearsome.

The world below kept on spinning, changing, and the seven other gods, they loved it. They gave the people gifts, and soon, the world was full of beautiful life.

The elves, capable of harnessing the elements. The Fae, strange and other, dangerously beautiful. The werecats, like us, shapeshifters, hunters. Humans, able to do so much, able to use magick.

It could have gone on like this. In peace.

But the Forgotten Goddess... She had been waiting too long, hate stewing in her blood until it poisoned her being, and rage overtook her.

This was when she descended to Erathien, and this was when the great cycle began.

"Keep going, Mammah! Please!" The little boy pleaded, not at all asleep. He tugged on his mother's sleeve, and she laughed.

"It's late, Coren. You have to sleep!"

"Mammah! Please! Just a while longer."

"Tomorrow night, lovey. I promise."

VI - In Which There is A Power Struggle

"COREN!" LINDARA CRIED, stepping inside the tent. She was tall, as tall as the boy himself, with warm brown skin and black, wavy, bobbed hair. Her intense green eyes glittered. "Coren, are you all-"

Her gaze wandered to the bed, her mother's bed, and she broke off. Her words twisted into a pained mewl, a sound that shook Coren to the core.

Seconds later, a boy stumbled into the tent, blinking the sleep from his wild, terrified, dark eyes. Sioch.

"Lin." he whispered into the tent, his posture expressing the pain that his *comitis*, comrade, partner in battle, was feeling. He responded aloud to something his twin must have thought. "Dead? Lindara -"

And his gaze fell on the blood. All that blood.

"Oh, my Lady of Stars." Sioch murmured under his breath. "Mother." Carefully, as if walking on eggshells, as if he were going to break the ground under his feet into a thousand bright shards if he fell, or trod too hard, he stepped across the glass-scattered ground, the hundreds of tiny fractured pieces reflecting the dimming lamplight like a million tiny stars.

Sioch knelt beside his sister, tears suddenly welling in his dark eyes. "My Lady of Stars." he said again, burying his face into Lindara's hair. "Mother."

Who did this? Who would do this to my family? Coren swiped at his eyes.

A small sound came from the entrance to the tent, and there - Gods have mercy - was the Chieftainess of the North. Their Aunt Myr.

She was fully clothed and armoured, her fingers tight on her rapier's hilt. Her long brown braid was coiled into a bun, and held in place by a silver net. A dark, finely worked leather band rested on her brow, clearly displaying her status.

"Kha-" She broke off when she caught sight of the dead woman. Her already pale skin grew even whiter.

Myr's eyes, momentarily startled and scared and grieving, hardened.

"What in... *Blazes* happened here?" She was never one to let her true emotions show. Lana softened out the Chieftainesses sharp edges, but when her wife was not there - Myr was cold.

Coren shook his head slowly, slowly, and his cousins just looked up at her with wide, terrified eyes.

Odd, how this woman loved them so much, and they loved her back fiercely, but there was a bit of fear mixed in with that unconditional love as well.

"Gods, *stand*!" Myr snarled, before closing her eyes and swallowing hard. Despite how hard she tried, her eyes were glassy with barely suppressed tears.

The three rose, shakily, holding onto each other, and exited the tent. The frost in the air stung against their wet cheeks, and bit at their throats.

"My sister - Who -?" Myr said.

It hurt. It hurt so bad. To cry. To hear the breaking voices. It made it hard to breathe.

Coren vaguely heard his name called, and he turned his head to meet Myr's cold, watery gaze. "You discovered the body."

The body. It was so damn distant, and so painfully like Myr. She couldn't say, *my sister*. She couldn't even say *your aunt*.

"Yes." he said, his face still blank, a practised mask. Shock was making his head spin, and oh gods, he still couldn't *breathe*.

"She was just as she is?" Myr demanded. Her face was almost as blank as his own.

He shook his head, slightly. "I touched the blankets. The lamp."

A crowd was starting to gather, murmuring and exclaiming about the cut-through knots, and the murder, the broken glass and the tears.

There was a rustle, and some shouts, as five armoured werecats shoved their way through the crowd. The Guard had arrived.

The Head of the Guard, an older woman with long, grey-streaked dreadlocks named Kortana, shouted an order, and the other four began to disperse the whispering crowd.

The woman came forward, and executed a curt bow from the waist to Myr, her Chieftainess, before getting down to business. "The first to discover the dead woman?"

Myr hesitated for a moment before responding in a clipped, formal tone. "Coren of the North."

Kortana nodded sharply, her dark eyes gleaming with an un-friendly edge that made Coren's skin crawl. The werecat gestured to her squadron. "Take him in for questioning."

Myr's brows drew together. "You are taking the boy into cus-tody?"

"Yes, Chieftainess. He was the first to find the body, and it is -" Kortana began, practically rolling her eyes at Myr, who snapped:

"Yes, I am aware, Kortana! But he is the nephew, and adopted son of the murdered. I cannot see that -"

Kortana cut her off, drawing herself up. The dangerous light in her eyes had only grown stronger.

"Chieftainess, I am aware of the familial connection, but I am the Head of the Guard, and, with all due respect, I do not take orders from you when it comes to killings and trials. Only in battle. I am a member of the Council, and we voted you into office. I understand that this is your family, but you cannot let family come in the way of your duties to the North." Kortana's tone was snappish, and Myr looked very, very angry. The tension had suddenly grown.

At the sound of Kortana's barbed words, Coren shrank away, wishing he could fade away into the woods. His pulse was roaring in his ears now, and the near-giddiness of shock was quickly morphing into fear.

Myr and Kortana had been rivals for as long as Coren could remember, competing for positions, for glory, for respect.

Myr had won the greatest battle eleven years before, at the age of only eighteen summers, winning the vote and becoming the youngest Chieftainess that the Band had ever seen. She had then led the North to victory in the Twenty-Years-War, and Kortana's hatred towards her had only grown in the years since.

Now Myr raised her chin, and snapped out a terse response.

"Kortana, Guardian and Councillor of the North. I am aware that I am not your superior in most situations. I am aware of my position, and my duties. I am aware that Coren is of my kin, and I understand how you must believe that that connection is blinding my judgement, but I assure you that I would have the same objections in any situation. He is her *son*, Kortana. Surely you must understand that."

"And I do, Chieftainess. I also understand the laws of the North, and I understand that they take precedence. This is procedure, and procedure *will* be followed in *any* situation." The older woman's tone was cold and condescending.

"What are you implying, Guardian?" Myr said, her jaw tightening. Lin, Sioch and Coren were watching with terrible fascination.

Kortana's eyebrows rose. "If you are too blinded by the fact that you are family to -"

"I would ask you to stop." Myr snapped, raising a hand to cut off the woman. "Murder is -" She cut off, and she whipped around, her eyes wide.

Coren smelled the smoke and heard the screams only a moment later.

VII - A Story, Part Three

CHAOS CAME TO ERATHIEN, after so long, a being forgotten by her own kin, left out of the great game, stranded, alone. *She felt so alone, after being abandoned in the empty space for years, you must understand that.*

All she wanted was to be known. To be hailed and feared and respected, and to rule.

She came to Erathien, and the second her feet touched the ground, the seven creators knew that she was there, and they came, to see, and to learn.

Their curiosity, the fact that they did not know their eldest sister anymore, enraged the Forgotten Goddess, and the land around her turned charred and barren, a desert, devoid of life. Her fists clenched, nails digging into her palms, and black blood welled in the crescent wounds.

She showed them, then, what it was she could do. War toppled empires, cities. The elves retreated to the depths of the earth. The world was divided, borders were created, plague ravaged populations.

The Forgotten Goddess's gift was destruction, and it destroyed the peaceful world that her seven siblings had created.

Her daughter became a shepherd, the kind presence leading souls to the Void, to their beautiful after. The hate that Chaos had given her daughter? It simmered inside Illira as well, but it turned, not towards her aunts and uncles, but towards her own mother, as she saw what a monster Chaos truly was.

Death was the gift that Chaos gave her child, a terrible burden that Illira hated her mother for thrusting upon her. It weighed heavier and heavier with each passing day, as chaos reigned on the surface

The seven creators did what they could, but they gave up in the face of this awfulness, than would not cease.

Plagues and wars, and harm.

No one knows exactly how it ended.

Some say that it was exhaustion that ended Chaos, and now she sleeps.

Some say the gods had one final battle, and they died, blades in each other's hearts.

One story, the one I believe, says that a band of mortals, one of elves, Fae, humans, werecats, came together, and they fought. They were brave. They gave their lives, and they ended it all.

All we truly know is that the gods no longer walk our earth. But they are out there, somewhere, and they gave us all we have.

"That's the story? That's all there is?" The boy asked.

"Yes, Coren, that's all." His mother snugged in the boy's blankets, and stood.

"That can't be it!"

"Oh, love, it is! But..." She trailed off, absently tapping the side of her nose with a slender finger. A dark shadow crossed her face.

"What, Mammah?!" The boy sat up, his eyes huge. His mother crouched back down, and began to speak again, her voice dropping to a sorrow-heavy whisper.

"They say that it was the beginning of a cycle, you know. A terrible one. They say that some day the gods will rise again, and there will be a time of peace, before a great war, and then, the gods will fall again. They say that this will go on forever, until one final victory, when the balance is upset, when the world tilts too far, and everything slips into the Void."

"That's awful." The boy murmured after a long silence.

"It is, Coren, it is." His mother said, her expression sad. "I truly hope that that story is just that. A story."

VIII - In Which Lady Illira & Lady Kinaar Have A Discussion

DEATH, THE WATCHER, saw everything. She had seen her mother's shadowy creature slip into the tent. She had watched the blade plunge down. And now she watched the women fight, watched the amber-eyed boy's expression as he watched them argue over him.

Death saw everything, and she was not alone.

Another goddess, her form pale and tired, stood, hazy, beside Death, her auburn hair swaying in a nonexistent breeze.

"Hello, Aunt." Lady Illira murmured to the woman.

"Niece." The elder goddess greeted.

A long moment of silence passed, as they watched everything unfold like some terrible play.

They watched the Chieftainess spin around, picking up on the *wrongness* in the air a moment before anything happened.

They watched a bloodied guard run up, a hand pressed to their heart, where a deep red stain grew by the second, and they watched as they collapsed, after panting out a laboured sentence.

They watched the werecats spin into motion as they finally realised that the North was under attack.

"Why are you here, Kinaar?" Lady Death finally snapped, and the red-haired woman sighed. Her hazy shoulders seemed to slump.

Lady Kinaar, mistress of the night and the day, the light and the dark, patron of the North, looked down at the child-goddess.

"Ah, Illira. These are my people. I am waking. I must be here for them."

"You're lying." Death retorted, immediately, and Kinaar laughed.

"I am."

"What is the truth, then, Aunt?"

Kinaar's green gaze wandered to the amber-eyed boy, his dusty brown hair tumbling over his brow, his bow already in his hands.

"You see that boy, Niece?" She asked with a smile.

Lady Illira frowned slightly. "Yes, Aunt."

Kinaar smiled. She was starting to grow faded around the edges. "He has power, Illira. He's been blessed. He is mine, and he is perfect. This boy is the answer, the cure. He will be the one to end this damned cycle."

IX - A Battle Begins

THE CAMP HAD BEEN THROWN into total chaos. Flames licked at the tents, turning the dusty canvas to charred black. Screams rent the air, and the crashing sound of steel-on-steel rang in Coren's ears.

Flickering, ethereal shadow-creatures were everywhere, smoking darkly, their weapons ranging from utterly real steel, to flaming shadows, all of them wreaking havoc, and drawing blood.

Coren caught sight of a group of children racing in his direction, the beasts chasing them, hands grasping, almost catching the back of the children's tunics. He screamed something, maybe a warning, maybe a battle cry.

Who would do this to my people?

He jumped, Shifting, and Shifting again, and when he landed, his knives were embedded in the slowly dissolving shadow-creatures throats. The children had stopped dead, terrified.

Coren lifted a hand. "You're not safe here! RUN!"

They were all too glad to comply, and the woods swallowed them up. Coren prayed that they would find someone capable of keeping them safe.

His knives back in his hands, he turned and ran towards the heart of the battle. Werecats danced around him, steel flashing in the flickering firelight, arrows whistling through the air, and bodies doing insane acrobatics, pouncing, leaping, landing on light feet.

A chill ran down his spine as he remembered, with startling clarity, his dream from just hours before.

Their howls of pain, fear and bloodlust rang out crisp and clear, despite the fact that their figures were blurred around the edges. Flames flickered around their dancing, frantic feet.

He shook his head, shaking away the memory, focusing on the fight, trying to see where he was needed. The full Council had gathered in the centre of camp, but they were backed up into a circle, each confronting two or more of the shadow-beasts at once. Their faces were strained, and black blood dripped from their weapons.

Kortana was there, her fangs bared, her dreadlocks whipping around as she ducked and spun.

Myr, across from her with her back turned, was snarling. The creatures seemed to be targeting her the most, their long fingers reaching for her, eyes burning.

He was about to lunge forwards to help, when a hand closed around his upper arm, it's grip strong as iron. He growled at the unexpected, unwelcome touch, and half-turned, his knife ready. He stopped just shy of stabbing Sioch in the eye.

His cousin let out a high pitched, frightened sound, and Coren instantly drew back, but did not loosen his grip on the blade.

Lin cried out from behind Sioch, her voice shrill with fear. "Coren! No! You'll be killed!"

"Our people are being killed! I need to be here!" He screamed back. A shiver raced down his spine as he remembered his dream, realising what he had just said, knowing Sioch's response before the other boy said it aloud.

"What are you doing? Cor-" Sioch screamed as a creature lunged for him, it's black form wisping. His *comitis* was there in an instant, her kris slicing into the creature, inky blood spraying everywhere, and leaving dark marks on the wavy blade. She fingered the gryphon wing that jutted out from one side of the hilt, staining her fingers black.

Sioch, the pacifist, looked sick at the bloodshed.

"No time to explain!" It hurt, but he spun away from his cousins, and continued towards the centre, leaving them to fight their way into the woods. "MYR!"

The Council was weakening. One body was already slumped on the ground, the cat's fur stained red and black. Myr's arms were gashed, and her hair was frizzing out from the gold-netted knot, but she was holding her own, her rapier a blur. She looked up for an instant at the sound of her name being called, and her eyes flashed dangerously when she saw him.

His stomach dropped, and he opened his mouth to say something - Every word died in a snarl as a searing pain blazed through his shoulder.

Coren Shifted, and reared, his massive claws raking across the shadow-creature's face. It's ember eyes guttered out, and it shrilled, making his ears twitch back, and his fur stand on end. He lunged, and his jaws closed around the monster's throat.

The thing dissolved, and he spat, running a hand over his mouth, trying to clear away the taste of the sulfuric blood. He shook his head, and felt the back of his right shoulder.

His fingers came away red, and wet was already starting to soak his tunic. Coren swore under his breath.

There was another hiss as a creature evaporated, much, much too close to his head for comfort, and he turned just in time to see a woman - a stranger - kill another shadow thing.

"Don't - mind - me..." She panted, her voice an unfamiliar cadence. The accent was not one that came from using his native tongue, the Old Language, regularly. She was human.

The woman was back to back with him now, her black cloak and midnight blue gown swirling out around her legs as she wielded her balisongs, her long silver hair flying. She was an old woman, but moved as if she were decades younger.

"Human?" He ask-panted, stabbing a creature that dared venture too close.

"Not quite." She laughed, and blue light flared. The creature looming before her went flying, and Coren's eyes went wide.

The old woman looked almost demonic when she met his gaze, with blood, not just black but also red, smeared across her hands, some splattered across her right cheek.

But that was not the striking part.

What had shocked him was the woman's eyes. She was a *maleficus*. A sorceress. And her eyes were her Tell. Their colour shifted, and not in the shades-of-the-same-colour way. No, hers... Gold one moment, and blue the next. From emerald green, to lavender, to brown, to red. A shifting kaleidoscope of colour.

"You are a *maleficus*. I did not realise..."

Sorcery was a dead art. There had been no known practitioner of magick since, well. Since the Fall of the Gods. So how...

"So much time has passed. It does not surprise me that you do not know me. My name is Theodosia." The sorceress said, expression grim.

"*Malefica* Theodosia." The Old Language word was strange next to the very human name. Theodosia's eyes caught on something over Coren's shoulder.

He spun, and managed to send an arrow through the shadow-creatures head, killing it, seconds before it could impale him with it's spear. The action shot a bolt of pain through his shoulder, and he bit back another curse, shoving the weapon back into it's quiver. It was useless to him in this state.

"And you, werecat?" Theodosia didn't even seem fazed by the thing, just blinked and carried on.

"Coren of the North." He didn't miss a beat, just swapped his bow for a blade. Then he froze, meeting the witch's gaze. "Oh gods. Myr."

Suddenly, he looked terrified, remembering why he was there. "Myr! Apologies, *Malefica*. I must-"

"Go."

The *Malefica* Theodosia, awake after hundreds of years asleep along with the gods, stared after him, her head cocked.

"So. That is who you choose, Kinaar?" The sorceress gritted her teeth, inhaled, and killed the shadow-creature that had been lunging for her.

She began to race across the battlefield, back into the woods. The injured waited for a good healer. More blood would be spilled today, and she was better at healing than hurting.

She had only wanted to catch a glimpse of this new *pupillus*.

X - In Which Lady Illira is Angry

THERE WERE TWO GODDESSES standing in the killing fields that day. Standing in the ruins of a home, watching it change into something charred, bloody and dark.

One was a child. Taking souls by the hand and leading them away from that grim place.

The other was that child's mother, and she watched through hundreds of eyes, moved with thousands of bodies, killed, and grew stronger.

Chaos knew that her daughter was watching, even if she couldn't see the child, and Illira, in turn, knew that the Wraiths were born of Chaos. She recognised her mother's fury burning in each of the dark forms's eyes.

Her tiny fists clenched, as dark memories filled her mind's eye, memories of crumbling marble, and dying flowers, and a familiar laugh ringing through it all, as the power drained from her small form, leaving her still and cold and sleeping again, atop a stone altar.

Chaos was taking all of these lives, this home, desecrating this place for her own gain. Chaos had taken life from her. She had burdened her daughter with witnessing death and destruction every moment of her life. And then Chaos had taken her strength, used it for herself, somehow.

Fury rose in Lady Illira's chest, and she remembered her aunt's words, spoken only minutes before.

He will be the one to end this damned cycle.

An end to the cycle of falling gods and endless sleep. An end. After all his time. Gods.

Illira didn't want to wait, to not act and find that the cycle would continue as her aunts and uncles predicted. She wanted to step in, to act. To finally give her mother what she deserved.

End this damned cycle.

Death looked around at the destruction, and the fire, and the blood, and she knew that this was not the end of it. This was the beginning.

XI - In Which Coren Learns Something Interesting

COREN CONTINUED ON, hauling people to their feet only to watch them stumble away, their fear all too clearly visible.

Whether it was fear of the creatures, or fear of him, he did not care to know. His shoulder throbbed, and his clothing was sticking to his skin, the bloodstain spreading, his armour growing darker.

The Councillors were still standing, thank the gods, but the crowd of shadowy forms surrounding them was growing thicker with every passing second.

The noises rang in his head, starting a pounding headache. Every time he killed a shadow-creature, or came across a body, bile rose in his throat.

Coren had to force himself to focus on the distance between him and Myr.

Steps. Count the steps. Ten more.

"What in the hells are you doing here, Coren?" Myr screamed at him.

"He's a fool! Just like the rest of his family!" Kortana laughed, the panicked sound shrilling into a wail as a creature gashed her cheek. The wound instantly welled red. Coren sprang forwards again, hurtling into the circle. Before he could think, his hand shot out, a silver flash of metal streaking from his fingertips.

The thing, about to deliver a death blow, dissipated, Coren's knife clattering to the ground. His arm, outstretched from the throw, fell to his side, and he thanked the Lady that he could throw with his left as well as with his right.

Kortana did not have time to hesitate, or to come up with a response, the next wave was upon them. She could only mumble something, perhaps thanks, under her breath.

Coren didn't respond, just pursed his lips and snatched up his knife.

He was finally where he needed to be. Fighting by his aunt's side, helping her keep the beasts at bay. They were thick here, their forms twining together until it was impossible to tell one from the other. Their target was the Council, this was clear.

"My Lady of Stars. What happened?" Coren panted. His shoulder burned, and new cuts had been opened along his arms, where cloth peeked out from beneath his armour, where he had been too slow to dodge the creature's blows.

"What happened?" he repeated, when he got no response, and Myr shook her head, striking at a creature, her movements growing slower as she tired. Her forehead was streaked with black and red where she had swiped at sweat with a wounded hand.

"I do not know. The other sentries are dead." She panted, and Coren took her place, allowing her to fall back and breathe for a moment.

He Shifted, and clawed at another creature. They just kept coming.

"Why did you run into this fight Coren? You could be in the woods now! Safe!"

"Needed to be here." He said, tersely, sliding his blade between the plates of a creature's armour. It shrieked, and dissipated, glaring at him with ember-bright eyes.

"Why?" Myr growled, tussling with a shadow-creature, before killing it.

He was quiet for a long moment, the wails and clashing of steel from all around him echoing in his head, dulling his response.

"A dream." He said, and then repeated himself, louder. "A dream."

Myr shot him a look, and paid with a sharp elbow to her stomach. She gasped, and Coren was there, evaporating the guilty shadow.

"A - dream?" she panted, regaining her breath, and allowed him to fall back.

"Last night. I've had that dream before, but this time it was... different. Something told me - aeh - that you would need me." He had killed four more before Myr spoke.

"A dream, Coren? That seems more like a vision."

"Hah." He gave a derisive laugh, cut off with a short gasp as a creature drew blood in a slim line down his upper arm.

"Who sent you?" he snarled. He expected no reply, but one came, in a voice of smoke and crackling fire.

"*Our Lady.*" The shadow-creature spat.

Myr stumbled beside him. It was then that he noticed that the creatures had frozen, listening. The werecats panted, enjoying the almost-peace while it lasted.

A goddess? Coren bit back a maniacal laugh. The gods had slept dormant for years. They had been banished from this world, and had not walked the earth for millennia. And yet...

"The gods sleep!" Myr cried, disbelieving.

"Our Lady wakes." Another beast murmured.

"She grows stronger, she sustains us. The others wake. They shall not rise for ages to come, but before they do, our Lady will have taken this world. She shall rule with an iron fist." Two more chorused in eerie unison. Coren's face was a mask, but he was reeling, and reminded of his cousins. The stunning pain of this was beginning to strike him. He had been living in a state of shock for hours now. He had to push on just a while longer.

"Which *dea* is yours?" Coren demanded, his knuckles white on the slick handle of his blade.

"Lady Chaos." The creatures murmured, and the name rippled around the ruined, flaming camp. *"Lady Chaos rises..."*

Myr and Coren went white. They had heard the legends. They knew the tales.

"She will take Erathien while it lies unprepared. This world will be hers."

XII - A Story, Part Four

THAT WAS THE STORY of the beginning. But the story didn't truly end with that last telling. It didn't end with the Fall of the Gods. No. It is just beginning anew.

The gods fell, exiled to their realms, floating between the stars, sleeping beneath the sea, blanketed by dust and trees, present in the passing of time. They were weak, and tired. They were not dead, as so many believed.

They lived, and they dreamed. They slept.

Death was the first to blink open her dark eyes. She was always present, you know. Always is. She is distant, but kind, and every soul that returned to the Void strengthened her.

She woke, and she smiled, and she lived. She ruled alone.

Chaos was the dreamer. The closest to waking, hanging in the in-between. She knew that her daughter was awake. She knew that the young goddess was leaving her, abandoning her, and she was alone again.

It felt like a knife twisting in her gut, and the anger and the rage swelled. She had given this girl everything. A kingdom, a gift, a life, and the child had abandoned her. Just like her siblings had, all those millenia ago.

Chaos felt for the tie connecting mother and daughter, and she pulled on it, and she felt all of Illira's strength, and in one brutal movement, she took it. In that moment, the tie was severed, as if it were nothing but spider's silk. She didn't realise this, until it was far too late.

The temple that stands in the middle of the Void, the temple that holds every memory, every thought and emotion of the dead, the Temple of Souls, it crumbled then, with the theft of the power, and the severing of the tie. Marble gave way to cracks and dust, and the fields of bloodied poppies that grew all around it wilted, and died.

And Death fell. Her legs gave out, and she tumbled back into sleep, and was forced to climb the slippery slope to consciousness all over again.

Hate and abandonment fueled hate, and something dark sparked in Death's chest.

A destructive cycle began again, as Chaos rose, and gripped the bars of her metal cage, staring, hungrily, out into the night.

In the beginning, there were nine gods and goddesses...

XIII - In Which the Situation Begins to Look Grim

COREN'S HEART THUNDERED in his chest, and his grip loosened momentarily on the hilt of his knife. The shadow-thing used this moment of shock to lunge at him, and Coren could not react fast enough to evade the creature entirely. His knife fell to the ground, sticking blade-down into the charred, dry soil. His nose was bleeding. The thing had landed a solid blow, and he shrieked, Shifting and matching the blow. The thing snarled back, it's edges wisping out. They were strange. Ethereal, and yet all too solid.

Sent by a god. Born of a god.

Myr screamed, and yelled obscenities from beside him, and he turned to see a gaping, red wound in her side, centimetres from the edge of her breastplate. Coren ducked under his attackers outstretched arm, rolling, wincing, and coming up with his dropped weapon.

Coren attacked the creatures around him with renewed energy, rage coursing through his veins, his nose dripped, unchecked, and his shoulder screamed. Myr continued cursing at the top of her lungs, her face twisted. Coren set his jaw, looking around for the Council, wondering why they weren't standing beside their Chieftainess.

When he had found them, he tripped, and choked, his blade pausing.

The Council was scattered. They weren't fighting behind them anymore. And Falyn was lying, glassy-eyed and limp, a few metres away. A spear jutted from between his shoulder blades, and his fur was matted red.

Coren could not stand in shocked stillness for long. A new thing's whip cracking across his shoulders. The impact was somewhat muffled by his armour, but gods above, it still stung.

And Falyn was dead. It hurt, even though the boy hadn't even particularly liked him. He was now yet another Northerner dead in a battle that no one knew the cause of.

An awakening goddess? And we are fighting her creatures.

There were only a handful of fighting Braves, most of them Guardians, scattered across the wreckage of the camp. Coren prayed that most of his people had made it into the relative safety of the woods, but he saw the corpses littering his home, and knew that they were his kin, if not by blood. He gritted his teeth, and glared up at a towering shadow-creature, blood thundering in his ears.

Myr, standing back-to-back with Coren, slashed at a shadow-creature's ankles. The creature, surprised, stumbled back a bit, and Myr used this to her advantage, leaping up, her lithe leopard form ploughing the creature to the ground. She pinned it with a booted foot, and stabbed it mercilessly until it faded away.

"Behind you!" she yowled, and Coren spun, just barely parrying a blow from a heavy longsword. He neatly disarmed the attacker, leaving it looking vaguely amused that a boy with only a knife, and a wounded shoulder to top it all off, was able to do such harm. It died with that stupid look on it's face.

"Thank you, Aunt." he panted, gripping his shoulder as it throbbed. This fighting was not doing it any good, but he *had* to be here. He was duty-bound, honour-bound, love-bound, to protect kin. Especially his mother's only living sibling.

"What in the god's names did they mean?" Myr snarled, scratching up the face of yet another in the tidal wave of beasts. The ridges and whorls of her fingertips were ingrained with drying, purplish-black blood. "Are the gods - ccheh - really rising?"

"I have no - godsdamnit - idea!" Coren bit out, hissing as another creature caught his flank with a sharp something. His mane flared as he whipped around to bite the thing's hand, like a cantankerous housecat, pestered by it's master. But his jaws *did* have a bit more force behind them.

"We're going to die here unless we get out!" He screamed over his shoulder, as yet more shadow-beasts converged on them. Myr yelled something back, but it was drowned out by the murmurings and crackles of the creatures.

How in the hells had she managed to get that far away from him?

"Aunt!" he yelled, but already she was disappearing behind the masses. New cuts were being opened across Coren's body, and he was feeling weaker by the second. A splitting headache had started to pound behind his eyes, and he could barely catch his breath.

He began to plunge towards Myr, but the swell of shadow pushed him back. They were here for her. But what else? There had to be something else, something that could slow them...

"Where is your goddess?" Coren screamed, his voice cracking. He waited, turning circles, knife flashing as he held the creatures at bay as best he could. When the response came, it was in a chorus of fiery voices.

"Everywhere. In us." They hissed, and a chill travelled down Coren's spine. "She uses our eyes. Our ears. We are her army."

Beyond the mass of dark shapes, where he couldn't reach her, Myr screamed. The sound was pure agony, and something in Coren's chest, perhaps the last thread holding him together, snapped, a brittle sound.

He roared, the sound huge and primal. It echoed around him, and the creatures' whispers increased in volume, until it felt like he was being hemmed in by the continuous, unrelenting, wave of sound.

He was desperate. He had to save his aunt. He had to be here. This was why he was here.

And then Coren did the one thing that no one, not even he himself, was expecting him to do.

He ran away.

He ran away, peeling off towards the woods at a dead run, his legs burning, and his shoulder lighting up with a new spear of pain every time his paw hit the ground.

Somewhere along the way, he Shifted, and then it was his boots pounding the burning earth, arms pumping.

Some of the shadows followed him, and he led them on a chase, circling around, a half-baked plan forming somewhere in the recesses of his consciousness.

As quickly as he had fled, he ran back into the fray, and now he had built up enough speed that it was harder to follow him. The beasts trailing him were caught up in the confused crowd, as he cut his way farther in.

Within seconds, he was slowed down, but it was enough. He was now feet away from Myr. She was on her knees, red from the wound in her side bleeding out into the fabric around the wound. It was bad, he could tell. The shadows were crowding in, and their wispy forms seemed to sharpen the closer they got.

Something was happening here, and *this was why he was here.* Coren fought his way through more of the creatures, until he was standing over his aunt. Her eyes were full of fear, pain making her words garbled and halting. "Get out - Coren! They want - me. Tell Lana - I love her. Tell her - to keep herself - safe. The ba-by -"

"Myr!" his voice was snappish, as he fended off a creature lunging for Myr's unprotected head and shoulders. "You will - ach - survive this. This is why I am here. If that really was a *dea* then she sent me for a reason. You *have* to survive this." Myr opened her mouth, but Coren cut in, through clenched teeth, through the pain in his shoulder.

"You are my mother's sister. A wife - and soon a mother. You are my *Chieftainess.* For all of our sakes... You must survive." He stared down at her, his amber eyes dark. "If that means I die, so be it. I am an Exile, as good as dead anyways. This cannot be the end of your story."

Myr stared past him, through him, and Coren turned and killed one more shadow-thing. The clouds above were growing denser, and they were tinged red, the last embers of the burning camp painting stark contrasts across them.

"It shouldn't be the end of yours!" Myr hauled herself to her feet, one hand pressed to her bleeding stomach. Her face was pale, and she swayed on her feet, but her grip on her soot-stained rapier was true.

She stabbed one more creature, her face going even whiter with the movement. The creatures were coming slightly slower now. It was one, maybe two at a time. They were waiting, waiting, waiting for the two of them to tire. Waiting for them to give up, and let them take the Chieftainess.

"We are going to fight." Myr whispered. "You won't let me - go - for my people, because I am your aunt, and I won't - let you go, because you are my sister's son. Heaven help us!" A manic laugh ripped from Coren's throat, and he set his jaw against it. His eyes were wide and glassy with fear, and tears.

"We'll both have to fight, then, I suppose." His left palm was beginning to burn where it was gripping the knife - probably just from the strain of fighting one handed, he thought. His bow was useless, just more weight thumping on his back.

Myr nodded, and her hair finally surrendered, the last wisps falling free from the braid, the glittering net falling to the ground. She looked wild, and he knew that he must look a bloody mess.

"We'll fight." Myr echoed, but she stumbled, her hand, scarlet red, falling to her side, her blade's tip trailing in the ashes.

Coren was so focused on her, he didn't notice the creature looming up behind him, wielding a wicked-looking blade, until it was too late.

His vision went white for precious seconds, the pain was so intense, and Myr screamed, the sound ringing in his ears. He echoed the sound, and Shifted, snarling, his teeth snapping at the shadow, crunching bone.

And as the shadow-creature faded away, his vision darkened.

He was curled on the ground, pulsing pain radiating from between his ribs.

The creature had come up from behind, and it's razor sharp blade had gone through his armour, meeting flesh and bone. Myr was swaying above him, barely fending off too many shadowy forms. He blinked spots from his vision, his breathing ragged as he stared up at his aunt.

Coren bit back a pained sound, and scrabbled for a weapon, coming up with one of his own arrows, the shaft snapped just below the fletching, and somehow he was standing, the wood of the broken arrow rough against his palm.

This was impossible. It was not possible that they could be alive now. He staggered back, into a creature, and somehow he brought it down. It fell through the bushes before finally returning to whatever hell it came from.

He couldn't breathe. His vision was blurring, intensely now, and his frantic mind could only latch onto one detail. *Bushes. BUSHES.*

Somehow they'd gotten all the way to the edge of camp. Myr had... carried him?

"Run!" Myr screamed in his ear. The wind was picking up, and it was only then that he noticed the rain that had begun to fall. Red skies had been replaced by a sickly green, and he growled again.

"You - the Band needs you!" He spat, black and red, and cursed. "Gods above. They need you!"

Myr stared at him, wild-eyed. It was life or death here, and it was serious.

Coren ignored her, and watched their opponents, his head still fuzzy. The beasts - His breath stocked.

The shadow-beasts were milling oddly, hungry, and yet never coming too close. As if...!

Myr followed his gaze, her hand pressed to her bleeding stomach, and she swayed, just a bit. A new light entered her eyes as she saw it, too.

"The woods!" The wind was whistling now, like a kettle left on the fire too long.

"They're scared. Not for long. Go!" Coren screamed over the noise of the storm.

One of them had to go.

One of them had to stay, and keep the wolves at bay.

Both of them were close to collapsing.

And the wind howled on. Myr's long hair whipped around her face, her eyes, the same shade of amber as her nephews, teary and full. "I am the adult. Let me -"

"You - you matter more!" He yelled, tears brimming in his eyes. "*GO!*"

Myr's reply was lost in the roar of the wind. Flickering lightning turned the darkening scene as bright as day, and the shadows screamed, anger crackling in their flame-like voices. Coren backed up, further into the woods, staggering, his broken arrow's shattered wood digging into his palm, drawing beads of deep red blood.

It was a stalemate. Neither werecat would leave, and so they were stuck - Facing an impossible situation.

Something moved at the edge of his vision, and he lurched around to face it, gasping when he recognized the woman running through the woods towards them.

"*Malefica.*" He whispered, and she nodded. Her eyes flashed deep black before turning a flashing, lightning silver, her long hair a flying halo around her head.

"MYR!" he screamed, and the witch's eyes widened. She had come back for the one person the Northerners would trust to lead them.

Theodosia snatched at Coren's hand, prying open his palm, and taking the arrow from him. He stumbled, and murmured a protest, but she just inhaled, sharply, and cast a quick look towards the shadow-things.

"The monsters will not hesitate much longer! I cannot hold them off for long." He said, and then a metal object was being pressed into his palm, and he closed his fingers around the hilt of one of - His own knives, picked up from where he had dropped them on the battlefield.

Theodosia spun away, hurrying to Myr's side, her black cloak swirling as she struggled against the wind. She said something to the chieftainess, whose eyes went wide with shock, and then narrowed suspiciously.

Coren staggered, the wind nearly bringing him to his knees. He turned to see the Wraiths, if that was what they were truly called, squaring their insubstantial shoulders, and moving in, towards them. The wind seemed not to affect them.

That was when he saw it. It stole his breath away.

A column of writhing wind and debris that he had only seen once before, from a distance, when he was small. It had wrecked miles of the forest, and trees had littered the surface of the lake, piling up around the *Conpitum*.

He turned, a new frantic energy burning in his veins, as he screamed something at Myr, who was ploughing away from Theodosia, and towards him.

"Get away!" He screamed, his voice fracturing and vanishing in the howl of the storm. She was not deterred. "LEAVE!" Myr yelled, gesturing weakly at the sorceress behind her. Coren shook his head, gingerly touching his ribs, where there was too much blood.

The sorceress's face was white and scared, as she stared at the pair of them, the ridiculous werecats having a ridiculous spat at the brink of ruin.

"What do you think - they'll do to me if I - If I go back?" He panted. "You saw - the Council. They need - you." His head fell back, as he tried to breathe. He had to convince her. She had to go while she still stood a chance.

Coren stumbled again, the wind tearing at him as the twister drew ever closer. The Wraiths were vanishing, one by one, as the storm drew near. Not dying, but simply vanishing, as if they had never been there.

They were being recalled as their mistress summoned a hellish, magickal storm. Theodosia was shaking, frantically looking between the pair, her gaze bouncing from nephew to aunt, back and forth, back and forth.

"Lana - she needs you." Coren muttered, and Myr staggered, as if physically assaulted by her wife's name. "She needs you."

Decide! Theodosia mouthed, her expression suddenly saddened, grim, and Coren gritted his teeth again, his fangs glimmering. "THEY NEED YOU!" he howled over the noise of the storm, and Myr stumbled. He exhaled roughly, and nodded at the sorceress. Myr shook her head again, but the movement was less convinced, and the light had gone from her eyes.

For a moment, it seemed that it was surrender, that she would leave, but that was not the case... Blood loss, exhaustion, stress - things that the Chieftainess had been fighting against - they were all catching up to her.

Myr swayed on her feet, and her eyes rolled back as she collapsed forwards, and Coren lunged, his side and shoulder exploding with white-hot pain as he caught her, falling to the ground himself.

He let his head fall back against the sooty earth, wind whipping through his hair, as his aunt's deadweight lifted. Theodosia, incredibly strong, slung the taller, lithe woman over her shoulders. She looked down at him, her eyes sad. She screamed over the roaring of the approaching twister, so close. Growing ever closer.

"ARE YOU SURE? I can only carry one of you. You deserve to live just as much as-"

"Yes." He whispered, and closed his eyes, listening to the roaring wind and the crunch or running footfalls.

The pain was so intense. The Wraiths - by some accursed miracle - were gone, but a storm was bearing down on him, and he had done what he had needed to do. Myr was gone. He had to believe she was going to be all right.

And he began to give in to the darkness as the wind began to pull at his limp arms and legs, rising and falling.

He prayed to the gods - the fickle gods that would allow this to happen - that Myr would survive, that his people would survive this new war.

And everything, everything went dark.

XIV - In Which Lady Illira Forms An Alliance

LADY ILLIRA CLOSED her dark eyes, her fingers trailing over the blossoming flowers growing all around her, the blood that bloomed on their petals stark against her moon-pale skin. The dark, hulking shape of the temple ruins were far behind her.

So many more souls had entered her kingdom in the weeks since her mother's rise. Hapless travellers who had happened to get in Lady Chaos' way. Werecats of the Cortach Range, slaughtered in their safe havens.

With every soul, she had grown stronger, just a bit, but with each new life taken by her mother's hand, her hatred grew, burning through her veins.

The thought of the Forgotten Goddess sent cold shivers down her spine, and she quivered with rage, her breath coming shorter as she remembered the cold face.

Lady Chaos. Mother of death, bringer of war, of unrest. Illira's lip curled, the expressions of hate and disgust so odd on the face of a child.

She thought of Kinaar, and the determined set to her aunt's face as she had spoken of ending cycles, and ending this.

She remembered the old laws, unspoken but known:

Only a god can defeat another god.

Well. What was Death, if not immortal?

And she was so much stronger now. She rose from the field of flowers, streaked in blood, and looked up at the pitch-black dome of the sky.

She whispered quiet words, words that she knew would reach the right ears, and those ears alone.

"Aunt. I will fight with you. Tell me what you need of me, and I will fight beside you."

Far away, there was a form hanging in the stars, glowing like an angel, words drifting soft and bright to her ears. Her eyes slitted open, golden light pouring from beneath the lids, and she smiled.

XV - Betrayal

Three Moons Prior

TWO FIGURES PLODDED on, over rough, gravelly, sandy terrain, a hot wind kicking up dust. The shorter of the two was grumbling under their breath, their hair falling into their eyes, and the older, a man, was pointedly ignoring them.

"Why the hell are we out here? Why did you not pack more water? Damnit, Kir?"

"Rane!" Kir, the taller man, snapped at his younger sibling. "You could have packed that water just as easily as I could have."

"But-" Rane wagged a brown finger at their brother. "I didn't know where we were going. Amma may not have, but I trust you, Kir. You are my kin."

Kir swallowed hard, his scar making it hard to close his mouth correctly. He had wanted this for so long... But it was hard, seeing the trust in Rane's eyes. Knowing that Rane was the only one left who actually trusted him.

He shook himself. This was what he wanted. What he needed. He'd finally get all that had been denied him.

Rane laid a hand on their brother's arm, stopping him. They set down their pack, and rummaged around, finally coming up with a long strip of cloth, and wound it around their head, covering the crown of their head, their shoulders, neck and face. "This should help with the sun. You want one?"

Kir shook his head. They were almost there. The water had run out hours ago, as planned. Soon, they would crest a ridge, and...

Rane bounded out ahead, their lithe, clouded leopard form bounding across the sands. A few yards ahead, they paused, and looked back, a hand shielding their eyes from the sun.

"I can see something. A city? If we hurry, and Lord willing, we can probably make it by nightfall." They closed their eyes for a moment, presumably praying to their patron god, Micha. God of the earth, of natural disasters and green life. Kir barely suppressed a grimace.

Chaos was rising, and she had chosen a select few to reign beside her. He planned on being on the right side of this war. He planned on following her, the goddess who had given him so much. Soon, she would give him a throne. He stared on ahead at his sibling's receding back.

Rane had to go. They would never allow Chaos to take the South, their people. No, Rane would fight, and therefore they had to be disposed of.

Kir smiled again, and trudged on. They didn't suspect anything big, and this would be over soon enough anyways. Soon he would exact his revenge, and the South would be his. He would gain favour with his rightful patron.

The only deity who had ever spoken to him, who had ever deigned to show themself to him, and learn his mind.

Soon he would have everything he had been denied.

RANE SIGHED, AND CONTINUED on, their paw pads aching. The stones and sand under their feet had been baking in the sun all day. It was easier to continue on when they had a full coat of fur between their skin and the sun. The heat didn't bother them, but they had been out here long enough that they could feel their human skin burning.

Kir was somewhere behind Rane, and that was bothering them, no matter how hard they tried to shake off the uncomfortable distrust.

Their mother, their amma, had always said that he had a dark future, unreadable. Amma had tried, again and again, to use the bones to read his future, but they always came up blank.

Every single one. And the bones had never once told a lie, when in the hands of the rightful Chieftain. Rane had yet to read them. They knew how, but the bones... They had always been Amma's. Rane didn't feel like they would ever be able to read the bones without feeling like they did not belong to them.

Rane shook their head, trying to dispel the thoughts. They had to focus here. They had to trust Kir, even if their mother hadn't. They ran a hand across their forehead, wiping away sweat. They almost laughed. This was so ridiculous. It really was.

Footsteps crunched across the sandy gravel behind them, and Rane turned to face Kir. "Where are we going, Kir? You have to have received more than you are letting on."

"I told you all I know, Rane. One of our mapmakers, our finest, was waylaid, and needs help. She was left with barely anything, and is afraid that it could happen again. She wants us to escort her home."

His claim was shaky at best, shady at worst, and this was part of why Rane was uneasy. But... Kir was their brother, and Rane had to trust him. Otherwise, what was the point of being family?

"But why am *I* here? I'm needed back home, Kir. There have been problems with the North, and silence from the East and West, and it's so close to War Council."

Rane was referring to the annual gathering of the Southern Elders, to discuss the coming year. The presence of the Chieftain was required for the War Council to convene. After all, the Elders couldn't pass new laws, or declare war, by a majority vote like the Northern Council. Rane was the sole person in charge of the entire band.

"Come on. She wanted you, she's that scared, and you couldn't go alone. So, I'm here."

Rane had never seen the message that Kir had supposedly received. And Kir was usually very, very careful when it came to rationing precious resources, like water and food. And Rane was always thinking back to what their amma had said about Kir. About how his future was dark.

Rane had had misgivings from the start, and now their water was gone, and their food supply was faring only slightly better. But they smiled, and nodded, playing the role of the unsuspecting. They sighed.

"We'd better get moving. It's noon." They gestured vaguely at the sun, and hoped that Kir would get the hint.

He did, dropping the subject, and picking up his pace. Rane narrowed their eyes at his back, and made a noise at the back of their throat.

Soon, they were back to the monotony of silence, the deadness of the landscape, and the aching in the soles of their feet. There was no time to rest. The days were short.

It was hours before they finally saw the blur on the horizon again. Only now the blur took the form of a city, sprawling across the desert like a lazy creature soaking up the sun, it's painted walls shimmering different shades of red, orange and yellow, with the occasional hint of green. It was still at least two hours away, however, at the pace they had been going, and Rane turned to tell Kir this, only to stop with their mouth gaping open.

He had vanished. Vanished, on nearly flat terrain. There was no sign of him anywhere.

"Gods! Kir, this is not funny. We have to go, the moons are rising! Come out! The city is still at least three kilometres away." They gestured at the nearly-full, silvery discs that were just barely visible in the early-evening sky. "This is not funny, Kir!"

Something prickled at the back of their neck. This whole situation already felt wrong. But... Family. Their amma's warnings, about messages in the bones, went unheeded. Maybe Kir really did need help. And if Rane left him - It would be all their fault.

There was a muffled sound, coming from somewhere, and Rane tried to focus on it, their eyes widening when they understood one word, one that quickened their heart rate.

"Trap!"

"Where are you?" Rane yelled, panic sharpening their voice.

"Behind you. Now leave!" Kir's voice was scared, and tired, but Rane frowned. They were not letting their brother go that quickly. They turned and raced away from the Painted City, eyes firmly on the ground beneath their feet, until they came across a disturbed patch of earth.

"Kir?"

"Rane, turn back! It's unstable! Get the mapmaker, and go back!" He snarled. There was something dark in his voice that didn't sit well with Rane, but...

"I'm not letting you go! I need you. And your map." Rane's attempt at humour fell flat. They stepped forwards, and plunged a hand into the sand, groping around hoping to find their brother's hand somewhere in the loose earth. Desperately hoping that they wouldn't regret this.

Of course, it was a mistake.

A hole in the gravelly sand opened up, and they found themselves falling, falling, until they crashed to the ground. The air was knocked out of their lungs, and they gasped, staring up at the blue sky ten feet above them.

Kir was nowhere to be seen.

Rane swore, softly, remembering the blank bones, and the hollow look in their mother's eyes. The way her voice had cracked when she had told her child that their brother was not to be trusted. But Rane had been stupid, and had trusted him all the same.

Because blood was supposedly the strongest bond. *Hah*.

"Kir," they whispered, "I trusted you." The words echoed around them, filling the sandy, empty space. Who knew how that trick had worked, that throwing of the voice. Some *magia* of sorts, surely. Rane's face felt hot, anger and embarrassment sending blood to their face.

"KIR!" They screamed, and his twisted face appeared over the lip of the hole. Rane glared at him, screaming: "I dared trust you! I'm such an idiot! DAMN IT!"

"Amma was right. You never should have trusted me." He sang back, softly, watching. "With you gone, the South is mine. Finally mine, after so long... Ah, little sibling! Your god has forsaken you, while my goddess rises!" His mouth was so twisted that it was hard to tell if he was grimacing, or smiling. "Don't worry. You won't be stuck down there for long. They'll come for you, take you to the Painted City."

Rane stared up at Kir, disbelieving. "You would trick me, leave me, for what? A false throne? A fallen goddess?" They shook their head. "Even Amma and Baba thought better of you, Kir. Our amma may have distrusted you, but she didn't think that you'd turn like this." Their throat was clogging, and they stared up, past Kir's leering face at the beautiful, dusky sky.

"Damn you, Kir. Damn you and all your pursuits."

XVI - In Which Lady Chaos is Pleased

Three Moons Later

THE GODDESS SET HER jaw, twisting a strand of stark white hair around her shadowy finger, her dark eyes flashing. Her movements were lithe as she stepped forwards, and leaned on the table before her.

The soldier facing her was unflinching, it's form wispy.

"We won." Chaos murmured. She tilted her head back, laughing, the cackle dark and bright and unearthly.

"We did." The Wraith said, it's voice crackly, static. "The North has fallen. Their leader was close to death when we last saw her... None of their medicines could have ever brought her back."

It was all things that the Forgotten Goddess already knew. She had seen it happen through many, many eyes. But she had wanted to hear it all again.

"Good." The Lady smirked. "We finally have taken the Cortach Range, and that, my soldier... That is all we need."

She leaned further over the table, the wire in the thin braids that framed her face glittering. "We are so close to vengeance. Soon, soldier... Soon we will end what we began so long ago. Soon, my siblings will regret the day that they forgot me. I will finally have a place in Erathien."

Her soldier stared past her with glowing, empty eyes, emotionless, and the goddess pursed her lips. A sigh escaped her, and she snapped her fingers. The Wraith vanished, bleeding into the shadows around the room.

Loneliness. Chaos's only permanent companion. She shook herself (Never. She would never let herself be alone.) and looked down at the table, tapping her fingernails against the wood.

A chequered surface, of dark, evil-looking shadows, appeared, tiny figurines covering it.

The *dea* found one small figure, a tall woman whose face was oddly feline. She extended one long, shifting finger, and tapped it, smiling to herself as it tipped over.

"Checkmate."

XVII - In Which Coren Survives

HE SHOULDN'T HAVE BEEN alive. That was his first thought. His wounds were too severe, the debris in the storm should have injured him further. He should have bled out.

His second thought: He was falling, the ground fast approaching, and there was nothing he could do. He was barely conscious, and the treetops of a vast, green forest, were hurtling towards him.

His vision began to blur out, and the pain hit him again, with the force of a landslide. His body was grazing the first sharp twigs, tens of feet above the ground, when the merciful darkness rolled over him again, and he wished - He wished that he would just die.

LADY KINAAR LEANED over the unconscious boy, examining him. Strong, and stubborn, broken, but fierce. Hers.

She slipped a slender hand into his calloused fingers, tracing a shape on his left palm.

The beautiful boy didn't even twitch as the mark sank, invisible yet, into his skin.

Kinaar stilled, a tugging wrenching at something inside of her. Her breath stocked, and her already hazy shape began to fade away, returning to her restlessly dreaming form, tucked away between the stars.

Her eyes stayed fixed on the bloodied, battered boy even as she faded away. Her boy.

With her help, he would be safe. He would live. But the mark was as much a curse as it was a blessing.

THE ELF STARED DOWN at the broken boy lying at his feet. He looked up towards the treetops, at the hole ripped through twigs and leaves, at the charred wood, fabric and grey ash that covered the ground, and shook his head.

He knelt, taking the boy's wrist into his hand, humming as he checked for a pulse. What he found left his eyes wide.

"Impossible." he whispered, pulling at the shredded leather armour that the boy wore, tugging at the bloodsoaked shirt. The wounds... In the ribs. In the shoulder. Gashes criss-crossing his arms, cuts marring his face. He should have been dead. But somehow, the boy was holding on.

The elven man picked up the bird-boned boy, and laid him in the back of his wagon. The horse tethered to the front of the cart whinnied softly, it's deep blue coat rippling as it turned it's head to roll an eye at the elf.

"We need to get the boy back to the healers, if we want him to survive." He said, patting the horse's neck. "Alright, Ladybird?"

The horse nickered, and as soon as the man swung himself up onto the bench seat, it took off, flashing through the trees, it's golden shoes, finely worked, flashing.

XVIII - Mourning

WIND WHIPPED ACROSS the top of the rock, tugging loose long strands of hair. Myr tilted her face up towards the sun, rising rosy in the east, her back to the setting twin moons.

Her fingers curled around the warm stone, and she sighed, tears slipping down her cheeks. Her side twinged, and she pressed a long fingered hand against the bandages wrapped there, the pressure reminding her to stay in the real world, out of her head. She wiped at her wet eyes, and schooled her face into its usual calm expression.

First, she had to stay calm for her people. Second, she had to stay calm for her wife, for her nephews and her niece.

But maybe... Maybe now she had to prioritise staying calm for *herself*. If she broke down, she would never be able to collect the pieces...

"Myr?" The familiar voice made her jump, and she tilted her head back, gazing at her beautiful wife. Both Lana and the baby were healthy, thank the gods.

"How did you know to look here, angel?" Myr asked, smiling.

"We came here so often during our courtship! You can't have forgotten *that* easily?"

"Maybe... You don't seem too forgettable, so I suppose I *must* remember, somewhere in this empty head of mine." She laughed wetly. The banter was easy, and soon Lana was tucked up into Myr's arms, where her tiny frame fit perfectly. It always had, even when the two were young.

They sat there in silence, watching the sunrise, scarlet and gold on violet blue. Lana ran her hand up and down Myr's arm, propping them up.

"You are worried about this. You are mourning your sister and our nephew." She stated softly.

"We all are." Myr's voice was low, quiet enough that she knew she could speak without the fear that it would break on her words.

"Yes. But you feel it the most. You watched..." Lana shuddered, and Myr's shoulders tensed, unwillingly.

"Yeah." Her voice crumbled. "I looked up to her so much. And my nephew... Gods. He's so much like Mai. Too brave for his own good." She whimpered, and Lana pulled her closer.

"The storm... I've never seen anything like it." Lana whispered. "We've lost so much."

Myr's lips pursed, and then they parted as she let out a pent-up breath. "So much. But not everything." She smiled and pressed a kiss into her wife's hair. "I still have you, dearheart."

Lana pinched her, lightly. "Ay, don't." But she was laughing.

They shared a kiss as the sun finally crested the horizon, and then Myr was pulling Lana down onto the mossy stone, and they were staring up at the sky as they had so many years ago, courting, new at love, never imagining that someday, they would be together, and happy. Never imagining the tragedies to come.

XIX - Mourning, Part Two

"SHIT!" LIN SWORE, HER throw going wide, her kris embedding itself in the tree to the side of the makeshift target, a bale of dried grasses.

"You're working yourself up, Lin." Sioch sounded sad, almost bored. "Throwing things never helps."

"You're - enh - wrong." Lin grunted, pulling the wavy blade from the bark. She ran a finger across the *luks*, the ridges singing under her finger. "Gods. I wish that we'd been able to find something stronger." She gestured grandly at the flask of wine sitting at Sioch's feet.

"You don't want to be drinking something harder when you're playing with knives." He said, shaking his head, his dark curls flopping. Lin pushed a strand of her own dark, messy hair, behind her pointed ear, and reached down for the flask, taking a swig and wincing at the taste.

"That witch could have gotten something better tasting, at least."

Sioch sighed, watching his *comitis* carefully. Her thoughts were uncomfortably jumbled, setting his nerves on edge, but he couldn't bring himself to sever the connection between them when she was like this, grieving and upset, even briefly. He cared too much.

"I don't care who I stab, at this point." The blade drew a bead of scarlet blood at her fingertip, and Sioch sighed again, rubbing his face. He hadn't had time to breathe, to think, to disengage.

He was spending too much time making sure that Lin didn't cause the next disaster to strike camp.

"Lin, it wasn't your fault..."

"If I had tried harder! If I had gotten up earlier! If I had kept him from running towards the godsdamned battle!" She snapped, throwing the knife harder, and this time it sank up to the hilt into the target. Sioch shuddered at the slew of fury-borne, gruesome images flashing through his sister's head.

"I wish you'd just mourn, Lindara." His voice was soft, and Lin's shoulders shook. She looked back at him, her eyes glittering wetly in the late afternoon light. Her anger had fizzled, snapped, worn until it faded into grief.

"I failed, See. It's always been my job to keep this family safe. And I failed."

Sioch shook his head, looking off into the trees. "No, you didn't." He whispered, nearly to himself, voice choked. "You and our brother have always thought it your sworn duty to protect our family, at all costs. You are both loyal to a fault. He... He has been - I don't know. He's been broken, I suppose, for a long time, Lin. He needed to be there for Myr, one last time, almost to prove to himself that he could still be here for us."

He ran a hand across the dirt, drawing spirals in the ashy dust. "I wish that we could have done something more, I do... But I think that we did a lot. You saved my life. You made sure that Lana was on her way. You saved so many children. We did all we could." He swallowed. "I still wish that this could have ended differently."

Lin gritted her teeth, her thoughts loud and angry, her voice even louder. "You don't understand! I made a promise to myself when we were young. I promised that I'd keep an eye out for you, and our cousin, and Mother. That promise has been my *life*." She looked up at him, and Sioch could feel warm streams tracking down his cheeks. "I failed myself. Mother is dead because I wasn't there. He is dead because I wasn't strong enough."

Her brother's voice was firm. "No." He tugged at her hand until she sat down next to him, and he rubbed her back. "Lin. Look at me! I'd be a godsdamn mess without you. You'd be bleeding out without me. You were Mother's golden child. Our brother..." He trailed off, without saying any more.

They sat in silence for a while, staring at the knife in the grass-bale, the ash-streaked ground.

Sioch inhaled, shakily, and laughed. "My point, Lin, is that if you failed, I did, too. I failed to remember how much we all need each other. How much we depended on Mother, and how much she depended on us. I failed to remember that if our cousin didn't have us, he was alone, and that wasn't good. I failed to remember that you need us to be safe for you to rest easy."

Sioch lay back, staring up at the sky. Lin reached for the flask, and he let her.

"To failure, then." His sister said wryly. "To failing a cousin, and a people. Heaven keep us."

She gulped back the last of the drink, and hurled the bottle at the target, where it hit the bullseye before thumping to the ground.

The twins sat, silent, red-eyed, crying, for a long while. There was nothing they could do now.

XX - In Which Coren Meets Queen Rosana

COREN OF THE NORTH'S eyes flew open, and he moved to sit up, but a hand pushed him back down, firm and insistent. The accented voice was sharp, the Old Language a native tongue, but his dialect foreign sounding in the speaker's mouth.

"Don't sit up. You'll reinjure yourself, werecat." the woman said, crisp and matter-of-fact. When he spoke, his throat felt raw as if he hadn't spoken in years.

"Where am I? How...? I should be dead." He muttered, disoriented. His vision was uncomfortably dull as his eyes adjusted to the dim light, pupils slitting.

"One of my people saved your life. Half an hour more, and it would have been much too late." Coren blinked as his eyes finally focused, and stared at the woman leaning over him.

Her ears were tapered into points, her eyes dark. For a moment, he thought that her skin, dark as the new, wet earth, was mottled, but as she reached up a hand to tuck a handful of tiny braids back behind her ear, he noticed that the mottling was actually a fine network of lacy spirals, inked into her skin. They reached from her wrists, to halfway up her neck.

He'd heard of markings like these.

She was an elf, and an elementalist at that. The spirals were her *Signo*, her Seal, the mark of her power.

Despite her protestations, he pushed himself up, sitting and watching the stranger closely. "I apologise, I have been rude. I did not mean -"

"You are a werecat." The elven woman interrupted, her eyes glittering, their sharp intelligence visible as she looked him up and down. "Our healers noticed your physical markings... Your people have not left the Cortach Range in hundreds of years. What changed, and what destruction did you bring with you?" She asked.

The words were harsh, but they were not meant as an insult, or a threat. She was curious, and spoke with the air of a woman used to command. She was a leader.

Coren met her piercing gaze. "I am Coren of the North. There was a battle..." he shuddered. "They set the camp on fire. They were everywhere. So many Northerners were murdered... We didn't do anything to provoke anyone. There has been peace with even the South for nearly six autumns. And yet... The Council has been decimated. My chieftainess may be dead, for all I know... We were the last two standing, fighting. The storm is the only thing that spared me from death at those... *Things* hands."

The elf stared, her eyes wide. "Who sent these creatures? If they are threatening peaceful peoples, I am duty-bound to act."

"They claimed that they were sent by one of our ancient gods. The Forgotten Goddess. A... *malefica*, I do not know where she came from, if she really will help my aunt, or if she will let her die... She called them Wraiths."

The elf's regular breathing stuttered, her eyes widened momentarily, and she touched the silver circlet that rested on her brow, nearly reverently, tracing the etched vines. Her face was wiped clean, shock erasing every trace of fear, or hope, or anger.

"So, you... Are the nephew of Myr, Chieftainess of the North. You awoke one morning to find Wraiths burning your camp and killing your people. You and the Chieftainess were the last ones standing. Everyone else had fled, or was dead. You... *sacrificed* yourself so that this stranger could take your aunt to safety while you held off an army. *By yourself.*" The words sounded strange coming from this elf's mouth, reckless and foolhardy. But they were true.

"Yes." He murmured, staring down at his hands, running a finger across his knuckles. A web of new scars criss-crossed the skin. Scars.

Suddenly, something came to him, and he shoved up the sleeve of the loose tunic that he was wearing, made of a strange material, alien to him. Where there had been deep wounds hours - days? - weeks? - before, the skin was pink and shiny, stretched into healing scars.

He pressed a hand to his ribs, wincing at the ache, the ache of a severe, but nearly healed wound, and he looked up at the elf, who was still watching him with that constant, stern stare.

This conversation was bouncing around, wildly, but he didn't care.

"You healed me? A stranger, nearly dead, and you healed me."

"It is my duty." She stood, and her embroidered gown rippled around her legs. "I don't believe that I have introduced myself. I am *Regina* Rosana, sovereign of the Elven Territories." She sighed. "I suppose it cannot hurt... Please stand."

Now it was Coren's turn to lean back, startled. He stood, slowly, his still-healing body complaining with every movement. But he still bowed to this strange, elven queen.

"My Lady. Thank you. You saved my life. I am sorry that I behaved... The way I did. I - There is no excuse. You owed me nothing."

Rosana smiled. "Coren. Please. It is my duty. But you... You shared something troubling." Her face was grave. "If this is true, and the gods wake... If the *Malefica* Theodosia awoke... The world as we have known it is ending, Coren... And your people began a new Great War."

XXI - In Which Coren & Rosana Realise Things

CW: The third part of this chapter contains a panic attack
COREN'S HEART THUNDERED. The network of tunnels beneath the Elven Territories that formed the underground city of Eire were extensive, and beautiful.

Artistic brackets with torches of warm, dancing flames illuminating the space, and paintings and carvings decorated nearly every available expanse of stone. Starry skies domed above their heads, gods, monsters, and mortals walked beneath their feet, battles and *magia*-wielding warriors adorning the walls with bloody, beautiful scenes. The beautiful painted faces seemed to be alive.

And yet, despite the beauty, Coren felt closed in, and his breath was coming in short bursts.

He realised, then, that the closest he had ever come to being in a building of solid wood of stone, was the Council tent. He had never *not* been able to hear the wind in the trees, the burble of a stream, never been unable to feel chill air seeping through the seams of the cloth, never been plunged into eerie silence, like that of these nighttime tunnels.

He hated it.

Rosana looked back at him, and her eyes softened. "Apologies, werecat. I know you do not... enjoy the way we have constructed our civilization. But it was the only way -" She stopped, and Coren tensed, but she just continued on, with a sweeping gesture, as if nothing had happened.

"We have so many *Elementae Terrae*. And with the young *Elementae Incendi*, it's safest for us."

He cocked his head, question on his tongue, and Rosana answered before he could ask.

"It is a term that I cannot imagine that the outside world has heard in millenia... It means Elementalist. You would know the elements, individually. Earth, *terra,* water, *aqua,* wind, *anima,* and fire, *incendi.* They are old terms, even for our ancient tongue."

The *regina* laughed, a bright sound. "Gods above. I forget, often, how long it has been since I have seen the sunlight. I forget how long it has been since my people have shown themselves. You barely know of us."

"There are legends about you and your people. My mother was a storyteller, so I know many of them. I knew what creature of this earth you were when I saw your *Signo.*" He smiled, and cast a glance at the lace-like design stretching across her skin.

Every time she used a bit more of her gift, the Mark would spread, like cracks across china. And she would shatter when they engulfed her.

She caught his glance, and pushed her sleeves up to her elbows, showing him the extent of the dark lace. It twined still further, up and under the rich cloth. "Do you know how old I am, Coren?" Rosana asked quietly. He shook his head, slowly.

"No, my Queen."

"Please, just Lady Rosana. My title has not needed to be dusted off in years." She laughed, but grew quiet again in moments. "I was a young woman when the gods walked the earth."

"I'm sorry?" He looked at her still black hair, her young face, and blinked. "You..." he trailed off, unsure of what to say, and Rosana laughed again, the sound bright, but earthen.

"We are near-immortal, but not quite." She said. "I will live until I am killed, until the *Evanida*, when my Marks consume me, or if I fall ill. Until then, I live as I am. Young, strong. But I do grow older, my Marks more extensive. And this war... This..."

The queen trailed off, stopping suddenly, and gestured to a door, whose wood was carved with a tree, done in silver and green, so realistic that it seemed to grow as he watched.

"Never mind me now. What is to come is a matter for the dawn. You are still healing, even if my people were able to speed the process a bit. You need to sleep." Shadows drew across her face, and Coren's gaze dropped to the ground.

The conversation, the long, awful day, was coming to an end. He was confused, trying to make sense of what the queen was not telling him, but a twinge in his newly-somewhat healed side stopped him. He stopped himself from saying anything, and bowed instead.

"Thank you for your hospitality, Lady Rosana. You saved my life."

Rosana opened the door, with a small smile and a nod, allowing the werecat to slip inside. He bowed his head, and she closed the door, softly.

"See you in the morrow, Coren of the North." She murmured, standing in the hall.

"In the morrow, *Regina*." Coren whispered back, his sharp ears picking up the sound, and a small, a real smile curling his lips. "Thank you."

THE QUEEN WAS PREOCCUPIED as she strode the dim hallways, alone, her dress sweeping the ground, and swishing around her ankles, its folds long and rich. She passed through a gorgeously wrought metal gate, entering the inner halls of her home, and paused outside a door, it's surface carved with a flaming bird, whose body was outstretched, swanlike, graceful. A phoenix.

Her hand stilled inches from rapping on the wood, and the elf sighed, turning away and continuing on to her thorny, rose door, the wood alive with reds and greens, entering quietly, and sinking into an armchair.

She sighed, and buried her face in her hands, and then sagged back, staring into the fire that was roaring in the grate, warming the chilled air.

Rosana had no idea what to do next. She had been dreading the day that the gods would wake ever since she had bound them, had prayed that she would die before that day. Now, a boy, barely younger than she had been when she had been called to act, had been dropped into her life, splintering his own in the process.

She closed her eyes, knowing that she would do what she could, without harming her people. She was bound to protect Erathien by oath, and her sense of duty would not allow her to break it.

She would have to fight.

COREN PACED THE FLOOR, unable to lie down, worrying at the bandages around his shoulder and midriff. His thoughts were beginning an all-too-familiar anxious spiral, and he couldn't drag himself back out.

He had possibly saved a life, but he had nearly been killed in the process. A godly, cursed storm had picked him up, and dropped him thousands of kilometres from home, in a foreign land ruled by near-mythical beings, who rivalled the Fae in the stories of their power and cunning.

They had healed him, by some miracle, and here he was.

Under the earth, surrounded by strangers, at the mercy of a powerful, ancient queen. A queen, who, if she was to be believed, had outlived nearly every mortal of this world. And now this elven woman was claiming that it was true, the Wraiths were truly born of Chaos, the eldest of the *deae*.

If it was true... It meant that the gods were rising again, that a new era of *magiae*, of wards and patrons, was coming.

Coren slid down the wall, his newly-healed shoulder twinging as he thumped the back of his head against the solid dirt and stone. He was weaponless, and this was bothering him. His clothing was strange, too loose, too soft, too unfamiliar, and he was lost. Without a map he would never find his way to the surface again, and even then...

Fool, if he should dream that he could go home again. Fool, if Myr would ever forgive him.

His breathing was ragged, coming faster and faster as he brought his knees tighter against his chest, and bit his lip anxiously. A panic attack. He hadn't had one in so long. But now...

He was alone. Closed in. Nowhere to run to, to see the sky and breathe clean, mountain air. There were no animals to hunt, creatures to track just for the fun of it. There were only earthen walls, and flames that were heating the place too fast, making his skin too hot.

The reality of everything that had happened was starting to hit him, pummeling his shoulders, raining down like hailstones, and there were no disasters or distractions.

His chest heaved, and he brought his head down between his knees, his amber eyes gleaming gold, wide-pupilled, as he struggled for breath. One more. And one more. And one more...

Just breathe, Coren. Just breathe. You'll make it through. One more breath. One more...

XXII - In Which Rane is Captured Three Moons Prior

WHEN RANE WOKE, IT was to the sound of nearby voices speaking in an unfamiliar tongue. They cursed again, and chose the less conspicuous form. Their clouded leopard didn't belong in the Solchar Desert. No cat like that did. But a cat that didn't belong was better than a humanoid creature with cat's eyes and fangs.

Most humans were too superstitious for their own good, and would kill a werecat like Rane in a heartbeat, hoping to save their family from their Devil.

And, gods, was Rane glad that they had Shifted when the bandits appeared at the rapidly darkening opening to the hole. They were a ragtag band, dressed in fine, but worn clothing, with badly kept, rusty blades hanging by their sides. There were maybe ten of them, seven men, three women.

Rane mewled, a pitiful sound. The humans above scoffed, and one woman elbowed the man next to her.

"See. Just a beastie. I told you so." She laughed, smirking down at the clouded leopard. The man hummed.

"Odd, though, innit? This cat... I ain't never seen sumthin' like it out here before."

"Aye, Conan, whadda you know?" Someone across the hole jibed.

"Shut yer face, Marck." Came the... original reply.

"The more important question, boys, is how we are going to get the cat out of this damned hole without it ripping our faces off." The speaker was one of the women, a girl really, her long sandy hair pulled away from her face, and braided down her back. The plait swung like a length of rope as she leaned over, trying to get a better look at Rane.

Rane stood and began pacing tight circles, baring their teeth at the cluster above them. Most stumbled back, but the girl held firm, her own white teeth glinting back down at the werecat. Rane choked back a laugh, a too-human sound. This girl... She spoke like a woman of a far nobler status than she surely was, and was much too brave for her own good.

The girl grabbed the arm of the boy next to her, who looked barely older than the young woman herself, and gestured down at the hole.

"This beast. We need a fighting beast, and now we have one. My father would be proud if we brought it back for his little games." She tapped a finger on the boy's arm. "This is what we need."

The boy looked at her with big eyes. "Prince. This is too -"

She lifted the finger up, and waved it in his face. "We are accomplished enough. We have taken down beasts before. We've raided alongside Father and his people before, have we not?"

"Yes, Prince." the circle chorused, any dissent masterfully concealed.

Rane cocked their head. *Prince.* Heh.

"Now. Do any of you lumps have rope?" The Prince asked, and one of the men from before, Conan, lifted a coil. She smiled.

"Well *done*, Conan! You remembered the rope." The man frowned at his Prince, and she laughed. "Aye, come on. You forgot it the last three times we came out to investigate."

"All o' the three other time, it warn't not'in.'"

"But! There was always the possibility that it *was* something, after all. Father didn't manage to take the Painted City without believing in himself."

"Yeah, but we ain't-"

"Shut it!" The woman, the first to speak, elbowed Conan sharply, but this didn't stop him from muttering under his breath. "*Capturin' a city.*" The woman jabbed him again, and he spat.

"Come *on* Larissa. Stoppit." Larissa smirked at him, raising a finely pencilled eyebrow.

The Prince tapped her booted foot, glaring at them, waiting for them to notice her icy glare. They quieted soon enough after that.

"We have rope, we can bind it. We just have to get the cat out of the hole." The banter went on for what felt like hours, leaving Rane to their restless pacing. The moons were soon exactly above Rane, their silvery light washing over everything, making edges shine, and even the tattered bandits looked like spun silver.

Finally Rane gave up looking menacing, and lay down, resting their head on their paws, staring down at the dust caught in their fur.

It was then that the Prince strode back up to the lip of the hole, flipping her braid back over her shoulder, her booted toes curling over the edge. Rane blinked their eyes lazily. The Prince's expression didn't change. She looked frustrated, but oddly calm, her eyes intelligent and lukewarm.

"Aye." She whispered, a quiet hello, flickering her fingers. Rane raised their head, closing their eyes and uttering something that fell between growl and purr. Maybe this Prince wouldn't be too bad. Maybe Kir hadn't left them to a fate too awful to bear.

"My apologies, beastie."

Their eyes snapped open, just as the Prince lifted a blowpipe to her perfect, cupid's bow lips. Rane snarled, fear glowing in their eyes. This could not end well.

They did not want to know what was in the dart that was falling towards them. They did not want to go to that in-between place, watching, but separate, with no control. Rane did not want to dream again.

But there was no place to run to. They felt the sharp sting of the dart entering their side, and then everything started to dim. And Rane had no choice but to succumb.

XXIII - In Which Coren Has Another Dream

Three Moons Later

THE FOG WAS BACK, THICKER than ever, and all he wanted was out. But his weapons were gone, his armour stripped away, and he could not see. He couldn't fight his way out, and the gods only knew how else he could escape.

Well done.

The voice... He snarled, his tail lashing, his fur bristling, ivory teeth bared.

You did right, werecat.

And he was kneeling on the wet ground, holding his burning hand, unable to unclench his fist. It felt like he was holding a glowing coal.

The mist cleared into a circular shape, ghostly, insubstantial walls hemming him in, and before him stood a woman, across the circle, still shrouded in wisps of the dream-fog. It looked almost as if she were being bound by the stuff. It was trying to keep her hidden.

Her gown was blinding, golden light, shifting as if it were being fractured by a body of water. It lent her figure a sort of halo, creating rainbows in the fog around her, turning the vapour into millions of tiny prisms. In an obscured hand, she carried a bow, similar to the carved one that Coren had made, and carried. The misty shafts of arrows were just visible over her shoulder... But this was all.

The fog was closing back in, before Coren could see her face. But the bow, it was so familiar...

"Mammah?" *he asked, a quaver entering his voice.* "Is that you?"

Oh, Coren... *The woman raised a hand, the fog curling around her wrist, binding her tighter.* Be brave, boy. You will need to be strong. You will need to be brave.

"Mammah?" *He asked again, but the scene was already shifting, bleeding away, colours blurring together. He reached out a hand to keep her there with him -*

The scene before him left his body cold, shock washing over him.

He had expected nothing more, really. Nothing more. But the reality was harsh.

His home was destroyed. The ground was dusted grey with ash. The trees were ripped up, their branches as bare as if it were the dead of winter. The storm had ruined just as much, if not more, than the fire had. He turned a circle, looking around, tears welling in his eyes. His home...

"Where are they?" *He whispered, and a small sigh came from behind him. He turned his head, and the scene changed again.*

He was standing in a circle of people. None of them seemed to see him, and it felt strange, to be invisible to them. Oddly, though, he didn't mind.

Myr was speaking, loudly, and Coren felt a rush of joy at seeing her alive. Underneath her shirt, he could see the heavy cloth of bandages, forming a lump in the fabric. But she was alive!

The malefica, *Theodosia, stood behind her, her kaleidoscopic eyes half-closed, her hands folded in front of her, her dress brushing the ground, and her cloak catching the breeze.*

"Northerners!" Myr said, her voice ringing clear and true. "A fire has destroyed our camp. A storm has devastated the forest. Creatures, Wraiths supposedly sent from Lady Chaos, the Fallen Goddess, have killed our people, unprovoked." Myr's mouth twisted, bitterly, on the last words. "But we endure. We have completed the rites for our fallen. We have found a new ally in the Malefica Theodosia, who slumbered with the gods. It is time we move on."

Murmurs rose from the crowd. Myr had to further raise her voice to be heard.

"We have always been a semi-nomadic people! We have other camps, which are small, but habitable. We will never forget the fallen, who gave their lives for our safety and well-being, but it is time that we set up a new camp. Malefica Theodosia will travel with us."

Myr bowed her head, looking up through thick lashes, her hair falling loose around her shoulders without the net to bind it. "I wish that we could stay here, in the home of our parents, of our fallen. But it is for our own safety, until we can properly form a war council, reach out to the other clans and tribes. Until we can properly defend ourselves. Please, collect what you salvaged. We break camp in the morrow."

And the scene faded.

It was replaced by four faces that he knew well. Lindara, Sioch, Myr and Lana sat around a fire, warming their faces and hands.

"What will we do?" the twins asked together.

"What our people have always done. We endure, and move, and survive." Lana said, twining her fingers through her wife's. "Myr was right to make the decision. This is what we need, what our people need, before we can do anything else. We need to mourn, and train, and regroup."

They sat there, quietly for a long moment, and Coren reached out, placing an insubstantial, unfelt hand on Sioch's shoulder. He squeezed, gently, and closed his eyes.

Oh, gods. What they must think...

As if they could hear his thoughts, the twins asked: "Do you really think that he's gone?"

"It is most likely..." Myr sighed, and Coren noticed dark rings under her eyes. She rubbed the bridge of her nose, inhaling deeply, and letting it out, blowing at a strand of honey-brown hair.

"But I can't help but hope. He's strong, that boy. Gods know we could use some good news."

Lana kissed her temple, lightly. Myr closed her eyes, and the twins shifted, settling in, pulling a blanket tighter around them. They were settling in for a cold night.

And just like that, Coren felt himself leaving the scene, coming back to himself, and his hand was burning worse than ever.

XXIV - Discussions

COREN SLOWLY BLINKED his eyes open, his great, tawny-gold furred form lying curled on the floor, the blankets from the bed draped over him. He twitched his tail against the stone floor.

He was used to camping, firm earth beneath his hip and shoulder, so, strangely, the bed had been too soft...

The boy Shifted, and rolled his shoulders, breathing deeply. Turning his head, listening to the still blazing fire.

Drowsily, he noticed the stack of clothes, and stood. When he lifted up the shirt, he grinned. It was nearly a perfect copy of the Northern style, as were the pants. Heavy cloth, dyed dark colors that blended with the earth, plants and grey sky. However, there was no armor, no familiar weight of knives and quiver, which made Coren feel oddly underdressed.

He brought his hands up to rub his face, and stopped, startled.

His hand, the one that had been itching, burning in his dream - All he could do was stare.

There was a mark on his palm, seemingly inked there, darker than the skin around it. An interlocking crescent moon, and sun, the rays soft and spiked.

Coren looked up at the dark ceiling. He felt sick.

Lady of Stars. His patron *dea*'s mark. His heart pounded, and his head spun with ideas, explanations.

Maybe the elves had painted it on, for some reason? They had patrons, other old gods, Lords and Ladies belonging to earth, water, wind and fire.

But Lady Kinaar was goddess of the light and the dark, the day and the night, and the in-between of the Veil. She was not Lady of an earthly element.

He rubbed at the mark, but it did not smear, it did not leave dark patches on his fingertips. It was not rubbed on with chalk, or any other writing tool that he knew of.

Coren licked a finger, and rubbed the mark again, but still, no change. He sat down, hard, his hands shaking as he remembered the dreams, Myr's words during the battle.

"A dream, Coren? That seems more like a vision." A vision. He released a pent-up breath, sitting in silence, studying the mark. So the gods were rising. Perhaps that had something to do with this. Perhaps the *dea* was claiming his people, as she was their patron.

Perhaps... He rubbed at it again, and then began worrying at the blanket underneath him, the fabric cool and smooth against the pads of his fingers.

He was so wrapped up in his own thoughts, and worries, that he didn't hear the door creak open, until a clear voice broke the silence.

Coren was on his feet in an instant, his hand going for his knife, only to grasp at empty air. The elf standing on the other side of the threshold shrieked at the expression on his face, and stumbled back.

Coren's shoulders relaxed. "Gods! Apologies! I did not mean to scare you... I suppose..." He trailed off, watching her confused face. "And... You can't understand my dialect. Shit." He thought for a moment, raising his hands, and repeated himself in the 'high' version of the Old Language.

The elf's eyes locked on his palm, where Kinaar's mark stood out boldly against his fair skin, and he dropped his hands. She considered him for a long moment, her smart, blue eyes glittering, her face softening.

"Apology accepted!" The elven girl bobbed a quick curtsy, grinned at him, and then waved a pale hand, silencing him as he tried to say something more. She turned, her impish smile broadening as she tossed her short, dark hair. "Never mind formalities, Northerner, just come! Lady Rosana and Lady Sora are expecting you!"

He blinked, startled, and then, biting his lip, followed.

He soon regretted leaving the room. People stared. He was a foreigner in a land far away from the sun, let alone other creatures. His clothes were different, and his eyes, his teeth, even his smooth, loping gait, were all more feline than human.

All he could do was tense his shoulders against the prickle of strange gazes in the now busy - no, teeming - tunnels, brightly clothed elves laughing and shouting, joking with one another, a handful of children running about, bumping into people and causing trouble. It was all he could do to focus on the deep violet of his elven guide's gown, and not get himself turned around in the constrictive maze.

At some point, he Shifted, and stayed that way. Somehow, the elves took less notice of a great cat than they did a strange human-like creature. His shoulders rolled as he moved, his paws padding quietly, his tail flicking. Scars marked his front legs, fur gone in patches where he had sustained cuts. He knew that there would be two particularly ugly wounds on his shoulder and side, but... He was a werecat. They all bore scars of some kind.

His mother had been missing two fingers on one hand when she died. Khara had had three raking, pale scars twisting around her ribcage and back. Lana had that mark across her nose and cheekbones. Myr - Myr had scars up and down her arms, from swordplay and more.

They were all scarred. They were all survivors.

He shuddered as his mind wandered back to the battle, the Wraiths closing in and the storm touching down. He had to force himself back into the present. His tail lashed, and he made a low noise in his throat as he bounded a few paces, catching up to the young woman.

She looked down at him, seemingly surprised at the fact that he was not humanoid anymore.

"Coren?" she asked, softly, and he looked at her, his great head tilting. Her luminous eyes widened. "Ay. I've never seen a werecat before!" She laughed, high and tinkling, looking around at the sea of people, thinning as they approached a somewhat darker part of the tunnels. Nearly every one of her sentences sounded like it should be ended with an exclamation mark. "They must think you are a Familiar of some sort."

He started to reply, forgetting that this form was limiting in that regard. She would not understand. Instead, he Shifted again, his form bleeding and reshaping in a matter of seconds, and shrugged, bowing his head. "It is easier to be a lion than a... non-elf here. I blend in more."

The elven girl laughed again. "It is a quite impressive brand of magic, being able to change your form. *Illusionis* are one thing, but actually, physically *changing*, that is old magick!"

Coren nodded. "Yes. But it comes as naturally to us as breathing. You should see the little ones, who barely have control. One second a baby is crawling, the next it has fur and is running all over the place...!" He suddenly realised something, and grimaced. "I'm sorry, I have been impolite. May I ask your name?"

The elf smiled. "They call me Corrine!"

"Like the city!" he said. Corinnestāt. One of the human cities closest to the Cortach Range.

"I suppose!" Her laugh was bright, and Coren Shifted again, without breaking stride, before morphing back a few metres later. Now, in these dim back tunnels, there were only a handful of people, and they were all quick to move on, their gazes barely resting on the pair, preoccupied. The paintings were growing more and more complex, and soon tapestries of fine threads, gold and silver and bronze, deep indigo and bright, bloody red, were adorning the walls.

"We are close to the Gates." Corrine said.

"The Gates?" Coren asked, rubbing the back of his neck nervously.

"The entrance to the chambers of the royal family!" The elf said, smiling.

"Oh. Does Lady Rosana have a family?" The werecat boy asked, curious. He regretted it as a sudden cloud drew across Corrine's abnormally cheery face.

"Her husband died. His name was Aleixei. It was a tragedy. An accident. There was nothing we could do."

"I am so sorry." Coren murmured, but Corrine just shrugged.

"It was a long time ago." She waved a dismissive hand.

"Hmm." He replied, a bit sadly, the noise low in his throat. Another moment of comfortable silence, and then they stopped.

Huge, intricate iron gates rose before them, reaching from the ceiling to the floor, it's spirals glowing faintly. Coren couldn't tell if it was reflected light, or generated by the metal itself, but either way, it was beautiful. The iron was bent into the shapes of delicate roses and birds, every detail, from thorns to feathers, precise. He studied it for a long time, entranced, following every whorl and twist. He had never seen metalwork like this before.

Corrine called out a name, and someone behind the Gates replied: "Their Highnesses, *Regina* Rosana and Lady Sora, are waiting for you in the Queen's Chambers."

There was a brief creak, metal hinges opening, and then silence as the Gates swung open, revealing the rest of the tunnel beyond.

An old elf, his hair long and grey, stood beyond, his hooded eyes glittering as he watched them pass through. He gestured for them to go along, and brought his hands together, once, twice. The Gates began to close, and then the pair was off again, rounding a bend in the hall.

Coren noticed doors, closer together and more ornate than the ones around the room he had been shown to. These ones... If possible, they seemed even more alive.

A fiery bird seemed to glow, it's feathers quivering. A waterfall tumbled and glistened wetly. A cluster of roses bloomed red, their branches twining around a white lattice. It was before this door that Corrine stopped, and nodded at Coren.

He looked at her, but she just shrugged, making a shooing motion, her smile infectious. "Go on! It was a pleasure to meet you!"

"It was a pleasure, Corrinne." He responded with a smile, turning back to the door. He reached out, hesitantly, for the blooming doorknob, the petals of the rose digging into his palm as he turned it, and stepped into the room beyond.

Everything was bathed in the warm glow of firelight, silhouetting the figures of two women, their heads bent, talking by the fireplace. One was Rosana, and the other, he assumed, was Lady Sora, heir to the throne. The elves looked up at him, and Rosana smiled. Sora looked mildly interested, but otherwise stern.

"Hello, Coren!" Rosana said, beckoning him closer. He walked over to the pair, and bowed his head.

"Lady Rosana. Lady Sora."

"Hello, Coren of the North." Sora said, watching him closely. Her angular eyes were deep brown, and her black hair fell smooth and glossy down her back. Her sleeveless gown was a deep red, belted at the waist with a thin band of braided leather, and it revealed the edges of Marks curling at the base of her throat, over her collarbones, and on her shoulders. A golden circlet rested on her forehead, engraved with a pattern of flames, licking at the metal.

"We have much to discuss," the *Regina* murmured, and she moved to sit down in one of the armchairs that surrounded the fire. "Come, please sit."

Sora and Coren obeyed silently, and watched the elven queen with curious eyes.

Lady Rosana sighed, and her fingers tightened on the armrests for a moment, before she relaxed, and stared into the fire. "Sora, dear - Coren, I have told her everything you told me - Sora, is there anything you did not understand, or more you wish to know?"

Lady Sora shook her head, her hair rippling. She kept on quietly snapping her fingers, a flame flickering on and off every time she made the movement. She was an *Elementa Incendi*. He watched the tiny flame dancing across her fingers until she closed her hand into a fist, extinguishing the spark.

"No, thank you, Rosana." She said softly. Even her voice had an element of fire, crackling and bright.

Coren glanced at her loose fist again. This was ancient magick, from the time of the gods. His own small magicks, magicks that all werecats possessed, had nothing against it.

Rosana sank back in her chair, closing her dark eyes. "I am so sorry, Coren... I tried reaching your people late last night... But our methods are old, and have not been used for many human lifetimes. I don't suppose that you've seen an elven-made medallion, a scrying piece, in your Chieftainesses quarters?"

Coren's brow furrowed. "No, I do not think so. Sorry, Lady Rosana... So many things were lost in the Twenty-Years-War..."

"You were at war?" Sora seemed honestly surprised, and Coren nodded, his eyes darkening.

"It was senseless. So many people lost their lives, over nothing. All it did was heighten the conflict between the North and the South."

"Oh, my Lord. Apologies, Coren..." Rosana murmured, and then sighed. "I suppose it was to be expected that we would not know of anything. We have not contacted the outside world in years... Although perhaps I could reach Theodosia..."

Sora cleared her throat. "Rosana."

The Queen's eyes flew open as she was wrenched from wherever her thoughts had drifted. She rubbed her forehead, a silver ring set with a gleaming amber stone glittering on her left ring finger. A wedding ring.

"Yes! Sorry. Coren... Until I reach your people, there is not much that I can do. I wish there was." She looked so tired. "All we know is that those things that you saw... They were her doing. And if there was no resistance from the other gods, they must still be too weak to fight themselves. Which means that we must fight, and do what we can, until they rise."

Coren exhaled, shakily. Gods rising. Old magicks. Cities under the earth...

Sora rose, her garnet dress swishing as she moved, kneeling on the hearth. "Werecat, how much do you know about the Great War?" she asked, picking up a few logs from the log rack, and examining them.

"Not much." he said. "My mother used to tell me stories... I know that that was when the gods left our world. That is all."

Rosana looked at him, her eyes sad. "They never left. They did not die. But they sleep, in the darkest, most remote corners of the world. And it was our fault."

XXV - In Which Kir is A Villain
Two and a Half Moons Prior

IT WAS BEAUTIFUL, IN a dark way. The fear in their eyes.

Kir stood before his people. *His* people. Rane was gone. Probably dead. He was scarred, powerful, and now he had an army to serve his goddess.

His people had grumbled, they had been weak and foolish, speaking of the old ways, and their patron god.

They had been silenced easily.

The South had a new patron now, one who would rise, and rule Erathien, and Kir would finally have the power that should have been his. It should have been his from birth, but his mother had been a fool, and she had given it to her second child, the weaker one.

Well. Wrongs had finally been righted, and he was a ruler.

The South had made the right choice. They would fight for the winning side, and Kir would be the one to lead them to glory.

When he spoke, his voice carried, as clear as a bell, ringing out across the fearful-silent clearing.

"We are fighting for the winning side, my friends! We have placed our fates in the hands of a powerful goddess, who will lead us to victory. We will rule, and we will stand strong, and proud. Nothing can stop us, not now, not ever."

There was silence. No roar of cheers, no grins spreading across adoring faces. Just a ringing silence, broken only by the rustling of the wing in bare branches, and the clank of weapons.

Kir's jaw tightened in frustration.

Perhaps... The start was not the best. But the end? It would justify all means.

XXVI - In Which Rane's Imprisonment Grows A Bit Worse

RANE PACED THEIR CELL, their tail lashing. They got halfway across, and then a tug at their left hind leg brought them up short, the heavy chain rattling as they moved.

The Bandit Prince, who's name, Rane had discovered, was Aralie, watched them with big, unfairly beautiful eyes. She pursed her lips, studying Rane's muscled form, their claws and their bright fangs.

Rane wished that they could just free themself from the chain, from the prison, from the Prince's stare, but there was no way... If they Shifted, the point of their disguise would be void, and even then... The shackle would crush their ankle before they even had the chance to pick the lock with the thin tools that they always, *always* had tucked into their high boots. Right beside the poisoned knives.

Rane bared their teeth at the Prince, making a growling sound low in their throat.

"Well, beastie... It will be up to you tonight. You have helped me greatly. But I do still wonder... How was it that a *clouded leopard* came to be out here in the Solchar?" Aralie frowned as Rane stopped, staring at her. They shook themself, a prickle building at the nape of their neck, and continued pacing.

Don't seem too human. Don't let her know that you can understand her.

"Yes, I read some books, learned enough. I cannot help but wonder if someone is playing us for fools." The Prince continued, a small smile on her face. "Aye... But it seems you cannot understand me, and never will. It doesn't even really matter, does it?"

Rane felt both ready to laugh, and a welling sense of dread as the Prince stood, dusting off her skirts, this one split up the side for freedom of movement.

She was growing on them, loath as they were to admit it. She was brave and headstrong, rakish and bold, and Rane envied her freedom.

But there was a dark glee to her, joy in the pain of her father's victims. She never seemed upset when prisoners were killed, didn't flinch at the sight of massive loss of blood... This was terrifying to the werecat chieftain.

Aralie turned away with a swish of skirts, making her way down the dark hall, never glancing around at the cells, ignoring the whimpers from around her. The creatures stuck in all of those cages, all fur and teeth, claws and gleaming eyes. And some humans.

Rane tried not to think about the way that these humans could stand to imprison their own kind for pleasure. It was unjust, cruel, and utterly heartless.

The heavy door clicked shut behind the Prince, and Rane snarled. The sound was too loud, too harsh, in the echoey space.

Low sounds answered them. Whimpers, human and animal. An answering roar or two, infused with so much emotion.

Anger at their captors. Longing for the wide open blue skies, the warm glow of the sun, the silvery gilding of the moonlight and stars. The feel of wind across skin, fur, feathers, scales.

Rane sank down, their paws tucked under them, their tail curled up over their nose, their wide brown eyes open and alert.

Gods. Whatever was going to happen to them, Rane wished it would happen soon.

METAL CLANGED AGAINST the cold stone walls, and rough, loud voices filled the space. A man strode out in front, his booted feet thumping, his cloak flapping.

Rane's lip curled, flashing their fangs. The man was neither young, nor old. He had a beard, salt and pepper hair, and his eyes were far too sharp and cunning for Rane's taste. He bore a sword, and carried himself imperiously. This was his kingdom. He was armed, and ready to defend, or conquer.

This was the King.

Aralie walked close behind her father, her face calm, outwardly. Her eyes were half lidded, her lips just slightly parted. Her hand rested on the pommel of her sword, the sheath drowning in the faded fabric of her skirt, and her sandy hair was in it's usual messy plait.

The King waved a hand at the guards behind them, and the four melted into the shadows, effortlessly. The Prince stepped forwards, her sturdy, heeled boots peeking out from under her dress. She walked up to Rane's cage, and wrapped her fingers around the bars.

Rane snarled again, but Aralie just laughed. Her father stepped up beside her, resting a heavy hand on the Prince's shoulder.

"Well done, Aralie." He murmured. "This beast is... beautiful. Look at the teeth and claws - and that pelt! And it is strong, as well. See the way the cat moves?"

"Aye. And, you must admit, my trap worked, did it not?" She turned, brushing away his hand. "If this great cat wins - you must admit that neither I, nor my people, are to be underestimated. We are smarter, stronger, braver than you and yours give us credit for."

"The underdogs are always the victors, eh?" The King smiled, a bit too condescendingly. His daughter set her jaw, and stepped away.

"Perhaps. This is the *last* time you assume that we cannot perform just as well as your 'select few.' The very last time." She stalked out of the room, her braid swishing.

Rane had to quell a chuffing laugh. This Prince... She was stubborn as hell, and not willing to give in to anyone. The more high and mighty they were, the more airs they gave themselves - the more the Bandit Prince would try to prove their assumptions wrong. She was a fighter.

The King sighed, watching her go, and pounded a fist against the bars, causing Rane to rattle at their chains.

"The more fool I," he muttered. "Headstrong girl. Never going to learn when it is best to obey and respect her elders."

He met Rane's darkly gleaming brown eyes, and the werecat snarled, long and loud, but the King didn't move a muscle.

"Guards! Get the cat in a muzzle, and into the Ring. We have a fight like nothing we have ever seen before us."

RING FIGHTING. OF COURSE. It befit the brutal Bandit King.

This time, Rane paced not a tiny, cold cell, but a large, dusty, outdoor arena, ringed with rough benches, carved into the earth. Tall walls had been constructed around the arena, trapping the werecat, despite the fact that they had been freed from their chains.

The structure was quite obviously from the days when the Painted City had been inhabited by honest people. The columns planted into the earth in twelve, evenly spaced places, and the designs caved into them were much too fine to have been done by the thieves that now called the city home.

The seats were slowly filling up, tattered, worn, but sharp people slinking in. There were men, women, some children as well. All of them looked thin, and angry, and like they had had to fight, and take the low road their entire lives.

Rane sympathised with these odd people, in some ways, but it was hard not to hold the pain the rogues were causing against them.

The King, the Queen Consort, and the Prince were all seated in more elaborate chairs, obviously brought in from outside the arena. The wood of the thrones was somewhat warped, but they were front and centre, and sure to provide a good view of the spectacle.

Finally, after a small eternity of praying and watching the sun travel across the sky, the King rose from his seat, his clothing finer than anything Rane had ever seen him wear before, all brocade and rich, unfaded cloth.

He cleared his throat, and the sound carried, by the genius of the architecture, throughout the amphitheatre. "Welcome, people of the Painted City, to the Ring. Again, we gather to protect our people! Again, we have captured a feral beast, that must die. Again, we let two strong creatures battle to the death. In one fight, we will kill a threat, without soiling our own hands."

There was a quiet roll of laughter.

"Today, we present you with an old champion, and your Prince's newest fighter, a beast that has yet to prove itself. We present to you a battle between the King's and the Prince's chosen champions." The King smiled at Aralie, who raised her chin, a ghost of a smile flitting across her hard face.

"Out with the old!" The Prince cried, earning herself laughter, a cheer here or there - a withering look from her father.

"Let the fight begin." came the cold command, and Rane spun around as a creaking sound filled the Ring.

They flinched away as they saw what was lumbering out of the rusted gates.

XXVII - Rosana's Story

I WAS THE HEIR OF THE Elven Territories, once, as Sora is, now. I was the heir after Chaos first came to Erathien, and I am too young to remember the move underground. I am too young to remember what the city of Eire was like when it was in the trees, not beneath the earth.

My mentor, and king, Soer, he was the one who chose to move. He was the one who guided our people to safety. I, as many did, loved him for this choice.

In time, however... I grew to despise him for it.

I would hear stories of the aboveground world, a world that I saw only once and awhile. I would hear tales as well, not of the natural beauties that existed out there, as one might think, but tales of war and disease, of all the things that afflicted the aboveground peoples.

My king told me that this was why Eire had moved to the tunnels beneath the Wood. He told me all about why we could never step in, for fear that it would ruin our people, our peace.

For years, I did not speak with him of the harm that had befallen Erathien. I did not question the choices that he made.

When I finally did speak with him again, he told me that I was not to worry myself with it. He told me that what was done was done. He told me that I was the Heir. He needed me here, in Eire, helping him, learning how to rule.

I was tired of running from the trouble that everyone but us was facing.

So I defied his wishes.

I left, one night. I told no one where I was going, merely left behind my crown, and a letter, telling King Soer where I was going, and why.

Somehow, I made my way through the Wood to the Great Road without losing my way, and I travelled for weeks.

For months, I searched for allies, for others who would be willing to stand against the dark force that had us all in it's grip.

But I found no one. So I worked to get money for food and lodging. I was a soldier, aiding in the destruction that was being wreaked. I hated it.

I was a hypocrite, spreading a message of peace even as I used my magick and my sword to kill.

When my army came to the city of Laeris I thought that it was all lost. I could not return home, for I had defied my king, and I had dishonoured the people by abandoning my duties.

But it was there that I met a woman, a Gifted healer named Theodosia. A sorceress.

And she believed me. She understood me. She had contacts, and friends, and before I knew it, I had abandoned yet another duty, for the sake of a dream - I had left the army for a true quest for peace.

It was... miraculous, what Theodosia could do. Her magick was like nothing I (admittedly, an Elementalist living among Elementalists, with no human mages among us) had ever seen. And she had a will of steel. She could convince people to do things with her silver tongue, or could trick them into it with a good bargain.

Soon, with her at my side, I had more allies than I had ever dreamed of, all of us fighting to do the impossible. It was me, the Faerie Imperator Quai, the human King Arthur, your Lady Forartha, the drakon king, Theodosia, and more...

We led the fight.

We plotted and planned and schemed, until we had a danger-ous idea, one so brilliant that it had to work. We found a canta-men, *a song-spell you see. Written on paper so old that it crumbled at the touch. A banishing spell powerful enough to do away with even a god.*

And so it was, that one day we found ourselves on the killing fields. Our army of Fae and drakons, humans and elves (yes, even some of my people had come to fight), werecats and gryphons and more, standing against a goddess and her Wraiths.

The bloodshed was terrible. So - Ach... So many died, that day. Heroes, all...

It looked as if we were going to lose, when Theodosia finally be-gan to sing the cantamen. *It was a last resort.*

There was a light, so bright that it burned. It washed over everything, engulfed all of us, and when it was gone, it was over. It left Theodosia asleep, unwakeable. I sat with her for four long weeks, before we laid her to rest in a mountain cave, with no hope that she would ever wake again.

The wards that had fought with us could no longer feel the pres-ence of their patrons, even if they still had godly magicks in their blood.

The gods had fallen. All of them, not just the one. And so there was no one but us, fallible mortals, to try and repair a broken land, shattered by unrest and plague.

XXVIII - Messenger

"WHY - WHY DID YOU TELL me this?" Coren asked, quietly. His heart was pounding.

Something inside of him cried as he thought of his mother, of the ending to the story that she had believed - And how that ending was the one that was true after all.

Something inside of him screamed, that this, this was it. It was the end and it was the beginning.

Rosana slumped, fiddling with her dark braids. She exhaled in a great burst, as if steeling herself to say something she knew would not go over too well.

"Because you needed to know... You need to understand what happened, then. I fear that the past is about to repeat itself. The cycle of time is very much real, and it can be so destructive. I -" She closed her dark eyes. "I needed you to understand what happened then, because the cycle must continue on, or, better yet, be broken. And to do so, someone must gather the people of Erathien. And you... You must be our messenger, Coren of the North. There is no one else who can do it."

Coren sat up straight, feeling a sudden surge of panic. "Oh, gods, no. I cannot bring together nations as you did! I am no king! No one would *ever* place their armies in my hands." He bit his lip, hard.

Sora studied him, her fire flickering across her fingers again. Her expression was stern, chiding, as if she were his elder sister.

"Coren... You must have been brought here for a reason. We believe in fate. We believe in reasons, and there must be one for your arrival. The gods rise, Coren, and we have not had a visitor in hundreds of years. And you have proven that you have a good heart." Coren opened his mouth to protest, but Sora waved a hand at him.

"You could have run, like the rest. Instead you stayed, you saved lives, and the gods brought you here. Coren - You have entered a territory perfectly placed to send out emissaries, and gather an army. It must be Fate's work."

Sora cocked her head, her circlet flashing as she examined him. "Maybe you are correct, and they won't listen to a boy. But they *will* listen to a queen."

It was true.

Coren bit his lip. "My queen, my lady, I..." He trailed off, feeling his face heating from embarrassment. "I would be honoured, but I have to get home. My family - They don't know what happened to me. They are all in danger."

Sora's lips thinned, and the room grew quiet.

"Yes. You're right. You mustn't abandon them." Coren's head shot up, and he locked eyes with Rosana.

"Then... You must warn them, tell them that an army is coming to help. You must tell them what a threat they face. And on your way home, you can send the same message to the peoples whose lands you will cross on your way." The queen said. "You can spread the word, and you will return home to your family in time."

Coren stood, unable to sit still, and Shifted without thinking, finding himself prowling before the fire. Thinking.

His family was in danger. He was their only hope? Ridiculous. But. He had seen those shadow-beasts, he had fought them. Their blood stained his hands.

To stop and play diplomat with everyone who came across his path would slow his progress home, yes, but some part of his consciousness niggled at the back of his thoughts.

All of Erathien deserved a chance, not just the North. And the North would need a hell of a lot of warriors on their side, if they were to face a goddess.

Coren turned to Rosana, and looked her in the eye.

"You say this is fate. I do not believe in such things..." He held the stare, and then bowed his head. "But you are right. I am the messenger, and gods help me, if this is what it takes to make it home, to save my family, then I am yours to command."

"Thank you, Coren of the North." Rosana seemed relieved, her gown rustling as she stood, and took the werecat's scarred hands. "And gods help us all."

XXIX - In Which Queen Rosana Panics

COREN'S HANDS SHOOK as he drew them away, blinking. Sora was watching him closely, but she just nodded, her long hair rippling across her Marked shoulders. She took his hands as well, and then leaned in, whispering.

"Thank you, Northerner. Maybe you'll be the one to finally get us out of these *infernal* tunnels."

"You hate being underground as much as I do?" he asked, startled, and Sora smiled, turning wordlessly to her queen regnant. Her smile faltered when she saw Rosana's expression.

Rosana's brows were drawn together, staring at Coren's hands. He tucked them behind his back, and the queen's jaw tightened.

Coren wanted to run when faced with her intense, nearly angry glare. She was usually so kind, relaxed. What could have upset her?

He remembered the symbol marking his skin, just as she darted forwards with impossible speed. She snatched up his hand, and his wrist wrenched uncomfortably.

"Rosana! What in the hells-" Sora exclaimed.

But Rosana was already tracing the mark. "Tell me, by all the gods, that that is just some sort of werecat tattoo."

Coren just shook his head, scared, and stumbled away from the suddenly mad-seeming elven queen. "I - I do not know." he stuttered, as Sora grabbed Rosana's upper arm, her fingers digging into the older woman's arm.

"Rosana! What has gotten into you? Coren - You had better leave. Tell the guard at the Gates that you need a guide to get back to your rooms. He will summon Corrinne for you." Sora had taken on a commanding air, and suddenly Coren could see exactly why she was the heir to the throne.

He didn't need to be asked twice. The expression on Rosana's face was shocked, eerily so.

"That mark holds so much more power than we could *ever* fathom!" She cried, twisting her wedding band around her finger. The light in her eyes was awful.

It was not unkind. It was terrified.

Coren fled the room, holding the marked hand to his chest, his head spinning as he tried to puzzle out what the elven *regina* could have meant. Right then, all he wanted to do was to lay down and sleep.

XXX - In Which Lady Sora Scolds Her Queen

SORA'S FACE WAS THUNDERCLOUD dark as she sat Rosana down in her armchair.

"What in Lord Duman's name? What were you thinking?" She shook her head, utterly confused, and she sank down in the chair across from her mentor. Her voice went soft again as she leaned out and took her mentor's hands.

"What did that mark mean, Rosana? Are... Are you all right?"

The addressed shook her head, her eyes fluttering shut as she squeezed the princesses fingers. "I haven't - Unless the other old gods are waking as well - that... Sora!"

She looked up abruptly, her dark eyes fearful. "That mark - I haven't seen it since-"

The old queen stopped, twisting the tarnished wedding band on her finger. Sora swallowed.

Aleixei.

"That mark has power, Sora, greater than we could imagine. Whole cities have been destroyed with that power. Cities, and whole lands. So many lost their lives."

Sora rubbed Rosana's back, trying to rouse her shocked queen from the state she was in.

The *regina* was shaking, and now Sora's own brow was puckered into a frown. "I don't understand-"

"That mark is a symbol of godly power. He has been blessed, but oh, gods... The *Honoris*, it comes with a burden. His patron chose him as her ward, gave him a fragment of her power - but that has *killed* wards before. It has brought down empires." Rosana still looked completely rattled. It was jarring to see her like this - Nothing like the calm, collected queen that Sora had learned everything she knew from.

Sora closed her eyes, her *Signo* seeming to curl across her skin as she stood.

"*Regina*, you are in shock, you aren't thinking straight - wait until tomorrow. You terrified the poor boy. Come lie down, perhaps it is nothing."

But a creeping dread was starting to fill Sora's heart, and she looked down at her own god-blessed gift flickering through her fingers, and extinguished it with a thought.

Fragments of gods and Lady Chaos and messengers...

XXXI - In Which Rane Fights A Tiger

Two and a Half Moons Prior

THE CAT THAT FACED Rane was massive, his dark, fire-orange coat matted, dark stripes like scars running through it. Real scars, patches free of fur, raked across his muzzle, across his stomach. He was missing a large chunk of his tail, and a few of the toes on his front right paw.

A tiger. How in Micha's name did they get a godsdamn *tiger*? Rane's eyes were huge, their heart pounding wildly, scared. *Damn* it.

As it was, tigers were usually at least ten times bigger than clouded leopards. And this one was large for its kind. The tiger snarled out a warning, and Rane backed away, their tail flicking slightly, laying their ears back and bowing their head submissively.

The tiger was having none of this, and snarled out another wordless cry.

"Please, lord. I don't want to fight my own kin." Rane tried, their call loud in the suddenly silent Ring. "Please, lord."

The tiger stopped his prowl, staring down the smaller creature. "You dare address me? Do you know how hard it was to survive these fights? And I am not your kin. You reek of halfling, and your speech is tinged with a human tongue."

"It is true, lord. I am not fullblood. But I have been chosen to fight someone who shares at least half of my blood, and I cannot do it. I cannot be responsible for the death of another kindred." Rane hung their head even lower, head nearly brushing the dusty ground. The humans watched the odd, growling exchange with bated breath.

How would the champion react?

The answer came too soon - and it was not in Rane's favour. They could tell just from the shift to the great tiger's stance.

He snorted, glaring down at the smaller beast. "You dare try to trick me? I see through all of your ploys. I know your kind. I know you, those who try and take me unawares, try to lull me into thinking that I have won without a fight..." The gleam in the striped cat's eye was sickly yellow-bright.

"Please, lord, I am not that kind of-" Rane tried, breaking off as the larger cat lunged for their throat. They danced away easily, sudden cold washing over them.

If they lost - Gods forbid - they would die. If they won - it would mean that they would have to kill. Rane felt sick, continuing the deadly dance around ivory claws and teeth, unwilling to dart in and strike, to hurt this broken creature.

The tiger was graceful, but old and tired. He walked with a very slight limp, because of the missing toes, and the lack of a full tail threw off his balance.

Rane could spot a million ways to get past his defence, but could easily see how this tiger lord had taken down so many others. He was strong, powerful muscles rolling under his mangy coat, and the fluid way he lunged showed that he had practice hunting.

I'm sorry, tiger lord. I wish that your fate had been different. I wish that I could have seen you when you were free. You must have been beautiful.

The tiger lunged again, claws *nearly* raking across Rane's chest, parting fur, and their heart sank.

It was time to end this. They could not stand watching this once-proud cat act so desperately. He was fighting for his survival, knowing well that if he won, he was only condemning himself to more fights, more torture, more starvation.

One last chance, before... "Please, lord. Please do not make me fight you."

His eyes narrowed to furious slits. "I will not fall for foolish children's tricks. I have earned my crown, I have chosen this life, I have chosen to survive."

"I see how they treat you, lord! You call this any sort of survival? We are pawns. Please, let us break their game. Please, do not fight me. I don't want to fight back. It will only continue this torture. I have been captured, taken away from my people. I know that you must have someone at home, someone who loves you..." Rane whispered.

"Everyone is gone." the tiger snarled, his voice rough around the edges. "I am the last."

"I see why you would want to live on, and fight me." Rane said. "But I have had enough of playing games. I went along with Kir's game, and I went along with my amma's. I will not play the King's by choice."

The tiger stopped, examining the werecat. "I've been playing this one for a long time. There is no hope, no point in resisting. It is simply better giving in. It is simply better, playing their game."

The soundlessness of the Ring was pressing in again, reminding Rane of the many, many stunned spectators. The many who had never seen the fighters talk. Who were used to the swiftness, the brutality of the Ring.

Rane raised their eyes to the Prince, who was sitting, calm, in her throne, her hands clasped in her lap, her eyes fixed on a point in the distance. They were glassy, unfocused. She was worried that she would fail. She was scared of what her father would do if she did. A loss would be yet another weapon that he could use to undermine her and her small, ragtag band of rogues.

Rane was so focused on the Prince, that they didn't notice the tiger shifting on his feet until he was in midair. Rane screamed, the sound human and unnerving, as they spun to face the great cat.

"For all your talk of trickery." They spat, choking on the tiger lord's rancid breath. It stank of rotted meat.

"I will not lose the game. I will go on, and I will survive, and they will free me! They will reward me." The manic gleam in his eye was back, and even more painful to see than before. Rane went limp under the great cat's claws, and he chuffed, softly. "I will make it painless."

"I'm sorry. But... You are mistaken, my lord." Rane growled softly. When the larger beast paused, confused, they whispered a soft apology, and then writhed free, spinning around and raking a sharp paw across his muzzle.

The tiger roared, the rumble carrying louder than anything Rane had ever heard. And the crowd erupted.

Their cheers made Rane sick. They didn't want to play a part in the power struggle between King and Prince, or to fight an innocent. But these people didn't think of that. This was all fun and games to them, and the beasts in the ring were nothing more than that... Just mindless, bloodthirsty monsters.

Rane bared their teeth at the tiger lord, and watched until the cat was unnerved, his movements faltering for a moment - and giving them an opening. Rane flew in, their small form now an advantage against the great cat, claws painting deep ruby gashes across the tiger's stomach, spinning away as the tiger roared, wincing as he stumbled.

He staggered forwards, pain making his movements erratic.

Rane gritted their sharp teeth, and sighed. There had to be an end to this, and it was better not drag it out. Even if they didn't want to do it... It was better than letting the ragged old beast suffer.

They watched for an opening in the circling tiger's movements, watching his limp, made even worse by the deep gouges in his stomach. Rane's bloodied claws dug into the earth. Their legs tensed as they watched, waiting.

The tiger stumbled, again, bleeding into the earth, red staining his already rusty coat, his mangled paw twisting under him as he put too much weight on toes that were not there.

Rane pushed off, and flew.

Their tail lashed, and they tensed for impact.

The crowd held its breath. Time slowed. Aralie half-rose, her hand on the pommel of her blade.

And... Impact.

The tiger went flying as Rane slammed into him, hitting him where they knew it would hurt, causing his legs to crumple under their combined weights.

The Ring was a blur of dust and sky and faces as they tussled. Claws scratched along Rane's foreleg, and they wailed, digging their own into the tiger's shoulders.

And then the training truly took over. In a blink, they were on top of the tiger, and he was limp. His eyes were glazed, the earth beneath him dark, dark red.

Too much blood.

But he raised his head, meeting Rane's eye. "Thank you, werecat."

Rane drew back, and the tiger blinked, leisurely. "It was time that I left this hell. I am sorry. The Painted City - It is hell on earth. Survive."

Rane stepped off of the tiger lord, and turned away, unable to watch as the life left his body. Unable to think.

Dear gods. Their thoughts were jumbled. Bile rose in their throat, and it took everything they had not to Shift and vomit all over the dusty, bloodstained Ring. They stared up at a shocked King, and a smug Prince, an emotionless Queen.

And they wailed, human and full of the pain that these fiends had caused.

These thieves had taken Rane's freedom. They had taken the tiger's... And he had chosen to force Rane into taking his life, just to escape them. And Rane keened on.

The crowd shifted uncomfortably, murmuring. They had gotten their game, and now... Now they saw the results. A body, as always. But the victor did not seem to want the title. Rane was too human in actions and expression. And it unnerved them.

But the game was over.

Rane had won.

And would pay the price.

XXXII - Lady Kinaar
Two and a Half Moons Later

THE DENSE DREAM-FOG was as thick as it always was, rolling in over a peaceful image of Myr and Lana, snugged up close. They were even holding hands in their sleep, their wedding bands gleaming...

And then they were obscured by the thick mist, and Coren shuddered, praying that he wouldn't have to face the shadow-woman again, wouldn't have to dream of his own death again and again.

The fog seemed to roll in faster the more he wished it would go away, and he could do nothing against it. Again, he felt heavy, unable to move away from the spot, only waiting. Waiting...

The woman stepped from the fog again, her bow still clasped in a pale hand, her blazing gown falling in glowing folds. And this time, the fog grew thinner, instead of thicker, as she stepped forwards.

Coren found himself sitting atop the Conpitum, *glossy black waves lapping on the stone around him. He sat on no-man's land, between the four crests. The woman was gone, and Coren stood, his heart racing. Waiting for something.*

Droplets spattered down from the sky, dampening his hair and clothing. His armour was gone.

Dripping echoed across the deathly silent valley. No smoke rose from above the trees... The blackened, shrivelled trees. Nothing moved in their shelter, no animals chirped, roared, howled.

Dead silent, under the rapidly darkening sky.

Coren stood, and was on the edge of the Conpitum *in a moment, staring down into the obsidian lake. He watched as the waves intensified, winced as the rain began to sting his face, and he knew he should move away from the edge, but he was rooted in place, unable, or unwilling, to move...*

The wind began to shriek, an all-too familiar sound as the clouds grew green-ish, dredging up painful memories.

The roar was all around him, below and above, and he could not escape, panting he tried to walk away, but he was stuck in place, a statue on the brink.

A wall of sound crashed over him, louder than the wind, louder than the pounding of his heart.

And the water before him exploded, sending him flying backwards, off the rock and into the waves. The dark closed above his head, and he thrashed, his clothes floating around him, his heavy boots dragging him down. He tried to lean down, untie the laces, pull them off, but they were already waterlogged, and his fingers were going numb from the bone-chilling cold.

Plants reached their tendrils up for him, out of the dark, their vines turning to hands that gripped his arms, pulling him away from the light, into the dark. The crash of waves turned into the murmuring of voices, and when he opened his mouth to scream, water rushed in, chilling, numbing, turning his heart and veins to ice.

It felt like frost was slowly creeping over his skin, as he fell, unable to do a thing. His eyes drifted closed as he floated down, helped along by the slick, colder than ice, hands.

He had given up, stopped fighting, stopped trying to breath, the tightness in his chest nothing compared to reopened wounds in his shoulder and side, which were streaming clouds of red, swirling in the water.

He was drifting down, no air in his lungs to keep his body afloat, the hands gone, not needing to aid his descent any longer.

And then he was falling faster, faster, the smooth silk of the water replaced by the tumbling, turbulent wind of a storm, tossing him about, and he was back in the storm that had carried him so far away from home.

Debris and ash coated his still-wet skin, as he struggled for a clean breath, drawing in only smoke, and stinging particles, grating against his skin. And he plummeted.

In an instant, he was flat on his back in a windswept field, clean and dry, unhurt, and able to breathe. Millions of stars twinkled above him, the twin moons shining, bright crown jewels in the black velvet sky. He turned his head into the grass, letting the soft blades tickle his face, the smell of green growing things reminding him of his home.

The voice was startling as it rolled across the valley, bright as summer sunshine, soft as the moonlight falling across everything.

I'll always be here for you, child. She murmured, and then she was leaning over him, offering him her hand, the light of her gown blinding him.

Coren's body moved of its own accord, lifting a hand, and she pulled him up, the light subsiding to a warm glow. The first thing that he noticed was not her face, not her weapons or armour, but the dress.

It was not glowing, as much as it was the light, it's rippling folds were the insubstantial turned solid. The same dark, diamond-speckled stuff of the night sky trimmed the hem, the flowing cuffs, the swooping neckline that accentuated a long, pale throat.

His eyes drifted to her bare feet, her bow and quiver, and then, finally her face.

His heart sank. Somehow, he had been hoping that this figure was his mother, a spectre come back to protect her only child, but this inhumanly beautiful woman was a stranger.

Her perfect cupid's bow lips were curled into a smile, her eyes a brilliant green, a dusting of freckles sprinkled across the bridge of her nose and her cheekbones. Her flaming hair fell in waves past her waist, so light it seemed to float.

And then he saw the crown.

It was a circlet, the traditional crown of Erathien, similar to the ones that Myr, and Queen Rosana wore. But the mark in the centre of this one was so familiar it hurt.

An interlocking sun and crescent moon, ringed with rays of light, done in silver and gold. Identical to the mark on his hand, and the one on the Conpitum. *His heart skipped a beat.*

This woman was no spectre, but for all of the mystery surrounding her, she may as well have been.

Coren knelt, his breathless voice breaking the complete silence of the field. "Lady Kinaar."

XXXIII - Invisibility

COREN SAT BOLT UPRIGHT, shaking off the gauzy remnants of the dream, shaking his head. He lifted his left hand to run his fingers through his hair, but the image inked there stopped him.

He cursed, staring down at the mark, and tried to forget the dream, the darkness hidden in it's folds.

He stood, his legs shaking, and wandered over to the mirror that hung above the glowing embers of the fireplace.

He hesitated, before looking up. To look in the glass would mean seeing exactly how much he had fallen apart since the Exile. He wasn't sure if he was quite prepared for that.

But exhaled, bit his lip, and raised his head to look in the mirror.

There was no reflection.

Coren turned in a circle, his breath suddenly coming fast, looking around, for what, he didn't know. Perhaps his own body, lying limp in a corner somewhere.

He tried to process, everything feeling very far away. When he looked down, he could see watery, faded patches of himself, so he had *some* substance. But when he raised his eyes to the reflective glass again, he could see nothing.

Coren swore, as long and as loud as he could. His brain was going into overdrive, thinking too far ahead, and descending into a spiral of anxiety and nerves.

He didn't know how this had happened. He didn't know how to fix it.

What would happen if the elves found him gone? Would they think that he had run away? Would this ruin his chances of seeing his family again? What if he never was visible again?

Panic was rising, freezing cold, as he replayed his dreams, replayed everything since his Exile. Every detail that could contain answers.

As his anxiety rose, a soft glow, barely brighter than the dying embers of the fire, caught his eye.

Kinaar's mark was shining in the centre of his palm. It was as if the tattoo were suddenly made of light.

"What do you want from me?" he cried, Shifting shape, and then returning to his human form, trying to lose the glow and the invisibility. But the tattooed mark just turned into a dark patch of fur, that shone with the same gilded radiance, and his body did not become any more substantial.

He froze when a wooden creak caught his ear.

The door to his chambers were opening again, and he bit back another curse as the energetic elf who had fetched him the day before stuck her head in. Her cheerful grin melted into a confused, somewhat fearful expression.

"Coren?" She asked, warily.

"Corrinne!" Coren tried, but she didn't seem to hear, or see, him. She couldn't see him, the glow, nothing. He began cursing again, but she still didn't do anything that would show that she saw him. His already too-fast heart rate ratcheted up.

The elf looked around once more, and then threw up her hands. "Gotta find Madame. Shitshitshitshit."

And then she was gone, the door closing heavily in her wake, and Coren screamed.

Come on! I can't stay this way... I can't ... I have to see the Queen. He pleaded, with whom he didn't know.

You've done it!

It was the voice of the woman from his dreams. Who took the form of Lady Kinaar, *dea* of day and night, light and dark, and the in-between. Patron of the North.

What did you do to me? He asked, even his mental voice trembling as he tried to form coherent words. *Why are you in my head?!*

You are my ward. She murmured, simply.

The hell? His legs gave out, and he sat down hard.

You contain a piece of me. You are strong. You are loyal, head-strong. You fought for the people who betrayed your trust, you chose to die for them. You stood up to my eldest sister, knowing full well that she is a goddess. You are the one I choose to bear my power. Her voice was serene, unruffled.

"This can *not* be happening. Not now. Not when I'm so far from home." He buried his face in his hands, tried to block out the voice. His *patron goddess's* voice! "There's too much happening. It's too much."

You wish to know what I did to you. I can answer that question. You need to trust me.

"You are in my head! You are in my dreams, my nightmares, my prayers, and now my head!" He yelled.

Yes. You are my pupillus, *are you not? A piece of me is inside of you. You are my eyes, my mouth, my hands, while I sleep. You will be my anchor as I wake.* Kinaar was so calm. So calm while everything around Coren seemed to tremble, blacken, and burn.

"I can't - I have duties - I have -"

Duties that will bring you to exactly where I want to be. My powers will aid you - you can draw on me to do incredible things. You have the ability to be the most powerful pupillus *I have ever seen, in all my years.*

Coren pressed his hands to the sides of his head, and forced himself away from the tight spiral of panic.

I can help you become visible again, Coren. Take a deep breath. The goddess murmured after a long pause.

It was all so much. Too much. But everything could be broken down into more manageable bits.

He inhaled, exhaled. Focused on the woman's voice in his head. That was all that mattered. Figuring this out was the first step...

Just visualise it. Strip away the layers of the Veil that you have wrapped yourself in. She sounded eager to see if he would be able to succeed.

"The Veil." He murmured, disbelieving. The in-between between the Void, and life. Lady Kinaar's domain.

He took a deep breath. Legends were real. This was real. It had to be dealt with. One step at a time...

Yes. Good. Now, try it. Like lifting a curtain, like pulling away a blanket. That's all. Kinaar murmured in his head.

He took another deep breath, his heart slowing down to a more normal rate. One step at a time...

Good. Again. Kinaar murmured in Coren's head.

Again and again, until finally, something clicked into place.

It was a blessed relief when he felt the heaviness of solidity return to his body. The mark on his hand was dark again. The first step was done, and his chest loosened a bit.

But the voice in his head was still there.

XXXIV - In Which The North Trains

THE BLADES CLASHED between them, and Lindara of the North screamed, her hair flying around her face as she spun and ducked, a whirling dervish surrounded by a gleaming force of silver-bright steel. Her opponent was breathing heavily, nearly finished...

Lin was strong and skilled, and had been drilling for hours every day, with her kris, with the bow, with a sword. It had paid off.

She brought up her serpentine blade, the opponent's rapier sliding off, metal screeching on metal from the force of the blow. Sioch was in her head, feeding her information:

Her side is still weak. It could be an advantage for you.

See how her grip is off? Use that.

Watch how she favours her left foot. Do something about that. Step on her toes if you have to.

For a second, Lin allowed her own gaze to slide up towards her brother, who was nestled in the branches of a nearby tree, observing the skirmish raging below with wide eyes.

WATCH OUT! Your left! I'm just another pair of eyes. Ignore me!

Lin brought her blade up just in time, parrying with deft movements. Even though she had the shorter blade, and had to get in close if she wanted to wound, she was winning. Although, that was probably because the woman she was facing was still recovering from a serious injury.

She had a feeling that Myr could have whipped her ass any other day of the year.

All around them, other pairs of Northerners clashed and fought, the oldest with greying hair, the youngest just barely fifteen seasons old. Training, training.

Myr was panting now, a hand pressed to her ribs where her wound was still healing. The skin was nearly done knitting back together, thanks to some of *Malefica* Theodosia's *magiae*, but she was still not in peak condition.

"Be careful, please love!" Lana sounded worried, rubbing her belly. She sat in the shade of the tree that Sioch had climbed to escape training. His logic was that he was a better asset up where he could spot for his sister. And it was true. Lin would have lost twenty times over without him.

Right side! He screeched, his mental voice loud.

In a flash, Lin had driven her kris up and around, twisting Myr's arm until she dropped her rapier. And then the tip of the wavy blade was at her aunt's throat, and Lindara had a grin on her face.

"And the queen falls." She said proudly, as Myr bowed her head in surrender.

"Well done, Niece. Although..."

"If you were healthy, I would be dead by now." Lin finished, smiling. Myr had said the same so many times by now, it seemed more like she was trying to convince herself, than the werecat girl.

"But she is *not* healthy, and really should sit down." *Malefica* Theodosia said, coming out of nowhere. Her odd Common Tongue accent was still strange to hear.

"I need to be seen training with my people." Myr protested, but the old sorceress was having none of it.

"You will not be doing anyone any good reinjuring yourself. Your people need to see you *well*." She responded, gripping the chieftainess by the arm, and escorting her over to Lana.

Lana grinned up at her wife, and pulled her down beside her. "Come snuggle."

Myr swallowed a grin, trying to look annoyed, but failing to fully quench it, the corners of her mouth turning up. "Just for a moment."

Lin wandered back to them as well, and stared up at her *comes*.

"Are you ever coming down, See?" she asked, but Sioch just shot her a lazy grin, and closed his brown eyes.

Possibly never. I'm away from you lot up here. He thought, and Lin laughed.

Theodosia made a small sound, studying Sioch for a long moment, her expression unreadable. Her eyes shifted colour, slowly fading from blue to violet.

"Is everything all right, *Malefica*?" Lin asked, a little alarmed by the intense study.

"Everything is fine, Lindara. Do not worry. Now, I had better get a bit of training in myself." She said, an odd look on her face as she absentmindedly drew and flicked open one of her butterfly knives, the blade shining razor-sharp.

"Aye." The twins murmured, watching her leave. Their aunts didn't seem to have noticed, until the witch was on her way. Then, their faces were full of questions.

"What was that about?" Lana asked, still rubbing her stomach, wincing as Baby kicked a bit too hard.

"No idea." Lin shielded her eyes from the sun, and looked across the field, watching the *malefica go.*

"My Lady of Stars, she moves fast." Myr muttered, following her nieces' gaze. They trailed off, watching the witch.

"It's hard to believe that after such a long period of peace, we are training again. Everyone is so scared, and tense. Including myself." Sioch said, suddenly. He looked serene and relaxed, nearly-bare twigs casting odd shadows across his face, the comment making for a strange juxtaposition.

"I know." Lana said sadly. "I was hoping that our child would be born to peacetime."

"I was as well." Myr wrapped a strong, tanned arm around the smaller woman's shoulder. The move was possessive, and tender, and for a moment the twin's thoughts flashed to their own mother.

They had never had the time to properly grieve.

"At least the training seems to be going well. We won't be going into this entirely unprepared." Lana murmured into her wife's shoulder.

"I wish we didn't have to do this at all." the twins said, their voices harmonising.

"Don't we all." Myr sighed.

XXXV - In Which Some Loose Ends Are Tied Up

Two Moons Prior

"SO, YOU RETURNED, LITTLE werecat?" Her voice was smooth and cold.

Kir raised his head to look the goddess in the eyes. "Of course, my Lady."

Power hungry, grovelling little boy. Chaos thought. Aloud, she said: "And it is done?"

"Of course, my Lady."

Her smile did not reach her eyes. "Well done, General. You are ready? The people accept you?"

"Perhaps a trifle unwillingly at first, but I soon... Convinced them. And you know that I have always been ready, my Lady."

"Of course, General!" Her laugh was screaming, as it always had been. Terrifying. She looked at her slave, at his ruined face.

He had sworn himself to her in blood and sweat and tears. Soon, though, he would make one final sacrifice for her, to help her regain her full strength. Soon, he would sell her his very soul.

"You are sure, General?" She asked, and stepped off of her dais of gold. As soon as her prison had lost its power, it had fallen to twisted pieces, and she had picked them up again. She had re-formed them into a throne of gold, of wood and of metal, the weave forming another sort of cage.

Her captured souls were trembling inside, howling. Their bodies were what allowed her Wraiths to *Acclarare*, Manifest, on this earth. For now.

Soon, she would be strong again. So strong, that she could form Wraiths from nothing but her own being.

"I am sure, Lady Chaos."

The goddess smiled and reached out her hands, palms up, to Kir. "Take my hands." she whispered to him, and he complied, as eager as a puppy. Oh, how he wanted to please her.

She let a fragment of her power surge into him, her Wraith curling around their intertwined fingers and into his body with a hiss of freezing air.

She could have let her first, ever-present, fully *Acclaratus* Wraith take him, but this was so much more *fun*. Kir trusted her.

He should have been smarter than that.

The goddess stepped away from his screaming mortal body. Kir had been a fool. She stretched out her hands over the body, twirling them as she gathered up his departing soul in her hands, before sending it into her cage. The shell on the ground was still twitching as the Wraith took over, the same inky darkness that she was comprised of slowly engulfing and dissolving flesh and bone, fiery coals replacing his eyes, slipping into the clothing that Kir had been wearing.

The new Wraith stood smoothly, and bowed before it's mistress, who laughed again.

"Kir of the South, you were a *fool*. A mortal fool. And now..." Lady Chaos gestured to the Wraith that stood before her. "You are gone, and your shell is mine to use. I suppose I should thank you. After all, you freed me. But stupidity... Stupidity is not praiseworthy, little werecat." She smiled over at the imprisoned souls in their cage, her silvery, razor sharp teeth glittering. "I thank you anyways."

WHAT DID BECOME OF the South, after Kir died at the hands of his goddess?

Nothing, and everything.

No one was killed. No Southern souls were imprisoned with the rest. Chaos kept her promise, in a twisted way, and the South was spared.

But the South... They would never join Myr's resistance. They would never fight for the Forgotten Goddess.

They would sleep, until someone woke them, silent, and cold, but alive.

They slept like their *deae* and *divi* once did, after the Fall of the Gods.

Rane still had a people. But that people slept.

And the West, and the East? Why were they unreachable? What had happened to them?

Everything.

They stood up, but were too proud to ask for help, and they fell.

One, and then the other.

Every single soul was killed.

XXXVI - Plotting

Two Moons Later

"COREN!" THE DOOR SLAMMED open, and a young elf stalked into the room. "The Madame is in a panic! She told me to check one last time, to see if you were still here, and I told her that you weren't -" She shook her head.

"Well, it seems that I was wrong!" She laughed, her usual light-hearted mood seemingly returned, and with a vengeance. She was making Coren's tired mind spin.

He had been sitting there for nearly the entire day, working with Lady Kinaar, and trying desperately to stay sane.

"Apologies, Corinne. I wasn't sure that you were coming to fetch me, so I left, and got lost... Someone told me the way back to my rooms, where I've been waiting for you. I am so, so sorry. I never should have tried to leave."

The lie slipped all too easily off his tongue, and Kinaar tutted something in the back of his head. He really needed to figure out how to block her voice.

But he had gotten a bit more control over his newfound powers. After first drawing the Veil away from himself, he had wound up flashing in and out of sight every couple of minutes. When Corinne entered, the flashing was mostly under control, but it cost him a lot of effort.

"Well, then! Come along, we must get you to the *regina*. She was quite worried, Northerner. Hurry up, I must report to Madame!" She skipped out, every trace of her frustration gone.

Coren sighed, following the elven girl, and quickly stripping away a threatening layer of gauzy magick.

"Coren. Where have you been?" Rosana's tone was concerned when she welcomed him into the huge, beautiful throne room. Coren closed the heavy side-door, the latch falling shut behind him.

"I am so sorry, Your Majesty. I found myself lost when I, ahm. Tried to get here myself..." Coren looked up from the ground, intending to meet Rosana's gaze, but instead found himself gaping at the architecture.

"Ah... I am so sorry. The tunnels must be confusing to newcomers." Lady Sora said, from her place beside the queen.

Rosana smiled at Coren, and then said, proudly: "As for the architecture... This is my own work. I was the one who designed it, the one who shifted the earth. It is still the grandest room we have down here."

The sharply arched Gothic ceiling flew high above them, stone benches facing the twin thrones at the front of the cathedral-like structure. The thrones themselves were carved of a dark marble, one with hammered gold veins, and a flamelike back, the other streaked with silver, it's back carved with elegant vines. The columns supporting the roof seemed too slender and delicate to possibly hold up the ceiling, but support it they did.

Before the thrones, there stood a plain wooden table, looking completely out of place. A large piece of paper was spread across the table's surface.

Coren gestured up at the vaulted roof above his head. "I have never seen anything like it." he murmured.

While the queen explained a bit more about the throne room, Coren examined the queen briefly, drawing a quick conclusion. Every trace of the somewhat crazed woman from the day before was gone.

Although... Coren now knew exactly why she had been so scared of the *Honoris* inked on his palm. When Rosana finished, Coren made a quick bow.

"My ladies. My apologies for yesterday. I did not mean to cause any sort of panic." He said.

"Apology accepted, werecat." Sora said calmly, stepping forwards. Her circlet glittered in the torchlight, as did the gold embroidery on the hems of her dark wine-red dress.

Rosana nodded at the heir, smoothing her own lilac skirts. "And Coren - I apologise for my actions. I am truly sorry that I frightened you." The ancient elf bowed her head. Her voice shook with something like embarrassment, gone in a moment, replaced by a business-like tone.

"Now. We brought you to the throne room for a reason. Come up here, please. We need to get you safely home. And we need you to help us gather our army."

When Coren reached the dais, and stood before the queen and heir, he could tell that the paper spread across the table was, in fact, a surprisingly accurate map.

It outlined every border, including the ever-shifting human ones. The borders of the elves, Fae, werecats, drakons, and every other magickal race had not changed since the time before the Fall of the Gods.

Sora cleared her throat, and tapped a pale finger on a point in the Elven Territories. "We are approximately here. The nearest exit..." She trailed the finger diagonally through the woods, eventually leaving it a couple of inches away. "Is here. Only a couple of miles."

"You have *miles* of tunnels down here?" Coren asked, unable to hide his amazement.

"We have been living under this earth for so long, and our people flourish... The tunnels have spread until they catacomb the entire length and width of the territory we have been allotted. Someday we may even have to spread underneath some of the desert!" Rosana laughed.

Coren gave a small smile, ducking his head. "So, if I am here, and the North, the heart of the war, I suppose, is here -" He tapped a finger on the centre of the Cortach mountain range, "Then which route would get me there the fastest? And -"

He paused to take a breath, and quiet the noise in his head. "And which people am I to visit on my way?"

"Well." Sora trailed off, running her finger along a road that cut through the forest blanketing the Elven Territories. "You will have to take the Great Road. It is the clearest of the paths, and the only one that will not mislead you. It will take you to..."

She traced along the dark line of road, and into a large sprawl of pale yellowish brown.

"The Solchar Desert." Rosana murmured. She raised her voice, continuing. "This is the fastest path. It is brutal, crossing the desert, but speed is of the essence..."

"I can handle it. I have to get home." The werecat's gaze was hard, his face entirely emotionless. Something flickered across Sora's face, but it was gone too quickly to identify.

Rosana continued: "All right. Now, you must remember that it has been too long since we have left the Territories. Our messenger does not often stop in the Solchar, so we are uncertain, but we believe that the closest city to our land is still the Painted City. We had steady contact with a man there for a long time, but we have not received any messages in recent times." The *regina* swallowed. "He was old... We think that he... May have passed on."

Sora cleared her throat. "But otherwise, the path is set through to the Faerie Empire. Auris, Corrinnestāt, and Laeren should be safe human cities. Well, as safe as any place could be. Auris is right here-" Sora tapped a dark point right at the place where the yellow-brown faded into an unmarked, lush green. "Right before Faerie. Now, the creatures in that place..."

"Nightmares." Coren muttered, remembering all of the tales that he had been told around the campfire. "They deceive you, and trick the senses. Even the map doesn't know what can truly be found there."

"Perhaps so, but you can trust *Imperator* Kalei. Fae is the descendant of *Imperator* Quai, our old ally, and fae seems honest in faer letters to us. Fae will surely offer you shelter for a few days, and you can try to gain the empire's support while you are there." Sora said. "Gaining Kalei's support would save us. Faerie's army, and sheer number of inhabitants, is immense, and they are all extremely powerful magick-users."

Rosana leaned over, taking over from her heir. "After leaving the Faerie Empire, I would try to proceed directly towards the Cortach Range. This would require travelling through the Drakon Lands, but I believe that their current queen should be hospitable. The drakons are unpredictable, however, so anything could happen while there. I would not count on them as allies, but we can still hope."

The Drakon Lands were shaded a pale orange, the same colour as a flame, and the legend seemed to indicate only wide open plains and a handful of lakes.

The drakons were loyal during the Great War, before the Fall of the Gods. The queen does not want to condemn them, but she does not know what their attitude towards a new war would be. They lost so many in the war. Kinaar said, suddenly.

Images of great scaly serpents falling from the sky, their shining armour pierced with flaming spears, flashed across the back of Coren's eyes, and he bit back a curse, biting his lip to ground himself.

When his vision cleared, the elven women were watching him with puzzled expressions.

"Apologies. Headache." He lied. "After the drakons?"

"After the drakons, it will be urgent that you make it home. You must warn them, and tell them that we are coming to aid them. Do not stray from the roads. They are the most direct path." Rosana dug her fingernail into the Cortach Range. "We will give you a map, and anything else that you will need. We repaired your armour and weapons, and will get them back to you as soon as we can."

Coren smiled again, his hand straying unconsciously to the place on his hip where his knives should have been.

"Everything still looks alright to you?" Sora asked, her brown eyes piercing. Coren shifted a little under her scrutiny.

"Yes." He studied the map for another long moment, mentally tracing the path, his heart skipping a beat. "I will be going from the far eastern border of Erathien to the centre, yes? How long will this take?"

"Weeks, if everything goes as planned," was the matter of fact reply.

Lady of Stars. Coren thought, a wave of anxiety welling up yet again.

Breathe, Coren. Kinaar murmured, and he wanted to scream. He closed his eyes, trying to break everything down again. Take it step by step.

"Everything alright, Coren?" Rosana asked. Coren nodded, and forced a smile.

"Yes. I'm going home!"

Rosana hesitated for a moment. Coren swore that her gaze darted to his palm for a second, and he curled his fingers around the *Honoris*. But then the elven queen stepped around the table, and pulled him into a tight hug.

"You have a long journey ahead, but I believe that you have it in you. We will meet you in the morning, with everything you will need. Try not to get lost again." Sora's joke was thin, but Coren's smile grew a little bit more real.

He had held it together, and was feeling calmer, after seeing the route all laid out. The stability that came with having a plan helped his anxiety so much. His shoulders sagged, just a bit, as he bowed.

"Thank you, my ladies. May I take my leave?"

"Of course, Coren. We will meet you at the entrance to the forest in the morrow." Rosana said.

The queen's smile grew visibly strained the second that the boy turned his back. "The mark was still there." She murmured to the heir, who sighed.

"My queen, please. You were so upset yesterday, and -" She stopped abruptly, and stared off towards the heavy door to the outer halls.

Her hands started to shake. "Rosana... Are you seeing...?"

The older elf had gone pale.. "I was right. Micha save us."

Their whispers didn't carry, swallowed up by the space, so when Coren rematerialized, he hadn't even noticed that he had been gone.

"Wait!" Rosana cried, as Coren reached for the door's handle. He turned, startled.

"Your patron is powerful." She whispered, and Coren's shoulders jerked, his fingers curling.

He stared across the room at the queen for a long moment, before taking his own wrist, and running a calloused thumb across the Seal.

"You knew what it was the second you saw it." It wasn't a question, and Queen Rosana did nothing to deny it.

"What happened to the other wards? Why are you so scared?" he asked, his voice shaking on the last syllable, despite every ounce of will he put into keeping a calm expression.

Total silence fell.

Rosana took a deep breath. She was twisting her wedding band again, and Sora was looking at it with tears in her eyes.

Corrinne's words rang in the werecat's head as he listened to the queen speak, watched her twist the ring around her finger.

Her husband died. His name was Aleixei. It was a tragedy. An accident. There was nothing we could do.

"I'm - I'm sorry, Coren. I would tell you, but... It's not my place." The queen bowed her head, and suddenly, she looked exactly as old as she truly was. Her shoulders slumped under the weight of the past. When she looked up again, her eyes were blazing. "Your patron, Lady Kinaar, she must be the one to teach you, to tell you of the laws of this world. Make sure that she tells you everything. *Everything*, Coren."

"She says that she will teach me. She swore it. And I will learn." Coren said, hiding any discomfort. Because this was... Odd.

Rosana was a great queen, and she had led hundreds of years of peace, but this side of her, it was unnerving.

"Please say that you still trust me, *Regina*. I am not a threat."

Silence. And then: "I never stopped trusting you, Coren. It's the gods who I have lost faith in."

Kinaar made a small noise in Coren's head, somewhere between hurt and grief.

"The world has changed, Coren. It is nothing like it was when I was young. I cannot help but wonder what would have happened had the seven bothered to remember their sister. If I had never made the mistakes that I made." Rosana turned her head away, still fiddling with her wedding band. "I wonder what the world would look like - what my life would look like - had the Great War never happened. I wonder what would have happened, had we found another way. Had the gods continued to walk this earth."

Coren's breath stocked as he tried to picture it. Kinaar fell silent.

There was a sudden rush of heat and noise as Sora extended her arms, breaking the silence. A tiny fiery bird exploded out from her palms, turning into a wave of golden heat. As it faded, she made a face.

"The world changed. There is nothing we can do about the past." She looked at her mentor, and her gaze went soft. "Rosana has been like a mother to me. I understand what she is feeling. But I - I think that the past is the past. What happened cannot be undone. We must instead work from that past to make a better future."

Sora could see Coren shift uncomfortably, could see the walls coming back up as his face settled into a stony neutral.

"I'm sorry, Coren. We're not helping much." Her laugh was wry. "Too much pressure for one person, yes?"

He bit his lip, his voice rough. "Yes. This all-" he waved a hand around, "It is all so much to process. I - I need time before I can talk about it. I *am* sorry, Queen Rosana. Lady Sora."

"It's all right, Coren." Rosana murmured.

"I need to sleep." The boy said, and bowed before leaving, swiftly.

"Rosana..." Sora murmured, her long hair falling around her shoulders as she leaned over the map. Her curled fingers blotted out huge swaths of land, and she had to quell the urge to set the whole paper world on fire.

"I'm sorry, Sora." Rosana said, her voice crumbling.

"It's all right. It's not me who you managed to terrify. Again." Sora looked up, and closed her eyes. "I'm sorry. I can't. Rosana. Mother. I love you, but you need to pull it together. That boy is scared enough. Please, don't comment on the *Honoris* again."

Rosana said nothing, instead sinking down onto her silver-and-black throne.

Sora came over, and touched her shoulder. "What happened to Aleixei was so long ago, Rosana... And Coren is a different person. Gods willing, it will all be all right."

When Rosana looked up, she looked to be on the verge of tears. "I know, Sora, darling. I know..."

"Good." Sora gave her queen, her mother-figure, a hug. "It'll all be all right."

XXXVII - In Which the Weight of the World is Placed on Coren's Shoulders

COREN'S FORM FLICKED back into sight, and he collapsed onto the too-soft bed, Lady Kinnar's voice finally silent. He was completely exhausted.

He had spent the entire afternoon practising with his patron, but for that amount of time, the reward was immense.

Invisibility and insubstantiality.

He had never been able to hold the simplest of *illusionis*, his entire life. Magick like this, being able to truly use it... It was incredible.

It was insane that it was he who was able to use it. Insane, but feeling more real by the second, and it was exhilarating.

He panted, and then grinned, his sharp teeth pricking at his lower lip. *Five minutes under full control!*

Well done. The goddess seemed completely unimpressed. *Child, how often do you practise your magicks?*

Ähm. Not often. No need. And... I am not terribly talented when it comes to illusionis, *or other small magicks.* He sighed, bracing himself for yet another disbelieving torrent of words. It came, right on cue. It hadn't been very pleasant so far, sharing his head with a goddess.

Lady Kinaar sputtered. *We slept for only a few millennia, and this is what I wake to. How many peoples have given up on the old ways?*

"I think... I think that the elves are one of the last. The Fae, perhaps, but many magickal arts have been lost. I don't know of any humans who practise any sort of magick. Aside from the witch who saved me in the North, but apparently she's hundreds of years old."

Kinaar made a choking noise. *After all that we did. All that we have given you. We sleep for a while, and then all of our work is undone! And the cycle is ready to be fulfilled again!*

"The cycle?" Coren asked softly. A memory surfaced at the words, a fond, dusty memory, of his mother. His mother, the storyteller, who had taught him so much, and who had known so much about the gods...

Silence.

"Kinaar?"

No response. Coren leaned his head back, frustrated.

"My Lady?"

Coren sighed, and then set his jaw. "Lady Kinaar. I have been trying so hard all day. I have endured you poking at me for not practising *dead arts*. This is all so new, and it's terrifying. Exhilarating, but terrifying. Please, tell me what in the hells you mean. It is the least you could do. You swore you would teach me. Start now."

The silence dragged out, and Coren was on the verge of giving up, when Kinaar finally spoke.

The cycle... It is... Life and death, birth, rebirth, everything in between. It is indescribable. It is our making, and our breaking. Everything is a cycle. But the one that I refer to... Is the cycle that we, the gods, are stuck in. We rise, we rule, we create, and then one turns against the others, and destruction reigns. There is no end to it.

It was Coren's turn to be stunned silent. "Is this what Rosana was speaking of? Are the wards destined to die when the cycle goes on, and you fall once more?"

Kinaar paused, surely trying to decide how much she should tell. *No. No, it's not. You are not. The cycle applies only to the gods, but the whole world is impacted.*

"Then why are you so hesitant to tell me about it, Lady Kinaar?" Coren whispered. His mind was already racing ahead, drawing out awful scenarios, and he had to force himself to breathe, and push the thoughts aside. There was only one truth, for all of the wild dangers that his mind had created.

Because if Erathien is to flourish, if we want to bring a balance to Erathien, the cycle must be broken. My sister... We were fools to forget her. When she returned, she upset our balance, and began the cycle. That must be righted.

"You-" Coren sputtered. Even his overactive mind could not have dreamed *this* one up. "You want me to restore balance to Erathien. Me. How? Look at me! I'm nothing!"

Coren. Kinaar's voice was suddenly thunderous, cutting through his anxious haze. *You are* not *nothing. I see you, Coren, and I see someone brave, and strong, and loyal. I chose you. I see something in you.*

Coren stopped. The goddesses words rang in his head, and his heart skipped a beat or two.

So the goddess did care, despite her chastising and frustration.

"Thank you, my Lady." He bowed his head, and closed his catlike eyes. "So... How am I to break this cycle?"

The goddess made a small, happy noise. *You are not ready, Coren of the North. Not yet. But continue on. Learn. And soon, soon you will be.*

XXXVIII - History

HOURS TICKED BY.

Corinne came by with dinner, which Coren ate ravenously, and Sora knocked to ask if Coren would like a tour of the tunnels. He declined, politely, in favour of training.

Kinaar continued to murmur softly in the back of his head, commenting and teaching.

It was slowly growing somewhat annoying, to say the least.

Coren flopped back onto the bed, and stared up at the vaulted ceiling, running through a mental checklist of everything that he had learned, in just one day.

Invisibility. And... Insubstantiality.

His head spun, trying to take it all in. Finally, he rolled off of the bed, and stood, stretching.

"Kinaar?" He asked, and the goddess made a humming noise. "I think that I'm going to go on a walk."

What? She said, as if she had been jolted awake. *Coren, you must rest. It's been a long day, you need to take a break. Sleep.*

Coren laughed. "Kinaar. I'm not going to die if I walk for a while. I just -" He wrinkled his nose at the walls. "I hate being inside like this. Closed in. Even if I can't get some fresh air, I need to stretch my legs."

Coren! Kinaar hissed, but he ignored her.

"I need to clear my head. Take some more time to process. Now shhh." He closed his eyes, and focused on the Veil, pulling it's folds around himself.

The Veil was Kinaar's realm. It was a thin thing, really nothing but a mist, separating the Void, where souls found peace, and his world. The deeper that Coren went into the Veil, the further away from his world he was. He grew more insubstantial when he pulled more of the Veil around himself.

Within seconds, he was completely invisible, and insubstantial. Strolling through the walls, and into the tunnels, was a breeze.

Walking along, Coren examined the painted walls again, and thought of his family, back in the North.

They still didn't know where he was, whether he was dead or alive. Chances are, they had decided that no one could survive being stabbed, hurled around in a twister, and then dropped hundreds of feet towards the ground. Usually, they'd be right in that assumption.

A thread of fear and panic had begun to wrap itself around his lungs, squeezing. And if he never made it home?

No. He couldn't think like that. He couldn't panic again. He had to keep it together.

Coren took a deep breath, and focused on one large painting, the one taking up the entire wall before him.

Shifting forms filled it, dark against a bloody bright background, rosy sunset, scarlet skies, vermillion earth, deep wine-red bloodstains.

There were half-way Shifted werecats, fighting alongside humans, and elves bending the elements to their will. Scaly, snake-like creatures filled the sky, and winged humanoids glowed with a fierce light, wielding otherworldly weapons. Drakons and the High Fae.

Each was battling one or more dark shape, while a huge black form rose above them all. Lady Chaos, faced by only a handful of others, each standing tall and brave and proud.

These were the leaders. These were the ones who had decided to fight back.

Coren traced a forefinger over the painted form of the werecat woman. The fabled Lady Forartha. Next to her stood an elf, with arms outstretched, cracks spider-webbing the crimson earth around her. Rosana, before she had taken the crown.

They seemed unreal, legendary, facing that ominous, dark goddess.

The sharp tingle of magick radiated from the werecat leaders figure, as Coren traced her again, and he drew back, startled. His eyes widening, he traced the form again, his brows furrowing.

The pulse of the magick grew stronger, twining underneath the pads of his fingers, and he barely swallowed back a startled cry as the corridor dimmed, and the mural began to shimmer.

The Veil slipped away from his control, and he flickered back into sight, as he gaped at the painting. The *living* painting!

Thunderous rumbles shook the earth below Coren's feet, as the painted cracks around Rosana spread, her comrades sprinting towards Lady Chaos. The elementalist made the ground ripple like water, sending allies and enemies alike tumbling to their knees. The tiny spirals of her Marks extended down her arms, growing and turning as she used up more and more of her power.

The painted elf dropped to her knees, and the earth stopped shaking, but the battle raged on. Tiny figures fell, werecats Shifted midstride. Drakons fell, burning, from the deep red skies. Lady Chaos' rumbling laugh filled the hall as Forartha tried to take her on, falling still with one blow from the goddess's broadsword.

King Arthur took the werecats' place, and on it went. One by one they fell.

Coren couldn't look away from the moving mural, watching in disbelief as one figure charged in from the sidelines, her dark cloak flaring around her. She summoned a glowing sphere of energy, a powerful spell, and the sound of her voice, chanting a *cantamen*, rang out from the painted stones.

It was the *Malefica* Theodosia, casting the banishing spell that had caused the Fall of the Gods. The sudden, brutal end to that war.

It happened so fast that Coren nearly missed it. The light grew, until it exploded out, blinding him, and when his eyes cleared, the painting was just ink on stone once more.

His eyes were wide, and Lady Kinaar's voice in his head, already far away, faded to nearly nothing. He shook himself, running his fingertip across Lady Forartha again, but this time, nothing happened. No rumbling. No movement.

He shook his head again, as if trying to clear a fog, and then, dazedly, started wandering back towards his rooms, Shifting as he went, his claws scraping harshly on the stone.

Gods only knew how he made his way back.

Stopping in front of his door, he drew the Veil close again, and stumbled inside, collapsing into his nest of blankets almost immediately. The exhaustion, and the shock, was a lot to process.

Never before had he seen *magiae* like what had been painted into the bloody mural. Never before had he felt so tired. He closed his eyes, replaying the intricate battle again and again, trying to memorise every little detail. Every little stroke of the brush.

Tiny puzzle pieces falling into place.

The reason that Rosana was so drained, why her Marks extended so far, twining across her skin, was because she had caused a major earthquake for the sake of the battle.

Forartha had finally fallen at the hands of the power that she had been standing against. That the North was now facing.

King Arthur, *Imperator* Quai, they had all given their lives.

Theodosia's *cantamen* had been the thing to finally stop the battle, and the gods only knew how much it had taken from her.

This was why Rosana was so afraid of this new war, maybe why she was so scared of the *Honoris* marking Coren's skin.

The werecat boy had known, of course, what was at stake. The lives of everyone he loved, the fate of the world... He had known. But watching the first Great War play out, in shades of the same red that had stained Khara's blankets, Myr's armour, his own skin... Knowing that this cycle could keep on going, knowing that this was what was going to happen again, unless something changed...

It was so much. He had never truly taken it in. He swallowed, and his pulse sped.

Lady Kinaar's soft voice crept back into his head. *You see now, Coren? This. This life, this world. This is what we fight for. This is why everything must change.*

XXXIX - In Which Lady Illira & Lady Kinaar Argue

DEATH WAS MEETING WITH Kinaar again.

Kinaar's being, her soul, I suppose, had slipped from her physical form, crossing her realm, the Veil, into the Void. She had stepped onto the cracked marble floors, and she had summoned Illira, by calling her name.

Death sat atop her altar, the marble newly restored. She swung her tiny legs, her toes smeared garnet-bright from walking through her fields of bloodied poppies.

"He is mine. He has power. He has harnessed more than I have ever seen from a ward of mine before, Niece. I was training with him just hours ago. The boy is so strong."

"You still believe that he is the answer." Death met her aunt's blazing gaze with her own black mirrored stare. Her ebony hair floated around her pale face like a dark halo.

Kinaar did not hesitate. "Yes."

"A boy. A *child*, Kinaar. Does he even know what the cost is? Have you truly discussed with him what it is we need? Does he even know about the Unspoken Laws?" Illira snapped.

Lady Kinaar hesitated too long.

"He doesn't." Death breathed.

The elder goddess did not answer, but turned her head away. Her grip tightened around her bow.

"I will tell him, Illira. But he is just coming into his power. To tell him of this now would be disastrous. We must wait. We still have time, yet."

Death glared at her aunt, and slipped down from her altar. When her feet hit the ground, she was grown, a beautiful woman as pale as the moons, her inky hair flowing like water. She was taller than Kinaar.

"We have no time at all, Aunt. My mother is as unpredictable as the weather. She could break any promise that she has made at any time. She could destroy everything overnight, she could kill us all, even if it would mean unbalance, and her own downfall." Death stepped closer, until there was barely six inches between the goddesses' faces. Her voice dropped to a hissing whisper.

"My mother would not hesitate to ruin us all, as long as she gets her vengeance. As long as she repays us for what we did to her. You must tell your ward everything. Everything, Kinaar."

Kinaar glared, but she had to nod, all the same.

"Good." Death murmured.

XXXX - In Which Coren Leaves Eire

COREN GASPED, AND HIS eyes flew open. He rolled over, his tail lashing against the cold stone floor, and flicked his ears.

The details of yet another dream were still spinning through his mind, bright shards of colour and emotion.

He had dreamt of the North. Again. He had seen his family, he had seen them mourning and training. He had seen the *Malefica* Theodosia. He'd seen the camp in ruins. It was all too much like the vision that he had had of the North, moments before it truly had gone up in flames.

"How... The visions of my family. Are they real?" He said, his voice quavering.

Hesitation. Stillness filled the gaps between his own thoughts as Lady Kinaar fell silent.

Yes.

The single word was enough to stop him in his tracks. He Shifted, sitting down hard.

"Every single one?"

Yes.

His laugh was hysterical, when it slipped past his lips. "So they truly think that I am dead. They have moved camp, they're training?"

I am sorry, werecat. She murmured. Coren shook his head again, and then bit his lip.

"I have to get home. I have to get home as soon as I can."

Deep breaths. Rosana was trying to find a way to contact the North. They'll know I am alive soon enough. And in just a little while, I will be above ground. I'll have my armour and weapons. The sun will set everything right. No more walls, just trees.

His shoulders slumped, and he took in a deep, shaky breath.

"Gods. I've been on the verge of a panic attack every couple of hours these past few days, haven't I?" He whispered, and Kinaar made a small noise.

Oh Coren, I am so sorry…

"There's nothing you can do." He laughed, and just focused on breathing, until his heart and mind had slowed.

"It's just my brain being an arse. Who knew that this whole saving the world thing would be so damn stressful?"

Seconds after the words passed his lips, a tapping echoed around the room, as someone knocked on the heavy door. He called out a hello, and Corinne stepped in. Her always bright face was cheerful as she looked him up and down.

"Ay, you're actually here! It was difficult, trying to find you yesterday. A needle in a haystack. But you couldn't hide for long." She wagged a finger, as if scolding a child. Her grin was infectious, and Coren gave a small smile.

The elf cocked her head, and her smile widened. "You may want to comb your hair… And then we'll be off." She whirled out of the room in a flare of lavender skirts and pink ruffles, and Kinaar laughed.

I like her.

Coren snorted, trying to flatten out a stubborn tuft on the back of his head. Finally, he gave up, and stepped outside.

Corinne didn't wait for even a second, off like a flash down the long, twisting hallways, talking at a rapid-fire pace as she went.

Coren followed, focusing on the elven girl, and her questions. Soon enough, he found himself relaxing.

And so they walked, for at least an hour, until they reached the edge of the Elven Territories, the furthest reaches of the tunnels.

Finally, Corinne stopped, faced him, and dipped into a short bow. "I have to leave you now, and return to the palace. It was a pleasure to meet you, Northerner! I wish you safe travels, and..." Her pretty face darkened. "Success. We need to win this."

"I will do all I can. I trust your *regina* and the heir. I'm just happy to be able to be out in the sun again." Coren grinned, and this time, he didn't have to force it. "I wish you all the best, Corinne. You and your people have been nothing but kind to me, even though I am a stranger."

Her smile was back, stretching ear to ear. "The Queen does not trust just any stranger, Coren of the North! She sees something in you." The elf nodded one last time, and extended a hand to shake, which Coren took.

Her grip was firm. "Fare thee well, werecat!"

And with that, she turned away, and was gone in a flash, leaving him to stare down the hall before him. It was plain, no murals adorning the walls, and it ended at an open, simple door. A lingering smile crossed his lips as he shook his head, and started down this last tunnel. He hoped that Corinne would never change.

When he stepped through the door at the end of the tunnel, he blinked. The room was a dead end.

His heart skipped a beat, and he suddenly wondered if Corinne had led him to the wrong place.

But there were Rosana, Sora, and a strange elf, a tall man with sandy blonde hair, a wooden cart, and a very blue horse, so... Somehow, this tiny room was the way out.

"Hello." Coren said, his gaze drifting to the ground. He could feel the mask slipping back into place as he took in the new place, the new person.

"Hello, werecat." The tall, pale elf nodded at him, extending a hand to shake. Coren accepted the gesture, still surprised, and a bit nervous. He had expected to be travelling alone.

Queen Rosana cleared her throat. "Coren, may I introduce Lord Elija of the Elven Territories? He is our messenger to the rest of Erathien, and provides us with news. And, sometimes, supplies."

"Pleasure to meet you, my lord." Coren said, and the elf smiled.

"We've already met." He laughed, the sound warm and full.

"I'm sorry?" Coren's head shot up, his intense amber cat's eyes meeting the elf's bright violet ones.

"I was the one who found you, and brought you back here. Well, me and Ladybird." He patted his horse's sapphire neck. Coren's slitted pupils widened, forming big, surprised circles.

"I... Thank you. I would have died if you had not found and saved me. I owe you my life." His voice trembled.

Too much at once again, damnit.

"I would have done it for anyone. You worried me for a few moments there. Completely motionless." Elija shook his head, and Coren could feel his cheeks redden. He had never thought about who must have saved his life, aside from the *regina* and her healers. The thought of so many seeing him completely helpless made him uncomfortable.

"Coren." Sora said, noticing the werecat's unease. A tendril of flame wrapped itself around her forearm as she made a small gesture with her hand. "We promised you a few things."

"Your armour. Weapons. A map. A way to contact us." Rosana said, and Coren's face brightened for a moment.

"I thought that my armour was ruined?" He said. Rosana's eyes sparkled.

"Yes, but we have some fine craftsmen, and were able to make a new set. Please, look in the cart."

Coren gave a small gasp as he leaned over the rail of the wooden cart. He picked up the armour, trailing a hand along the smooth, well-tooled leather. It looked exactly like the set he had lost, whole and... His gaze fell on three small runes etched into the underside of a corner. They were nearly unnoticeable.

"It's enchanted?" he asked, looking up at the three elves. Elija nodded again.

"It is stronger than regular leather. Will hold longer."

Coren gently set the armour back down, and reached back in, his smile widening.. A belt, like the one he had worn, equipped with perfectly weighted knives. A fully stocked quiver, and... A bow.

His bow. All of his whittled carvings were there, some scratched, but it wasn't splintered, as he had feared it would have been.

Glancing down at the quiver again, whatever attempts to keep his face schooled into a neutral were abandoned, as his face split into a toothy grin.

He recognised it, as well. It had been made by his mother, the designs pressed into the leather with fine tools that he remembered clearly. It was the last thing that he had that connected him to her. And he had thought that it was lost.

"Thank you." he breathed, starting to strap on the armour. Nearly reverently, he fastened the belt, and slung the quiver over his shoulders. The smiles he received in return were enough, and he felt his heart lighten a bit.

"One more thing!" Sora said, and she reached into the deep pockets of her scarlet dress, pulling out a tightly scrolled piece of parchment, bound with a silver charm. She tossed them to Coren, who examined the tiny, flaming bird. A phoenix.

He looked up at the heir, and she nodded. "The paper is a map. You will need it. The pendant is a scrying piece... My queen has it's twin. To speak to us, just state Rosana's name, and read the rune aloud. Please, do not hesitate to contact us."

The werecat's eyes still carried traces of his happiness as he unwound the charm from the map, hanging it around his neck, where it came to rest at the base of his throat. When the charm touched his skin, the bird glowed with a strange internal light for a brief moment. He fiddled with the paper, rolling it tight.

"Thank you, again, my ladies. My lord."

Elija flashed a smile, and raised a hand. "Don't thank us too fast, Coren of the North. Supplies." He heaved a knapsack from the front seat, and untied the top, showing him the dried fruits and meats inside. A large, corked flask of water, marked with an eternity rune, sat on top, and a bedroll and tent were strapped to it.

Coren gasped as he took the heavy bag, but recovered quickly, and grinned.

He looked back at the elven royalty, and bowed again. Rosana tutted, stepping forwards to embrace him.

"Travel safely, Coren. Go home, find your family. We will be there within the month, I swear it. I will also continue trying to contact the North before you arrive." She straightened her skirts, and then fixed her silver circlet, doing something to occupy her hands. "We will find a way to defeat Chaos again. We'll recast the *cantamen*. We'll do anything we can..."

"I will get home. I won't fail, *Regina*." Coren said, solemnly. "I know that we'll find a way."

"I trust you, Coren of the North." She responded, her braids gleaming as she turned her head towards Lord Elija, who had strolled over to his cart, and swung himself up into the seat, hands gripping the gilded reins.

"Come on, werecat. We really do need to make the Great Road by sunset, before the paths shift. The maps take at least an hour to reset... And I, for one, do not wish to be stuck off of the Road where the beasties can get me." The lord said it with a smile, but the back of Coren's neck tingled as he leapt up to sit beside the taller man.

"Travel safely, werecat." The queen and her heir responded in unison, making Coren's heart ache for his cousins.

"Gods preserve you." He replied.

XXXXI - In Which We Check Up On Rane

RANE WAS PACING AGAIN, their chains rattling across the floor. They were honestly surprised that they hadn't worn a groove into the floor in the past couple of months that they had been there.

Fights had come and gone, and Rane had long ago hardened their heart against their opponents. They would have lost their mind long ago if they hadn't.

Most of the time, the creature they were forced to fight was bigger than them, but old, tired, maimed and clumsy. It was too easy, and they knew it. Soon they would be forced to take on someone actually strong enough to stand a chance against them.

Soon enough, Rane would be pitted against a new champion that they could not possibly defeat.

And then... Then they would die. Alone. In a brutal way, they were sure.

Rane shook their head, determined. They didn't want to die. They couldn't die. They had a people, one that needed them to lead.

But... The South was surely in Kir's hands now. And he would be destroying it, from the inside out. Destroying it with talk of forgotten gods, and war, and blood.

If Rane ever got out, would there even be a Southern Band to go back to?

They truly hoped so. Every name, every face was remembered, and held dear, and they swallowed back a small, keening cry. It was hopeless.

It truly would take a miracle to get out of the Painted City alive.

XXXXII - In Which Coren & Elija Run From Monsters

NIGHT WAS FALLING, and quickly, making Elija seem tense and twitchy. Every noise from the depth of the Wood made him flinch, and it just served to heighten Coren's own anxiety.

Soon, one of the moons was visible, pale ivory against the rapidly darkening sky, and Elija swore, loudly.

"Come on Ladybird! Just a little bit further! Just a few more metres..."

An animal scream rang out from somewhere in the trees, and Ladybird screamed back, her golden horseshoes flashing as she sped up. The cart rattled, and Coren found himself clinging to Elija, who was muttering hasty prayers under his breath.

Something crashed behind them, and the scream came again, much, much closer than it was before.

The Wood thinned ahead of them, and Elija yelled something, made completely incoherent from stress and the rattling of the wagon. Ladybird gave one last burst of speed, her blue coat lathered with sweat.

Coren closed his eyes, sure that whatever creature that was after them would be eating him within minutes, but then there was a new rattle, and Elija whooped as the wagon skidded to a stop.

"Not today, my dear!" He yelled back into the woods, and the creature screamed in response.

"Holy hells." Coren whispered, slipping down from the cart. His legs were shaking.

Elija nodded, and jumped down on the other side. "Never, ever, allow yourself to cut it that close. The Wood is a dangerous place when night falls. The only safe place is the Great Road, where we are now." He made a sweeping motion at the wide, dirt-and-gravel road stretching out before them, and then went about tending to Ladybird.

Coren's heart was still racing. He shook his head, a smile tugging at the corners of his mouth. "Elija - How often have *you* cut it that close?"

The elven lord patted Ladybirds nose, and grinned. "Too often. Especially when I was younger. I've escaped the Wood so often by now, that I wouldn't be surprised if it's creatures have it out for me."

Coren laughed, and started to rummage through his pack, coming up with some food, matches, and his bedroll. Soon, he had a crackling fire going, and was ready to spend a night under the stars.

No more tunnels for him, for as long as he could manage.

He looked down at the handful of nuts and fruit in his hands, and closed his eyes. For a long moment, he listened to Elija puttering about, and considered praying. He had always prayed before every meal, ever since he was old enough to understand what it meant.

Well. Before every meal except for the ones he had eaten in Eire. To be quite honest, he had been so stressed that he had completely forgotten.

But now that he had the time to think about it, he found himself having difficulty deciding whether to do it or not. The goddess that he would be thanking, the goddess that he would be asking for guidance, she was literally in his mind.

She could see every thought that he had, moment to moment. And... She seemed more *real* now. No more mysticism. No more unknown.

Just Kinaar.

She was quiet as Coren mulled it over. Finally, he pursed his lips, and started to eat. No prayers. The goddess saw every thought he had.

Every moment now, was a moment of prayer.

Elija settled himself on the other side of the fire, and took a bite out of a red-skinned fruit.

"So, Coren... I know pretty much nothing about you, aside from your name, and where you hail from. May I ask you some questions? About you, and about your home?"

Coren paused, watching the elf closely. His expression was open and calm, and his eyes still danced with humour. After a beat, Coren nodded, and Elija grinned.

"What is it like, in the Cortach Range? I've never been."

Coren's eyes shone, and his hands flew as he spoke. "It's beautiful. The mountains aren't really the highest in Erathien, and they are blanketed in trees. The shape of the range is the strangest thing - a nearly perfect circle. In the centre is a lake, no-man's-land, and in the middle of the lake is the *Conpitum*..."

They talked late into the night, and Coren grew more and more animated, the more he spoke about the people and places that he loved. Elija was a rapt audience, his eyes wide, and his laugh deep and ready.

He was a smart man, that elf. He had seen how stressed and uncomfortable Coren was, and had found a way to fix it.

Stories are the best medicines, and they can fix so many unseen hurts and aches. Reading them, listening to them, forces a break. It forces your mind to still, and focus on one thing for a while.

Gods only knew that Coren had needed that break.

XXXXIII - In Which Coren & Elija Say Goodbye

WHEN COREN AWOKE THE next morning, Elija was already awake, feeding Ladybird. He was dressed in clean clothes, looking as if he had just come from a good night's sleep in a feather bed, as opposed to a night spent sleeping on the hard floor of a rough wooden cart.

Coren rolled over, and then stood, shaking the pins and needles from his paws, and then picking bits of leaf from his hair. Elija looked over, and grimaced.

"You might want to check your hair again, werecat."

"Good morning to you, too Elija. I assume you are heading back to the tunnels?" He asked, slipping over on silent feet.

It felt so good to be outside, in the fresh air, and wearing proper armour and weapons. It felt a little more like home.

"Yes. It's my daughter's birthday. She's only three, and I promised my husband that I would be back by the evening."

"Happy birthday to her, then, and safe travels." Coren laughed. He didn't like meeting new people, but the friendly elf had grown on him, and he would be sad to see him go. "Gods keep you."

Elija patted Ladybird's side. "And you, Coren of the North. It was a pleasure to meet you."

"I hope we will see eachother again! In peacetime, of course..." He trailed off, and Elija's smile slipped for a moment.

It was back soon enough, and he swung himself up into his cart with grace and ease.

"Of course! Well... Safe travels, werecat! Oh, and when you reach Corrinnestāt, be sure to find *Medice* Racha, she's a good friend of mine, and will give you good, safe lodging for a night."

"Thank you. Fare thee well, Elija!"

"Farewell, Coren. Remember to stay on the Great Road, especially after dark!" And then the cart was rolling off of the road, taking Elija with it, and leaving Coren behind.

There was nothing left to do but pack up, and that Coren did, brushing dust from the blanket and rolling it up tight, before grabbing a couple of slices of a pale pink fruit to eat, and tying up his bag.

Looking around one last time, and satisfied that there was nothing else that he could do before continuing on, he was off.

Sometimes, he would hear a sound from the woods, branches snapping, low growls, but nothing ever ventured onto the Great Road.

He passed the long hours by thinking of home, and sometimes conversing with Lady Kinaar. Trying to practise using the Veil while walking however, was too much. As was thinking about home.

When night fell, he slept under the stars, and he was off again before dawn's first light. Every so often, he would bring out the map, tracing the road, trying to determine where he was, how many kilometres there were yet to walk before the Solchar Desert.

It was the same routine every day. Sleep, wake, walk, rest, eat, walk, practise, eat, sleep. And repeat.

Two days later, there was a shift in the air, the very impression of the woods, and the Great Road. Everything grew drier, and dustier, the trees were not as large as they had been in the heart of the woods. The air no longer smelled of moist earth.

The landscape was shifting, and as the day wore on, it grew more apparent. Great trees became shrubs, became grasses, became weeds, and dust and gravel.

In the evening, the sky crimson and blazing orange, the silver discs of the moons rising above the eastern horizon, Coren stopped, and looked around himself.

He swallowed, and dust coated the inside of his mouth. Lady Kinaar made a happy noise.

The Solchar!

"We are here?" the werecat boy asked, taking a long drink of water from his flask. "This is really the end of the Great Road?"

And the Elven Territories. You are now officially on human land, and will be for at least a week and a half.

"Dear gods..." Coren tucked the water back into his bag, drawing out a thick piece of orangey-yellow fruit, and a thin slice of a meat that he didn't recognise. Dinner.

Settling down onto a smooth, pebble-free area of the road, he closed his eyes, letting himself relax. The Great Road was ending, but nothing truly dangerous lived in the desert, aside from a chimaera and a phoenix or two. And the handful of human cities.

He wrapped himself up in the *Rica*, letting it seep in deep, until he was confident that he could take his mind off holding it in place, without it falling away. His *Honoris* prickled, with the sensation of magicks.

What would I have to do, if I wanted to kill a chimaera? He asked, trying to distract himself from the Veil.

The chimaera? The poisonous, four-headed monster? He could imagine Lady Kinaar's eyebrows raising.

Yes.

Avoid the tail, cut it off, no matter what. It is where the viper is, you know. Cut off the snake's head, and the poison cannot get you. The drakon head spits fire, but it takes a while to work up a flame. The ram has only horns, and you know the strengths of the lion's head. For each of the three main heads, the eyes are vulnerable. Even the drakon's scales are weaker there.

A chimaera can fly, you know, because of the drakon, it's forelegs are lion, it's back ram... Kinaar droned on about the chimaera, moving on to gryphons after that, for hours. By the time she finally stopped, she made a sound like a clicking tongue, and laughed.

You didn't flicker once, and you had completely forgotten about the Veil by the time I had finished speaking about the chimaera. Well done, Coren. My last ward was not nearly this adept. I highly doubt that you will need much training.

Coren smiled at the praise, something new and remarkable when coming from the somewhat cantankerous, stubborn goddess.

However, when he finally stripped the Veil away from himself, his hands were shaking from the exertion. His eyelids were heavy. The training, the early mornings, and the late nights were catching up with him.

Sleep, werecat. You've trained enough for today. Tomorrow, you face the desert.

Coren didn't complain.

XXXXIV - Important Events

LINDARA WAS FIGHTING Theodosia this time. The *malefica* was using magicks, and the werecat was Shifting. No blades, this time. Only armour, a thin magick shield, and Lin's *comitis*, helping from the sidelines again.

The sorceress's hair and cloak flared out around her as she whirled, a cage of electric light forming around her, tossing her much younger opponent back. Lin's hair stood on end, her small lynx baring its teeth, tufted ears flat against its head. Theodosia focused the energy, her kaleidoscopic eyes flaring electric green as she did so. Lin ducked as the witch hurled the bolt.

It hurtled overhead, striking a nearby tree, and shaking it, but causing no other damage. Had Theodosia put more force into the spell, it would have been incinerated.

Lin spun in seconds after the spell blazed past, driving a series of quick blows into *Malefica* Theodosia's midriff before Shifting and leaping out of reach, her emerald eyes sparkling with the elation that came with training.

Theodosia retaliated with a new *incantatio* that flew from her hand like a net, swallowing Lin in its folds. She searched, frantically, for the edges, tearing at it as it grew warmer against her skin, temperature rising with every passing millisecond. She Shifted, and wrenched at it, but the bright, blue light was as strong as rope. A few strands snapped under the force that she applied, but most held strong.

The net was still growing warmer, and she knew that it would have been singeing her fur, had it not been for the thin magickal shield that covered her. And... A wicked idea came to the werecat girl, and her brother groaned.

Lin reached one hand through the hole, and beckoned to Theodosia, frantically. "The heat, I think that something is wrong!" She sent a high note of desperation into her tone, and the sorceresses' eyes widened, flaring a panicked grey-brown.

She raced forwards, trying to get close enough to dismantle the *incantatio.*

Dirty move. Sioch whispered in her head, but Lin ignored him.

Compassion is her greatest weakness, See. If I have to go down, I'll bring her down with me. Lin thought. In battle, there was no time for chivalry.

The sorceress was close now, and the magickal net was drawing sweat from Lin's pores. The witch swore the second she saw the smirk on Lindara's face.

"Really?" She asked, planting her hands on her hips.

It was too late to end the counterspell, and the net went supernova. Blinding light flared around them, a wave of heat washing over the field, sudden and harsh, and gone quickly.

When it cleared, Lin had an arm around the woman's neck, that she could tighten and turn into a stranglehold if she wanted to.

Malefica Theodosia sighed, and tapped Lin's hand three times, surrendering.

"You fight dirty, Lindara of the North."

"I can't deny it, but... Would you hesitate to do the same to an enemy?" Lin's face was hard, her smile devilish.

"I've got to say, *Malefica*, your talent is incredible. I have never seen anyone wield magicks like that." Sioch said, strolling up to them.

The sorceress bowed her head, smiling. Her eyes brightened to a pale lavender. "Thank you, Sioch. Magick is a gift. A rare one. I'm blessed to have it."

She seemed to study him a moment too long as she said this, and Lin wrapped a protective arm around her brother's shoulder.

"Come on. Let's go find Lana and see if she-" Lin cut off at the sound of a small shriek. Sioch's voice shrilled.

"What in the hells?"

Malefica Theodosia staggered back a step, as a light shone from underneath the collar of her dress. She held up a hand to calm the twins, but her smile was weak.

With shaking fingers she pulled a necklace out from under the fabric. The pendant was a small quartz crystal, inscribed with a rune, and it was the source of the light.

Lin's fingers dug into Sioch's arm, and he had to pry them away.

"What the-"

"What is that?" The pair asked.

Theodosia looked up from the necklace. Her face had gone very pale. Even her eyes had taken on a milky colouring. "It's - It's a scrying piece. Harder to make than just scrying using a liquid, but infinitely better. You can only scry the person with the twin of your piece, but you can speak with them at any time, from anywhere. This - This piece hasn't been used in..." She trailed off. The colour had still not returned to her cheeks.

The witch tucked a strand of grey hair behind her ear, and continued to stare at the pendant.

"Who's scrying you?" Sioch asked in a hushed tone.

Theodosia looked up with a small smile.

"Queen Rosana of the Elves."

XXXXV - In Which Rosana & Theodosia Make Contact

THE ELVEN QUEEN ADJUSTED her heavy silver circlet, straightened out the cuffs of her heavy brocade gown, shifted in her seat, fiddled with her own pendant. Twisted her wedding band.

It had been ages - literally hundreds of years - since she had spoken with Theodosia, and she was finding herself... Nervous.

She took a deep breath, and as she focused the scry, she tugged on her crystal, the facets catching the light. A rune, carved into the surface, began to glow with the same silvery light as scrying water, and heat up in the palm of the elven woman's hand.

An eternity, contained in a few minutes, stretched on that way, the queen staring at the glowing piece of enchanted stone.

Finally, a sound like the clinking of glass rang out, and Rosana's eyes crinkled at the corners with a smile. The surface of the crystal cleared, and a slow smile crept across her face, and she stood, leaning in.

A figure in deep blue robes, with a flowing black cape, and long, once blonde, now white-grey hair, was shown on the surface of the crystal. She looked shaken, her kaleidoscopic eyes changing colour rapidly.

The *malefica* just stared down at her pendant, the twin of Rosana's, taking in the sight.

Tears filled Theodosia's colour-shifting eyes. They flared a soft grey, before turning a contented light blue.

Something warm and wet trailed down Rosana's cheeks as well. It had been *so long*. So long since she had seen Theodosia awake. So long since she had laid the witch to rest, believing it to be the last time that she would ever see her face.

"Rosana?" Theodosia asked, a quaver in her voice. "Is that really you, old friend?"

"Dear gods." Rosana sat down hard. "It is. And... It's you! You have the necklace, after all these years?"

The sorceress laughed wetly. "Of course. You made sure it was with me when I was laid to sleep, and when I awoke, it was still with me. Stone, metal and magick... Always strong."

Rosana sniffled, and turned her face away, wiping at a stray tear. "Oh, gods. Theodosia, I have so much to tell you..."

"And I as well." Theodosia murmured.

Two voices broke in, then, and the moment passed. Reunions could wait, anyways.

"Did you say... Queen?" The voices asked, and Theodosia grinned at someone out of sight.

"Sioch and Lindara of the North... May I introduce to you Her Majesty, Queen Rosana of the Elven Territories. My oldest, and dearest friend. Our ally." She added, speaking the syllables as if testing the word on her tongue, making sure it wouldn't crumble to dust.

XXXXVI - In Which Lady Chaos is Furious

LADY CHAOS CLENCHED her fists, the silvery basin in front of her rattling against the stony earth. The liquid inside shone like moonlight, casting an electric glow across everything around her. The goddess herself seemed to absorb the light, her wispy shadow-form as dark as ever.

She murmured lines, the *cantamen* for an ancient spell, and the liquid shivered, and rose from the basin in a smooth motion. Lady Chaos moved her hands through the air, her fingers flicking as her eerie voice rose and fell. She twisted her wrists, and the water rippled through the air, strands weaving together until they formed a glowing orb, a mirror of the one moon that peeked through the tree branches. It's twin would not rise for at least an hour yet.

Chaos's voice reached a new, high pitch, and she held the note as the cloudy, moonlight liquid cleared. It's glow faded slightly, as an image solidified. An image that made Chaos's blood boil.

The *dea*'s nostrils flared as she watched the scene, her hands forming tight fists, the water rippling each time her fingers tightened.

But the image stayed, and her cursing grew more intense with every passing moment.

A woman, her long brown hair flying around her face, whirling and ducking as she parried the strokes of a man's blade.

Her hard blue eyes gleamed as she brought her rapier up, resting it lightly on her opponent's breastbone. Her mouth moved, but no sound escaped the watery sphere.

The woman removed the blade, and adjusted her leather armour, rubbing a hand across her midriff for a moment before tossing her hair, and grinning at three people resting in the shade of a nearby tree.

The oldest of the trio waved, the scar that ran below her eyes wrinkling as she made a face at her wife.

Lady Chaos released the liquid, and it plummeted back into the bowl, splashing up and soaking her boots, but she ignored it.

So. The Chieftainess of the North was alive. They had fled camp, their numbers decimated, their people frightened and wounded, but their Chieftainess, and their hope, were very much alive. Stars, she should have scryed the North so much sooner than she had.

Cursing, she began the song-spell anew, her eyes burning with a dark fire.

This time it was so much stronger, and her white hair lifted up, floating around her face, making her look even more unholy.

The goddess hissed the last sentences of the *cantamen* again, a shadowy radiance beginning to show around her form. The orb looked like a fallen star, illuminating everything for miles around.

Finally, the glow flared one last time and began to dim, the liquid clearing as Lady Chaos peered into it. She hissed again, her face contorting into a mask of fury.

Seven other forms filled the surface, each form's surroundings different, but distinct, turning the scrying water into a mosaic of colour.

There was a woman with deep navy blue, scaly skin, and hair like seaweed, suspended in a watery deep. A woman wearing a shining gown trimmed with stars hung like an angel in the skies, silhouetted by sunlight. And more. Fire and earth, time, sky and season's change.

Her brothers and sisters.

As she watched, Lady Kinaar stirred, her eyes flickering open before she relaxed, and sank into sleep again. Lady Nyx flicked her fingers, and the water around her erupted in a storm of bubbles and foam.

Having shown all it needed to, the sphere began to sink towards the bowl, but before it made it that far, it began to glow again, a star going supernova.

The visions of the gods... It was far too much for this simple scry.

The surface of the water began to boil, and finally, it exploded, sending a mist of glowing liquid everywhere, coating the trees, the earth... Until everything looked doused in silver.

Chaos was furious. Kinaar and Nyx were nearly awake. And...

"Mother of all darkness." Lady Chaos swore. Her dark eyes drifted closed as she remembered a tiny detail.

Kinaar, her sister, with her glowing gown and auburn hair. Wakening, stirring, opening her sunlight eyes. And there was a mark beginning to form and glow on the inside of her wrist. Her mark, but wrought in silvery light, shifting like water in the sun. She had taken a ward.

She was *conscious* enough to take on a ward! And she had always been powerful, so who knew what this new player could bring to the game.

Lady Chaos slunk back to her throne, draping her shadowy, wisping limbs across the golden metal. Anger was still fizzling through her, demanding that she lash out, somehow. Do something.

She had to fix this. She had to move everything back on track.

Chaos swore again, and snapped her fingers, and a Wraith materialised in front of her, summoned from wherever it had been slumbering. The soldier's coal-like eyes blazed with an intense heat, and it's armour, noticeably Southern, clicked and rubbed loosely as it moved.

"Hello, soldier." The goddess on the throne greeted it, and it bowed.

"My Lady Chaos. Whatever can I do to serve you?" It asked in a raspy monotone.

"My sister is so close to awakening." She said, closing her eyes, her stark white hair drifting around her face as she grinned menacingly. "She has taken a ward. I want to know who they are. I want to know *where* they are. And I want to utterly destroy them."

"Yes, my Lady." The Wraith hissed, and wisped away, already on the hunt.

Chaos watched the point where the Wraith had stood for a long moment.

Forgotten once, defeated once.

She never wanted to be forgotten again. Never wanted to be scorned by her family, by Erathien, again. But... They would never trust her, never worship her like they trusted and worshipped her siblings...

Not unless she succeeded here. Not unless they were all under her rule.

She would build her army until she became a force so powerful, every one of these new enemies would cower before her. She had a mission, now.

Gods save the ones who stood in her way.

XXXXVII - The Costs

COREN STIRRED THE EMBERS with a long, scrubby stick, snorting when the ends caught fire, and he had to tamp it out with a booted foot.

He was about to head off to bed, to finally rest, when Kinaar spoke up, her voice tentative. Something that immediately made him pause, and listen. (A goddess, tentative? Never.)

Coren of the North... There is something that I must discuss with you.

He sat up a little straighter, surprised. "My lady?"

It concerns the war. And the gods. And Chaos herself.

Coren froze. "What is it?"

There was a long pause, as if Kinaar were steeling her nerves before she spoke. And even when she finally did, it was an avoidance. *My niece has wanted me to tell you for a while, and I have been... Putting it off.*

"*Death* knows about me? About *everything*?" Coren asked. His voice splintered. "Is this about everything that Rosana couldn't tell me?"

Be calm. She is working with us. She didn't respond to the last question.

Frustration was beginning to rise in Coren's chest. More secrets, of course... "Please stop putting it off, Kinaar. Tell me. Tell me everything."

Coren... The goddess was hesitating. The nape of his neck prickled.

"Kinaar." He said. Just her name. Just that. It was enough.

I - She sighed. It was less fed up, and more... Sad. *Before the Fall of the Gods, we were there to take wards, and to guide them. The wards were merely hunters and party-trick makers. It was... Fun. There were no great wars, no dangers to anyone, until Chaos came to Erathien. It was then that we discovered the catch of having a ward.*

Coren's breath stocked. He knew, just knew, that he wasn't going to like what came next.

Kinaar paused, as if to take in a deep breath, before continuing. *The Great War involved all of our wards. Perhaps twenty in all. All seven of us had at least one. (Neither Death nor Chaos can take a ward - there is simply something about their nature that forbids it.)*

They fought in that final battle. And they fell. Three survived, and that was all. The others either perished by steel, or by the ripping of their souls from their bodies.

Coren could feel the blood draining from his face. He pressed a hand into the still-warm sand, and stared up into the starry sky, imagining his patron's face, there in the velvety dark.

"What?" He asked, and his voice was a weak thread of a thing.

They used their powers too fast, without waiting for a moment of rest, to replenish their gifts. They used up what was at the very core of them, the piece of their patron's soul that was linked to theirs. Because the soul-piece, and the whole of theirs, were intertwined, their own dissolved as well, fuel for the fire, in a sense.

Those wards, who used all of their power in the Great War, died. Every single one.

Coren's hands were shaking. "All of them?" He asked, the quaver in his voice all too present.

Yes.

"So that's why Rosana was afraid... Or part of why... But." He hunched his shoulders. "That fate isn't set, yes? So I don't need to worry about it..."

Kinaar was quiet for a long time.

"Kinaar?"

When Rosana spoke to you about your being my ward, she mentioned the Unspoken Laws. Do you remember, Coren?

He swallowed. "Yes."

They are the rules that govern our universe. They are what determines the kings and queens and rulers of all Erathien, they are everything.

Coren's heart was still racing, and he looked up at the stars, listening.

They are as follows: Any action has consequences, for the better or for the worse. Only a god can defeat another god. The balance of the universe must be upheld. And someday, everything must end.

Four rules. Simple. They echoed in his head (in his own voice, not Kinaar's), and it seemed, somehow, that he had heard them before. The longer that he turned them over in his head... The more they seemed to click.

Only a god can defeat another god. The balance must be upheld. The deadly results of the overuse of a ward's powers. And then there was Kinaar's wish to end the cycle of rising and falling.

"What are you saying, Kinaar?" He whispered.

I am - She paused for a long moment. *I am saying that if Theodosia's catamen is cast again, the cycle will continue on, and Erathien will plunge into chaos. The gods are already unbalanced, because Chaos is stronger than all the rest of us. Erathien itself is unbalanced because, despite magick being it's heart and soul, it has slowly faded away since the Fall of the Gods. I can feel it in my bones. We need to restore the balance, and end the cycle.*

"I don't understand!" Coren said. "Give me a straight answer. I need to understand exactly what needs to be done. I *have* to."

Another pause. *We need to defeat Chaos, and restore the balance, but without causing another Fall. And only a god - or godly powers - can kill another god. You have godly powers, and some of my soul is twined with yours. Illira and I, we have tried to think of any other option. But... We think that this is the only way.*

Coren's heart had begun to race again, and he bit his lip. He tried to process, but what Kinaar was saying - It just didn't make sense.

To restore the balance amongst the gods, and to help Erathien flourish once again, Chaos must fall. She cannot sleep, because it would spell out doom for this land, as all the gods would sleep with her. She must be killed - or come as close to death as a goddess can - to bring her back down to our level. To restore balance. But she cannot be defeated unless it is by another god's hand. Illira cannot hurt her mother, and I am still too weak so it must be you.

Coren shook his head. *No. No way in hell.* "It would kill me."

There was a long silence, longer by far than all of the ones before, broken only by the crackle of the fire. *I know, Coren of the North. But it's the only way. I am so, so sorry.*

Coren closed his amber eyes, and his fingers curled into fists. It was all so much, and he wasn't getting any kind of break from the pressure.

A hero, a ward, a messenger, a sacrifice.

How much more was he going to have to give?

Everything.

XXXXVIII - In Which Coren Meets Prince Aralie

ON THE SECOND WEEK of travel, halfway through the Solchar Desert, Coren began to run out of food. He had never lacked for water, thanks to a spell cast on his flask.

He sighed, looking out across the flat, scrubby terrain, Lady Kinaar humming something in his head.

It had been only a few days since the goddess had told him what he had to do to save Erathien.

He had yet to truly accept it, putting off processing it until he could get more food. Until he could afford to rest.

It would be only a few days more until he reached the closest human city on the map, where he could restock. And maybe he could take the time to rest, as well...

His eyes closed as he remembered what Kinaar had showed him of the Painted City. Walls streaked with bright colours, sometimes murals, sometimes just for the sake of it. Sandy domes and gleaming spires. Not at all a bad place to stop for a while.

His ears twitched, and he shook his mane. Only a couple of kilometres more, until he could eat a good meal, until he could sleep soundly, until he could relax for a while. Until he could process.

Only a couple of kilometres more.

THE GATES WERE BRONZE and wood, the finely grained brown peeking through beneath the amber-gold. The murals upon the walls were more faded than they had been in the memories that Kinaar had shown him, but they were still beautiful. Rich greens depicted what could only be the Wood, deep burnt oranges painted sunsets and sand, misty greys and blues coloured the skies.

The murals were beautiful, in an abandoned way, and the city's domes and spires still rose into the sky, strong and gleaming, but something still felt... off.

Coren had been standing before the gates for a while, but still, no one had called down to him from the ramparts. There were no guards standing before him. He yelled something at the gates, but of course, there was no response.

Finally, after waiting for a couple of long minutes, he just pulled the Veil tight around him, and strolled right through the main gates.

The city beyond was... not what he had expected. The buildings of the Painted City had seemed in good condition, when seen from beyond the city's walls, but standing before them, Coren could see the truth of it.

Their painted walls were faded and chipped, and some even bore hairline cracks. The heavy scent of animals and unwashed skin hung in the air, and every few yards, Coren could see an empty bottle of spirits, a pile of droppings, or something of the sort. The Painted City still stood, but it's inhabitants did not seem to be the most... Clean.

"Dear Gods." He whispered, flickering back into sight, and scaring a poor dog, who started barking, loudly. He Shifted and snarled at it, and it ran, mangy tail tucked between its legs.

Kinaar immediately set about giving him a pounding headache.

What happened here?! The Painted City was the *most well-known human scholar-artist city, before the Fall. I can't imagine that things have changed so much...*

"My Lady, it has been hundreds of years. I'm sure that *some* things have changed. Besides, the elves haven't left their tunnels in so long. It's entirely likely that they didn't think to check if the cities were still the same. If they were still safe." He stared at the empty streets around him, his lip curling.

Leave. Kinaar snapped. *If there is anyone here - It seems they are all drunkards, too lazy to look after their own animals and their art!*

"I need food, my Lady Kinaar. I have to check and see if there's anyone here. Or anything. I could always kill one of the horses that made those..." He mused, gesturing at one of the brown piles.

Coren.

He rolled his eyes. "My Lady. I have to. I promise, I'll leave the second I start being haggled by drunks."

"Hello, traveller." came a voice, speaking the Common Tongue, scaring him. He spun, drawing his knife, his eyes narrowing, and his fangs showing.

"Dear Lord." The young woman examined his face, her own the picture of nonchalance. Her dress was a deep grey, the ribbons trimming the sleeves, and the ruffled petticoats wine-red. She carried a rusted sabre, and her mouse-brown hair was plaited over one shoulder.

"You are not human."

"No." he answered, his Common Tongue heavily accented, words drawn out and warped. Clearing his throat, he raised his chin, matching the girl's stand-offish pose. "I am not."

"Then what in the name of God are you?" She asked. He noted her singular usage. She was entirely human.

"Why do you wish to know?"

"Because if you are something that means us harm, I should have tied you up the second I noticed you."

An uncomfortable feeling crept up his spine, but he tried keeping up the stiff banter. "And when was that?"

"Only a few moments ago. You were speaking to yourself, in what I would assume is the Old Language? Which means that you are a magickal creature. And your appearance would confirm it." Her tone was light, silk over a wicked blade.

Coren... Kinaar murmured, a warning creeping into her tone.

"I am a magickal creature, you are correct." He answered, his eyes cold slits. "A werecat."

The girl's eyebrows rose sceptically. "A werecat. You are supposed to be legends."

"Like the Fae? The chimaera? The drakons? The elves? And yet they are very present in your paintings."

Coren, be careful. She's baiting you.

He lapsed back into the Old Language. "I know, Lady Kinaar."

"What the hell did you say?" The girl asked, and Coren's grip on his blade tightened.

"I don't believe it concerns you, no?"

"I believe that it concerns my entire people, what strange travellers say when they enter our city."

Lady of Stars. His entire body was a live wire, ready to run, or fight, or hide.

People in shabby clothing began to creep from the shadows, weapons drawn, expressions hungry.

"'Ow the 'ell did 'e get in 'ere?" A man asked, blinking his one eye.

"Good question, Warren." The girl replied, her gaze fixed on the werecat boy. He cursed in the Old Language, and Kinaar went silent, slipping away. *Thanks, Kinaar.* He thought dryly.

"How did you get past the gates?" The brown-haired girl asked, her hand resting lightly on the pommel of her sabre.

"Magick." Coren replied, completely matter-of-fact, and she barked a laugh.

"Don't fool with me, werecat. Magick is dead."

"Prince, just tie 'im up. Get 'im into th' cells. Yer father will be happy." The one-eyed man said.

"I would be surprised if he doesn't fight us." The girl, the *Prince*, said lazily, looking him over again.

"I agree with your Prince." Coren responded in his rough Common Tongue.

"You are outnumbered, werecat."

"I've come this far." Was his tense reply.

"Boys..." The Prince said, and the circle drew tighter, cruel eyes pinning him in place. Great gods, there was no way he was going to win. But, heaven help him, he would try.

Cursing again, his new knives found their way into his hands, looking much too fine against the rusted blades of these raggedy people.

Someone slipped towards him, and he spun, kicking out the woman's legs with one hard blow. She fell, hitting her head on the way down, and didn't rise again. A man cried out, and rushed to the woman, pulling her away, his eyes full of anxious fear. Coren felt mildly ill. These weren't shadow-monsters, with no souls or emotion. These were people...

Someone else stirred behind him, and he whirled, deftly dis-arming the person. They fell, as well, but rose and tried to attack again. With only their bare hands.

Coren scrunched his nose, and went in, driving a couple of hard blows to their stomach and diaphragm, and a clean one to the jaw, felling them. Someone behind him made an appreciative noise, and he turned, glaring.

There was no escaping this. He snarled, and Shifted, his lion baring his sharp ivory teeth, his claws digging into the dirt. Every time one person came close, he snarled and lunged, biting some of them so hard, that bone crunched between his fangs.

He flinched every time someone's blood dripped into the dirt.

But Coren was tired from walking all day, and this was too much. No matter how much he fought, there were always too many more. Finally, his breath coming heavy, he Shifted back, and held up his hands. His accent was even thicker as he tried to think.

"Enough!" he snapped. "I surrender. Take me. I don't want to hurt any more of you, or take any lives. I surrender." He let his hands drop as the thieves, or bandits, or lousy drunks, or who-ever they were, backed off, their Prince stepping forwards. Her smile was cruel and smart.

"I thought so. The rope." A small man handed it to her, and she stepped forwards, but when she reached forwards to take his knives, he Shifted, and snarled at her. They could capture him, but there was no way in hell that he was giving up his newly restored, and perfected weapons.

She sighed, and slipped a tight noose around his neck. "Fine then. You wouldn't be able to shapeshift out of the shackles anyways. They would crush your ankles."

XLIX - In Which Lady Chaos Plots Some More

LADY CHAOS SAT ON HER twisted, broken throne, staring out at the dead woods all around her, without really seeing anything.

Instead of gnarled trees and dying undergrowth, dead-eyed Wraiths and evening shadows, she saw dusty roads and scrubby grass. She was seeing through her Wraith, the one tracking the new godling.

Finally, she closed her eyes, and when they opened again, they were sharp and alert. Her fingers curled around the armrests of her throne, and she growled, the sound rumbling deep in her throat.

She wanted her vengeance on her siblings so badly, and she was *so close*. The Cortach Range would have been hers, were it not for this godling, and now he, and the entire North, were within her sights.

Once the godling was gone, hope would slowly fade, and nothing would stand between her and the Cortach. Once he was dead, there would be no way to defeat her without destroying Erathien.

And the mortals were *so* fond of their lives.

Chaos slowed her breathing, a slow smile curling up the corners of her mouth. Either way, she was so close.

Soon, she would have those cursed mountains.

Very nearly the centre of the known world, and the site of her first defeat, all those years ago, they would be reforged as her new throne.

L - Inmates

RANE LIFTED THEIR HEAD as the heavy prison door slammed open.

No one should have been coming in at that time. It wasn't mealtime. There were no Ring fights scheduled.

Their head was fuzzy from exhaustion, but when they saw who was coming into the Painted City's prison, their eyes widened, and they struggled to their feet as they watched the Prince walk in, with a new prize on the end of her rope.

A lion, his coat thick, dusty but smooth. He walked placidly, not a spot of crimson staining his fur, but the Prince's people skirted him warily. His amber eyes gleamed with a dangerous light as the Prince led him to a cell right next to Rane's...

A new competitor. Fuckfuckfuck. They had thought that they were done with the damned fights, at least for a while. It would seem that the gods were not on their side...

The bandits shackled the lion in the cage next to them, and they watched him carefully. They could smell something about him - something changeable and familiar.

The lion raised his head, muttering something, curses perhaps, as he glared down at the shackle. A few moments - and then his head snapped up, and he stared at Rane.

Oh, gods, *no.*

"Werecat." he growled, his voice a low rumble, his face stone cold. Rane flinched away at the sound of the word.

"Ach." His eyes drifted half closed as he strengthened the deliberate mask, trying to gauge how bad the situation was. "Well, this whole mess can go straight to hell."

"Who in the hells are *you*?" Rane's voice broke, rusty from disuse.

"Coren of the North. He, him, please..." The lion said, meeting Rane's brown gaze.

The North. *The North.* The situation, it seemed, had just gotten a whole lot more complicated.

Another werecat. A Northern werecat. The curses came to mind easily. They were the *Chieftain* of the South, and here they were, stuck next to a *Northerner*. Rane's mind whirled, trying to find a way to get themselves out of the mess that was coming. Coren was staring, obviously awaiting a response.

"Rane. Rane of the... East. They, them." They blurted.

The East. Gods! Liar, liar, liar. They tried to justify this to themself, but it wasn't quite working. It was dangerous, but it was safe, and... The East hadn't killed Northerners. That was all that mattered.

Rane looked away, examining every memorised brick and bar and shaft of hazy sunlight. Their thoughts wouldn't sit still. A Northerner, a supposed enemy, in the Solchar. What was happening? What had happened to the Cortach? To Kir?

They looked back at Coren, over their shoulder. "How did you get here, Northerner?"

The werecat looked up, his amber eyes darkening with some difficult memory. There was a long silence before he said a word.

"There was a battle in the North. Against these... These shadow-creatures. They said that they were sent by Lady Chaos." His voice dropped to a whisper as he spoke the name. Rane felt a chill run down their spine, and their hackles rose.

Kir, what have you done?

"The Wraiths destroyed the camp. They killed most of the Council. And they tried to kill me. I was caught in some sort of magickal storm. Landed in the Elven Territories. I am on my way home, to help. And to try and - I don't know. Help build an army."

The Northern werecat's voice grew even more reserved as he turned his great head away, and his laugh was barking and short. These were painful, bloody memories, and he had the scars to prove it. Two new-looking long marks, slashing across his shoulder and side.

Absolute silence filled the prison. "A godly war. The North in ruins." Rane whispered.

"Yes." Coren said softly.

"What happened to the others? The other bands?" Their voice shrilled painfully on the last word, and they fought to keep their tone under control. No, no, no. The North, decimated. *What had happened to the South?*

"Oh, Rane." Coren's gaze was sad. "We haven't had contact with any of the other bands in months."

Rane's heart felt like it had plummeted out of their chest.

LI - In Which Coren & Rane Plot

COREN SWALLOWED, AND he felt like he had done something very wrong as Rane sank to the ground, resting their head on their paws. They made a small whimpering noise, and Coren's heart ached.

"I'm so sorry, Rane. I really am."

"There's nothing you can do. I saw it coming. I should have been more careful..." They turned away from him, and muttered under their breath.

Coren turned his head away, wishing for all the world that he hadn't been the one to cause that pain.

Gods damn it. Now he was sad, angry, and tired. The pad of his great, tawny paw, where the *Honoris* was inked, was itching like crazy, and he was *so* tired. So tired, and so thirsty, and so hungry.

He didn't know how he was going to survive here. He didn't know how Rane had survived.

Dear gods. It was a small miracle, at least, that they were Eastern.

But if Rane had been Southern - He was sure that they would have killed him by now. Or, at least tried to. The bad blood ran so deep. The name did seem oddly familiar, though.

He shifted uneasily, turning his thoughts away from everything, and to Kinaar instead.

Well, my Lady?

Coren! You can get out of here. You have to. Your abilities...

He snorted, and nearly responded aloud, but remembered the werecat in the next cage just in time. *Well, I wonder why I hadn't thought of that.* He thought, sarcasm dripping from his words. *Kinaar! There are so many prisoners here. I can't just escape on my own, and leave them here to die. It would be cruel. Inhumane!*

You have to get home. Kinaar said, unruffled.

I have no food, Lady Kinaar. Coren said, gritting his teeth.

Steal some on the way out.

And wander for hours trying to find the stores? I may as well free the others, in that case.

You still haven't gotten yourself out of those chains.

Not the time. But when I do, I will take as many of these people as I can with me.

Kinaar made a sound, beginning to protest, but Coren tuned her out, and closed his eyes. Kinaar was no help. Rane was... grieving? Sleeping?

There was no point. As long as he was here, he may as well try to sleep.

THE SCENE. AGAIN. THE woman, and her blade. The dark, starry night, and the blood, and the too-weak armour, and the burning as his power grew with nowhere to go.

The woman tossed her white hair, her pitch-black eyes staring straight down into him, through him. He tried to say something, but the words couldn't escape his lips, and...

And the blade was swinging down. Silver streaking through the air, slicing down towards him. A death blow -

The scene changed, as swiftly as it had come. His family. They were watching Malefica Theodosia with wide eyes as she told the story of the Great War, and the Fall of the Gods. That story narrated the rest of the dream.

He could feel so much power coursing through the air around him, and when he tapped into it, the ground around him rumbled, tossing fighting forms to and fro.

He was Shifting, running at the goddess, falling beneath her blade.

He was flying, his huge, tawny wings beating the air around him as he fought a Wraith with a glowing Fae weapon.

He was casting a spell, the blinding light consuming him, and he was falling asleep, leaving himself, leaving the scene.

As it all fell away, as he made the slow journey back to consciousness, his thoughts whirled. He had been in the Great War. With its heroes as they fought, and fell...

This, this was what the coming war would be like. But worse. So much worse.

Coren awoke with a start, his chains clanking. The small werecat in the next cell, Rane, opened one bleary dark eye, and sighed.

His heart rate slowed to a more reasonable pace, and he bowed his head. "Sorry. I didn't mean to wake you."

"'S fine." Rane murmured sleepily. "Probably time to wake up anyways." They stood, and shook, their tail lashing, and their ears twitching. Then, they settled back down, staring down the dark prison corridor beyond the bars.

"What happened to this place?" Coren whispered. "I heard tales from the elves, tales of a beautiful city, full of scholars, and heroes. Some of the best minds in the known world. What happened?"

Rane looked over, and the darkness in their eyes was chilling. "Maybe the Painted City was great years ago, but it was taken over by thieves and liars. Now, it is nothing more than a place where the bandits can rest their heads, and host their damnable fights."

"Fights?" The word wavered, and he hated it.

"These bandits are... Monsters. They host fights. Between their captured beasts. In an arena called the Ring. I was chosen as the Prince's champion, and, unless I wanted to die, I've had to kill for her. I despise it. But I have to get home. My brother -" They stopped short, their jaw tightening. Their eyes gleamed wetly.

"Gods above." Coren murmured. "You don't have to explain... I'm so sorry. I -" He stopped. Despite barely knowing them, his stomach twisted as he thought of what Rane must have gone through over the past months. That was simply his nature.

He had to get out of here. And Rane had to as well. It wouldn't be right, kind, or just to leave them here, at the mercy of the Prince and King. And as for the others...

"How many people are in here?" Coren asked, hesitantly, after a pause.

"Maybe fifteen others." Rane said.

"Rane... Last night, I was thinking. I think I know how to get out of here, and I can fight, but I don't want to leave any one of these poor prisoners behind. I need help."

Rane's head whipped around, and their face broke into a grin. Any trace of the sadness that had been there before was gone. "Are you asking me if I want to help you? I've been here for three fucking months. If you think that I'd give up my shot at getting out of here you're absolutely insane! What's the plan?"

"I - it's complicated." Coren stammered, laughing a little, stunned by Rane's sudden enthusiasm. "Old magick. But I think that I can do it. I've never tried before, so if I fail, we're done for. But at the least, I think that I could get the two of us out. Besides, we're heading in the same direction."

Rane examined Coren, their eyes glowing with a light that definitely hadn't been there when Coren had first arrived. "And where is that?"

Coren looked at them, a smile curling his lips into a smile for the first time since he had been caught. "Home."

LII - Joy

THEODOSIA'S EXPRESSION was alive with something new when she strode into the clearing, her scrying crystal swinging hypnotically.

Sioch and Lindara were, respectively, sitting in, and leaning against a tree, while Myr and Lana sat nestled together.

"Well?" Lin asked, before the *malefica* could seat herself. Sioch sent her a mental nudge, a warning. Truth be told, however, he was just as curious, and his *comitis* knew it. She shot him a look.

"What news from *Regina* Rosana?" Myr asked, leaning forwards.

The witch smiled. "I have some wonderful news. But..." She looked around, before continuing. "You may want to sit down.

What? Lin asked her brother, telepathically.

No idea. He responded, and slid down the tree trunk to join his twin on the snowy forest floor.

Malefica Theodosia looked down at the ground, before meeting each werecat's eyes, one at a time, her own a shifting kaleidoscope.

"I have news... Concerning the war, concerning a messenger who is on his way to the North."

Lin's throat went dry, her nerves jangling. A messenger?

"A messenger. Who has visited other peoples along the way? Is he finding new allies?" Lana asked, and her eyes were so bright and hopeful, it hurt.

Theodosia's voice was barely a whisper. "Yes... He will be travelling to the Faerie Empire and the Drakon Lands before arriving."

Myr's usually schooled expression broke into a smile, and she held her wife a little closer.

"Is there more?" Lin asked, her throat tight. This time, it wasn't from tears. It was hope.

"Yes. This is the best part. Concerning the messenger himself."

She nearly stopped breathing. There was a slim possibility -

"Coren is alive. He's coming home!" Theodosia said, her face breaking into a smile.

Lin screeched, and keeled sideways onto the ground, her hair flying. "Oh my Lady of Stars! He's alive? Why didn't you tell us that first? And when did you - Oh my gods." Her heart pounded quick and happy, and her thoughts were a mess.

See! He's alive! Neither of us had to worry or cry or anything. Oh my gods. We didn't fail. He's alive!!

Sioch laughed, and his smile was so wide, it threatened to crack his face in half.

"Rosana just told me. That forgetful elf." She shook her head, with a small smile, but soon grew a bit more serious. "It sounds like he was in pretty terrible condition when he landed in the Elven Territories. He nearly died."

Lana held up a slender hand, her nose wrinkled in confusion. "Wait. The *Elven Territories*? What in all the gods' names?"

"The storm that came after the battle was goddess-made, as we assumed. It carried him that far, and wreaked havoc along the way. Coren would have died, had he been left just a few moments more, but the elves found him, and saved his life. He's on his way home! The queen has been in steady contact with him."

Lin screeched again, and hugged Sioch tight.

Beside them, Myr rose. When she spoke, her voice was shaky, and when Lin looked at her, she was stunned to see tears streaking her cheeks. "Thank you, *Malefica*. Thank you so much. It means... Everything... Thank you." She whispered, before burying her face in Lana's long dark hair.

"Our brother is alive. He's on his way home!" Lin whispered.

LIII - In Which Rane Learns Coren's Sort-Of-Secret

COREN SAT UP FAST, his paws splayed on the cold floor, his eyes wild.

The nightmare scene, again. He didn't know how many times he had dreamt it, didn't know where it came from, but it seemed more real, more intense every time. And now he could remember every detail, even in waking.

And it terrified him. As his fear and frustration grew, his chest tightening, a hot pressure building behind his eyes, his paw began to prickle, where the *Honoris* was inked into his skin. There was a sudden rush of chill air as he lost control of the Veil, and his form flickered in and out of sight.

"Damn you, Kinaar! Damn this whole war." He swore, and roared, his scream seeming to shake the prison bars.

I don't want this.

He collapsed back onto the ground, his head resting on his paws, the golden glow from the Seal gilding everything.

And then he remembered something. Something important, which he probably should have remembered before his powers went haywire. Before he screamed at the entire prison.

Rane.

He could feel their eyes focused on his left forepaw, where the Seal still glowed gold. Reluctantly, he turned his head to face them, their gazes locking. Amber and deep brown.

"What are you?" Rane asked, the words no more than a whisper, a mewl. Coren closed his eyes. Damn it. He hadn't wanted to show them this way.

"I... I am a ward. A godling. Lady Kinaar is my patron." He whispered.

Rane's gaze intensified, and he turned his head away, biting the inside of his lip.

"The gods rising again. A war. A *patron*? What the hell is going on, Coren of the North?" They didn't sound upset. Didn't sound scared. Just pleading. "I already said I'd do anything to get out of this hell on earth. I don't care how, I don't care when. Just tell me."

Coren turned to them again, his eyes full of an emotion that was maybe fear, maybe hope, maybe pleading.

"I-" He swallowed, and gave a frustrated growl. "I'm sorry. I don't know who to trust. I don't even really know what I can do, and it scares me. There's too much going on. Too much stress. Just - too much." He shook his head before continuing. "All I know is that I can vanish. And if I wrap the *Rica*, the Veil, tight enough... I can walk through solid objects."

Rane was very still, balanced lightly on their toes like a fighter preparing to fight, or flee. "Oh. Oh, gods. You could just stroll out, invisible, insubstantial, anytime. But you're still here - Because you want to help us escape?"

"Yes."

Their eyes were huge, shocked mirth filling them as they laughed shortly. "You're so much *better* than I could ever be. I would have left hours, *days* ago... But, Coren. War?"

Coren looked away for a second. "That's what this all means. Me being a ward. Lady Chaos's Wraiths attacking the Cortach.

An attack on anyone would mean war, but the Cortach... It's the centre of the world. If she had it, then she would have all of Erathien. The stakes are so high. It's why I have to get out."

"Gods. I thought you were joking... Dear gods." Rane swallowed, sitting down. "Damnit."

"Yeah." Coren tilted his great head, his mane flopping. "Damnit."

"And..." The hesitance was painful. "And did I hear you - Can you speak to Lady Kinaar?"

Coren looked up. "Yes. I've been having dreams... Visions of the - I don't know. The future, or a possible future. Dreams of my family. All it does is remind me of how much danger we are all in. How terrible this war is going to be. All I want to do is be home with my aunts and cousins right now. Home, in peacetime."

THE PRISON WAS SILENT. The other people could have been dead, for all Coren knew.

Rane stretched again, their claws extending and raking shrilly across the stone floors. Coren's ears twitched back, and Rane chuffed.

"Sorry, Northerner!" An awkward pause. "So... D'you have anyone waiting for you at home? Family? Someone special?"

Coren laughed. "No one special. I've never really been attracted to someone in that way." He shrugged. "It doesn't bother me, and it doesn't bother my family. Not their business anyways. As for family..." He looked down, and shrugged. "Well. My father was killed in the Twenty-Years-War when I was five winters old. I don't really remember him. My mother, I remember. She was a storyteller, the best we've ever had. She died from the plague only a few years after my father passed. My aunt, who took me in... She - also passed recently. The twins, her children, are like siblings to me."

"Oh." Rane said. "I'm so sorry about your aunt. Your parents."

"It's all right... I'll always miss them, but I guess I have to keep on going." Coren flickered for a second, but smiled through it. "Besides. I have my aunts Myr and Lana, and the twins. And you?"

Rane blinked, and tried to hide their shock. *Myr.* The name rang in their head, but they tried to hide it.

The Chieftainess? Of all the fucking people to be trapped next to, it has to be the nephew of the woman who killed so many of my people. The one who drove my parents to their early deaths.

Oh. I should probably respond -

"My parents are dead as well... And my brother... Well. He's as good as. And no, there's no girl back home." They laughed. "I'm just going home for myself. No one's waiting for me."

No one except the entire South. If there's a South left to go back to.

"Your brother has to miss you?" He was so quiet, calm. How was this boy related to Myr of the North?

Rane chuffed quietly. *Why am I still talking? Talking to this boy?*

"Well, I don't think that my brother is exactly the picture-perfect example of a sibling, Northerner. He's done some awful things. But I still love him. Which may make me awful, as well."

Coren laughed. "It doesn't make you awful, Rane. Far from it, I'd think... My parents killed other people, people just like us, in that godawful war, and so did my aunts. I hate the fact that they did, but that doesn't make me love them any less. My cousin Lin can be moody sometimes, and See is stubborn as hell. We all have our faults."

He - Hates what they did during the war?

Rane laughed. "I guess so..."

The rest of the day passed slowly, as the werecats swapped stories, and plotted, both wishing themselves away from the dark, grey prison, and both thoroughly enjoying the other's company.

Although, Rane felt severely discomfited by all of their lies. Someday, they knew, they would come back to bite them in the arse.

Coren repeated the plan for the hundredth time, smiling a little as Rane rolled their eyes at him.

"Yes, Northerner! Yes. It's all settled." They laughed.

"Lady of Stars." Coren settled his head on his forelegs. "I suppose so. Nothing else to do."

"So. Now we just... wait?" Rane asked, a confused, slightly frustrated expression on their face. They curled their lip, exposing one fang as they growled.

"I'm going to try and sleep. I didn't really, after last night." Coren said, shrugging.

"Alright. I won't stop you." Rane laughed, and he rolled over, turning his back to them.

Rane just watched him for a long moment. A Northern boy. Related to Myr of the North. By all means, the enemy. What would happen if he knew who they really were?

He probably never would have dreamed of freeing them.

Even if he had... They would have to travel home separately. Coren would never trust them. Rane could hardly even believe that they were finding themself trusting him. But... But, but, but.

There was no point. No point to trying to logic their way out of this. They liked him. Even with all of his strangeness, they liked him.

They turned their head away, and settled down. It would be best if they got some sleep as well. No use to being sleep-deprived while planning a rebellion. A jail break.

And maybe if they got some sleep, their thoughts would be a bit more organized.

LIV - In Which There is A Jailbreak

WHEN THE PRISON DOORS creaked open, Coren was ready. He had been ready for hours, just watching the door.

The two werecats had known that the thieves would have had to come to feed them eventually. They had been planning on it.

But the people who stepped through the door were not who they had been expecting. Instead of a handful of filthy bandits, carrying nearly spoilt meat, or something of that sort, it was the King, and his daughter. The Prince's head was held high, her mouth set in a thin line.

"Do we go through with it?" Coren hissed, desperately.

"*Yes*." Rane muttered back, their eyes shining with a dangerous, hateful light as they watched the bandit royalty walking towards them.

"So this is the werecat." The King said with a sneer, and Coren growled at him. He seemed entirely unfazed, leaning towards the small cage, and the shackled boy with a grin.

Coren made laughing sound, and Aralie's brows drew together at the sight of his toothy smile.

"Father!" She warned, much too late. Coren lashed out with a heavy paw, delivering a swift blow to the King's hand. He screeched and cursed, pulling away, deep crimson dripping down between his fingers.

Coren snarled out a 'NOW!' to Rane.

The cluster of bandits watched with gaping mouths as Coren made a show of drawing the Veil tight around him, slowly vanishing, like a spectre. Soon, he was insubstantial, and his shackle, untouched by the Veil, clanked against the stone floor, as it fell away.

Invisible, he slipped through the bars into his neighbour's cell.

Rane was watching the King with a cold, impassive, utterly catlike expression. They did not flinch when Coren touched their shoulder. Their eyes betrayed not even a trace of emotion, not even when they felt the chill, light waves of the Veil washing over them. Not even when a man cried out, his eyes nearly popping out of his head as he watched the clouded leopard fade away, just as the werecat boy had.

When Rane looked around themselves, they grinned. They could see nothing of Coren, or of themselves, but they swore that they could feel cold fingers digging into their wrist.

And then they were being tugged forwards, towards the bars of the cell, and they were going to run into them... And then Rane was being pulled through, out, out of the shackles, and out into freedom.

Seconds later, they were on the other end of the prison hallway, blocking the only exit, while the bandits stared with terrified eyes at the two empty cells.

The King cursed, and turned towards the door, which is exactly when Coren decided to drop the Veil, and they flashed back into view.

Rane's joints cracked and popped as they pulled themselves up to their full, if not great, height, and grinned, flashing their fangs. Coren stood beside them, his head cocked to the side, his knives flashing in his hands.

He really was pretty, Rane noticed, with pale skin, honey-brown hair, and a dusting of freckles across his nose. His eyes were just as amber as they were when he was a lion, and scars arced up and down his arms. A finely-etched quiver, and beautifully carved bow were slung across his back.

Rane turned their attention back to the bandits. "Hello, my King. My beautiful Prince." They said with a mocking bow.

Aralie's eyes were huge. "Who the hell-"

"My name is Rane of the East. I am a werecat, as is my friend here. And I believe... That I fooled you all."

Coren watched Rane with a grin. They were lithe, their hair a natural, flaming red that looked even more bold against their light brown skin. A moonstone pendant dangled from around their neck, and they had earrings of the same stone. They wore panelled armour that Coren didn't know Easterners wore, but that was no matter. Rane carried a battle axe, and obviously knew how to use it.

"And I believe... That I fooled you all." They were saying, their dark eyes blazing with that same dangerous light as they fastened on the King.

Coren called up the Veil again, vanishing, to the great discomfort of the bandits, and he slipped into a nearby cell, where an elderly, human man was huddled on the floor, watching Rane with a toothless smile.

The werecat boy wrapped long archer's fingers around the lock on the door, cleanly removing it, and setting it behind him. Turning around, he held a finger to his lips, and the old man's grin grew. Coren helped him to his feet, and then motioned to the door.

"Wait here. I will be back with others, and get you all out of here." He whispered in his heavily accented Common Tongue. The man nodded, leaning against the wall, and then Coren was gone, darting from cell to cell, freeing the other sixteen trapped people.

Rane was almost elemental in a fight, fast as light, brutal as a storm, elegant as the wind. And gods, were they cold. They fought like a Fury, kicking people until they collapsed, darting in with poisoned knives, and once... Bringing down their battle axe.

Coren couldn't say that the inhabitants of the Painted City didn't deserve it, but Rane was being so brutal... It was like nothing he had ever seen before.

He finally reappeared, as Rane was standing over the dead body of the Bandit King, lying in a pool of crimson. Aralie was sagging against the bars of Coren's old cell, a hand pressed to her mouth, her face green.

Coren felt sick.

"RANE!" He screamed, and they turned sharply, their face twisted with pain and fury. The Old Language was smooth on his tongue as he lapsed out of the Common Tongue.

"What in *all* the gods' names do you think you're *doing*, Rane?"

"They were the reason for so many deaths, Coren! Just... Let me punish them for all the harm they caused." Rane's knuckles were white on the handle of their battle axe. Their eyes were wet and angry.

"No! They don't deserve that! They followed their King, out of loyalty. You killed him, *and* his most trusted. That must be enough. Leave the others. Now. Or I take the prisoners, and leave you to fight your way out alone." Coren was shocked at the commanding tone of his own voice. Magick prickled against his skin, and he knew that the *Honoris* on his palm was shining.

He looked like an avenging angel. Glowing with the energy of godly *magia*, his amber eyes filled with a commanding that Rane had not expected, dual knives held loosely in scarred hands. And he looked just so... Furious at what Rane was doing.

So, the axe sank. Their eyes lost the sharp edge, and a sickness rose in their chest as they took in the bodies scattered around them.

They looked over at Prince Aralie, who's eyes were filled with terror, pain, and confusion, for she couldn't understand what Coren had just commanded.

"You don't deserve to live. Not after what you did to me, did to all of those creatures you forced me to kill. You're so damn lucky that Coren has a better heart than I do. We're letting you live. Do better than your father. Lead these people towards a better fate, a better afterlife." Rane spat at her in Common, turning on their heel and marching out of the prison.

Coren looked around at the blood-stained floors, and shook his head, looking even paler than usual. Whimpering came from the cell where the former prisoners were huddling.

Finally, he walked over, and extended a hand to the Prince. She glared at him, but took it, struggling to her feet.

She looked down at her father's corpse, and for a second, grief flashed in her eyes. But then it was gone, and she was perfectly composed once more.

"He was disgusting." she finally said, and then gestured at her remaining people. "Stay here. We're *escorting* these damned were-cats out of the Painted City."

And that, Coren mused, was how one managed to get seventeen malnourished humans, and two werecats out of a thief-held city in the middle of the desert.

He kept his eyes half closed, somewhat threatening, somewhat darkly amused as they were led out of the Painted City, and at one point he slipped away, stealing as much food as he could fit into his pack. Nuts, dried meats and fruits, and one or two unfamiliar orange fruits with a tough skin.

When he loped back up, slowing to walk next to Rane, he got no response. Their eyes were shadowed, tired, their blood-spattered axe strapped across their back.

"Why did you do that?" He asked, after a while. Rane turned their face to him, their brown eyes dark.

"They deserved it."

"That doesn't mean you had to kill them. It's not like I'm marching over to the South and murdering the person who killed my father. I had to grow up without a father, and then without a mother. They sure as hell deserved it. But I'm not just going to go and kill them." He shook his head.

"And why not? If they deserved it?" Rane asked, a sharp, dangerous edge creeping into their voice.

"Because I'm sure that that person has a family, just like my father did. Because I can't just go and kill someone on a grudge. I'd lose my mind." Coren's smile was sad, and dry.

The dark look in Rane's eyes had gone on to shadow their entire face, and something told Coren that he should have shut up a while back.

"Maybe I'm made of a sterner stuff than you are." Rane hissed, but Coren just shrugged.

"Maybe so."

"Maybe I didn't want the King and his people to continue holding the Painted City like some sort of mad fortress. Maybe I didn't want them torturing anyone else." Rane added.

"Rane, there are other ways that we could have made that happen." Coren said, and blinked slowly at them. Rane set their jaw.

"You know what - Damn it, I'm not arguing about this with you, Northerner." They threw up their hands, and fell back, allowing Coren to go on ahead.

He shook his head, biting his lip. "I don't want to argue, Rane. I just... I don't know. Wanted to know why you had to kill them. Sorry. I'll see you on the road."

And he was gone, racing out into the desert.

Finally, finally free, but left with a heavy taste in his mouth.

LV - In Which Coren Scrys Queen Rosana

THEIR CHEST HAD FELT tight, with fear and rage. Anger at their brother, anger at the situation that they were in. Anger that couldn't be taken out on Kir, or the Prince, so it had been turned on the Northern boy, for stopping them.

Even if he had been right.

Rane had gotten the fight that they had wanted. Some of the tightness had eased.

But now they were alone in the desert. They cursed under their breath, and sighed heavily, giving up and sitting down on the hot, gravelly sands.

So they had escaped. Finally! After months, and months. Killing and surviving and praying for this very moment, and then? Then they just sat out in the desert, without a plan, without food, even! Just weapons, and their dreams. Shattered dreams.

No word from the West, or the East, or the South. No word for months.

Gods... What did that mean for them? *No word.*

Kir had said that he had sided with Lady Chaos. Perhaps the South was safe, but under the Forgotten Goddess' control? The thought was not comforting in the least.

And if the worst had happened... Then everything that Rane had given up had been for nought.

Rane looked out across the barren land to the sunset, which stained the skies and the earth in shades of orange and red. The moons were already brightening on the opposite horizon.

The Painted City lay behind them. The Cortach Range lay before them.

Home. Home to ruin, or home to a people. Home, either way.

They struggled to their feet, head spinning. Their stomach ached, and they sighed, staring up at the stars.

Amends had to be made.

THE DESERT AIR HAD grown chill, and a slight wind had picked up, stirring up dust.

Coren had pitched his tent only a few hours out from the Painted City, but he wasn't worried about anyone trying to attack him. The nearest sign of life was that cursed place, and he didn't think that it's inhabitants would be too keen on hurting the werecat who had helped kill their King.

As for the others... Rane and the prisoners had immediately scattered to the winds, and Coren prayed that they would find shelter, or food, or water, or... Anything, soon. He didn't have too much hope.

He sighed, and was about to rise and go to bed, when he swore under his breath, remembering something.

Coren touched the base of his throat, exhaling in relief when his fingertips found the silver chain, warmed by his skin. He pulled the tiny phoenix pendant from beneath his tunic, cradling it in the palm of his hand.

He had checked in with Queen Rosana only once before, when he had been about one day out from the Wood, three days to the Painted City. As they had bid eachother good night, he had promised the queen that he would contact her again when he reached the desert city.

It had been six days now.

She must be frantic.

Turning the little phoenix over, the boy reread the inscription on the bottom, before reciting it aloud.

The rune, just barely visible on the phoenix's surface, lit up, and the metal bird grew just slightly warm in his palm, buzzing with something like static electricity - the feeling that always came with magick. The silver surface blurred and twisted, before resolving in the form of an elf, a silver circlet resting on her brow.

"Coren!" *Regina* Rosana cried, her voice heavy with relief. "You're all right! Where are you? What happened?"

Coren bit his lip, lightly. "I... Well, I'm all right. I am around four hours out from the Painted City."

"What?" Lady Sora asked, leaning in so that Coren could see her.

"Yes. I ran into some... Difficulties." Coren said, turning his head away, just a bit.

"What sort of difficulties?" Rosana asked nervously.

"The city has been overrun by thieves. I, äh... Managed to tick them off. And got myself captured." Coren bit his lip a bit harder, before telling the Queen and Heir everything.

When he finished, there was a shocked silence. Flames licked around Sora's fingers, and Rosana was twisting her wedding band, around and around.

"Dear gods. I'm so sorry about the Painted City, Coren." Rosana whispered.

"I'm all right, really!" He ducked his head. "I'm safe, and I doubt that Prince Aralie will be as brutal as her father was. It's all right."

"We should have known. We should have checked that it truly was safe." Rosana said, rubbing her forehead.

"Really. I'm safe. All the prisoners are free. It's all done!" Coren said, smiling a little at their concern.

They care!

"It could have played out differently..." Sora said, her brow creased.

"That's true. But everything turned out for the better." Coren said. He raised a hand to cover his mouth as he yawned, and Rosana shook her head.

"Oh, Coren. Go sleep! Scry us soon, or else." The queen shook her head again, smiling herself.

They exchanged farewells, leaving Coren staring down at the dark pendant, still warm against his skin, with a half-smile on his face.

Too tired to train, too tired to do anything else, Coren tucked the scrying piece back underneath the collar of his shirt, and yawned, ready to head to his tent for the night.

It was then that he spotted a dark figure racing across the desert plains.

They were charging straight towards him.

He was on his feet in an instant, an arrow nocked and ready. He was tired, and in no mood for foolishness.

LVI - In Which Coren & Rane Are Reunited

AS THE FIGURE DREW closer, Coren's bow sank, and he slipped the arrow back into his quiver. He forced himself to relax.

"Hello, Rane." His tone was more curt than he had wanted it to be.

"Hello, Coren."

A pause. A heavy exhale. "You need a place to sleep tonight?"

"You'd be willing?" Rane scuffed a booted toe against the gravelly sand.

"Of course! We're going the same way, anyways. Come sit." Coren said, gesturing at the fire. After a beat, he continued: "I'm sorry we fought."

"No, I'm sorry. You were right. It was wrong to attack those damned bandits so blindly. I shouldn't have done that." They bowed their auburn head.

Coren cocked his head, walking over to the flickering flames, his grip on his bow loosening. "S'all right. Come on, come sit."

"Thank you." Rane murmured.

Coren bit his lip, and turned back to the other werecat. "Do you need anything? I was just about to head to bed. I don't plan on travelling tomorrow, so feel free to settle in. You're welcome to come with me when I do continue on."

The decision, both not to travel and to invite Rane, was abrupt, and he surprised himself with it. But a day of rest would be good... And he needed a travelling companion aside from the cranky old *dea* in his head.

Rane looked at him with a grin, fangs glinting and eyes glowing. "Really? Thank you Coren. I'm sorry about everything."

His own small smile was relieved. "It'll be a hard trip, with some diplomatic stops along the way-"

"Hey! It's fine. Go sleep." Rane interrupted, their head tilted to the side.

Coren laughed. "Sorry. I'm just tired..."

"Good night, Coren." Rane said.

"Good night."

LVII - In Which A Wraith Draws Nearer

THE WRAITH'S EYES DRIPPED fire as it squinted against the hot sunlight beating down upon its shoulders. The pebbly, dry land around it was empty, aside from the faraway blur of a city on the horizon behind it.

It had tried the Painted City, but had found nothing except for a mourning group of raggedy criminals. Utterly useless.

To its satisfaction, the Wraith had found one starved human, just outside of that useless mess of buildings and cracking paint, who had known something.

He had nearly shat himself first, but he had been able to show the Wraith in which direction the ward had been headed.

It was good information. Needed information.

The shadow-creature had killed him anyways.

The Wraith tilted it's face into the wind, trying to pick up the boy's scent. So close... So close to finding him. Soon enough it would find him, follow him, kill him.

Soon enough, one of the greatest threats to Lady Chaos' rise would fall - and the rest of the enemy forces soon after.

LVIII - In Which Coren & Rane Relax

THE MORNING DAWNED crisp and clear, the sandy earth already warming under the sun's light touch. Small creatures scuttled for shelter, as a wind swirled across the terrain, and scrubby plants tried to survive with everything they had, somehow staying green. Somewhere, out in the distance, a large creature screamed, echoed by a second beast, even further away.

The campsite was quiet, slowly waking with the sun. The fire had burned to ashes long ago, and as a faint wind picked up, some of the grey powder dusted the side of Rane's canvas tent.

A rustling came from Coren's side of the site as he pushed his way out into the sun, rubbing sleep from his eyes, his hair even messier than usual. He was surprised by the second tent at first, before remembering the night before.

The exhaustion-addled conversation, the hasty invitation.

He called out Rane's name, but the sound was swallowed by the sheer expanse of the Solchar.

He figured that, since the other werecat's tent still stood by the fire, they would be back from wherever they had gone soon, so he went about grabbing one of the fruits to eat, and finding his location on the map.

Pale juice dribbled down his chin, and he swiped at it, absentmindedly tapping where he assumed he was camped. Just west of the route, so he would have to bear northeast if he wanted to get back on track.

To the human city of Corrinnestāt, and then to Auris. And then to the Faerie Empire, and the Drakon Lands, and so on… Until he reached home.

Sighing, he began to roll up the map, jumping as a shrill whistle split the air. Spinning, the map abandoned for his knives, he snarled. The snarl morphed into a choked laugh as he found the source of the whistle. Rane was striding towards him, shaking their head and tsking.

"Gods. You're jumpy." They said.

"Why, yes. I have nearly died, become a goddesses ward, and then been imprisoned all in a matter of days. I do believe that I am a bit jumpy." He said, deadpan.

"Hey, tone down the sarcasm, werecat." Rane smirked.

"You're in a good mood."

"I'm free! And *clean*." Rane grinned, running brown fingers through their damp hair.

"Where did you find water?" He asked, laughing a bit.

"There's an oasis or something only a kilometre or so away. It's tiny, probably isn't marked on your map, but it was enough. I had to get the grime off. It took forever, getting the clumps out of my hair and pelt." They Shifted, and, sure enough, their spotted fur was smooth and gleaming.

Coren smiled, and sat back down. "Hungry?"

"Starving." Rane responded, settling down across the fire ring. Coren handed them the second orange fruit, and a handful of dried meats. "Where did you get this?" They asked, slowly peeling the fruit.

"I stole it from the Painted City."

"Honest?" Rane laughed when he nodded. They took a bite out of the fruit, and rolled their eyes as the sticky-sweet juice slid across their fingers. "Mmm."

"When was the last time you ate?" he asked, concerned.

"The last time the King's people brought me something. Maybe four days?" Rane tapped their fingers on the dusty ground, and then moved on to drawing spirals in the ashes.

"Lady of Stars!"

"It's not that bad. I got used to it." Their shoulders drew together, like a turtle entering its shell.

"I was so hungry after only a day or so. Rane, you... Gods." He shook his head, a dark look crossing his face. "Maybe those bastards really did deserve death."

"No. You were right. I shouldn't have killed them." Regret hung heavy on every word. Coren shrugged, his form flickering for a second as the Veil slipped.

The fruit's citrusy smell filled the air as Rane flicked the peel into the cold fire pit, and took another bite.

"Are you sure you are up for travelling, tomorrow already?" He asked, and Rane's head shot up.

"*Yes.*" They said, vehemently. "We have to get home. I have to get back to my people. You need to get to so many others, to gain allies... We have to move out tomorrow. You already lost two days. We can't lose another."

"It really would not be so awful, if we waited. Rested another day." Coren tried, but Rane shook their head, red hair flopping into their eyes.

"No. Go, head to that oasis, clean up, rest. We're leaving tomorrow." Rane said.

Coren wasn't about to argue. He stared at the peels, bright against the dull ash, and then up at the slowly climbing sun.

"All right then, Rane. Rest here, eat something. I have water in my pack. It won't run out, so drink as much as you want."

"Alright. Head east, towards the sun. See you in a bit, Northerner." Rane wiggled their fingers, flicking the last bits of pale juice off of their fingertips, and closed their eyes.

Coren shook his head at the other werecat, and then smiled to himself, before digging out a change of clothes, and heading off towards the oasis.

LIX - In Which Coren Cleans Up

COREN STARED DOWN INTO the dusty water, at his own reflection. Had it really only been a couple of weeks since everything changed?

Only a few weeks, but he looked... Different. He was different.

Clean and shaved again, his light brown hair hung damp across his brow, his freckles just barely standing out against his tanned skin. His eyes seemed harder.

The new scars on his arms were pale reminders every time he looked down to nock an arrow, or draw back his bowstring.

Every so often, now that he wasn't concentrating on keeping it back, the *Rica* would slip in and surround him, and he would flicker in and out of sight. It was so exhausting, keeping it back.

He hadn't really noticed the strain until he had forced himself to let go of the Veil. It felt as if a huge weight lifted from his shoulders.

Trembling slightly, he stood and stretched his palms towards the sky, damp pebbles crunching under his booted toes.

There were so many changes, but he had a goal. A mission. A message. A destination.

He just had to focus on that. Just had to focus on getting home. The changes would come, the reminders would surface, and the truth of the end would stay set. And yet...

Coren looked away towards where he had set up camp, but paused, and sat down instead.

Kinaar.

Coren.

I - I want to know more about the Unspoken Laws. I want to understand everything. The cycle, the consequences. I need to know.

The goddesses' silence was painful and long, and he worried that she wouldn't respond, but... She did.

There is not much to tell...

That's a lie, my Lady, and we both know it. He leaned back, gravel digging into his palms. He ignored it, focusing on the goddess in his head.

You know that it is becoming a cycle, the fall and the rise. You know that we need to break the cycle, so that the universe can keep a balance, and heal.

Why did the gods fall in the first place? What caused enough imbalance to make that happen? Coren asked. The question had been weighing on his mind for a while.

We left out one of our own. We forgot her. Her power wasn't used, and she stayed strong while we used ours, and weakened. When she came to Erathien, we were not strong enough to face her. Kinaar's voice went soft, ashamed, at the end.

And then Rosana fought... And won. Coren said, tentatively.

Yes. But the universe saw it as a way to regain balance, and when she fell, so did we. Something happened then. We regained synchronicity in our strength. Until Chaos found a way to wake, leaving most of us behind.

But - Coren paused. Something didn't make sense. He had to continue aloud, slowly making sense of his thoughts. "But if Chaos rose - and how is that even possible - then that means that your strengths just regained their imbalance again? That would mean that the Fall was meaningless! It means that when, if, we defeat Chaos again, it will just restart the imbalance."

Kinaar paused, as if contemplating what she was about to say next, if it would be sensible to say so much.

The 'how' is possibly the easiest to explain. Chaos and Death are mother and daughter. They share a unique bond. The gods were all in balance as we slept, but then Chaos discovered that bond, somehow, and drained her daughter's strength through it. We're not sure if she would be able to do it again.

Coren's hands shook. "How awful..."

Another long quiet. *Yes. Chaos is my sister, but I don't... I do not truly know her. She is crueller than I, or any of the others.*

Kinaar exhaled, long and slow, regaining her composure.

As for what you said about imbalance returning... You are correct. To kill her, or force her to sleep, wouldn't kill us, but it would cause irreparable damage to Erathien, and to us. So, the key is to harm her... But to save her before she dies. I myself - She swallowed. It seemed that the next words were painful for the proud goddess to utter.

I myself do not fully understand what is to be done. My niece, Lady Death, has a plan that involves a prison in the Void. She has no power over the Veil or the Void, so she would be trapped, but would be able to stay strong, and the balance would remain.

Coren rubbed his temples. "Wait. Wait, wait, wait. The balance - If she dies, you all suffer. Does that mean that if I wound her - and it does have to be me, yes, because of the Unspoken Laws - all of you would bear the same wounds?"

I - I do not know. Maybe not physically.... But we will weaken, I know this.

Coren stood, and began to pace, ruffling his wet hair absently. He turned to face the oasis, and began going over everything again, from the beginning. It was his way of making sure he understood.

"So. To uphold the Unspoken Laws, I must be the one to defeat Lady Chaos, because I have a fragment of your soul in me. However, to keep the balance, and break the cycle of rising and falling, I must not kill her, but instead wound her, weaken her enough so that Lady Illira can imprison her in the Void, or Veil, where she has no power?" He hesitated, but then plunged on. "And this - This will most likely kill me because - Because to wound her, I must use up that bit of your soul that is intertwined with my own. The wounding will weaken all of the gods, until all nine have the same amount of strength, and balance is returned?"

He swallowed hard. It became so oddly real when he spoke aloud. More real, more clear, that it had been when it had been in his head.

Yes. Was Kinaar's short response. She sighed. *Yes... I think... That is all.*

Coren's shoulders slumped. There was a long road before him. A hard road, that would end in pain for his family, pain for himself. A hard road, but one that had to be travelled.

The werecat boy rubbed his face with a hand.

It had to be done.

LX - In Which Rane Faces A Wraith

A RUMBLING, HISSING noise broke the silence, waking Rane.

"Northerner?" Rane looked up blearily, eyes widening the second they understood what they were seeing.

A dark form, made of writhing shadows, wearing... Southern, panelled armour. Carrying... Their elder brother's broadsword?

What in the hells?

The heirloom sword was unmistakable, from the golden wire-wrapped hilt, and the cloudy, shimmering moonstone pommel, to the ornate sheath.

Rane sat up slowly, creeping into a crouch, picking up their battle axe. Somehow sensing the movement, the creature whirled towards them. It's eyes were pulsing coals, glowing flecks like tears shining in the corners.

Rane sprang up, axe at the ready. The Wraith, for that was the only thing that it could have been, strode towards them, and they widened their stance, ready.

The creature's voice was the crackling of fire. "Werecat... Where is the boy?"

"What boy?" Rane asked, forcing an easy smile. Pretending that their fists weren't tightening until their fingers were numb.

Where the hell had the Wraith gotten that sword?

"The one you travel with, Child of the South." The shadow-creature hissed, and Rane's spine stiffened. How, by the Lord of Earth and Life, had it known where they were from?

"What the hell do you want with us?" They snapped.

"I want only him." It responded, too calm, too impassive.

"If you want him, you'll have to go through me. I owe him my life." Rane snarled at it, their fangs bared in a demented grin.

The dark monster began to creep closer, hand on the hilt of Rane's family sword. The pommel stone grew cloudy grey at the shadow-creature's touch.

"Where did you get my brother's sword?" They hissed at the thing, anger burning through their veins.

"I had it when my Lady created me." It responded, drawing the blade with a hiss of steel on leather.

"You are one of Lady Chaos' soldiers." Rane shifted uneasily on their feet.

There was no response but a dark smile. It was preparing for a lunge, Rane could see it in the creatures stance. They brought their battle axe up into a defensive position.

"Why do you have my brother's sword? Why doesn't *he* have it, the traitorous son of a bitch?" They screamed, the words tearing at their throat.

"He is no more!" The Wraith thundered back, and Rane's axe dipped, just enough. Just enough for the Wraith to dart in, and try to drive it's blade into their heart.

Rane was too fast, spinning away, and jumping as the Wraith came for them again, turning the jump into a Shifting leap. They landed feet away for the Wraith, still struggling to understand the news.

He is no more. Not dead, but *no more*.

What does this mean? What does this mean for the South?

They snarled at the Wraith again, lunging forwards and swinging the battle axe, driving it into the Wraith's side. The blade slid over the tough leather of it's armor, before settling into a chink, drawing tiny beads of black blood.

Rane drew the weapon back as swiftly as they had driven it in, preparing for retaliation. The Wraith's eyes were glowing brighter, the burning tears blazing. It swung the sword, but Rane's axe's metal handle caught and deflected the blade in a swift motion, sending the shadow-creature stumbling.

It was the same mistake that Kir had made time and time again. A bitter taste rose in the back of Rane's throat.

As they had time and time again, Rane darted in, and struck again. This time, there was no holding back, like there had been in training.

The battle axe's blade bit at the same chink, and this time their aim was true. The panels separated, the tiny metal rings split, and blood, so much black blood, welled up, staining everything it touched, but the shadow-creature fought on.

Rane spun away as the Wraith swung the broadsword, ducking low and swinging their leg out, toppling the creature.

They planted a booted foot on the creature's chest, and neatly disarmed it, resting their axe's curved blade against its throat.

"Who are you, Wraith?" Rane growled, staring down at the creature's face. Only now did they notice a strange tilt to its mouth. A memory of a terrible scar.

"I am Lady Chaos's soldier, little leopard..." The Wraith hissed. "Nothing, and no one more."

A dark pool was spreading from the creature's side, and the ember-glow in its eyes was slowly fading.

Put it out of its misery.

Rane closed their eyes.

Exhale. Swing. Whistling blade. Thump. Head rolls. Dark vapour as the Wraith dissolves, leaving behind the bloodied armour, the cracked sword belt.

Rane spun away from the bloody spot, a tight, choking feeling filling their chest and throat. They roughly cast aside their battle axe, barely hearing it clatter against the gravelly sand as they picked up their brother's broadsword.

The cloudy pommel blazed the second their hand closed around the hilt, as the sword accepted it's new master.

Rane held the blade aloft for a moment, watching the sunlight glint across the metal. Closing their eyes, they let their arm fall back against their side, the sword's tip cleaving the air with a whistle.

"Fuck you, Kir of the South." Rane whispered.

Someone cleared their throat behind them, and Rane jumped, spinning to see Coren, standing awkwardly at the edge of the campsite.

"What in blazes?" He asked, skidding down the rise, his claws digging deep into the earth.

"Wraith. Came for you." Rane responded shortly, their tone clipped and sharp.

"Is that sword... Glowing? What in the hells?" He asked, dropping his bundle of fabrics into the dust.

Striding over, he frowned, touching a finger to the dark, bloody patch in the sand. His fingers came away stained and sticky.

"The sword... It is my birthright, now I suppose. That Wraith... I think - I think that it may have been my brother, once." Rane choked out in response. Coren's brow puckered as he looked up at them. Rane misinterpreted, fumbling for words. "My brother was a despicable person. I am not like him."

"No, stop, Rane! I know. Are you all right?" He asked, stepping over, a hand outstretched. He looked like he meant to pull them into a hug, or place his hand on their shoulder, or something so... *Familiar* like that, but he stopped when Rane gave him a blank stare.

"Yes." Rane snapped, holding the sheathed sword flat across their palms. Their eyes welled, and they turned away from Coren, staring out at the horizon instead.

How could he be so understanding? So calm? And gods above... What would happen if he knew who they really were.

There was a soft scraping noise as Coren picked up the discarded battle axe. He touched Rane's shoulder, and handed the weapon back to them without a word.

It wasn't until he had slipped back into his tent that Rane noticed that he had cleaned the axe's head for them, wiped clean on his shirt.

They swallowed hard, and tears began to slip down their cheeks as they gazed fixedly at the weapons in their hands. Their axe, and the sword.

Their sword.

Gods above. Kir was dead.

In his tent, Coren lay looking up at the dusty canvas. Words that he should not have heard tumbled through his head.

Fuck you, Kir of the South. Rane's brother.

LXI - An Ultimatum

MYR SCREAMED, AND DROVE her rapier up, hard. The shimmering blade whipped through the air, impaling itself hilt-deep in the Wraith's chest.

Black blood misted through the air, spattering the Chieftainesses' armour and sword arm. The Wraith evaporated around the rapier's blade, and Myr panted, crumpling the white sheet of paper in her fist. Lana came waddling over, as fast as she could. The twins, and *Malefica* Theodosia were in hot pursuit, but the pregnant woman made it there first anyways, asking her wife a million questions a minute.

"What in the Lady's name-" Her niece and nephew asked in unison, while the Sorceress Theodosia stood there in silence.

Myr shook her head, dropping her sword into the dying autumn grass beside her, silver bright against brown.

Lana touched Myr's arm, her nose wrinkling, twisting the scar that arced across it. "What did that foul thing want?"

"Isn't that what we all want to know." Myr responded wryly, handing Theodosia the wrinkled, stained scrap of paper. "It had a message. For whoever was in charge here. I figure..."

The witch pushed the scrap away, with an incredulous noise. "It's for you, Chieftainess Warlord. You are the leader of this army. I am just... A helper."

Myr took in a deep breath, then nodded, and began unfolding it. Lana began to read over her shoulder, and pressed a hand over her mouth.

"What does the Lady Chaos want?" asked Lin, an arm slung around her brother's shoulders. A small crowd had gathered around them, the remnants of the North, and they were all holding their breaths.

"It's an ultimatum." Myr said, meeting her niece's gaze. "She wants us to surrender to her before two full moons have passed, or else prepare to be utterly destroyed."

Instant chaos.

It took Theodosia standing, and shooting a whistling flare into the air, for the people to finally quiet again.

"What are we going to do?" Someone in the crowd asked, their question repeated until it had formed a new kind of roar.

Myr shook her head, leaning on her rapier. The decision she made was split second, but she knew it was right. It had to be right.

"What do we *always* do?" She asked her people. "We fight."

She took a deep breath again, calming her nerves and setting her face into a small, determined smile. The tips of her sharp fangs gleamed as she spoke. "In times of emergency, and in times of war, I take on full responsibility for the North. This, more than ever, is a time of emergency."

Lana shifted slightly, as if to slip away, but Myr stopped her, taking her hand. The Chieftainess's gaze was not on her people when she spoke again. "I do not make decisions lightly. I have a family. A people. Lives are at stake. But we would suffer just as much, if not more, under Lady Chaos. She is the embodiment of plague, war, strife, crime...

"If we don't want to truly lose everything, We have to fight back. For our families, our homes, our legacy, we must fight.

Even if we lose, we can be remembered as the people who fought back."

Now, Myr looked out at the crowd, looked past them, out into the mountains.

"We have to fight. It's what we've always done."

LXII - In Which Rosana & Sora Are Tired

ROSANA SIGHED, LETTING the crystal scrying piece fall back against her chest. Sora let out a similar sound, tilting her head back to stare up at the soaring ceiling of the throne room.

Rosana tapped her foot, and a tiny tremor ran through the floor. "So. An ultimatum from Lady Chaos, requesting their surrender. Theodosia says that they will not respond at all, declining, but also giving the North time. Two months. Eight weeks."

Sora pursed her lips, and a tongue of flame danced up her arm, twining on her skin, and casting strange shadows all around her.

"Have hope, my queen. We must have hope."

A beat of silence, and then the queen snapped her fingers. "Ah. Have we heard from the emissaries to the minor forces yet?"

"We have received a message from the dryads. Sadly, it's not good." Sora's flame flickered faster between her fingers. The mood in the room dipped even lower.

"They declined our request of allyship, didn't they." Rosana said, simply.

Sora tried for a smile, but it didn't come out quite right. "Well. Yes... But they also said that they would be remaining entirely neutral for the duration of the war, unless some force disturbed their home. And that would be the Elven Territories. So, if we don't bother them, and Lady Chaos does... One ally for us."

"And no word from any of the others?" Rosana sat down on her throne, rubbing her brow.

"No. But I'm sure we will receive word from the other Elven Territory inhabitants soon. Best keep a positive outlook."

"I suppose."

LXIII - In Which Coren & Rane Argue (Again)

THE WERECATS WALKED in silence, having slowed from their initial run, the sun blazing behind them, the sky shining in shades of pale rose and delicate blue.

They had risen before the sun to beat the heat, packing up camp with the speed of practise, and ate while they walked, all under a rough silence.

Coren glanced over at Rane one more time. After hearing their bitter words last night, little pieces had fallen into place.

Rane had avoided talking about the details of their life, because, well. Coren was Northern. Their people had been at war, not so long ago, and many had lost their lives. And Rane's armour really was in the Southern style, it wasn't just Coren losing his mind.

It didn't matter to Coren where Rane came from. He just didn't know how to tell Rane that, especially since it seemed that Rane didn't trust him enough to tell him themself.

He bit his lip lightly, and looked over at the other werecat once more. Fine, he wouldn't talk about what he had heard, but the silence between them was painful.

"Rane. Please. Can we talk about what happened yesterday?"

"No. I do *not* want to discuss this. He is dead. I am *alive*, and free. That is all that matters." Rane's face was stony, their teeth clenched.

Coren raised his hands, supplicating. "Lady of Stars, Rane. I am not your enemy. If you would let me-"

"You don't understand!" They bellowed, their chest heaving. Coren's eyes blazed as he stared at them, his hand reflexively drifting towards one of his knives.

"Maybe I do, Rane, but if you are going to snap at me every time I try and speak, then it will come to nothing."

His tone was infuriatingly calm, as opposed to Rane's wild anger.

"You will *never* understand. Your family *loves* you. My only family was my brother, and he did *everything* in his power to-" They stopped, staring at the ground. "He would have done everything in his power to hurt me, if he could have. And now he is gone, and even after - after he betrayed me, tricked me, trapped me, sold me... Even after all of that I will still miss him."

Coren suddenly felt very tired, and he watched as Rane's face twisted with emotion.

"He was your brother. Of course you loved him." Coren said softly. "We have no control over whom we love. We all have done wrong, and yet we still love, and are loved."

Rane was silent, and when Coren looked over, he was startled to see tears glistening in the corners of their eyes.

"I'm sorry." He murmured.

Rane's jaw twitched, and for an agonising moment it seemed like they would run, like they had at the Painted City. Instead, their shoulders hunched, and they stared down at their boots.

"Don't be. You were trying to help." They said, "I'm sorry."

A beat. "Loss is hard. And I should have just let it be."

Rane looked up after another silence. "No, you're right. I need to talk about it. Just... Not today."

"All right." Coren tapped their shoulder, a small smile tugging at the corners of his mouth. "Let's go?"

"Let's go."

LXIV - Corrinnestāt

TWO DAYS LATER, THE werecats finally made it to the sprawling city of Corrinnestāt.

Before daring to approach the gates, Lady Kinaar walked them through how to cast simple *illusios*, disguising their eyes and fangs. After the Painted City, and knowing how superstitious some human clans were, one could never be too safe.

This city's walls were pristine white, with bronze-roofed watchtowers every couple of metres. It's guards wore simple mail, under white tunics and boots, and carried swords at their hips. Neither of the soldiers posted at the gates gave the disguised werecats a second glance.

Coren grinned at Rane after making it through, and Rane laughed, spinning in a circle.

"Hey, look! A market!" They exclaimed, stopping suddenly, and pointing down a side street.

Coren inhaled, and his eyes got big. "I smell meat pies."

"Let's go, then!" Rane hooked their arm through his, and dragged him down to the stall, where they devoured the savoury pies.

Walking through the rest of the market, they stopped at booths pedding everything from brightly dyed cloth and glittering jewellery, to exotic spices and foods.

Coren stopped to purchase some pale linens and thread to sew himself a couple of new, clean shirts, while Rane took full control of the food inventory.

Soon enough, they had enough dried fruits and meats - plus some more of those orange fruits - to last weeks, and were searching for a place to stay the night.

Of course, it was then that Coren remembered the elven Lord Elija's request - to find the *Medice* Racha, a human doctor, and his contact in Corrinnestāt.

"Oh, damn it." He reached out a hand, tapping Rane's shoulder. "I forgot. I am supposed to find *Medice* Racha here in the city. She is a contact of a - a friend of mine. An elven lord. She was going to let him know that I made it to Corrinnestāt. And Elija said that she would give us lodging for the night."

"Oh, wonderful!" Rane screwed up their nose. "How do we find her?"

"Not specified..." Coren murmured, biting his lip. "Maybe people know her?"

Rane shrugged. "Worth a shot!"

Coren smiled, complied, and followed Rane as they made a sharp about-face, racing back towards the Corrinnestāt Market.

It didn't take long to find someone who knew the doctor. The very first person they asked was able to give them directions to her house, which was only a short ways away.

Sunset found the werecats standing before the healer's pale green-painted front door, watching the brightly lit windows.

"Knock." Rane murmured.

"She's a noble?" He asked, for the second time, staring up at the arched windows, the carvings around the door.

"Ach, she can be a healer and still be a noble." Rane said, rolling their eyes.

"I guess... I wasn't expecting something like this." He murmured sheepishly.

"Oh, gods above." Rane strode up the short path to the front door, and rapped the knocker once, twice, the sound echoing through the quiet street.

The sound of scuffling rang out from inside the house, footsteps, and the sound of small voices bleeding out onto the street.

The door swung open with a clang, revealing a panting boy, maybe twelve years old. Two more children were standing behind him, pouting. The boy pushed his shaggy dark hair out of his bright scarlet eyes - Scarlet? Coren stared for a long moment.

"Ah. Ach, hello." He finally stammered. The boy extended a hand, smiling, his pearly teeth oddly sharp.

"Hello! I'm Farse. You're looking for my mother."

"Yes, we are. I'm Coren." Coren said, quickly getting over the shock and taking the sticky palm.

Children. And... They were not human. He looked around the quiet street, and then over at Rane, before dropping his illusion.

The boy didn't look surprised by this slight change, while the third child, a little girl in a grass green dress, gasped a little.

"I'm Rane." They said, and shook Farse's hand next, also shedding their *illusio*.

The second child, another boy, turned and raced back into the house, calling for his mamá and revealing a long, serpent-like tail.

The little girl, maybe seven years old, stepped up beside Farse, looking up at the werecats shyly. She reached out a hand to touch the knife hanging at Coren's waist, and he knelt in front of her.

"Careful. It's sharp." he warned as she drew it from the scabbard, staring into the blade. Something flashed in it's silvery surface, and when he looked down, he caught the child's reflection.

She looked like herself - but with silvery, pupil-less eyes, and thin snakes for hair, instead of tight curls. The little girl was a medusa.

"What's your name?" he asked her, carefully taking back the knife, and returning it to its sheath.

"Valeria." She whispered, shuffling her feet. "You're like us."

"Is that right?" Rane asked, looking down at the kneeling werecat and the tiny girl.

"Not human." She said, looking up.

"You're right." Coren responded, standing. "We're werecats. See?" He Shifted quickly, and Valeria grinned. She held out her arms, imperiously, and Rane stifled a laugh as Coren picked her up, deftly balancing her on one hip.

Farse waved them in, storming off down the hall and disappearing around the corner.

"Not what I expected." Coren said again, and Rane shook their head, closing the door behind them. Valeria laughed.

"Mamá!" She cried, wriggling out of Coren's arms as a middle-aged woman, leaning slightly on a cane, came into the entry hall, Farse close behind.

"Hello! I'm *Medice* Racha. The apothecary is closed at the moment, is there any other way I can help you?" She asked, a hand on her son's shoulders. Her smile seemed a bit strained.

Coren swallowed, mulling the Common Tongue over in his head before he spoke.

"*Medice,* we thank you. We aren't here for medicines, but instead came to speak with you. My name is Coren of the North.

This is Rane of the East, my travelling companion. We were sent by Lord Elija of Eire."

Medice Racha's grin turned real, and she tapped her cane briskly against the floorboards. "Oh, wonderful! You must come on back to the kitchen to eat with us. You can stay in the guest rooms tonight. How did you meet Elija?"

"It's quite a long story..." Coren murmured, but the healer was undeterred.

"I have time. And four energetic kids who could use entertainment!"

"Oh. It's not really... It's not a story that children should have to hear." He said, his voice dropping. Racha cocked her head, a shadow drawing over her bright face.

"I see. Farse, Valeria, Heor, go get Leon, and play upstairs, please. I'm going to talk to our new friends for a bit, and then we'll all have dinner together, all right?"

Valeria nodded, and smiled shyly at Coren again. "Come play with us later?"

"Of course!" he smiled, and she squealed, running off after her brothers. Rane hip checked Coren.

"You've made a friend!" They said in the Old Language.

Racha laughed. "Head on down the hall to the left - the Blue Parlour is the first door on the left. I have to go check on the kitchen, I'll be back in a moment."

With that, she strode off down the hall in the opposite direction, leaving the werecats to find their way alone.

LXV - In Which the Werecats Explain to Medice Racha

THE MANSION'S PARLOUR seemed to double as a waiting room for *Medice* Racha's apothecary.

A sign hung on the door, encouraging people to come in (after they had signed in across the hall), and make themselves comfortable. The room was large, with enough chairs and sofas for maybe twenty people, and enough standing room for ten more.

Coren suddenly felt filthy, thinking about the dust and sweat of the road as he stared around at the pristine room. Rane seemed to have no such qualms, immediately sitting down on a cornflower blue armchair.

Coren took up a seat on a deep indigo sofa.

It didn't take long before *Medice* Racha was back, sinking down into another blue chair and sighing as she extended her bad leg.

"So, travellers. You are friends of Elija's? What brings you here? And so far away from the Cortach Range?" She asked.

"War." Rane said, their expression grim. Racha sat back, her shoulders slumping, eyes closing, mouth sinking into a line.

"I see. Against?"

"Lady Chaos, the nameless goddess of the magickal races." Rane said.

"My gods, too." *Medice* Racha said, nodding.

"Really?" Coren asked, leaning forwards. Fascination steered him away from the more pressing topic. "I didn't think that humans..."

"It's a common mistake. Most magickal beings don't realise that some of us believe in the nine gods. Myself included. After all, I tend to call on them, use their magick in spells when I'm healing someone. It would be hard not to have faith in them after that." Racha shrugged.

"You practise magick?" Coren could feel his eyes widen, and Kinaar's voice grew to a roar in the back of his head.

"I do. I am one of the last magickal healers in the known world." Racha said proudly, her eyes sparkling. "When I found Farse, he was gravely injured. I didn't think that he was going to survive. Thinking about this poor little boy dying because of a human's cruelty - Something snapped in me, and somehow... I suppose I unlocked my magick."

Kinaar laughed. *This is incredible - A miracle! Magick isn't dead! Look at her - Look at what she's built! Magick...*

"It's incredible, *Medice*." Coren whispered, echoing the goddess. "What you've built - Magick."

"Thank you, Coren." Racha said.

"Your children, you adopted them?" Rane asked curiously.

"Yes. Farse is a vampire, Valeria a medusa. Heor is half Fae, and Leon is human. They were all orphaned, and wounded. They needed a parent, so I thought... Why not me? It can be hard sometimes, being a single mother, especially with them being so young, and magickal, when I'm human. At least scrapes and bruises heal quickly in this household." The doctor shook her head, strands of pale hair wisping out around her face.

"Ay, look at us! Don't let me distract you. What brought you to the Elven Territories?"

"Oh." Rane looked over at Coren. "He'll have to tell that story. I didn't meet him until the Painted City."

Racha leaned in. "Go on."

So Coren found himself recounting the entire story, from the murder in the North, to Corrinnestāt again.

He struggled with the Common Tongue, so Rane had to help him along with some of it, and together, they made it through.

When Coren finally ended the story, his throat was hoarse, and Racha was looking at him with a new sort of intense, motherly light in her eyes. She stood up, and gave him a hug. It was unexpected, and Coren flickered for a moment, but the healing woman didn't seem fazed.

"Poor duck." She whispered, and then drew him to his feet. "Come on, the pair of you. Let me get you some food. I'm sure Valeria will be thrilled to see you again, and Leon is much friendlier than either of his brothers."

The kitchen was warm, and filled with the sound of laughter, and the clinking of silverware on porcelain. Dinner was a soup, filled with vegetables and sausage, which Coren and Rane ate ravenously, the meat pies feeling like an eternity ago.

The children, however, only picked at the vegetables, and Farse wandered off halfway through dinner, coming back with a vial of a reddish liquid - one with an all too familiar iron tang.

Immediately after dinner, Valeria looked up at Coren with huge eyes, before tugging him down the hall, and upstairs.

Rane laughed, but it wasn't long before Leon did the same to her, with Racha the only one left standing.

So, Coren wound up spending the next hour playing with the children, to the infinite amusement of Rane, who had somehow managed to get out of it, and was leaning by the door, watching.

After a while, Racha tapped her cane on the floorboards, and made an *ahem* noise. "All right, Farse, Valeria, Heor, Leon! Time for you to get ready for bed. Our new friends need some space!"

Reluctant good nights were said, and the werecats were shown to their rooms, where they were able to take baths (after figuring out the running water) and sleep away from the elements.

Coren even wound up sleeping in the bed, he was so tired.

LXVI - In Which Kinaar Wakes

AS COREN'S EYES SLID shut, heavy with sleep, Kinaar's blazing sunlight eyes slipped open, the light intense, blinding. Her fingers twitched, and she sighed, a tired smile slipping across her face.

She hung in a space between the stars, pinpricks of light illuminating the darkness all around her.

Her gown shone like the sun, and she looked for all the world like an angel, haloed in warm yellow light.

The Lady of Stars sank to the ground - A hard surface like glass separating her from the emptiness. She pressed her fingers to the obsidian-smooth surface, relishing the sensation of touch after so many years of stillness, the nothingness of the in-between.

She looked up then, and smiled, tilting her head to the side. Awake. After millions of years. She had finally fully awoken. Just in time for a war.

LXVII - In Which the Werecats Leave the City

MORNING CAME TOO EARLY, complete with tiny, stampeding feet, and the return of the blazing sun.

There was a rapping on the door, and Farse's voice was unmistakable as he called Coren down to breakfast.

"And Mamá has supplies for you!" He added, before thundering off, a squeal and a thump following shortly after.

Coren rolled out of bed, thumping down to the ground. The blankets came with him, and he groaned, standing.

He went to open the door, stopping short when he caught a snatch of *Medice* Racha chewing Farse out for running Leon over.

Grimacing, he decided to just drop through the floor, into the room below - which happened to be the kitchen.

Rane, who was wide awake and cooking breakfast, didn't even blink, just laughed, and said a cheery good morning.

Heor's tail was wrapped around their arm, and he was cuddled up in the dip of their neck, waving around a wooden spoon. His eyes went wide when Coren rematerialized, and Rane just barely caught the spoon before it hit the ground.

Coren snorted. "Ay, sorry Heor! Made a friend, eh, Rane?"

They responded by baring their fangs and waving the serving spoon at him. It wasn't nearly as threatening as it could have been, not with the rosy-cheeked six-year-old bouncing on their hip.

There was a shriek, and Valeria came racing in, Leon on her heels, and a thoroughly scolded Farse trailing them both. The medusa shrieked again when she saw Coren, and nuzzled her head into the back of his knee. He picked her up, sitting down on one of the kitchen chairs, and bouncing her on a knee.

"Sorry Rane, if I had known that you were already cooking breakfast, I would have been down here a while ago." Coren said with a smile.

"Pfft, yeah right sleepyhead." Rane responded.

Coren was about to reply, when Farse cut in, his eyebrows drawn together in confusion.

"Excuse me? What language are you speaking? I know the Old Language, it's what Mister Elija speaks. You aren't speaking it."

Rane shot an amused look at Coren. "All yours."

He frowned. "Rane!"

"Mister Coren?" Farse asked, looking even more puzzled than before.

"We do speak the Old Language, it's just a different dialect, a different type, than, ah, Mister Elija. My apologies." He said, looking down at the red-eyed boy, who smiled and bounced on his toes, satisfied by the answer.

In that instant, a smiling *Medice* Racha came bustling in, laughing when she took in the scene.

"Good morning, all!" She greeted, setting a full bag in front of Coren on the table. "Food, and some medicines. Free of charge." She waved away their protests.

"Your cause is enough. A world of peace... That is the best re-ward."

Breakfast passed quickly, and soon enough Racha, her children, and the werecat messengers were gathered in the hall.

Valeria and Leon did not want Coren to leave, wrapping themselves around his legs, hindering his movements. Of course, this just meant that he dragged them around, to their delight.

While he dragged the children, Rane and Racha were dragging out their goodbyes.

"Really, *Medice*. Thank you so much for all that you've done. We'll never forget your hospitality."

But Racha just waved them away, yet again. "It was nothing. I am going to speak to the Lord Ruler of Corrinnestāt, and see if xe will send forces North for the war. If I pull that off, then we can speak about payment."

Coren laughed, and Rane shook their head, smirking.

Finally, it couldn't be put off any further. Racha smiled, and then tapped her cane. The children's heads swivelled towards her, with a look of dread.

"All right, Valeria, Leon, get off of Coren. He has important places to be, and we can't keep him."

Valeria looked crestfallen, and Leon's eyes grew large.

"I don't wanna you to go." Leon said, giving Coren a tight hug.

"Me neither." Valeria chimed in, adding to the pile. Coren swayed, in danger of falling, and Rane leaned forwards to grab his upper arm, pulling him upright.

"I'll miss you!" Coren said, leaning down to return the hug. Farse, Heor, and Rane joined in, and Racha topped it all off. When she pulled away, she brought her children with her.

Rane opened the door, and Valeria sniffled. Coren leaned in. "It'll be all right. Stay brave, little one." Valeria just bit her lip, her eyes watering, and Rane could see Coren's resolve wavering.

"Thank you again, Braves." Racha said, in the nick of time, waving. "Stay safe in Faerie. I'll be praying that the Emperor chooses to aid you."

"Good bye!" The four children chorused, as the werecats stepped out the door.

Rane was only dragging Coren a *little* bit.

"I promise I'll try and come visit you all. And maybe I can borrow a Western courier hawk to send a message. Thank you, *Medice* Racha."

"Goodbye, and good luck, the both of you!"

LXVIII - In Which Coren Receives Some Good News

ONCE AGAIN, THE DESERT spread out before them, the horizon a thin line, smudged with the faraway blur of prairie grass.

The sun was setting crimson and gold on the edge of the world, and the temperature was beginning to drop, when Rane stopped. Coren nearly ran into them.

"Do you think we should stop now, or should we go on a while longer?" They asked. Coren hummed.

"Ay. Well... I need to scry Queen Rosana tonight. I should have done it in Corrinnestāt, but I fell asleep too fast. I don't wish to wake her too late at night, either."

"So, you're saying that we should stop here?" Rane asked, laughing.

"Yeah." He ducked his head, grinning.

"I'll start the fire, you scry your queen." Rane said, waving away his protests and rummaging through their pack for the sticks they had gathered as they walked.

He smiled again, and sat down in the sand, whispering the words to the spell. The pendant heated up, just a bit, in the palm of his hand, and then Rosana was staring up at him, her eyes shining.

"Coren! How good it is to see you! How was Corrinnestāt?"

He laughed. "It's good to see you as well, my lady. It was wonderful. We stayed the night at *Medice* Racha's house last night, and we are perhaps seven hours out from the city now."

"We?" Rosana cocked her head.

"Oh!" Coren shook his head at himself. "Gods, I can't believe I've forgotten to tell you. My friend Rane, from the Painted City... They caught up to me, and we are travelling together. They know the message, and what is at stake. They are willing to fight." He said, nodding shortly.

"A travelling companion! How wonderful." the queen said, after just a short pause.

"Is everything all right, Queen Rosana?" He asked, hesitantly.

"She's nervous. Paranoid." Lady Sora said, leaning in over Rosana's shoulder. She pursed her lips, and shook her head affectionately.

Rosana rolled her eyes. "How much do you know about-"

"Rosana! Gods. We trust Coren's judgement, remember?" Sora chastised. "Now. The North. The news?"

Coren felt a little... Discomfited by the elven queen's instant distrust of someone that she had never met, but he let it slide. She may have looked young, but the queen was old. And she had seen too much war and betrayal to be healthy for any mortal.

And then Lady Sora's words sank in.

"What of the North?" He asked, his heart pounding. He leaned in closer over the pendant.

Rosana's expression brightened. "My friend, the *Malefica Theodosia*... Coren, she is staying with the North. And she still has her scrying pendant, after all of these years. I didn't think to try and contact her until recently, when I realised that... If the gods were rising, maybe she was as well."

Lady Sora cut in, sighing. "Queen Rosana forgot to tell you the last time we scryed Coren, I am so sorry. You must forgive our lapses in memory."

"You have been in contact with the North? How is my aunt? My Aunt Lana? The twins?" He asked, too frantic to know anything and everything to care. He barely noticed Rane slip up beside him.

"That is your friend? Rane?" The queen asked, and he nodded distractedly.

"Yes, yes. My family?!"

"Well, Coren... The good news is that they are all alive, and they have received our message. Myr was wounded, as you know too well. But she survived. And now... She is raising an army. Training the North to fight. The bad news is that she received an ultimatum from Lady Chaos. Surrender within the next two months - moons - or die."

Coren's heart nearly stopped. "Within *two moons?* When was this?"

Rane touched his shoulder gently, reminding him to stay grounded.

"The message was received only a few days ago, don't worry, Coren. It just means that... I suppose you'll have to travel fast." The queen said. She looked at Rane. "And this is Rane?"

"I am, Your Majesty." Rane said, bowing their head.

"A pleasure to meet you." Lady Sora said, and her queen nodded.

"And you, my Lady, Your Majesty."

Coren waited a beat, and when no one spoke again, he asked, "How much time does this give us?"

"Not long. It will take you a week, perhaps less if you move quickly, to get to the Faerie Empire. The landscape of Faerie itself is unclear. It could take you a week, maybe two, to get through, or perhaps only a handful of days. As fast as you can would be good." Sora paused. "And then travelling through the Drakon Lands and the small human queendom will take at least four days. You'll be cutting it close."

Coren's heart pounded. "Too close." he muttered.

"It'll be all right. We can do it." Rane said. "Maybe the goddess won't be precisely... Punctual?"

"Maybe." A pause. "We have to get out early tomorrow morning. We need to make it on time. I have to be there." The fire in his eyes was something fierce and dangerous.

Rane nodded firmly. "We leave at first light."

LXIX - Six Letters

REGINA Rosana steepled her fingers under her chin, her thin braids falling loose around her face. The phoenix pendant hung, warm, against her collarbones.

Coren was safe.

The North was... In a constant state of training and preparations.

And six letters had come back.

Six letters. Four allying themselves with the elves and werecats. Two no's.

The gryphons, and three human kings.

No's from the phoenixs and chimaeras. Not surprising, as they preferred solitude, but disappointing.

The war was beginning, truly. And their army was slowly growing.

LXX - Laeris

SIX DAYS LATER, THE desert had slowly faded into grass-lands, the thin road that the werecats were travelling barely visible amidst the waist-high plants.

Coren shielded his eyes from the sun, and looked ahead, stopping when he saw it.

The city of Laeris. It rested exactly on the border to the Faerie Empire, and rumor had it that the quarter that lay on Faerie land was nearly as dangerous as the Faerie capital itself, full of illusion and magicks.

They reached Laeris only hours after spotting it for the first time. They came prepared with *illusionis* cast upon them, but nothing could have prepared them for what the city was like.

The guards before the city gates wore no armour or weapons, but carried a gleaming bronze horn apiece. The horns were carved with ancient runes, and Coren didn't want to know what they could summon.

The soldiers cast the pair of them a cursory glance, and then opened the gates for them. All seemed in order, until they stepped forwards. Then, a rushing, burning sensation enveloped the pair of them, and when Coren looked around, everything was tinged a deep red.

The guards snapped to attention, raising their horns in preparation. Rane's form was cast in the same red light as Coren was.

"Show yourselves!" The one soldier barked, her eyes sharp, calculating.

Coren raised his hands away from his weapons, and Rane followed suit. They dropped the illusions together.

"Just werecats." the second soldier said, a smirk on his face.

Just werecats? Coren mouthed to Rane.

"Illusions." The first soldier muttered under her breath, before spitting onto the ground. "Step back out of the gates, try again. Apologies. With all of the Faerie magick around here, we must make sure that the people who enter our city are what they seem to be. I would not try another *illusio* until you leave our walls."

Rane executed a short bow, and Coren nodded. "Thank you, soldiers."

When they braved the gates again, there was no flash of light, no raising of horns. The soldiers gave them quick salutes before fixing their gazes on the horizon again.

Laeris was quiet. Completely still. Unlike Corrinnestāt, there was no market here. There were no gatherings of people at all. Anyone they did pass on the street shot them wary glances and rushed on.

Once or twice, the red of a person cloaked in illusion would flare up, but for the most part the city stayed colored in every other shade.

That is, until Rane and Coren rounded a corner, after wandering aimlessly for a long time.

Everything, everything within sight was tinged red. Deep crimson cloaked every person, object or animal, and the second that Coren and Rane stepped onto that street, they flared red as well. The Fae had twisted the spell until it was impossible to tell what was red because of the warding spells - or red for no reason at all.

This street was bustling, odd compared to the quiet human streets. For the people of this part of the city couldn't have been anything but Fae.

This was the famed Faerie Quarter.

"Gods." Rane said, staring down at their red-tinged skin. Their already fiery hair looked ablaze under the odd light.

"I know..." Coren murmured, staring at the magickal beings all around him. High Fae, with their human faces, curling horns and massive, feathery wings.

Goblyns, with their grey skin and knobby, six-jointed fingers worked at stands, serving as locksmiths and watchmakers, their deft hands crafting intricate, beautiful things.

Sprytes, with their tiny, whirring, dragonfly-like forms, and pixies, similar, but closer to butterflies, spun through the air.

Ellylldan, with their lanterns, and wicked, needle smiles bobbed through the crowds, misleading the innocent.

Brownies, small, with wrinkled brown skin and long dark hair picked pockets as the werecats watched.

Banshees, withered women with hair that floated around them, spectre-like, their lips too wide, too stretched, twisted in perpetual screams, slunk through the crowd, while fauns danced on street corners, playing panpipes and singing.

Selkies walked among the crowd, their seal-skin clothing, and the wet footprints belonging to all the watery Fae, giving them away.

Everything was so red, it was like viewing the world through a lens.

"Gods." Rane said again, and a High Fae turned towards them, faer[1] eyes a disconcerting black. Fae fluttered faer wings, and took off, turning flips as fae flew.

"Lady of Stars." Coren breathed, as an ellylldan waved faer lantern at him, and a brownie slunk closer, her hands shoved into the pockets of her dress.

Coren snarled at the small Faerie, and she glared at him before shuffling away, caught.

"Well." Rane turned to Coren, hands in the air. "I suppose we should find a place to sleep?"

"Yeah. In a human hostel. I'm not sure... I don't like the feel of this place." This earned Coren a titter from a nearby swarm of sprytes, their dragonfly wings flashing metallically.

LXXI - In Which the Werecats Meet Fyeren

ONE NIGHT IN LAERIS. That was all the time they devoted to the place.

The humans were all skittish when it came to the werecats, with their magickal tendencies, so similar to the Fae, and the Faeries treated them with either cold amusement, or disdain.

It didn't ease any of Coren's fears about meeting the Faerie *Imperator*.

They had crossed the border into the Faerie Empire when the sun was out and bright, hoping that it would diminish the strength of the illusions that the Fae were so well known for.

The woods were even older than those of the Elven Territories. Trees as wide as two metres rose high into the sky, branches so wide that Coren could pitch a tent on them scraped the air.

And the Fae were everywhere, if you looked close enough. Leaves on the trees turned out to be pixies, with moth-like wings in shades of brown and black.

Shadows were dark-furred brownies. Boulders were sleeping goblyns. Large lakes were inhabited by selkies and kelpies, beautiful and elusive.

"How the hell are we going to *find* the Faerie capital?" Rane asked, after tripping over a root for the twentieth time. "I can't even stay upright for more than five minutes."

"Straight on, I hope... The map doesn't know a thing about the Faerie Empire." Coren responded, stepping gingerly over a vine, before helping Rane to their feet again.

"Gods. This forest is out to kill us." Rane muttered, and someone laughed.

The pair of them jumped, and looked up into the thick, russet foliage of a tree. Straining their eyes, they were just able to make out the form of a High Faerie, faer wings the same shade as the leaves around them, faer clothing and hair mottled for camouflage.

"Lady of Stars." Coren hissed, before raising his voice to address the Faerie. "Hello!"

"Hello, travellers." The Faerie stepped off of the branch, free falling for a moment, before faer wings snapped open, catching faer, and bringing faer to a gentle landing before the werecats.

The High Faerie made a mocking bow, as faer clothes shifted colouring, until they blended in with the tree behind fae. Faer long hair and curving horns made the same change, until they were mottled in shades of brown, instead of orange.

"What do you seek on Faerie lands?" The High Faerie asked, feathers rustling. Was it just Coren's imagination, or had faer tawny wings taken on a brownish colour as well?

"We seek your capital city, and your Emperor." Coren said firmly, hand on the pommel of one of his knives.

Never trust a Faerie. They are masters of illusion, trickery, deceit.

"You do?" The Faerie grinned, leaning against the tree.

"Yes." Rane said, meeting the High Faerie's eyes with their own steel and fire.

"Ah. I see." Fae said, faer eyes gleaming amethyst bright. "You will need a guide. No non-Fae creature can make it to the capital without a Faerie escort. Let me be yours." Faer voice went sing-song at the end, mockingly pleading. Faer eyes half-lidded, as if fae couldn't care less what the answer was.

Coren set his jaw. There had to be a catch.

"What will we owe you?" Rane asked, matching the strange Faerie's expression.

"Nothing..." Fae said, examining faer midnight blue lacquered nails. "Just the message that you carry."

Coren's eyes widened, and he grabbed Rane's upper arm, squeezing hard when it looked like they were about to answer.

"No." He snapped.

"No?" The Faerie leaned forwards, faer lips curling into a wickedly cruel smile. "Then you'll be lost. Never heard from again. The message will never arrive."

Silence, Coren examining fae, Rane's eyes still angry.

"Trust me." Fae sang, high, and sweet, and dangerous.

"We have no other choice, do we." Rane said, wrenching their arm free from Coren's grasp.

"Rane!" Coren began, panic rising, but the other werecat just held up a hand, their red hair tousled by the wind.

"No, you don't." The Faerie said, twirling around.

"Then we have to. And if you don't like it, I'll go alone. I know the message." Rane said, and Coren's jaw tightened.

"It's our only option, Coren." Rane hissed.

"It really is." Again, the strange Faerie's ears were too sharp, picking up the quietest sounds.

"Godsdamn it. All right. Be our guide." Coren said through gritted teeth.

"Tell me the message first!" The Faerie commanded.

"I want your name before I tell you anything." Coren responded, arms crossed tight over his leather breastplate.

"Fine!" The Faerie sang. "It's Fyeren of the Faerie Empire. Now. The message, and I will lead you there."

"Swear not to leave us. Swear that you will deliver us safely to *Imperator* Kalei. Then, we will tell you." Coren bartered.

"I swear it, on my honour." Fyeren rolled faer bright eyes.

"I doubt you have any honour, trickster." Rane said, their mouth twisting.

"I swear it on my life, on my parent's graves, on the stars in the sky, on the leaves on the trees, on the Emperor faerself." The High Faerie sang, twirling again until fae were a blur of shifting colours. Faer wings really were tinging the same colour as their surroundings, it was obvious now.

Fyeren raised an eyebrow, faer grin slick. "Happy?"

"Very." Rane said. "Want to seal the deal, Coren?"

"We are carrying a message to the *Imperator* regarding the fallen gods, and the Great War. We carry a message of a coming war, and the need for an allyship. Without the Fae, we're lost. We will not have a great enough force." Coren spat out. He didn't like this Faerie - fae sent an ugly, creeping sensation of mistrust through his veins.

"Happy?" He mimicked.

"*Very.*"

LXXII - In Which The Faerie Empire Reveals It's Dangers

CW: This chapter contains suicidal ideation, and vomiting
FYEREN TURNED OUT TO be true to faer word, if sarcastic, fleet, and constantly getting on Coren's nerves.

Every time either he or Rane dared ask where they were, the High Faerie smiled, and found a way to change the subject. Coren was of the right mind to tell the Faerie to get lost... But this was their only chance of getting to the unnamed capital city of the Faerie Empire safely.

Fae laughed at any attempt to bribe faer for information, and oftentimes would travel through the treetops, far away and hard to see - hardly a proper guide.

At night, fae would vanish to gods knew where, leaving Rane and Coren to brave the night alone. Night... It was full of noises, illusions, dark things, and so much magick.

It took tremendous effort, but Coren would wrap the Veil tight around the campsite, forming a wall-like structure. It made it that much harder to practise with Lady Kinaar, but it was nice, being ignored by the Fae, instead of being constantly pestered by them.

The dangers of those woods were not completely revealed, however, until the fourth day of travel through the Faerie Empire.

The day was chill, the seasons change obvious once out of the desert, and Rane and Coren were exhausted.

His head still felt stuffed full of cotton from the strain of using his control over the *Rica* to ward them every night, so Coren barely noticed when they walked out of the woods, and onto a pebbly beach. Fyeren had vanished again, and was presumably somewhere nearby.

Hopefully somewhere nearby.

An obsidian-dark lake lay before them, unlike the others they had seen in those woods. The surface was impenetrably dark, unnaturally still, and a black, rocky spire rose from the centre. It reminded Coren of the *Conpitum*, in a sick way.

Rane opened their mouth, turning to Coren. They looked as if they were about to say something, their posture tense, fearful, ready to run, when their head snapped around, towards the lake. A faraway look entered their eyes, and a slow smile spread across their face.

"Oh no..." Coren murmured.

There was one more Faerie that they hadn't yet seen, and, *gods above*, had he prayed that they wouldn't.

Syrens.

Syrens, singing people into the water, to their deaths. Their songs would be charming, drawing you in, and then would dredge up every fear, every hurt that was lurking deep inside of you, amplifying it until you lost the will to swim.

They would drag you down, the fears and the syrens themselves, with their cold, clammy hands.

He knew what was going on, tried to plug his ears in time, but it was too late. Gods *damn* his sharp hearing.

His heavy pack fell to the ground, side by side with Rane's (he couldn't see them - where had they gone?) and then he was up to his ankles in the water.

Kinaar, and the remaining autonomous part of his thoughts, were screaming at him, but the voices were muted by the song.

The voices were an unearthly choir, tendrils wrapping around his consciousness, pulling him in, deeper into the liquid silk of the obsidian lake.

A blink of the eye, and he was up to his waist, his boots sticking into the heavy muck at the bottom of the lake, his linen pants sticking to his skin.

The voices reached a new crescendo, and sudden memories came crashing down. How he hadn't woken his cousins, when he should have. All of the dark blood on his hands. The memories of the dead Councillors, who he could have helped.

Being lost, people probably believing him dead. And now, a war. One that would end with him sacrificing his own life. What was the point of trying to survive the way home, if he was to die anyways?

How was he going to tell his family that he was going to die? How was he going to tell Rane?

He had waded in until his mouth was just barely above the water, and the song went on and on.

Every fault, every flaw, every argument, every mistake.

Dear gods. He took a gasping breath, and then... It was too much. Anything to stop the pain of the song, anything to put an end to it.

He was stepping forwards again, and there was a drop off, and then he was falling through the water.

Just like in that damn dream, so long ago.

The water was so dark when he opened his eyes, and it stung every inch of skin, it was so cold. He could feel the numbness creeping into his fingers, into his toes.

The boots dragged him down, his armor was waterlogged.

Blue faces swam before his eyes. Long, webbed, goblyn-like fingers touched his face, scales glittering up and down slender arms. Billowing fabric the same colour as the water. Their voices...

Dear gods, the voices went on, even beneath the water. He thrashed trying to get away from the unholy sound, but he was *so* cold...

A last breath escaped his numb lips, the bubbles only slightly lighter than the dark liquid around him. His vision was fuzzy... His chest was tight.

This was it. A way away from the world waiting for him. Away away from the war, from the gods, from everything.

A way away.

He closed his eyes, and sank, the water flowing silky cold over his skin.

A way away.

The syren's grip on his arms loosened, and he was falling of his own accord, his chest was so tight... It couldn't have been more than a minute or two. No water had yet entered his lungs. He could fight if he wanted to.

But he didn't.

He opened his mouth, and the water came rushing in. Silt swirled up around him, scraping, and it was over. He was on the bottom, and when he opened his stinging eyes, the light that filtered through the waves was so weak. So cold...

He closed his eyes.

So this was what dying felt like.

And he lost consciousness.

Rane couldn't see Coren, but no matter. The music, the syren-song. It was everything, drawing them in. It was a rope, dragging them towards the water, and in an instant, they had swum out, close to the rocky spire in the middle of the black waves.

It was then that the song turned dark. Right when they had been so close to the source, a beautiful syren sitting on the rocks, faer long, blue legs dangling, faer voice the sweetest melody.

The song was suddenly reminding, painful. It was their amma, chastising.

I told you, child of mine. The bones never lie. I told you not to trust your brother. I told you, I told you, I told you, I TOLD YOU.

It was their brother, throwing nasty words, leaving them.

Worthless. Worthless, and unworthy to lead. They'll finish you, and then it will all be over. You should have listened to Amma.

It was their own voice, hissing and spitting nasty things.

You should have listened to Amma. You never should have trusted Kir. You never should have killed that tiger lord. You killed the Bandit King, and his closest people. You have been lying to Coren since you met him. You, you, you, you...

Too much. They clapped hands over their ears, trying to drown out the noise, but then they couldn't swim, and they sank.

Better off drowned. Everyone would be better off without the lies. Without the betrayal, the fear, the hurt.

Better off.

Hands curled around their ankles, stilling the fruitless kicking, stilling the struggles.

Better off...

They stopped fighting, and sank, down, down into the lake, the water closing over their head with a tiny sound. The syrens were all around them. They didn't open their eyes, but they could hear the voices, could feel the webbed, too-long fingers on their skin.

The water slid across their skin, through their clothing, all around them, in every pore, leaving them shivering. It was so slick. Cold.

Icy cold, syrup smooth.

And then it erupted.

Swarming bubbles prickled across their numb skin, and they lifted their chin up, just up, nothing else.

Something had happened.

The singing had stopped.

And suddenly Rane wanted to fight again.

There had been wrongs. They had made mistakes, been *human*, for gods' sake.

Lord of Earth and Life, were they cold.

And wanted to *breathe*. Opening their mouth, they got nothing but water, but kicking got them nowhere, they just sank again.

Their thoughts had devolved into a swarm of *shitshitshitshit*'s, and this... This could end in two ways. Life or death.

And then cold hands were clasping around their forearms again - and gods, the syrens were back. They kicked out, feebly.

Damn, damn, damn! The water was too dark, they were blind, and weak and -

"Stop fighting, damn you!" A voice, garbled by the water, hissed in their ear. A familiar voice.

Warm, feathery wings enveloped Rane as they shot upwards, and Fyeren screamed something at the forms beginning to swarm back up towards them. The High Faerie was sopping wet, but somehow managed to fly out of the water, struggling with faer waterlogged wings, and Rane's near-deadweight.

Safe?

Rane's head felt heavy, their body even heavier.

"Stay awake, damn you!" Fyeren snapped, pinching Rane's arm hard enough to bruise.

Seconds dragged on, until they felt like minutes, and then there was cold gravel beneath Rane's back, and the Faerie was standing above them, planting a boot on their stomach.

Rane was barely able to choke out a 'no' before Fyeren stepped down, inducing vomiting.

They were so preoccupied with this new development, that they didn't notice the High Faerie's absence until they heard another splash, and a geyser of dark water shot into the air.

Coren. Coren!

They spat into the gravel, wiping their mouth and staggering to their feet, watching the water with anxious eyes. A second ticked by. Two. Five. Twenty.

Their breath was coming faster again, nothing in their stomach to heave up. There was no water in their lungs, so why was it so hard to breathe?

One minute. Or maybe only half. Maybe Rane had been counting too fast. Or maybe too slow. Maybe it had been two.

A piercing shriek rent the air, and a dark, winged form exploded out of the water, flying higher and higher, struggling up, water streaming away from faer.

One second, two, and Fyeren was falling again, back towards the shining lake, and Rane's heart leapt up into their throat. At the very last moment, the Faerie's wings snapped out, and fae coasted towards the beach, crashing to the ground in a tumble of feathers and twisted limbs.

Fae fell still, and Rane stumbled over, rolling the Faerie onto faer back, revealing the sodden, crumpled werecat beneath faer waterlogged form.

"Coren..." Rane breathed, rolling him over as well, and pushing a hand in front of his mouth. Gods above, please, please, please...

Nothing. Not a breath passed his lips. A hard look entered Rane's eyes.

They knew what to do, years at the *Conpitum*, and the lake beneath it, had taught them.

They curled their hands together, and began pushing on the werecat boy's stomach. Compressions. Pump out the water. Push air in.

Seconds stretched again, who knew how long it took, until Coren began to cough violently. Rane turned him on his side, and the water came up in a filthy stream.

They shot up a quick prayer. Thank the gods.

Tears were streaming down their cheeks as they held Coren's shoulders, waiting, helping, continuing as best they could. And then, when he took his first shaky breath without coughing, Rane grinned through their tears, and hugged him tight.

"Shit, Fyeren." They said, suddenly, pulling away, and trying the limp High Faerie for a breath. "Thank the gods, faer breathing. Alright, what the hells, I'm returning the favour."

And Rane kicked the Faerie in the gut, in just the right place, where you were to aim if you wanted your enemy doubled up, unable to breathe for a bit... Fyeren spasmed, coughing, before rolling faer eyes up at Rane, glaring.

"Damn. You." Fae spat, sitting up and scooting away.

"Thank you, Fyeren. We would have died." Rane said, making a short bow. Coren had stumbled upright, and was leaning heavily on Rane's shoulder. He nodded his head.

His eyes were eerily empty, but he thanked the Faerie all the same, and extended a hand to help faer up, which really just ended with Rane hauling the two of them upright.

Fyeren shrugged. "The syrens know me. They are going to regret touching you."

Rane examined faer for a second, a question in their eyes, before turning their attention back to Coren.

He was looking out at the lake, at the rocky spire crowded with shadowy figures. "I need to get away from this godsdamn lake."

"Agreed." Fyeren said, back to faer usual aloofness. "Your bags are a couple of yards that way. I will meet you in the trees." Fae pointed off to the left, before disappearing into the thicket.

Rane realised, belatedly, that this was the first time that they had seen the Faerie just... Walk.

They sighed, and followed Coren. He already had his pack slung up on his shoulders, and he was walking slowly towards where Fyeren had entered the treeline, an arm wrapped around his stomach, where Rane had been pushing.

Rane followed, only a bit faster, still shaky from, well, nearly drowning. They caught up, and walked beside him in silence.

"It was awful." They finally said. "That song, what I heard... Gods. Every regret that I have. They kept on saying that the world would be better off without me. I believed it." Their eyes welled again, and this time they didn't wipe the streams away.

Let him see them cry. They had travelled together, nearly died together.

"I-" Coren broke off, blinking away his own tears.

Rane could only watch as a wall came slamming down, blocking off the open, kind boy they had come to know. It was back to the frightened, upset, closed-off werecat they had first met in the Painted City.

"Every regret, every mistake. That's what they say about syrens."

LXXIII - In Which Lady Chaos is Frustrated

LADY CHAOS'S HANDS curled into fists, her silvery fingernails digging into her shadow-woven palm.

The syrens, turned to her side, hadn't worked, and a second Wraith had been killed at the gates of Laeris. She wasn't going to be able to send another one of her shadow-soldiers into the Faerie Empire.

The godling boy was still alive, that much was obvious. Damn the High Faerie, and the other werecat. Without them, he would be dead.

He would be dead, and Lady Chaos wouldn't be so desperate. He had to die.

He would know the full extent of his powers soon, if he didn't already.

Damn it. The goddess drew her sword, and stabbed it into the ground.

Even she didn't know the terrain of Faerie, and would never find the way to the hidden capital.

There was nothing to do but wait until they left the Faerie Empire. Then a Wraith could begin tracking again.

For now, she would wait, and plan. There was still a war that had to be waged - on the North, and their weak army.

LXXIV - Secrets

WHEN THE SOAKED, BEDRAGGLED werecats entered the trees Fyeren was waiting for them, somehow already dry. Faer lacquered nails didn't show even a whispering sign of chipping, and faer long hair was braided back, spiralling horns gleaming.

"What in blazes?" Rane sputtered, as the High Faerie smirked.

"You're welcome, by the way. Now. Come. We'll set up camp in a kilometre or so, I doubt that the two of you will be able to make it any farther.

Rane noted that Fyeren didn't try to fly, either, walking ahead. Fae were more tired than fae were letting on.

There was no way in hell that Rane was letting Coren vanish the campsite that night.

"I swear on all of the gods, I will knock you out if you even try. Heavens, you're so tired you'd blow up the campsite before properly warding it." They snapped, when Coren tried to protest. The empty look was still lurking in his gaze, and they were determined to extinguish it.

"But-"

"What?" Fyeren interrupted, crossing faer arms over faer chest. When fae had heard the story, fae smirked again, twisting the ends of faer hair.

"I see. You, my dear godling, will not be warding this campsite tonight. You will be resting, after nearly drowning. I will take care of everything, don't worry." Fae said, whirling away into the woods with a rustle of feathers.

"Settled." Rane nodded, mirroring Fyeren's smirk.

"What the hells? We trust Fyeren to protect us? We could be killed by ellylldan tonight."

"What in the hells is wrong with *you*?" Rane retorted, anger flaring, their voice dropping to a whisper. "Fyeren saved our lives out there. Show some gratitude. If fae want to help us tonight, then I'll let faer. Besides, fae haven't flown since the Lake of Glass. If Fyeren *can't* fly, then that's on us."

Coren set his jaw, biting his lip hard enough to draw a bead of blood. Reluctantly, he bowed his head. "Sorry."

"You'd do well to remember what fae did for us." Rane crossed their arms, but after a second their expression softened. "You remembered some terrible things in that lake, didn't you. I did too. I - I kept on hearing that the world would be better off without me."

Coren shook his head, closed his eyes, obviously struggling with what to say. Finally, his fists clenched, and he spat out the words. "They said that - It would be better if I died there, than in this pointless war. I saw - *Every* mistake that I have ever made. *Every* bad choice. Every awful thing that I am going to have to face."

"Coren..." They put a hand on his shoulder, and he met their eyes. "Coren of the North. You have done amazing things. You have come *so far*. You're doing the *right thing*. Can't you see that? Everyone makes mistakes, and you... You have done nothing wrong. Your family loves you. They'll welcome you back with open arms." They said, and Coren started to cry. He looked up at the sky, his lips moving, no sound coming out.

"Hey, Coren! Coren, it's all right." Rane's breath stocked, as the panic that they had said the wrong thing set in.

"Thank you, Rane... Just... I - Kinaar - Chaos... " He choked on the words, and Rane watched him anxiously, saying his name again and again. His nose and eyes were red now, the tears coming quick.

"I'm going to die, Rane. Soon."

The words felt like a punch to the gut. *"What?* Coren, *what?"* They asked, loudly, hands on his shoulders, forcing him to look at them again.

"I'm going to die. I have to. To prevent the world from ending." He pressed a hand to his mouth, to his bleeding lip. Rane's eyes were wet, their mouth open as they watched him.

"No. No fucking way, no." They whispered. "You've got to be shitting me. Please."

"I'm not." His voice broke. "That's what the syrens were singing about. They said it would be better if I never went home. I'd never hurt my family again."

Rane said nothing for a long moment, their heart pounding, and then drew him into a hug. "Oh, Coren. I - I'm sorry."

He closed his eyes, and sniffled. "I don't want to die."

Tears spilled down Rane's cheeks. "I don't, either. I don't want you to die, I don't want to die, myself. I want - I want to go home. I want to see my people. I want to fall in love. And I want to live."

Coren's chest heaved, and he swiped at a tear, breaking up the hug. "I want to meet my baby cousin. I want to see Lin and See find the people they want to spend the rest of their lives with. I want to help train new warriors. I want to hunt, and swim, and live. I don't want to die."

Rane closed their eyes. "Is there any other way?"

Coren looked away. "No."

Rane swore softly, their heart sinking in their chest. "Fucking syrens."

This time, the Northern werecat laughed a bit. "Damn right."

A long silence stretched between them, and Rane's heartbeat thundered in their ears. Coren, the person who had become their best friend, was going to die. And they were still lying. And the syrens had fucked everything up.

Rane had realised, sinking in that godsdamn lake, that they didn't want to run anymore. No running from the truth, or the past, or their issues.

They took a deep breath, tapping nervous fingers on the pommel of their sword. Coren looked up, his amber eyes red from crying, a question held in them.

"I know - I know this isn't the time. But in that lake I realised that I want to live, and I realised that I don't want to lie." They swallowed and the tightness in their chest was back, but they pushed past it. "I have something to tell you."

They could feel Coren's gaze pinning them in place. He wasn't being hostile, just... Watching.

"I'm from the South, not the East. And - And I'm not just anyone. I'm the Chieftain." The words tumbled from Rane's mouth, and after they blurted it all out they waited with bated breath for Coren's response. They expected him to recoil. They expected shock and pain and hatred.

But this amazing boy's response was a laugh. A small one, quickly growing, until the Northerner's shoulders were quaking.

"What?" Rane asked, incredulous.

"I knew it!" Coren wheezed, holding his side. "I knew it. Your armour, the way you fight, and when you swore at that damn Wraith. I just hadn't figured out the chieftain part yet."

Rane sat in silence for a long minute, and then they started to laugh as well. The rumbling sound came from somewhere deep inside of them, somewhere that hadn't been open in a while.

"Fucking *hells*, you're telling me that I thought I was being so discreet, such a good liar for so long, when you had me figured out the second we met?" They cackled.

"Pretty much, yes." Coren laughed, and they hugged again.

"Look at us. Scared of dying, scared of the war. But finally being open because of it." He said, his voice crackly.

"Yeah. We're idiots." Rane hiccoughed.

"Oh. Hello." The new voice was unexpected, and they jumped apart as Fyeren strode back into the clearing.

Fae looked at them, that crooked smirk splitting his face. In faer hands, fae held a broken circlet, dripping wet and covered in algae.

Fae laughed, and sat down in the dirt, scraping green sludge from the crown. "The syrens will do that to you."

LXXV - The Nameless City

AS THE DAYS WENT BY, the woods grew denser, more Faeries appearing all around them, watching and murmuring.

Fyeren was back to faer usual self, just a blur in the treetops, occasionally handy with a sarcastic remark.

Coren and Rane's friendship seemed more solid now, easier now that they knew the other's secrets.

They spoke as if they had known each other for years, and while the weight of the war was still heavy, they bore it together now.

One afternoon, the woods grew dense enough that Coren simply grabbed Rane's wrist, and vanished the both of them, walking *through* the bushes instead of trying to cut them away.

Of course, this didn't faze Fyeren in the slightest. Fae simply hollered Coren's name, and blinked lazily when he reappeared.

"There you are. Come along, it's not far until the capital, and you will have to stay close." Of course, the Faerie then took off through the trees, and Coren had to sprint to keep up.

When they finally found a clearing to reappear in, Rane released a long breath in a scream.

"Dear gods, don't *ever* do that without warning me again. A *tree* was hurtling towards my *face* and I was sure that I was going to crash into it and *die*."

Coren laughed, shrugging. "Sorry. But we kept up with Fyeren."

"You did! Now," the Faerie in question said, dropping from a tree branch, brushing faer now green hair from faer purple eyes.

"We're just a short walk from the city walls. Come on, keep up. And stay close. I don't want you getting killed."

Coren swallowed, hard, and Fyeren smirked, flying back up. He extended a hand to Rane, who took it, and the Veil slipped over them both.

When Fyeren dropped down in front of them again, they came to an abrupt stop, the Veil falling away leaving them inches from faer chest. The High Faerie curled faer wings around faerself, raising a mocking hand. "Ah-ah... no touching. Be careful where you step."

The werecats dropped their hands, stepping back, and away from each other.

"The gates to our city are just ahead. We'll be walking from now on. Oh, and I would recommend... Staying visible." Fyeren said, faer voice singsong and high.

Turning away from them, fae whispered something under faer breath that neither could pick up. There was a long pause, and then fae smiled, gesturing at the thicket before the three.

"Come along, messengers!" Fae sang, faer hair and clothing shifting colours - browns and greens and reddish-oranges. Rane and Coren pushed through after the High Faerie, trying to keep branches from slapping back into their faces behind Fyeren.

When they cleared the thicket, Coren was about to snap at the Faerie, something about the etiquette of bushwhacking, when the words caught in his throat.

The capital city of the Faerie Empire, it's name unknown, lay before them, greater than any civilization that Coren had ever seen before.

Glowing, twisting spires reached into the sky, Faeries flying in and out of dark openings on the sides. Carvings adorned the walls, and the streets teemed, everything tinged faint gold.

Coren was awed, and a glance to the side showed the same stunned expression on Rane's face.

"My Lady of Stars..." He breathed, and Fyeren smirked.

"The Nameless City, to you. Our capital. Come along, now. The *Imperator* waits." Fae snapped open faer wings, and glided down the hill, leaving Rane and Coren to stumble their own way down.

The gates were ornate, carved with a familiar scene, remembered clearly from all of the stories that his mother once told.

They depicted the gods holding court. All nine of them were present, with Lady Chaos, the eldest, in the middle, the seam between the twin doors cutting her in half.

To her right was her daughter, Lady Illira. Death. Then, Lords Varien and Titor - Time and peace. Beside Titor, sat Lady Kinaar, staring straight ahead with cold stone eyes, her hands resting on the armrests, curled loosely. Everything about her was exactly as it had appeared in Coren's dream.

To the left were Lord Micha, Lady Nyx, Lady Ria, and Lord Duman, symbolising the earth, the waters, the skies and the seasons respectively.

The traditional godly court.

Did they carve it correctly? Coren asked, consulting the goddess in his head for the first time in a long time.

Yes. Although... Illira does not usually present as an adult. She said, slowly.

"Death is a child?!" Coren blurted, earning him some very strange looks from his travelling companions.

Yes. Kinaar said simply, before retreating, put out because of the rude summoning.

"Kinaar?" Rane asked, simply.

"Of course."

"You have a goddess in your head." Fyeren stated, one eyebrow rising.

Coren didn't respond, so the Faerie just smirked and whistled shrilly. At the sound, the gates swung open, slowly.

"No guards?" Rane asked, and Fyeren nodded.

"No need! We are the most obscure people in the known world. The only ones who can find this city are the ones who know it's true name. Let's not keep the Emperor waiting." The High Faerie strode forwards, and as fae passed through the gates, faer tunic went a deep blue that matched faer lacquered nails. Faer hair turned the same colour, and the Faerie's curling horns went the same russet-bronze as faer sweeping wings.

The camouflage was changing to fit in with the city people.

Coren stopped before the gates, staring up at the walls for a long moment.

This was the capital. A simple yes or no from *Imperator* Kalei, and then there was only one more stop before home.

He stepped through the gates.

LXXVI - In Which An Army is Mobilised

THE CLEARING, DUSTED in the silver light of a scrying spell, and dominated by the twisted throne, filled with words spoken in a language older than the Old Language itself. The tongue of the gods.

Lady Chaos stared into the sphere of enchanted water, hovering inches above her open palms, and read the Chieftainess Warlord Myr's lips.

'To win the war.'

She had been watching.

She had seen all of the Northern Chieftainesses speeches, seen all of the opposing forces gathering, and with this knowledge, she had sent Wraiths to delay the coming armies. The Nameless Goddess was the silent puppetmaster, orchestrating the entire war.

From her golden throne, the seat that should have been her prison, she watched as her siblings stirred.

She had been watching when Kinaar's eyes had finally opened for good, and she had slumped to the 'ground' in the starry place she had slept in.

Chaos obsessed over these stirrings, faint panic and rage flooding her veins every time she saw movement. She worried that they would wake in time to defeat her.

Yes, she had been overlooking her own daughter, who was awake and plotting, but she believed there to be no reason to worry about Death. The more fool her.

Now, watching this speech, this call to arms, she smiled. Her long, shadow-woven fingers fluttered, and the watery orb drifted to the ground.

The smile still clinging to her lips, she exhaled, a plume of shadow chasing the breath, twisting around itself until a Wraith stood before it's mistress, it's ember eyes pulsing.

"We have waited long enough, General. There is no more planning to be done. We move out at dawn." Chaos hissed.

LXXVII - In Which Fyeren Becomes Slightly Less Mysterious

THE CAPITAL CITY OF the Faerie Empire was worse than the Faerie Quarter of Laeris.

The Fae were everywhere, of course, peddling illusions and tricks, fleet fingers grasping for any semi-precious thing that could be resold.

Rane had to keep a firm grasp on their moonstone necklace, lest the pixies lift it from around their neck.

Goblyns hawked fine watches, even finer gold- and silver-smithing...

It was magickal. All of it. But Fyeren just kept on ploughing through the crowd, unstoppable, a midnight blue blur. It must have been so familiar to faer that it wasn't worth stopping.

Or fae just wanted to be rid of the pesky werecats. Fyeren had the gossip early, fae may as well complete the task, and then leak all of the information.

When the High Faerie held up a hand to stop said messengers, they nearly crashed into fae.

They had stopped in front of a building, rising high above the ground. It was, by far, the finest, tallest structure in the entire city. A palace.

The doors were grand, carved with hundreds of tiny faces. The vast majority were High Fae, with their great horns, but some were tiny sprytes or pixies, some goblyns, and a brownie or two.

"Our Emperors." Fyeren said, before turning away from them, and gazing up at the top of the spire. Fae examined faer nails one more time, looking up lazily.

"Go on. I'll announce your arrival to *Imperator* Kalei." Fae made a shooing motion, and Coren bared his fangs, tail lashing.

"Come on, Coren. We're so close, don't start a fight." Rane muttered, as Fyeren made yet another signature, mocking bow, before shooting up, until fae were nothing but a speck in the sky, swooping in to the highest entry port of the palace.

Coren shook his head. "I still really dislike that Faerie."

But he pushed the doors open all the same, and they entered the spire together.

About 4,000 steps later - Rane had stopped counting somewhere around 100, deciding to estimate instead - they reached a gilded, circular room. Rane immediately flopped down onto a bench, sighing, while Coren, as was his fashion, examined the room for a bit.

Vases full of flowers sat on pedestals spaced evenly about the room, benches placed between them. Three spaces were left free, to make room for a check-in desk, the door that Coren and Rane had used to enter the room, and a space simply dropping off into open air. The room bore no trace of any way to ascend further.

A compass was carved into the floor, and Coren moved to stand at the Northeast point.

"That direction. That's home." He said, that lonely look entering his eye.

"We'll get there. You'll see your family again." Rane said, patting his shoulder, and he nodded, slowly.

"I can only hope."

"You'll get there, if you survive this." Sang a voice, startling the werecats. They spun to face the voice, finding only Fyeren, lounging in the armchair behind the desk. Faer camouflage had shifted to match the coppery walls.

Gods only knew if fae had been sitting there the whole time, or if fae had only just arrived.

"The Emperor will see you now." The High Faerie said, lazily clapping out a simple rhythm.

The ceiling shifted, wavering, and a staircase spiralled down, the end touching down right at Coren and Rane's feet.

"I'll be right behind you." Fyeren said, standing, and prowling around the desk. "Wouldn't want to keep Emperor Kalei waiting."

The throne room. That was where the stairs ended. It had a vaulted ceiling, forming what could only have been the tip of the spire, and a raised dais stood in the centre. Upon it stood a High Faerie, faer hands clasped behind faer back, below faer wings.

The stairs rose back into place soon after Fyeren had reached the top, and fae instantly dropped into a short bow, before walking over to faer *imperator*.

"The messengers." Fae said, and the Faerie ruler turned - Revealing a familiar face. Coren's breath stocked.

It was Fyeren - Almost. This Faerie had a truer smile, and a crown.

"What?" Rane sputtered, and Coren nudged them gently, bowing low to the High Faerie.

"*Ave, Imperator* Kalei." Coren said, and Rane repeated the greeting.

"Hail, Emperor Kalei."

"*Ave*, Coren of the North, and Chieftain Rane of the South. Welcome to our nameless city." The Emperor's voice was smooth and friendly, the opposite of Fyeren's. Fae looked over at the guide, and shook faer head.

"I see that my brother didn't tell you that we are related... I am the eldest. Fyeren answers to me. Even though he was lost for *so many months*. I am sorry that he did not tell you this." Kalei murmured, studying faer sibling with something akin to disgust. Fyeren curled faer lip, and turned away, wings fluttering.

The Faerie *imperator* stepped off of faer dais, instead sitting gingerly on it's edge, beckoning the werecats over. Coren's head was spinning.

So, they were related. And, even though fae had been speaking to strangers, Emperor Kalei had used faer sibling's personal pronouns - highly impolite.

There was bad blood between the pair?

Rane bowed low again before sitting, cross-legged, before the *Imperator*. Coren went through the same motions, keeping his head bowed.

Fyeren stayed standing, leaning against the far wall. Faer eyes were closed, faer wings curled around fae, blending into the walls. The guide was obviously listening, but trying to pretend that fae was not.

"Werecats. You have come from the Elven Territories, through the Solchar Desert, just to get to the Faerie Empire, and deliver a message. Is that correct?" *Imperator* Kalei asked, and Coren stiffened. Even Kinaar, constantly murmuring, fell still.

"How did you know where we were travelling from?" Rane asked defensively, and Coren winced. Rane bowed their head, muttering an apology.

"I have my sources. Now, what was this message?" Kalei waved a hand, and with that, Coren had to revise his mental image. Kalei was not like Fyeren... But fae were nearly as cold.

Coren took a deep breath. "War is coming. The gods are rising. I, myself, am a ward of Lady Kinaar, goddess of the Veil, the night and the day."

"I know what my own patron *dea* is the goddess of." Kalei snapped, and Coren flinched. "Apologies. Continue. War is coming..."

"Yes. Lady Chaos is rising again. She had shaken off the slumber that the *Malefica* Theodosia placed upon her, and she has already waged war upon my home, the North." Coren took a shaky breath, and Rane reached out, squeezing his shoulder, moonstone ring glittering.

"My aunt, the Chieftainess Warlord Myr of the North, was severely injured, as was I. I forced her to leave with the *Malefica* Theodosia, so that she would stay alive to guide our people."

Emperor Kalei's expression did not change throughout the entire tale, even as Coren's breathing grew laboured, the story's weight drawing his shoulders down. Finally, he finished, the final words leaving the throne room steeping in silence.

"Please, on behalf of Queen Rosana of the Elven Territories, and the Northern Band of the Cortach Range... We ask for your help in this coming war. Military and strategically. Please, join us, become our ally, as *Imperator* Quai was during the first Great War."

Kalei's expression did not change.

LXXVIII - Ally

COREN'S LIP WAS BLEEDING again, iron and salt on his tongue. Rane was cursing under their breath, a mere moment away from hacking the furniture to pieces.

I will think about it. Leave me. The Faerie emperor had said. And there Coren had been, thinking that Kalei was better than faer arrogant, sarcastic sibling.

Fyeren faerself had said nothing as fae led the werecat messengers to their rooms on a lower level of the palace.

Nothing. No 'I'm sorry that I didn't mention that the Emperor of the entire Faerie Empire - a whole *quarter* of the known world - is my older sibling.'

No 'sorry that my elder sibling is an ass.'

Just silence, and to be quite honest, there was a good chance that, had Fyeren dared say anything, Rane would have separated faer horned head from faer shoulders. In fact, Coren may have beaten them to it.

But now, there was nothing they could do but wait in the infernally golden rooms. Technically, Rane was supposed to be across the hall, but they had come into Coren's chamber to talk everything over. Strategize.

So far, strategizing had turned out to be a whole lot of sitting in silence.

"*Damn* those High Faeries." Rane finally spat, their hand closing around the hilt of their sword. The scuffed moonstone pommel shone like a beacon, before dulling to a pale, pulsing glow.

They stood, and stabbed a pale silk pillow before sitting back down, leaving the broadsword sticking into it. Coren stared at the impaled pillow for a long moment, and then sighed again.

"Well, this was... An adventure." He said, and Rane grimaced a smile.

"Without the Fae... We'd be even more dead than we already are." Rane muttered, sliding down the wall until their head was at an uncomfortable-seeming angle.

"Maybe they'll still join us." Coren said, halfheartedly.

"That 'maybe' seemed a lot like a 'no.'" Rane responded, screwing up their nose.

"Damn, damn, damn."

He couldn't stand it any more, so he stood, Shifting back and forth as he paced, his claws leaving little divots in the fibres of the pale blue carpet.

"Clawing up the carpet won't solve your problems, godling." Fyeren laughed, causing Coren and Rane to jump again.

This time, the Faerie was lounging on the bed, the blanket wrapped around faer shoulders.

"My Lady of Stars." Coren swore, and the High Faerie slipped off of the bed, landing lightly on the floor, faer wings neatly folded.

"Where the hell do you come from?" Rane barked, but Fyeren just smirked, and tsked.

"Secrets are not meant to be shared, little werecat."

"What do you want, Faerie?" They snapped back at faer.

"I want to *survive*." Fae tapped a slender finger against the side of faer nose. "But. I also must do what is right for the people. See, my brother does not want to join this war."

Fyeren sat down on the floor beside Rane, stretching out faer legs. Fae leaned in, conspiratorially, as if sharing a secret. *"He is scared.* But letting Erathien be taken by Lady Chaos would be disastrous."

"We know." Coren snapped.

"Yes... So you must also know that you *need* the Fae." Faer smile was wicked, but it soon grew more serious than Coren had ever seen it get.

"I just wanted to let you know that, no matter what Emperor Kalei says, I will bring an army to the North to fight by your side. I stand with you."

Fae stood, dusting imaginary dirt from faer camouflaged trousers.

"Good night, messengers." Fae paused at the door, turning back towards them. "And I think that you've known me long enough to stop using those obnoxious formal pronouns. He, him, his, please."

And then Fyeren was gone, the door clicking shut behind him.

"What the actual hell." Rane said, standing up and staring after the High Faerie. "Did that actually just happen? Did fae - he - actually just say that he'd fight with us? *Disobey his emperor?* Oh, gods."

They made a small shrieking sound, and then twirled around the room, hugging Coren briefly before dancing away.

"We have an ally! A small army!!"

Coren made a shocked noise, frantically trying to process. "Oh my gods! We do."

LXXIX - In Which A Different Army is Mobilised

THE TUNNELS OF EIRE, their home, were slowly emptying out. Only the youngest of the elves, the oldest, and some parents were staying behind, safe and hidden.

Rosana sat astride her blue horse, her eyes sharp, her circlet gleaming at her brow.

She nodded to Sora, who smiled, and clapped her hands together. With that one strong movement, the torches that lined the walls guttered out, plunging the space into total darkness.

A snap, and they roared to life again, leaving every eye on Rosana, their queen. She nodded, her braids swinging. Her crown seemed made of light.

"People of Eire. We ride, today, to the Cortach Range, the home of the Northern Band. We ride to face an old enemy, one we faced millenia ago. We ride, and we fight for the good of all of Erathien.

"We waited as long as we could, to strengthen our armies, and train, but it is now time. We will march with discipline, and calm. Do you understand?" She said, her voice ringing through the echoing cavern.

The response came back just as clear, a rumbling, echoing *yes*, spoken by many tongues.

"Then we leave." The elven queen turned her horse, and the doors before them opened out, into the Wood, into a bright blue day.

LXXX - Conflict of Interests

THE THRONE ROOM WAS silent. The Faerie *imperator* stood on faer dais, just the same as fae had been positioned when Rane and Coren had first met him.

A surge of anger and grief swelled up in Coren when he saw Emperor Kalei again. The bastard was going to refuse to do the right thing, so much was obvious. And the way that the Emperor had treated the pair of them?

Comfortable chambers, yes, but no food. No meal, no bath, and now a curt, out of the blue summons in the middle of the night, to discuss the war plan.

Kalei turned, the metal winding around faer horns catching the light. "Werecats. Thank you for coming."

We didn't have much choice. Instead of voicing that thought, Coren bowed before the Emperor, smiling. "Have you come to a decision, your Imperial Highness?"

"Yes, I have." Kalei returned the smile, although faers was colder. "I have decided that my troops shall not enter into this coming war."

Coren had known that this was coming, but his heart still sank, his carefully blank expression just barely covering his anger. Rane, beside him, tensed, their jaw tightening, lips pursing.

"*Imperator* Kalei, you do understand that this war will impact *all* of us? If we lose - and we will, without your military force - the Lady Chaos will not spare a single soul." Rane's voice quavered on the last words. Maybe remembering their own brother. Their people.

"She cannot seize what she cannot find. We will be increasing our already strong security measures. No one will be able to find this city, not even our own Fae, and no messages will be able to enter or leave it, unless they are sanctioned by myself."

The High Faerie was convinced that faer people were safe. From a goddess. Fool.

"I'm sorry, but... The Lady Chaos is a *dea*. She will be able to find you! We need to fight. We need you. Please, your Imperial Highness." Coren added, and suddenly... He realised exactly how much this failure would mean to him. The queen of the elves and her heir were surely waiting for his reply. They would be hoping to receive some good news.

I was hoping to gain an army, not whatever ragtag band Fyeren manages to scrounge up. The thought felt bitter, and he winced.

"I have made my decision, and it is *final*. Fyeren will escort you from the city. Thank you for the message." The Emperor said, waving a dismissive hand.

Fyeren was there in an instant, appearing, yet again, from gods knew where.

He was wearing the broken crown.

The Faerie shook his head at his sibling. He crossed his arms, his wings flaring out, making him seem bigger, stronger. His voice was smooth, calm, cold.

"Kalei, you are making a big decision, are you sure that you do not need more time to deliberate?"

"Are you questioning my judgement, little brother?" Kalei's chin rose, faer back straightening.

The back of Coren's neck prickled, as a cold, dangerous feeling pervaded the air.

"Yes. I am." Fyeren said with a smile.

"Leave me." *Imperator* Kalei commanded, faer own wings flaring.

"No." The Prince of Faerie said, blinking leisurely.

"Oh, Fyeren, little brother... I am Emperor. You are but a Prince. I command you. Now leave me. My decision has been made." Faer tone was ice, faer eyes like dark, cold water.

"Our crown is won by force. It is only rarely that it is passed down without violence, and you know this well, Brother." Fyeren said, stepping closer, drawing a sword from somewhere. It's blade was as golden as the walls.

Kalei took a step back, spreading faer wings, searching for an exit. Fae carried a weapon, a sword, studded with jewels - more for show than for true battle.

Fyeren laughed. His clothing faded back into blue and bronze. He wanted all eyes on him.

"A toy. Fancy, yes. But useless." He spread his own wings wide, ready to take to the air, should that be that path that his sibling chose.

Coren had stopped breathing. Rane had stilled. Their axe was resting in their hands, as if they were preparing for the fight to turn to them.

Gods above.

"What in all the hells is he doing?" Rane hissed.

"He's taking the crown. And when he gets it... All the armies of the Fae will be at his command." Coren murmured back. Fyeren's plan was starting to make sense. Terrible sense.

"You, my useless little brother, wish to be the Emperor of Faerie?" Kalei scoffed, even as his eyes belied his panic.

"I have served you my entire life. Ever since you killed our father for the crown, even though it was already going to be yours. I was quiet for *years*. I ran from this life, but no longer." Fyeren said, his voice carrying through the throne room. He advanced towards his elder sibling, further and further, until they were close enough to kill. "I tried to warn you. It's over now, Kalei."

"Had I not killed him, someone else would have, *Prince*." *Imperator* Kalei spat. "I got my throne. You were always the weaker one. I made sure you knew your place."

Fyeren's face set, anger flashing in his eyes. He readied his stance, and Kalei did the same.

"Oh, *shit*. They're actually going to fight." Rane swore, and Coren shook his head, still disbelieving.

What a bloody crown Faerie had. And it was about to be doused anew.

"I was never weak, Kalei. You just failed to see my strength." Fyeren snapped. He tucked a long, blue strand of hair back into its loosely bound tail. And then, his sword held tightly, he spoke.

"*Imperator* Kalei, ruler of the Faerie Empire, I, Fyeren, Prince of Faerie, challenge you to a duel for the crown."

LXXXI - Duel

KALEI PALED, AS IF fae had not truly believed that faer brother would truly fight faer. Fae exhaled, adjusted faer grip on the bejewelled sword.

And then -

"Fyeren, prince of the Faerie Empire, I, Kalei, Emperor of Faerie, accept your duel for the crown. A duel to the death."

The last words chilled the air, and Coren's lungs felt suddenly tight.

If Fyeren won, they would have an army of hundreds. If he failed, then they would be leaving the Faerie Empire with nothing. Perhaps they would not be leaving at all.

Fyeren's easy smirk had gone murderous and dark. His sibling's wings had extended, and fae gripped faer sword with experienced hands.

The prince was the first to move. He lunged across the space, his wings bearing him up, and then he dropped, falling to the ground and stabbing. His sword cut through the rich fabric doublet that the *Imperator* wore with ease, drawing first blood mere seconds into the deadly game.

But it missed it's goal. Instead of the heart, the golden blade met shoulder, collarbone, and a line of emerald blood rose along the wound.

Kalei roared, and swung faer own blade up, before faer brother had the time to escape. Fyeren made not a sound, even as his clothes were cut. There was a soft clank, and a betrayed look stole across Emperor Kalei's face.

Fyeren laughed, the bright silver shine of chainmail gleaming from beneath his torn shirt.

"Oh, elder brother. Were you wiser, you would wear mail yourself, and you would carry a sharper blade." He taunted, rising like a dark angel, and he plunged again.

Rane watched every movement, every motion, but Coren could not. He had to look away from this butchery of brothers. Away from the duel that would decide this war.

Only when a scream, more terrible than anything he had heard before in his life, rent the air, did he look back, and what he found left him reeling.

The Emperor still lived.

The Prince still fought.

But one lay on the ground, in a growing pool of green Faerie's blood. The tawny feathers of a coppery wing lay, severed from the body, five feet away, the tips already heavy with clotting fluid.

Fyeren's smile was demonic. A streak of emerald arced across his cheekbone, as he stared down at what his blade had done.

Kalei, wounded. Kalei, bleeding. Faer remaining wing fluttered helplessly, and fae screamed again, the sound turning Coren's stomach.

"I was never weak enough to lower my guard, Brother. I was never stupid enough to shame the people around me, and think that they would not fight back. Had it not been me, it would have been another one of us, plotting your demise." Fyeren spat, casting aside his broken crown.

He smiled, one last time, and the golden blade plunged down, right into his brother's heart.

Then, with still, reverent fingers, he lifted the circlet from Kalei's blood-streaked head, and he crowned himself Emperor of Faerie.

LXXXII - In Which One Brother Survives

WHEN FYEREN, A KILLER, a schemer, an emperor, a friend, turned back to Coren and Rane, he was smiling. He waved a hand at the corpse at his feet.

"I am sorry that you had to see this. Let us... Go to a nicer place." With a clap, the staircase spiralled down, and the were-cats, shocked, had nothing else to do but follow him.

In the room below, Fyeren sat behind the desk, kicking his booted feet up onto it, laying his still-bloodied blade flat on its surface. He was enragingly calm.

"You killed your sibling." Rane said. Their tone was flat. Still disbelieving.

"I did." He said, tapping the circlet at his brow.

"Why did you not tell us what your plan was, Fyeren?" Rane snapped. Coren touched their shoulder, a silent warning that Rane shook off. Something roiled in their chest.

Maybe it was the flippancy with which the new Emperor treated the killing of his kin.

Maybe it was the memory of killing their own brother - Or the Wraith that had once been him. Maybe it was that.

The roiling tightened into that familiar feeling, the one that came before beginning a fight. Rane's fists clenched, and they would have said something disastrous, surely, had Coren not stepped in.

"Fyeren - Emperor - Disregard Rane, please." He shot a hard look at his travelling companion, pulling out his diplomat voice. "But... We would greatly appreciate it if you did tell us why you duelled him. What your plan was."

The *Imperator* of the Fae snorted. "It was bound to happen soon. My brother and I hated each other. He murdered my father, when the crown was already promised to him. He treated me like scum. This -" he gestured around, at anything and everything. "This was the perfect opportunity. I have my revenge, he has what was due to him. And you have an army."

"Why didn't you tell us what you had planned? I thought you trusted us." Rane snapped.

"I didn't tell you because you surely would have tried to stop me. You would have tried to convince me that there was another way." Fyeren swung his feet down from the desk, and leaned in, his eyes flashing. "Let me tell you something. There was no other way. No army would have followed me, had I not carried the crown. Even those already dissatisfied with my brother would not have thrown their lot in with me. I played at being weak, and they believed the lie."

"I'm sure that's not-" Coren began, but Fyeren cut him off. His usual grin was completely gone, the Faerie blood on his face already darkening and flaking away.

"I am that person, in some ways, truly. But it was time for my brother to see what *else* I can be. Stronger than he ever was. Kalei was willing to kill our father. I was willing to kill Kalei."

Rane's stomach dropped. The Fae played games, they all knew that. But playing a game of crowns and murder for so long...

"Let it go, now." Fyeren said, softly. "I did what needed to be done, that is all. I got you an army. I will fight by your side, for the good of all Erathien. Forget you saw this. Let it reside in the past."

Rane watched Fyeren for a moment, before looking at Coren, who was still examining the new Emperor. As they watched, his shoulders sagged, just a few centimetres.

"All right, Emperor. All right." He looked up at the Faerie, his amber cat's eyes gleaming. "You are a friend, Fyeren. You saved our lives in the wood. And you saved us again just now. I will not forget that, at least. Thank you. I owe you a debt."

The tightness in Rane's chest had not eased. They did not trust themself with more words than were necessary, the immensity of Fyeren's deeds not soon forgotten.

"*Ave, Imperator* Fyeren."

Hail, Emperor Fyeren.

LXXXIII - In Which Death Welcomes One More Soul

LADY ILLIRA OPENED her eyes again, watching Emperor Kalei of the Faerie Empire's face fade away to nothing before her.

Her hands dropped, child's fingers curling around the cold stone edge of the table upon which she sat, and swung her legs.

She had seen her mother in her dreams again. She had seen the futile trainings that the tiny allied army was undertaking.

Their ranks would be decimated. So many would fall. Only one side would win.

She pursed her lips, still kicking her tiny, bare feet, her long dark hair floating around her face.

She prayed to whatever was out there that was more powerful than the nine of them. She prayed that the careful plan that she had crafted with her aunt would work. She prayed that the boy would be strong enough to do what needed to be done.

Hatred bears hatred. Chaos bears Death. It was only fate that the daughter should despise the mother. Only fate that both Chaos and Death sought vengeance, and would kill to get what they wanted.

Illira cast her dark gaze around what she could see of her realm.

Look! She thought, *Look at my crumbling kingdom! Look, Mother, at what you have done! See the crumbling columns, the cracks in the floor! This is your doing. Maybe I can't fight. Maybe I can't cheat, and change the tide of this war. But I can resent you, hate you for all eternity, and when you return to the Void - for you must at some point, to rest - I will hold you there. I will be your jailor, and I will grow strong. There is a war coming, Mother. Many will die.*

Her visions of death were never wrong. After all, she was it's mistress.

LXXXIV - In Which the Werecats (Finally) Leave the Faerie Empire

THE WOODS OF THE FAERIE Empire were darker now. They seemed more menacing than they had with the Prince of Faerie by their side.

But that prince was now an emperor, and had had to stay behind in the capital, organising his new army, solidifying his claim to the crown.

Coren shivered, against his will.

"So we have an army." Rane said, swinging their axe at a tree, and wedging it deep into the trunk. Again and again, they hacked at various plants, taking out some sort of tension or rage.

"So we do."

"He lied to us. And then he murdered his brother." Rane looked up from their work, their eyes dark.

"Yes he did." Coren paused, and then continued. "But... It was a duel. Kalei knew what fae was getting into before the fight even started. I wouldn't say it was murder, exactly. Even if it was..." He trailed off, unable to finish the sentence. Remembering the scream.

"Awful." Rane sniffed, finally replacing their axe in its usual place, hanging across their back. "You think that everything was an act?"

"No." Coren laughed a bit. "I think... Who he was with us was truly who he is. It's hard to act that annoying without truly being it."

Rane snorted, and smiled. Coren was relieved to see any expression but the murderous one cross their face.

"It really was awful." He said. "But... We are so close to home. And we have an ally! An army, a strong one! It's hard not to be happy about that. Even if the means were terrible."

Rane nodded slowly, and pushed their way between two thorny bushes. They gasped audibly, and Coren tensed, his hand straying to his knives.

However, when he joined them on the other side, there was no threat in sight, just rolling plains, almost glowing in the sunlight.

It was beautiful. The deep faerie wood faded into long grasses, soft hills hidden beneath their waving stalks. And crowning it all, far off on the horizon, were the mountains, grey-blue smears where sky met land.

"Home." Coren whispered. Absently, he fingered the phoenix pendant around his neck. The Veil slipped over him, leaving him flickering. A manifestation of his absentminded nervousness.

The metal shocked him, softly, when he rubbed the rune the wrong way, and with the small shock came the larger one of a nearly forgotten truth.

You're almost home. *Home, with your family... And then you'll have to tell them, and...*

He tried to pull himself together, sighing, turning his thoughts away from the North.

Examining the horizon, he pointed. "There! The road, see it? That's where we want to be. It will lead us directly to the Cortach Range."

"Perfect." Rane nodded, their own gaze far away. Before Coren could ask what was bothering them, they were racing down the hill they stood upon, lithe form and lashing tail being swallowed up by the grasses.

Coren was only moments behind them.

LXXXV - In Which Coren & Rane Meet Drakons

THE TRIP TO THE ROAD was easy, with no conflicts or obstacles, and as soon as Coren's paw hit the dusty gravel, he knew he could relax. It was a trader's road, a peaceful place. No blood could be shed on it's earth, by Common Law.

So passed three calm days and nights. The pace was quick, and ground was covered much faster than it had been when trekking through the desert, and the undergrowth of the Faerie Empire.

It was on the fourth day of travel along the traders road that Coren saw the drakon.

It was a bright, bloody red, vibrant against the turquoise skies. Upon closer inspection, a second, snow-white form flew beside the first.

The twisting, snake-like creatures began to plummet, straight down towards the earth. Right before they could hit the ground, they flared their wings, and coasted along the road towards Rane and Coren, smoothly coming to a halt before them.

Coren could feel his hands begin to shake the second the massive beasts landed.

One eye alone, was half as tall as Coren was, and the whole head, crests included, was four times that. The scales ranged from the size of his fist, to the size of his torso, massive, shield-like plates.

And they were *long*. So long. From the nose to the tip of their barbed tail, they were at least fifteen metres long.

The scarlet drakon lowered their head to the ground, until they were staring directly at Coren. Their eyes were pure black, ringed by those fire-red scales, their head crowned by two bony, red and black mottled crests. The drakon's six legs, almost stubby on the massive creature, were placed just before the wings, underneath the where the wing met the body, and then finally a few metres behind. Their claws were as black as the drakons eyes, and just as sharp.

"Who seeks entry to our lands?" The drakon thundered, the voice rough and low, unused to their sharp, clipping Old Language dialect.

This time, Rane stepped forwards to do the introductions.

"I am Chieftain Rane of the South. This is Coren of the North, my travelling companion. We seek an audience with your queen, Her Majesty, Queen Wyeran."

The scarlet drakon's head swung towards Rane, and their huge eyes narrowed.

"And what do you wish to discuss with Her Majesty?" The white drakon asked. Their eyes were just iris, like their companions, but the colour was a startling blue, as were their claws. Their white-and-blue crests flared as they leaned down to examine Rane.

"We carry a message from Queen Rosana of the Elven Territories, concerning all of Erathien, and news from the Faerie Empire." Rane said, their voice coming out smooth and unwavering.

"Do you carry a seal to verify this?" The white drakon thundered, their wings beating at the air.

"Yes. Elven made. I can scry Queen Rosana of the Elven Territories using it." He said, pulling the silver phoenix charm out from under his shirt and breastplate.

"He tells the truth, Sister. I can smell the magick on it." The white drakon murmured after sniffing the pendant, and the scarlet drakon bobbed her massive head.

"Well then. Welcome, travellers. I am Asoban, Guardian of the Queen. This is my sister Kelaban, Guardian of the Queen."

Kelaban bobbed her head, as Asoban had, white and scarlet together.

Rane and Coren bowed crisply in response, and the white drakon lifted her head.

"The city of-" Here, Kelaban made a series of harsh, guttural noises in the language of the drakons, unintelligible to the werecats. Her sister translated.

"The Burning City."

"It is our capital." Kelaban added, shifting from foot to foot - odd to see when one had six.

"And it is just ahead." Asoban finished.

"Climb up, please. We will carry you to the city - just to the gates, lest we lose our posts. Someone else will guide you the rest of the way." Kelaban extended a snowy wing to Rane, who smiled, bowed again, and climbed up the smooth, scaly surface.

Asoban mirrored her sister, and soon Coren was perched on the drakon's back, between the crest and the wings. The warm scales beneath him were oddly flexible, but he had a feeling that should he try to drive a blade into them, they would prove to be as hard and unyielding as diamond.

He shrieked as the drakon flapped her massive wings, lifting her serpentine body from the ground. With a snake-like movement, she lifted off, her sister close behind.

Within seconds, his fear had fallen away with the ground, and they were soaring so high that the air was slightly thin.

Rane whooped from somewhere behind him, and, holding on tight to the spines of Asoban's secondary crest, he turned to see them with both fists pumping the air. Kelaban dove, and Rane whooped louder, clinging tight.

Too soon, a sheer cliff dropped away before them, falling away towards the faint sparkle of a river at its bottom.

The drakon guards corkscrewed up above the cliff, before plunging straight down, leaving Coren holding on for dear life, his stomach somewhere in the clouds.

Asoban drew up abruptly, jerking up and down as her wings struggled to keep her long, heavy body hovering. Her barbed tail lashed as she turned her great head to look behind at Kelaban.

The white drakon soon drew up to hover beside her sister, and Rane waved excitedly at Coren.

We're riding drakons! they mouthed, and Coren grinned back.

"Our Burning City lies ahead, in the caves." Asoban said, bobbing her head.

"I do not think that we will be bringing you much further than this. We have duties at the border..." Kelaban added. "Someone else will guide you."

As if she had summoned them, a drakon plunged out of the caves below. They rose before the four of them, banded in black and grey, their smoky gaze sharp.

They snapped something in guttural drakonic, and the sisters flinched.

"Bringing messengers to the city, General, sir." Kelaban said in the Old Language, lowering a wing for a brief moment to show Rane to the general, who bobbed their head.

The General made the switch to the werecat's native tongue as smoothly as could be. "Ah, I see. I assume that you have questioned them."

It was a - somewhat displeased - statement, not a question, and Asoban nodded.

"Of course, General, sir."

"Good. I will hold the trader's road. Bring the werecats directly to Queen Wyeran, and entrust them to no one else." The General soared upwards in a wingbeat, leaving no chance for the other drakons to question them.

Asoban sighed mournfully. "I should have guessed that the General would have wanted us to bring you to Her Majesty, as we found you."

"Our responsibility." Kelaban added.

"Apologies, I understand that this is not usually a part of your duties." He said, the barest tinge of sarcasm seeping into his tone. Rane hid a smile.

"Oh well." Asoban sighed, beating her bright wings, and then dropping down, before landing neatly in one of the caves, once again leaving Coren's heart in his throat.

Kelaban's landing was rougher than her sisters, but Rane slid off unharmed. She lashed her snowy tail and snorted, warm air and sparks flying from her nostrils.

"Come along." The white drakon finally said, before scurrying into the dark.

Coren looked at Rane, who shrugged before following Kelaban. Asoban took up the rear, her hot breath warming Coren's back.

After a small eternity of walking in the dark, the only light coming from the pommel of Rane's sword, and a wavering flame that Keleban held in her sharp-toothed mouth, Asoban spoke.

"The Queen Wyeran's nest is close. When you meet her, bow low. Do not make eye contact until she addresses you. Do not speak until she addresses you. Is that clear?" The red drakon snapped, and Rane and Coren nodded crisply.

"Good. Are you ready?" Kelaban asked, turning and lowering her head until Coren was staring straight into one of her huge, pure blue eyes.

"Yes." He said, his spine straightening, and Asoban huffed.

"You had better be. We're here." She spat an orange tongue of flame, illuminating the massive stone door that stood before them.

The flame died, and Coren had to strain his eyes, watching Kelaban scuttle forwards. She blew a blue flame against the seam between the rock slabs, and the doors shrieked open, painfully slowly.

The harsh sound grated on Coren's ears, but neither he nor Rane flinched. It was too late to stop now.

The room beyond the doors was a huge cave, resplendent in natural beauty. Never before had Coren seen *anything* like what lay before him.

Stalactites hung, smooth and gleaming, from the roof of the cave, the shortest just barely nubs, the longest brushing Asoban's crest and folded wings. There were jagged protrusions, too, where longer stalactites must have once hung - broken off by a wingstroke, or a rearing of the head.

Stalagmites bristled on the floor, mirroring their hanging twins, and forming a glistening maze, through which the massive drakons had to weave their serpentine bodies to avoid being scraped.

The space should have been dark, but every damp surface glowed with an otherworldly light. Tiny bacteria in the water, Kelaban explained, when she noticed Coren staring.

Rane nudged Coren's side, pointing up, and he grinned when he saw what they had been pointing out. A lizard, pale as Kelaban's scales, with rheumy eyes, clung to one of the stalactites. It blinked its milky eyes at them, before crawling away across the cave ceiling.

Long moments passed in the pale blue glow, before the light shifted to something else entirely - warmer and brighter - and the rock formations dropped away.

A clearing lay before them, in its centre a nest of stone, pelts, and rich fabrics. Lying atop it was Queen Wyeran.

Her scales gleamed golden, her claws and wing membrane a glittering bronze. Three crests crowned her head, one after the other. Upon closer inspection, the first was a brighter gold, a true crown. Rings inlaid with obsidian and milky quartz adorned her razor claws, and a medallion in silver, imprinted with a dark flame, hung around her neck.

Rane and Coren bowed as one, as deeply as they could.

The drakon queen snorted, brilliant sparks floating down, and the werecats straightened, eyes still fastened on the ground.

"Guards, who do you bring to me?" She asked in the Old Language, as a courtesy to the werecats.

"We bring messengers from Queen Rosana of the Elven Territories, carrying a message of the utmost importance." Asoban said, before lowering her scarlet-scaled body to the ground, even her wings flattening out. Kelaban had already sunk into the position.

"I see." Queen Wyeran murmured, standing. She lifted her head, her wings flaring, and Coren choked back a whimper. She was easily twice, possibly three times, the size of the drakon sisters.

Standing before the messengers, she lowered her head until she was staring into their downcast eyes.

"Look at me. I will not tolerate such shyness from the messengers of a fellow ruler." She rumbled, the ground seeming to shake under the weight of her voice.

The werecats obeyed, and the drakon queen cocked her head, her gleaming crest-crown glittering.

"Welcome to our lands, messengers. Welcome to the Burning City. You've come a long way. Now, what message is the message that you have carried all this way?"

LXXXVI - In Which There is Nervous Waiting

THE DRAKON QUEEN HAD listened to the message, and huffed a jet of golden-orange flame, making a series of clicking, guttural sounds that, judging by the reactions, were probably obscene.

Queen Wyeran had then lowered her head again, her crest-crown catching the light.

"Thank you, messengers. For the message, the warning. I wish that I could do something now, but I'm afraid that I must consult my son and my advisor before I can do anything. I am truly sorry, Coren of the North, Chieftain Rane of the South. You will have to wait outside."

The drakon queen had turned then, her tail whipping through the air, her wings flaring for a moment. She had looked back over a shoulder, her head cocked.

"Asoban, Kelaban, you did well. Asoban, please take them back outside, and Kelaban... Fetch Lord Wrisan and Prince Zephyran, would you?"

Both of the sisters' jaws had tightened at the command - obviously not a task that they would usually undertake. But this was their queen. They had to obey.

And so... There they were. Waiting in the hall before the great doors. Asoban had her great black eyes closed, as if she were asleep, but the way her crests twitched at every noise belied this appearance.

Across the wide corridor, Rane was sprawled out on their back, tossing a shirt knotted into a ball, up into the air, and catching it deftly.

They were silent, and seemed unwilling to talk, so Coren's thoughts were free to roam. In an instant, they had turned back to the topics he had been avoiding.

He scraped the tip of his knife across the floor, tracing the faint outline of an interlocked sun and moon.

Kinaar. Going home. The war. His patron, his newfound abilities. Everything would have to be explained, again. This time to the people he loved most in the world.

And he would have to - Even his thoughts faltered - He would have to *tell* them.

One life for the many.

Closing his eyes, his knife slipped to the rocky floor, his head thumping back against the stony wall.

Rane missed a catch, the balled up shirt dropping on their face. They made a frustrated noise, and resumed the repetitive movements.

Coren closed his eyes, spinning his blade and envisioning his family, after the war. Imagined them healthy and smiling.

That was what he had to hold on to. That vision. It was the only way to make it through.

LXXXVII - In Which the Waiting Ends

THE HEAVY DOOR SCRAPED across the floor with a bright blaze of familiar blue flame.

Kelaban slipped through, the doors slamming shut the second that the tip of her tail whisked across the threshold.

She held her crested head high, her electric blue eyes cold, snakelike.

"The Queen, Heir and Advisor have come to a conclusion. Please, come along." She said, turning back towards the door. A cerulean spark, and they opened again, the sound sending shivers down Rane's arms. Asoban stepped through, her wings folded, her head held high, and she joined her sister on the other side.

The drakons didn't look back to make sure that Rane and Coren were following, they just sank into conversation and continued on, everything tinged with that unearthly glow.

The cave was still gorgeous, the second time around, but this time Rane's mental energy was focused on something else entirely. What could happen.

It had seemed as if Queen Wyeran would join them, if she alone had the choice, but she had had to confer with two others. If they had changed her mind...

Rane was so wrapped up in their own thoughts, that they nearly walked into a stalagmite. It was only Coren dragging them to the side that stopped them from sustaining a particularly nasty bruise... In a particularly sensitive area.

A moment more, and then there was that telltale shift in the light, and they bowed again before the drakon queen.

This time, the regal creature was not lying down, but standing at her full height, the spikes of her crown pressed up against the cave ceiling.

Beside her stood a drakon with gleaming black scales, wearing a silver pendant similar to the queens, with the same imprinted flame. He could only be one person - Prince Zephyran.

So, the silver drakon standing to the queen's left had to be Lord Wrisan, her advisor. He was small, smaller than the drakon prince, but he held his head high all the same.

"Messengers." The queen greeted. "We have come to a decision, regarding the Lady Chaos, and the coming war..."

Rane held their breath, afraid of what the answer could be.

"We have counted our warriors, weighed the odds." Lord Wrisan said, bowing to his queen as he continued. "We have determined that your odds would increase, should we join you."

Rane's heart couldn't decide whether it wanted to plummet, or leap. *Should we join you.*

"Not only that," Queen Wyeran said, glaring at Wrisan, "But it would be best for not only you, but the entire known world, if we joined you in this battle. We understand that the losses will be immense, as they were in the last war. We understand that this could be our downfall, or perhaps our making, and... We are willing to take the chance."

Oh gods.

"We choose to join you in the coming war."

A small sound escaped Coren's lips, and Rane's eyes widened. They relaxed, visibly, and whirled, hugging Coren tight.

"Thank you. Thank you so much, Queen Wyeran." Coren grinned. He bowed, and Rane followed suit.

"Is there anything you would like us to do for you, Your Majesty? Deliver a message, or..." Rane asked.

"Thank you, messengers, but that will be all. I must rally my people, and you must return to the Cortach Range. Lord Wrisan can try to scry the elves, and tell them of our choice, if we can find the godsdamned pendant." Queen Wyeran mused, before nodding.

"You may stay in the Burning City tonight. Asoban and Kelaban will escort you to the border in the morrow."

"Thank you, Queen Wyeran. Thank you!" Coren said again.

Rane had stopped breathing a long time ago. This was it! Two strong allies.

And now... Now they were on the last leg of their journey. They were heading home.

LXXXVIII - Bonding & Friendship

THE NIGHT AFTER THE drakons joined them, Coren didn't sleep a wink. Which was only part of why he was dragging his feet.

They had crossed the invisible line separating the Drakon Lands from the tiny human kingdom of Pheria hours ago, and the mountains were looming dark before them.

He stopped to stare at them, at the deep green of pines, and the occasional smattering of golden leaves, the peaks that he knew sloped off slowly on the other side, dipping down to cradle the Conpitum.

Rane walked up beside him, and he exhaled when he noticed how grim their expression was.

"You're not looking forward to heading home either?" He asked tentatively.

"Nope." Rane said. "I... Have no idea what I'm going to find. I don't know what my godsdamned brother did to the South with me gone."

"Yeah..." Coren bit his lip, crossing his arms. "I honestly don't want to go home."

Rane laughed, clapping his shoulder. "We should form a club."

The corners of his mouth turned up in a small smile, but his expression grew somber again after a second. "Really though. Would you... Be okay with delaying going home for a bit? Just a night out here. Just one."

"Always." Rane plopped down where they stood, stretching out their legs and staring up at the sky. "Alright, so no club. Instead it's a new country, where everyone is running away from responsibilities." They clapped the ground. "I officially declare this our capital city."

Coren grinned, and sat down, shrugging off his pack. "What's the city called?"

"Uhm..." Rane wrinkled their nose, and pointed accusingly. "Quit making me think."

"City of Runaways and Magickal Freaks." Coren made a 'phoot' sound, and Rane kicked him.

"Hey! You're not a freak!"

"Hmm." Coren laughed, the rare sound throaty and full, letting himself flicker in and out.

"I absolutely forbid begging to differ."

"Damnit."

They sat in silence for a while after that, starting a small fire and making a meal out of the near-last of their supplies.

"So... You've got to be looking forward to some things about going home, yeah?" Rane asked, poking the fire with a long stick, and sending a shower of sparks into the sky.

Coren leaned back on his palms, staring at the stars. "Yeah. Seeing my aunts and my cousins will be really good."

"Lin and Sioch, right? Practically your siblings."

Coren smiled, ducking his head. "Yeah."

"You got dealt the good hand sibling-wise."

"I'm sure I can convince them to adopt you." Coren grinned, and Rane smirked.

"You sure they'd want all this?"

"Pfft, of course." He leaned forwards. "You're my best friend. Whether they like it or not, you're family."

LXXXIX - In Which Nightmares Become Reality

THEY LEFT AT DAWN, leaving no trace behind but the ashy remains of the fire, and made it to the foothills by tenth hour.

Coren only hesitated for a second before clapping Rane on the back of the head and taking off into the trees, claws digging into the dirt path as he ran.

"Fuck youuuuu!" They screamed after him, close behind.

The trail wound sharply through the trees, slowly snaking its way to the southern peak of the Cortach Range. Coren had never been South before, so had he not had Rane with him, chances are he would have completely missed the Southern camp.

The path continued on, up a little ways further before dipping down to the lake, but Rane led him down a barely-there thread of a trail, twisting off in the opposite direction. They had to be careful not to lose their balance as they walked along it, carefully stepping over roots buried in fallen leaves, and iced-over puddles.

The camp came out of nowhere. There were trees all around them, and then there was a clearing, and... A sea of destroyed white tents.

Rane stared around themself in horror, and their eyes began to well with silent tears. Coren had fallen still, his eyes wide as he took in the scene.

It was like something out of Rane's darkest night horrors.

Everything was still and calm. Tents torn and tumbling. Only the central tent, in a deep shade of indigo blue, stood unharmed.

"Oh, Rane." Coren whispered, but Rane just shook their head, flinching away from his touch.

Coren flickered for a second, and Rane shook their head again, running towards the indigo tent. *Their* tent. The tent that they had lived in, performed trials in...

They could hear Coren's soft footfalls following behind them, and nearly lashed out at him again, but stopped. *Vicious cycle.* One of lashing out instead of taking comfort as it was offered.

They threw aside the heavy flap of fabric closing off the tent from view, preparing for a message, perhaps, from Kir. Gloating about this latest horror, even from death.

What they found instead, was perhaps worse.

Rane sank to their knees, just outside the tent. It felt like the entire world had shifted under their feet. Too late. Too late. They shouldn't have fallen for Kir's trap, should have been here, could have prevented this...

The only sound was that of the breathing of maybe one hundred people, soft and rhythmic, and *slow*. So slow.

Rane looked again, taking in the faces. The people. Their people.

Sleeping. Row upon row of sleeping forms, as unmoving and cold as death, only the soft sounds of inhales, exhales, filling the silence.

Teary, Rane moved to step inside, but before they could, a strong archer's hand grabbed their upper arm, holding them back. Rane struggled, and whimpered, and made to move in again, but Coren dragged them away.

"NO!" Rane screamed, and beat at him frantically. "I have to be there - They're my people - Gods above, why? Why?!"

Coren was silent, unmoved, dragging, until they were in the woods again. Rane screamed again, and finally sank to the ground, their shoulders shaking, gaze pinned on the indigo tent.

Coren let them slip out of his vise-like grip. "Rane." He whispered. "Are you all right?"

Rane's shoulders shook, as they remembered the tent, the sleeping bodies. They had known every face. Every single one. And many had been missing. Where they had gone... Rane was absolutely certain that they knew.

"Rane." Coren said again, and Rane managed to meet his amber gaze.

"They're cursed." They whispered, their voice fracturing. "It's my fucking fault. I left, I trusted my brother even after Amma warned me against it. It's my *fault*."

"It's *not*." The words came out forceful, and Rane looked up, startled. Coren shook his head, biting his lip. "Sorry. But it's not your fault. It's your brother's fault, and it's Lady Chaos's fault. Which is why we're fighting this war, to stop her."

"They're *cursed!*" Rane's fists clenched, their shoulders tensing.

"There's a *malefica* with the North. She can probably help, Rane, we just need to find her." He said softly. Rane knew the look in his eyes, the one that said that he was thinking hard, trying to figure out the right thing to say.

The only problem? Nothing he could say would fix this.

Rane struggled to their feet, and Coren reached for their arm again. "What are you doing?"

"I have to go to them." They insisted, their voice broken and small.

"Rane. You can't go in that tent because you don't know the spell. What if - If the spell impacts everyone who enters that tent, and you fall asleep with the rest of them..." Coren faltered, closing his eyes. "Please. We need you. I need you. They're safe, Rane, that's all that matters."

Rane choked, tears spilling over. "I -"

"Please, Rane." Coren said, squeezing their shoulder.

They turned away from him, wiping at their eyes and staring into the woods. This was all so *wrong*... Anger swelled, and they drew their battle axe, driving it hard into the closest tree. The bare branches rattled, dry as bone. Their thoughts swelled in a whisper to match the branches, hissing and turning.

They're safe, aren't they? They're safe, and will be safe, and you have a duty, don't you.

Your brother is dead. You are the Chieftain, there is no one to combat that claim, and besides... They sleep. They have waited at least a month. They can wait a while longer.

Rane turned back to Coren, salt tears tracking down their cheeks, and wrapped him in a hug.

"I'm so sorry, Rane." He said, patting their back stiffly before giving in and relaxing a bit.

"We'll go. We'll fight. And when it's all over we'll wake them up." They said, pulling their axe from the tree, and looking back at the tent one last time.

"Let's go? Please, I can't be here any more."

Coren's eyes were welling, his attempts at blinking away the tears failing. "We'll - You'll be back Rane, I swear it."

"I'll be back…" It was a promise and a prayer.

XC - In Which Coren Returns Home

COREN EXHALED, ROUGHLY. His fingers danced over the pommels of his knives, he bit his lip, and shifted uncomfortably, a ball of nervous energy.

There, just through the trees, was the encampment. He could see the makeshift tents, smell campfire smoke, could hear the sounds of the children playing. It was home. It was terrifying.

Every fear and anxiety was coming up to the surface, showing itself in a variety of imagined situations.

There would be shock on their faces, that he was alive, that he had come back. He would be a ghost, back from the dead, and scorned for hurting Myr. He tried to calm his breathing, tried to convince himself that everything would be all right.

Coren glanced over at Rane, whose ears were flicking back and forth nervously. Their tail lashed, and they Shifted, huffing.

"Now or never?" They said, their voice pitching up at the end, turning it into a question.

"Yeah." He replied, ducking his head.

He took in a deep breath, closing his eyes and taking in one last moment of peace before stepping out of the trees.

It took only seconds before they were spotted, every thought of fleeing quickly scrapped.

Coren knew most of the North by sight, if not by name, but it seemed that either they did not know him, or they thought him to be a threat. In an instant, weapons were bristling at them from every direction.

Coren raised his hands supplicatingly, his thoughts going completely blank. What did you say to a group of angry werecats?

Coren could tell that Rane was about to try something, maybe pull rank, and he glared at them, hoping they would be smart and shut up.

Something, a spearhead, it seemed, jabbed Coren in the ribs, and he snarled, baring his teeth at the werecat, who held his ground, glaring back.

"What do you want here? The hunting patrol returned two hours ago, and you were not in it."

"I -"

"Coren of the North." Kortana. Of course it was Kortana. Of course she had somehow survived. Of course, of course of course. He could have laughed. How naive, to choose to believe that she had died.

Murmurs rose at the sound of his name, and his shoulders tensed.

"Kortana, please!" he said, raising his voice until he could be heard above the murmur. "I made it back. I have been travelling for weeks, and I would really like to see my family."

"Silence! You disobeyed direct orders from the Chieftainess, and have brought a stranger back with you! How are we to know that you aren't one of those bloody Wraiths?"

"I did what I had to do, and you are not my Chieftainess, Kortana of the North. I wish to speak with the person who has true power here." He ignored the sudden rush of murmurs at his words, ignored the way that Kortana's face paled. Ignored Rane, standing at his shoulder, ready for a fight.

Something sharp poked him again, and he drew his blades, snarling at the werecat who had dared.

It seemed that violence would break out when one voice, screamed above the clamour:

"PEACE! EVERYONE!" Myr screamed, striding towards Coren and Rane, parting the sea of people all around her. Lana, and the twins, and the *Malefica* Theodosia, walked in her wake.

His aunt stopped just before him. Her face was so schooled, it was hard to tell what she was truly feeling. Her tone, however, was warm. "Greetings Coren, Nephew! Where, in all the world, have you been all these weeks?" Her gaze wandered to Rane, something flickering in that mask - Of course his aunt would recognise Rane as the Southern Chieftain.

Coren squared his shoulders, and met his aunt's gaze. "I have been to the Elven Territories and back. I am a messenger for Queen Rosana of the Elven Territories. I come bringing allies for the coming war, and I apologise for leading you all to believe me dead."

Murmurs spread, and Myr let them, focused only on her nephew. "And who do you travel with?"

Coren looked over at Rane, who looked determined, fierce. He hesitated for merely a moment.

"My friend and ally, Chieftain Rane of the South."

And everything exploded into sound.

XCI - In Which Myr is A Good Aunt

TENSION FILLED THE air. Rane could feel the prickle of all of those eyes trailing down their spine, examining them.

They could hear the whispers.

He went against the Chieftainess' direct order.

He saved the Chieftainess's life.

And... Who's that?

He called them the Southern Chieftain.

Southern?

Yes.

How do we know that we can trust them?

How are we to be expected to trust either *of them?*

The woman with the long brown hair and the rapier, Chieftainess Warlord Myr of the North, raised a commanding hand in the air.

"SILENCE!" When her people did not comply, she bellowed the word again, and the petite, pregnant woman at her side touched her arm gently. Myr sighed, and wrapped an arm around the woman (her wife?), before screaming one last time.

Silence finally fell, and the eyes shifted from the two newcomers, to the Chieftainess.

"Although Coren of the North disobeyed an order, he saved my, and many other lives on the battlefield. Including yours, if I remember correctly, Councillor." She shot a burning glare at Kortana. "Chieftain Rane of the South is not responsible for their mother's deeds. They are our ally, and I will not tolerate any complaints."

Suddenly, Rane saw why Coren had been nervous about returning home. This woman was seriously frightening.

"The Chieftain and my nephew come here today as messengers from Queen Rosana of the Elves. They bear her seal, and the *Malefica* Theodosia can support their claim, as she is in direct contact with the Queen. We are preparing for a war, and they bring allies."

Her sharp glare intensified as she scanned the crowd again. "Does anyone wish to contest this decision?"

Absolute, ringing silence. Even Rane felt scolded, even though they had done nothing wrong.

Myr turned towards Rane and Coren, then, and cocked her head. Her long brown hair swished as she turned, holding her wife's hand.

"Come. All of you. We have much to discuss."

XCII - In Which Coren & Rane Talk

RANE STEPPED OUT OF the woods, and into the ruins of the old Northern camp. Everything was painted in shades of grey, from the steely skies, to the dark ash still covering the ground.

Coren stood in the centre of it all. A few scraps of scarlet fabric flapped, pinned underneath fallen wooden poles, the only movement. He was staring at a point somewhere in the distance, at something beyond anyone's range of vision. He didn't notice Rane enter the clearing.

They crept to his side, standing, silent, waiting for him to say something first. Which he didn't. So they wound up having to talk anyway.

"Coren?" Was all Rane said. Just his name. Almost startled, he looked at them and sighed, gesturing at the burned out remains of the Northern camp.

"Look at this... We have other camps we can go to, we already did move, but this... This one was our true home, the one we always returned to. This was where I was born, where my parents, and the twin's parents, and Lana and Myr got married. This place is special. And now... It's ruined." His gaze was hollow.

"I'm sorry, Coren. So sorry. About this, and... And about the South, I shouldn't have..." Rane trailed off, and Coren smiled his lopsided smile, his fangs gleaming.

"It's all right, really. They are your people, and you're loyal to them." He knelt in the ashes, and worked the scrap of red fabric out from under the pole, holding gently, as if worried that it would crumble away under his touch.

"Yeah." Rane paused for a while, trying to think of what to say next. "Are - How are you doing? That discussion was a bit... Intense."

Myr had brought them all into a very tattered tent that seemed to be serving as the Northern Council's meeting space. There had been a few moments of pure happiness that Coren was home safe and sound, which Rane had awkwardly watched from the corner.

That had turned into yet another recounting of the whole story, from the Elven Territories to the Painted City, to Faerie (omitting the Lake of Glass), to the Drakon Lands, and then finally home again.

When it was all over, the talking had begun again, discussions and planning for three new armies to converge on the Cortach Range, all conversations that Coren and Rane felt they couldn't be a part of. They were just the messengers.

It had been so chaotic that Coren had vanished and slipped out of the tent without anyone but Rane noticing.

"You didn't tell them about the goddess." Rane added, when Coren still said nothing. He sat down in the ashes, a puff of grey filling the air around him. Rane coughed, and then sat across from him, trying to read his face.

He was back to that anxious, cold expression, the one he had worn back in the prisons of the Painted City.

He exhaled shakily, flickering in and out of sight. "I was surprised that they didn't know already... I also don't want to... Don't want to tell them about the end. What the end is going to have to be. I *just* got home."

Rane tapped his foot with theirs, watching him carefully. "You're going to have to tell them eventually."

"I know." He bit his lip, his eyes dark.

"I guess it can wait. Take some time with your family." Rane said after another quiet moment. "Want to head back?"

"Not really." Coren half-laughed, staring at the sky. "They all look at me differently now. I can't remember how long it's been since one of us travelled as far as we've gone. They all know me now, and not in a good way. I'm the kid who disobeyed an order, and something like that isn't really looked kindly upon."

"You're a hero, Coren. You've done so much. They're looking at you because you've done so much, and seen things that they probably won't ever, and don't want to, see." Rane nudged his foot again. "Get out of your head, Northerner. It's all going to be okay."

Coren exhaled again, running a hand through his messy honey-brown hair. "It's all gonna be okay..."

"That's it! Use that mindset." Rane threw a handful of ash like confetti, regretting it immediately when they started to cough on ash.

Coren's lopsided smile was back in an instant, and a sudden mischievous twinkle came into his eye. "All right, so since my mental breakdown is mostly done, want to talk about Lindara? She was totally checking you out."

Rane could feel themself blushing, and they hid their face in their hands. "Coren!"

"It's true!"

XCIII - In Which Various Armies Arrive

IT SEEMED THAT MAGICK made travel much, much easier.

It was only a day before the allies started to arrive, somehow managing to both give Coren hope, and make him anxious, especially since they all knew that he was a ward, something he had somehow still managed to avoid telling his family.

The first to arrive were the Fae, sweeping through the woods and neatly encircling the camp. The North was so nervous that they nearly started attacking, before Coren stepped in.

Fyeren stepped out of the ranks to meet him, smirking.

"You made it home, eh?" Fyeren laughed, twisting a strand of his long hair around a slender finger. As Coren watched, the colours of his clothing, hair and horns changed, until he looked just as he had in the streets of the Faerie capital: All blue and bronze.

"And Rane as well." The High Faerie made a brief, somewhat mocking bow, as Rane surfaced from the crowd. They grinned as they greeted the Emperor. A murderer. A friend.

"*Ave, Imperator* Fyeren. Welcome to the North."

"We didn't expect you so soon!" Coren added, smiling faintly.

Fyeren's easy smirk spread across his face. "Don't underestimate a Faerie, werecat! This is my army. Smaller than I would have liked, but here all the same, and at your leaders command."

The aforementioned leader - Myr - said, stepping up and offering a hand to shake. "Welcome, *Imperator* Fyeren of the Faerie Empire." Fyeren stared at her for a long moment, eyes resting on her circlet, noting her leadership, before taking the proffered hand.

"Thank you, Chieftainess." He made a short bow, before turning back to his army, clapping his hands to get the attention of a couple unruly sprytes. "Make camp around the set up tents. Do *not* disturb the Northern Band, or you *will* have hell to pay from me, mark my words."

A snap of the fingers, and they were off, gone within minutes. He grinned again, his eyes flashing with something like glee.

"Have the others arrived yet?"

'The others' flooded in that very afternoon, filling the skies and storming the forests.

Coren raced to the edge of the camp to watch and wait for the rulers, staring at the creatures around him. Drakons spiralled through the air, searching for a place to land, gryphons among them. Elves, humans, and ghostly dryads came next, starting to set up camp without being asked. The noise of all of those new voices was deafening.

Coren barely caught the sound of his name yelled over the clamour, and turned to see Rane bounding over to him, their face alight.

"They came! You were worrying for nothing. They're all here! We have an army!" Rane threw their arms around Coren's neck, and he spun them around, allowing himself a small smile.

"Coren of the North!" A new, welcome voice broke through the crowd, as a tall woman strode towards them, her circlet gleaming, her braids pinned up elegantly. Next to her walked a massive, bronze and gold drakon, her wings half-extended.

Coren dropped into a deep bow, and everyone around him followed his lead. "Queen Rosana. Queen Wyeran. Thank you so much... It means so much to see you here. Thank you."

"Coren, we said we would come. We never break our promises. Please, rise." She extended a hand, and helped the werecat to his feet. The drakon queen rumbled out a similar greeting.

Myr pushed her way through the crowd, and soon the rulers were slipping away into the woods, surely to discuss their plans.

"We really did it, didn't we." Rane sighed, looking up at the teeming sky, watching the laughing warriors all around them, clothed in bright colours, in metal and leather, razor-steel shining on their backs, at their hips, in their hands.

"I think we really did. We gathered an army."

"Now, the only thing to be done... Is to win the war."

XCIV - Secrets No Longer

THE DAYS PASSED IN a blur of training. Each army had something new to share, from obscure swordplay techniques to magick, and everyone was eager to learn.

Coren had taken to slipping away into the woods when he wasn't needed, and just closing his eyes, and talking with the goddess in his mind. Lady Kinaar shared much of his people's past with him, tales of the Lady Forartha, stories of the way that the world once was, before the Fall of the Gods.

He trained until he could stay invisible, insubstantial, for hours without really trying, even if it did leave him feeling drained.

Every day was a blessing, but for Coren, it brought with it more anxieties. The month that Lady Chaos had given them had been up for days. The attack was imminent. Coren still hadn't told his family about everything, and avoided any talk of why he vanished every day as best he could.

He probably would have continued hiding it, if it weren't for his cousins stepping in.

He'd been avoiding them since he returned home, telling himself that it was for the best, but still feeling sick every time he avoided their gazes.

They were his best friends, why wasn't he being open with them?

They finally just ambushed him in the woods one day. He had his eyes closed, legs crossed, just concentrating and talking with Kinaar.

You must talk to them, werecat. She was saying, not for the first time.

I just need more time -

"Coren!"

"We need to talk."

Coren jumped, and his heart sank as he lost control of the Veil, flickering. He turned hesitantly, risking a small smile at the twins, whose identical glares just grew more intense.

Shiiiit this is not good.

"Okay, now we *really* need to talk." Lin snapped.

Rane crept up behind the twins, waving awkwardly. "I tried to stop them, sorry."

"This is a conversation that needs to happen, Southerner." Lin crossed her arms and turned her death glare on them.

"She's right." Coren said reluctantly, leaning back on his palms. His heart was pounding out of his chest, anxiety thrumming through his veins. Shit. Kinaar was right, he should have told them a long time ago, he should have -

"Coren." Sioch tapped his shoulder, snapping him back into the present. "You're okay."

"We're just... Worried. We want to know what's up with you." Lin added, spinning her kris in a flashing arc.

Coren looked down, listening to his heartbeat pounding in his ears.

"Was that magick?" Sioch chimed in again, gesturing vaguely at Coren.

Moment of truth, yeah?

"Um. Yes." Coren said before he could chicken out.

"When did that happen?" Lin asked loudly, and Sioch shoved her.

Coren bit his lip. "The Elven Territories. I thought maybe Queen Rosana would have told you, and then she hadn't, so I was nervous, and -"

"In your head again." Sioch said, crossing his arms.

"We aren't mad, we just..." Lin started, letting See finish the thought. "Wish you'd told us sooner."

"You know, Theodosia could help train you, get the magick under control... You know all of the old stories about untamed magick."

"So, about that..." Coren winced slightly. "My magick isn't exactly normal? It's not like Theodosia's, to just be unlocked and tamed, it's um... I kind of have Lady Kinaar in my head? My powers are because of that. It's part of why I didn't really want to tell you guys."

Sioch's eyes widened, and Lin's mouth hung open. "Oh my gods. So you're a -"

"I'm a ward. The first one since the gods fell."

"I can't believe you didn't tell us!" The twins said in synch, and Rane raised an eyebrow at Coren, a blatant I-told-you-so.

"What does that mean about the war?" Lin asked, plopping down onto the grass and dragging Sioch down with her.

"Can she hear us? Oh my Lady of Stars, are *you* a god now?" See added, his eyes wide.

Rane settled down behind them, leaning against a tree. Coren looked at them when he was speaking instead of at his cousins, it was just easier.

"Yeah. She can hear my thoughts, so she can understand what's going on around me. I'm definitely not immortal though."

Hello, cousins. Kinaar said coldly. Not that Coren would pass it on.

"And the war?" Lin asked again.

"That's... A little more complicated." Coren closed his eyes and tried to just breathe, tried to not completely lose his mind. "I can fight, and I can fight well. I... I think I'm going to have to fight Lady Chaos myself. There are rules -" he made a vague hand gesture, "about balance and the gods that are going to be broken and twisted unless Kinaar and I step in."

"Oh." Lin said, paling a bit.

"We're not quite sure how to feel." See added quietly.

"Either excited or scared." Lin finished.

Rane finally came over from where they had been trying to fade into the background, and took a seat next to Coren. "It took me a while to get my head around it, too."

"You told them before us?" Lin shrieked, glaring.

"Hey! I was travelling with them, and couldn't talk to you guys. It was a bit hard to hide at first." Coren protested, ducking his head and smiling.

"Are you going to tell Aunt Myr? I can't believe Theodosia didn't tell any of us." Sioch cut in, wrinkling his nose.

"I..." He trailed off, biting his lip.

"Your aunt is terrifying." Rane said, laughing. "I don't blame Coren if he's not quite ready yet."

"No, I have to tell her. It... Really wasn't fair of me to not tell you about this. Especially since I should probably know some more details now, huh."

You really should have told them sooner, ward. There was nothing to worry about, your head was just twisting everything again. Kinaar scolded.

I know, my Lady, I know. Coren's shoulders slowly relaxed, and he smiled a little. This would be okay. At least for a little while.

There was a meeting that night, and then he'd finally tell Myr and Lana.

He would also have to tell them the one last detail.

XCV - One Last Secret

THE FIRE CRACKLED IN the centre of the circle. Coren tried to take in all of the faces. Humans and elves, Fae and drakons, gryphons and werecats, all gathered around the same fire.

As he watched, Lady Sora gathered up an armful of wood, and reached into the fire, rearranging the burning logs, adding more, until the blaze rose higher, burned warmer.

She dusted sparks from her skin, and then returned to her seat. If she noticed the amazed stares from the non-elves, she did not let it show.

As soon as Sora was seated, Queen Rosana rose, spreading her arms wide.

"Welcome, allies. Friends. We gather here to discuss the coming war. We gather tonight to publicly discuss the training of our armies, and to finally go over our final plan. We need to end this, as safely as possible."

She paused to look around at all of the faces, and lifted her chin. She looked so regal, standing there, Marks spiralling, circlet shining. "Thank you for standing with us. I would call Coren of the North to speak?"

Murmurs broke out from the people who didn't know about his powers, including Myr and Lana. They looked at eachother, and then back at him, brows furrowed. Lana rubbed the scar across her nose, and Myr leaned forwards, looking a little angry.

Coren had known that this moment was coming, but his stomach dropped all the same. He cast a quick glance over at the

363

twins and Rane, who mouthed various words of support. Thank the gods for them.

He stood shakily, before the assembled leaders, and generals, and they were all watching him, waiting for him to speak, the fire roaring in his face.

A spear of panic shot through his chest, but he took a deep breath and continued through it.

It was time to tell a story, one last time. The full story, not just the bits and pieces he had told in the past.

Inhale. Exhale. Speak.

"My name is Coren of the North. I am the ward of Lady Kinaar, goddess of the night, the day, and the in-between. I am the first ward to be taken in a long, long time."

Murmurs spread again, but one flick of Rosana's fingers set the ground trembling, and silence fell once more.

Myr and Lana were staring at him now, and oh gods, why hadn't he talked to them before now?

"I have been training with Lady Kinaar since I was in the Elven Territories. I've learned so much." he swallowed, looking back at his cousins. "One of the things that Kinaar taught me about were the Unspoken Laws. They keep the universe in balance, and one of them impacts our war." His voice shook only a little as he went on. Rosana and Sora exchanged a frantic look. They hadn't known about this next part of his speech.

"You see, only a god can defeat another god. We cannot use the curse that ended the last great war without causing a great imbalance, one that could end the world. To end the cycle that Erathien seems to be trapped in, and return balance to the world, I must defeat, but not quite kill, Lady Chaos. Only I can do this, because I have a piece of Lady Kinaar inside of me. This is what she has told me. There is no other way."

Murmurs filled the air again, and Coren moved to sit down, his hands quaking, but *Regina* Rosana shook her head before he could. He forced himself to meet her eyes.

"Wait, Coren. I do not understand." Her brows were furrowed, and she twisted her tarnished wedding band around her finger. Her voice dropped to a near whisper. He could see people straining to hear. "That power, the power you would have to use... It is tied to you. To your soul."

"I know." He said, and returned his gaze to the fire, crackling leaping and burning.

Lin and Sioch understood immediately, rocketing to their feet. "Coren! You'll... Burn out!"

He looked at the ground. "It's possible, I know. *Possible.* Maybe-"

"Coren! I have never, in all my years, never seen a ward survive overusing their gifts." Queen Rosana said, angrily.

Myr had stood now, too, and for the first time that Coren could remember, she looked unsure as to what she was to do.

Coren forced himself to look away from them all, and into the fire instead. He was afraid that his eyes would betray how scared he was.

Kinaar's running commentary grew louder, and he wrestled her down, forcing her to leave his thoughts alone.

"I know, my lady." He said to the queen. "I know. But I have discussed this with Lady Kinaar over and over again. And it is the only way. Were we to repeat the spell, all the gods would be hurled back into sleep, along with Sorceress Theodosia, which we do not want."

He looked up now, meeting Rosana's dark eyes. "We want to weaken Lady Chaos, enough so that Lady Illira can pull her, and imprison her, firmly in the Veil. Taking her to the Void is impossible, as she has been barred from it long ago. Even if it means my death.... This is what has to be done. Please, please understand."

XCVI - Shock

COREN SAT DOWN, BACK in his place in the circle. Everyone was silent.

Rane and Myr sat as well, leaving Rosana the only one standing. She was visibly shaken, and the earth trembled under their feet as she turned, watching everyone again.

"This can't be it. We can't stand to lose Coren. He has done so much. We have to find a way that would not mean such a sacrifice. We have to." She said. "I have seen wards use their powers like this before. I have seen them try and use it all. Never once have I seen a ward keep their sanity - or their lives - after doing such. Godly power, pure power, is too much for a mortal to bear."

Rosana turned back to Coren. The raw anguish in her eyes was painful. Awful to see.

"My husband - Aleixei. Not many know this, but he was once the ward of the Lord of Time, Varien." The queen twisted her tarnished ring again, gleaming silver-bright against her dark skin. "He... He was my one and only."

The *Malefica* Theodosia, paling, rose to put an arm around her friend's shoulder. Maybe she knew what was coming. Maybe she had never heard the story before. But she understood the pain in Rosana's eyes. The pain of loss and love.

Coren thought of his mother, his father, and his aunt, and his heart twinged.

"I also had a child, once. Or I would have." *Regina* Rosana's voice hitched. She looked at Lady Sora, who had tears glittering in her eyes.

"The child came too soon. Much, much too soon. Four months too soon. I lost my baby. And my husband tried to turn back time, tried to retrieve what had been lost. He tried, and he tried, but nothing worked. What has happened is set, and not even the ward of the God of Time can reverse it." Rosana choked on a sob. "I lost my child and my husband on the same day."

Sora stood to take the queen's hand, and led her back to her seat in the circle. Theodosia was close behind.

Coren felt his throat close up, thick with emotion, sadness for someone else's pain.

"That is why we cannot allow you to do this, Coren. I have seen a ward die. It is long and painful and cannot be reversed. I cannot allow it again. I cannot allow you to make that sacrifice, Coren. I cannot."

The werecat and the queen sat perfectly still, eyes locked. There was silence.

Coren saw Rosana's grief, and her determination to never let what had happened to Aleixei happen again. Finally, he understood the panic that she must have felt when she saw the Seal on his hand - Probably much like the one that Aleixei had once had.

In Coren's eyes, Rosana saw his grief, for what she had lost, for what he had lost. And she saw his resolution to do whatever he had to. Even if it meant his own sacrifice.

Even if it meant breaking Rosana's heart.

"I'm sorry, Rosana."

Despite what Coren had said, despite everyone knowing that this really was the only way, the fireside deliberations went on. Night after night. No plan was made.

Tensions were high, with the threat of an attack at any moment looming over their heads.

Some sided with Coren, knowing that as awful as it was, it was the only way. Surprisingly, Rane sided with him as well. They made it very clear that they hated what he was doing, crying, but they understood why it had to happen.

("I believe in you Coren, if anyone could be the first to survive, then it must be you. You're really the bravest out of all of us.")

Rosana, Coren's family, and some others, believed that he should not be a sacrifice, for fear of what could happen. What he could do. For his own safety.

Perhaps he should have been glad that they cared so much for him, but he was also furious that they were trying to stop him when this was so clearly the only way that they could win. Kinaar herself agreed, telling him this over and over, until he was nearly insane with it all.

It went on evening after evening, bleeding into night, until the fire went cold and the moon washed everything in shades of silver.

Every night, the same points were made. Every night, the conversation was the same.

Coren's head spun from it all, and frustration caused raging headaches.

Finally, he stopped going. There was no point. Everyone knew that there was only one way to defeat Chaos, and keep the balance. Everyone knew that this was the best way. The only way that they had a chance of surviving.

Surely everyone noticed him missing from the deliberations. Surely they noticed him slip away into the woods, to train instead of talk.

They didn't mention it to him.

XCVII - In Which the War Truly Begins

IT WAS SNOWING.

The skies were iron-grey, the flakes stark and clean and bright, turning the trees to shimmering lace, piling into small drifts. Coren sighed, and let them settle in his hair, clinging to his lashes. This was his favourite time of the year. Winter.

It has been so long since I have felt snow. Lady Kinaar murmured in his mind.

"This is the best season. Everything is quiet. Quiet and clean." Coren raised a hand, catching snowflakes on the soft fabric of his gloves.

Quiet and clean... His patron echoed.

Frozen branches behind him cracked and swished, and he startled, whirling to face the newcomer. It was Rane. Their face was pale, their laboured breath white fog in the chill air.

"What is it?" He asked, frantic. "Is something wrong?"

"Wraiths! Surrounding camp. A Faerie entered the wood, never came back. Friends went to investigate, barely made it back." Rane struggled to catch their breath, hands planted on their knees, supporting them. Their eyes were dark. "It's here. It's time. The battle's begun."

Coren stared, and then hugged Rane tight. "Let's kick some godly ass."

It has begun. Kinaar whispered.

There was a sick feeling of deja vu as Coren raced up the path through the woods, just as fast as his legs could carry him.

Rane raced behind him, not even trying to make conversation, just trying to get back.

It was time. It was time and they still didn't have a solid plan, even after all of those debates.

Kinaar was running commentary, her voice annoyingly calm. She didn't seem to care how this ended. She didn't seem to care if all else failed, and they wound up having to get the *Malefica* Theodosia to chant the *cantamen*, the world might very well end.

When Coren finally reached the camp, his heart lodged in his throat. Rane skidded up behind him, barely catching themself on the ice.

"Coren." They said, softly, and he looked their way, snow falling soft around them both.

"I... Thank you for always thinking the best of me. For forgiving me when I was an idiot. You've been a good friend, Coren. I trust you."

He was speechless for a long moment, examining the other werecat's face. "Oh, Rane. Thank you. For enduring my needling and fears. I trust you too. And we'll make it out." His face hardened. "We have to."

Maybe one of them would have said something more, then. Maybe the conversation would have continued on, if not for the time, and the place.

A hissing rose in the air, the whispery, rasping tones of spectral voices, voices that had haunted Coren's nightmares since the day the camp had been destroyed.

Wraiths stepped from the woods, and the pair spun into motion.

The shadowy forms fell at their feet, dissipated, but more kept in coming, five for every one of them. Rane was soon lost to the chaos, flipping and hacking, their strange, elegant form of combat keeping them alive, a spinning battle axe and worn, chinked armour their only defence.

It was too close range for archery, so Coren was fighting tooth and claw and blade, his dual knives flashing out. Soon, black blood was dripping from the shining steel, and new cuts were marking his forearms.

No mercy. No relief.

He couldn't see his friends in the crowd. The drakons, swooping and diving, were the only things that really stood out from the trees and the bloodied snow. Already, allies had fallen.

High Fae lay crumpled, horns snapped and wings twisted. Werecats had fallen, half-Shifted. It was that awful, red mural from the city of Eire, but in hues of white and grey and black.

XCVIII - War Is Ugly

RANE FLIPPED BACK, propelling themself head over heels, flying over the head of a Wraith, and bringing their axe down on it. It faded, gone but for a stain on their weapon, and they smiled a sharp, fanged smile.

They were fighting. They were doing something. It was death. It was destruction. It could cost them their life. But this was something other than diplomacy, something that they were well and truly gifted at.

This was how they would get their people back.

They missed a blow, and then there was someone beside them, a lithe form with loose, black curls and startlingly green eyes. Lindara drove her kris towards Rane, and for a moment their heart stopped, thinking that she would kill them, despite the irrationality of the thought.

But the wavy blade just hissed past their ear, taking out a shadow-monster that had been ready to impale them.

Lin smiled fiercely. "Any idea where Coren is? Or Myr? Or the elves, or the witch?" She punctuated each question with a jab, a parry, a strike.

"No, Coren bolted, just got back from getting him." Rane said, whirling and dropping, avoiding a blade and dropping a Wraith with a well aimed kick. In a moment, Lin and Rane were back-to-back, trapped in a circle of foes, and Rane traded the axe for the sword, the pommel-stone flaring. It drove back the Wraiths for an instant, and Lin whistled under her breath.

"Lady of Stars." She murmured, at the same time that Rane called on their god: "Lord of Earth and Life."

"A blessed blade." Lin said, tripping and stabbing one of the odd beasts.

"Thank the gods. Some help at last." The second that the blade, wielded by a creature bound to it by ancient blood, skimmed a Wraith's shadowy skin, it vanished without a trace.

The pommel stone blazed, matched by an unexpected shine from Rane's necklace and ring.

Lin's eyes widened, and she was in Rane's face in an instant, so close that their breath was mingling, Lin's blade driving past Rane's ear, black blood dotting the back of their neck.

"Should have seen that coming, Chieftain." Lin commented, an eyebrow raised.

"Should have. Didn't. Next time." Rane said with a smile, as a new beast came running up, it's feet barely seeming to brush the ground. Rane ducked it's blow, turning the movement into a smooth roll that brought them behind the monster.

It spun, but it was too late. Rane had already slit its throat with the blessed blade. The thing didn't even have time to widen it's ember-eyes.

Lin was barely fending off a Wraith in full metal armour off to Rane's side, and they narrowed their eyes, running and flipping, killing the monster.

Where was everyone else?

Lin's eyes unfocused for a moment, and Rane screamed, lunging forwards and killing the Wraith headed straight for the werecat girl's face.

"What the *hell*? Lindara, we're in the middle of a-"

"Battle! I know! I'm back." She panted, terror painted across her face. "It's Coren. Something's happening."

XCIX - The Only Way

WHAT DO I DO? Coren asked Lady Kinaar, frantically searching for anything even vaguely godlike. Even she, the immortal, seemed scared.

I... I do not know. For the first time, perhaps ever, Kinaar seemed rattled.

"Shit!" He swore, dodging a Wraith's silvery blade. He drew the Veil around him, fading away, and the Wraiths moved on. He stood there, the sounds of a war raging around him, a still, invisible point in the chaos.

We never decided on a plan because they were so busy arguing! I can't see anyone. Not even Queen Wyeran. We don't have a plan, *Lady Kinaar!* He thought frantically.

Kinaar barely seemed to hear him. *Erathien needs the old gods again, or the balance will be upset, and the world will crumble. Magick, the Veil and the Void, they are what hold our world together. And the gods are needed to make sure that they are used well, and not forgotten.*

I know! Coren snapped back, moving his lips, the sounds never escaping, the Veil preventing it. *What else is there to do?*

We must go through with it. The leaders may disagree, and they will be furious, but it has to be done. It's the only way, the last option. There's no other way out.

The last option. The sounds all around him dulled, and his breath turned ragged at the edges. The last option.

You're sure that Lady Death will help.

She must. Illira must. She knows the costs.

Coren flickered into sight just long enough to kill a Wraith. *And if she doesn't?*

Then Erathien will never be the same again, and Chaos shall reign. Coren could almost picture the goddess rolling her eyes at him, waving him off. *But I have talked with her. She hates her mother, she will come through for us. She has to.*

His heart skipped a beat, two, three. He released a pent up breath. *My Lady of Stars save me, and keep me.*

It's time Coren. You can do this.

He stopped in his tracks, in the middle of the battlefield, ignoring the blood and screams around him.

This time when he drew on that invisible tide, it came not from the air around him, but from somewhere deep inside of his chest.

A hot light, warmer than he had ever felt it, began to radiate from his form, and his hand, the one marked with the Seal of the Lady Kinaar, burned.

This is the only way.

C - Determination

DEATH WAS PRESENT ON the killing fields, hidden from her mother's eyes. Maybe Chaos could not see her, but she could feel her presence. Stealing the last fragments of life away from those just barely hanging on, with the simple press of lips on a cold cheek.

Chaos smiled. The enemy lay strewn about, weak, and falling. Yes, they were taking Wraiths with them as they fell, and every single one gone left a prick of pain in its place, skittering across her black, smoky skin... But... She could always create more.

She was hidden in the crowd of forms just as dark and cruel as she was, untouchable. No one could find her, but she could see all.

The girl and the Chieftain (Damn you, Kir, you couldn't even kill them) fighting side by side. The pacifist, hiding in the trees, helping the wounded stagger away, keeping an eye on his *comitis*. The godling sometimes in sight, sometimes vanishing, even from her. The Chieftainess Warlord, her rapier singing. The *malefica*, the *regina*, and the heir, spells flashing, ground rumbling, fire sparking... And Marks spiraling, growing.

All searching for their allies, all searching for her.

She smiled, her stark white hair falling in front of her face, obscuring one obsidian eye.

No one could bring her down. Not even the godling. The balance... The balance was too important.

She was unstoppable.

She did not see the light growing around the godling boy. She forgot that she had a daughter who she had used one too many times.

CI - Finally It Begins

HE WAS FLASHING LIKE a strobe light, the glow around him charging the air, steady and constant, but his own form flaring in and out of sight. It felt like the sun's fire was coursing through his veins, and gods above, it hurt. It hurt so bad.

Only a god can truly harm another deity.

Kinaar's voice in his head was faint now, as her power was released, but she was there, reminding him of the steps, of what had to be done.

Find Chaos. As fast as you can.

Use the Veil, as I showed you! Lady Death must be here. Find her, if you can!

He closed his eyes, trying to tune out the world around him. The glow was scaring away the Wraiths. Even his own allies shied away, scared of this strange occurrence. Even the Fae, with their constant illusions, looked afraid. Of him. The quiet, nervous boy.

Lady Illira! Lady Death, where are you? He thought, somehow *knowing* how to project the cry through the Veil.

Hello, little boy. The voice was new to him, somehow slipping into his guarded mind. It was a faint whisper, that seemed to echo, just a bit. It was a child.

Lady Illira. You're here. Relief coursed through his veins, under the fire. He was barely biting back a scream.

Yes.

Please, Lady Death, I... I need your help if the balance is to be restored. If you want Lady Chaos defeated.

Lady Illira barely gave him time to finish. *You need to imprison her... Awake. And to do that you need my help, as I am the only goddess aside from Kinaar who can manipulate the Veil.*

Yes, Lady Death.

Call me when you need me. She was gone as quickly as she came, and there was no time to feel anything, and Kinaar was screaming at him. *She's found you! Lady Chaos! MOVE!*

He opened his eyes, the Veil pulsing around him, crashing like waves, the static heat oppressive around him. The surging, fighting crowd was being parted, as if by a giant hand, and a woman in fine silver armour was walking through it, her long, white hair wisping around her face. Her sword was gripped in a hand as shadowy-dark as her Wraiths.

"Hello, godling." She hissed. The voice was the one that had haunted his dreams. Her face was the one that he saw nearly every time he dared to dream. She was the one who had taken his life, over and over again.

Suddenly, the flickering was gone, something inside of him had either clicked into place, or finally snapped, and he was solid, out of the in-between. His knives flashed as he spun them, holding them tight.

The glow was as bright as the sun, hotter than a flame, and his eyes burned with an intensity that was almost feral.

"You really think you can chain me?" The goddess asked, her loping gait smooth, carefree. "The balance will be upset. Hasn't my baby sister told you that?"

He stayed silent. It was what he did best. She began circling him, drawing ever closer.

It was then that Coren realised he wasn't sure how exactly he was supposed to bring her down. All he knew was that the release of all of the godly magicks stored inside of him had something to do with it. Kinaar had fallen silent. Or maybe she was just being drowned out by the roaring in his ears.

He planted his feet a bit firmer in the earth, still biting back a howl. The liquid fire just ran hotter, faster, as his heart rate ratcheted up.

The glow seemed to be intensifying, until even Chaos backed up a pace. She mimicked his pose, sword in a defensive position, waiting for him to make a move.

He wasn't going to be that foolish. She was an immortal. He could never take her on, if he began the fight. If she started… There would be a bit more of a chance.

Who am I kidding? There's no chance. He kicked the thought away, waiting.

The war around him seemed to dim. He didn't see his friends slowly making their way through, saving allies, killing Wraiths, stopping, terror-stricken, seeing the goddess. Seeing him.

Too late. Their hours of bickering were over.

Any interference, and the gods only knew what would happen.

Lady Chaos cocked her head, meeting his stare with her own obsidian dark, glassy-dead gaze. "What do you mean to do, little boy? Fend off a goddess? What harm can you do?"

Every word felt laced with a power, driving him deeper and deeper into the ground. His heart thundered, his body screaming. He couldn't last much longer.

The shining aura around him blazed even brighter, until the snow gleamed gold, melting around his feet.

Finally, after what felt like ages, Lady Chaos lunged, and the entire clearing, stopped, stared, holding its breath.

CII - Watching

RANE NEARLY SCREAMED. Lin's fingers were like claws, digging into their arm.

The second that the brilliant light had begun to radiate from the centre of the battlefield, they had started to run as fast as they could.

The light had drawn everyone towards it, like moths to a flame, and there they had found their allies.

They stood together, and everything was still, as they watched, horrified. The fighting, so intense a moment ago had ceased, a tense stand-still, watching. Waiting.

A woman made of shadows, none other than the goddess of war and destruction herself, facing off against a boy, no more than eighteen winters old. None of the watchers, be they peasant or Queen, could intervene.

Snow steamed and melted at the heat of Coren's powers, bleeding into the air. Charging the surroundings. He didn't look at them. He was just watching her, his knuckles white on the hilts of his dual knives.

Rane had never seen his powers do anything like that before, so that... Couldn't be good.

Please gods, don't let it hurt him too much.

They inhaled sharply as they watched the Wraiths around them dissipate. As they faded away, Lady Chaos seemed to stand taller, stronger. The shadow monsters were truly a part of her.

Rane risked a look away, across the forest clearing that had been their camp, for a few short weeks. Rebels were sobbing over the dead, and helping the injured away.

How was it that a barely ten-minute long fight had done *this*?

When they looked back at the scene before them, they caught a glimpse of Coren's face as he looked behind him for a moment, and their heart nearly stopped. His eyes were glowing a molten gold, the same shade as the light all around him.

Lin's fingers pinched tighter, and Rane blinked away a haziness, tears, or sweat, or both. They reached up, and pried her fingers away, clasping them tight.

This was it. The *true* beginning of the end. One on one, armies at a standstill, all force devoted to this one battle.

CIII - Stay Calm

HE WAS BURNING. EVERY inch on fire, his blood boiling.

The glow was so strong, it was a miracle that he wasn't blind. Any shape beyond it, aside from the *dea* herself, was a blur, vague, and indistinct. Washed out. He finally, finally gave in, screaming.

It hurt so bad. Gods, it hurt.

Lady Chaos laughed, narrowing her eyes, striding closer, closer. He was so stunned, he could barely react. And he felt so heavy too. This wasn't a blessing, it was a curse, embedded inside of him, and he couldn't rein it in.

Even if he could have, he couldn't. Gods, that didn't make sense.

He gripped his knives tighter. The dark goddess circled closer.

What the hell am I supposed to do now?

Nothing but react.

Finally, seconds stretched into an eternity blurred by fire and pain, the goddess made her move. She lunged for his throat, her silver blade arcing through the air.

Memories of training with Myr, her making the exact same movement, flashed through his slow brain, and he brought up his knives, crossing them before him, blocking the movement.

Lady Chaos was all sinew and fluid grace. She spun, her snow white hair flaring, and struck again. Coren danced away. The glow was sharper, stronger, brighter. He was just barely fast enough.

The wicked sharp blade nearly ripped open his stomach - a twisting move was all that spared him, and even then, it slashed across his arm, drawing a line of red and gold... Gold. The filaments of something, magick, the Veil, fire, something, twined across his skin, along with his own blood.

Chaos snarled at the sight, and struck again, and again. Years of training, with his family, with Rane, kicked in, and he managed to avoid, or block each one. Barely. 'Barely' was enough.

No counterattack. Stay calm. The edges of his vision were blurring out, the light finally taking its toll. He could barely make out anything but the black void that Lady Chaos' form made. He couldn't hear anything but the screeching of metal-on-metal, and the pounding in his ears.

CIV - A Fight, A Healer, & Death Herself

RANE SCREAMED AS THE blade arced down towards him, a sob catching in their throat as their friend somehow managed to block.

The light was growing brighter, a supernova, an explosion - slowed down and dragged out.

The silver blade came down, again and again, and he managed to dance away each time. He staggered, once. He was bleeding, from a long gash on his arm, and the blood was twined with golden light.

"He's holding her off. Lord of Life... How?" Rane whispered, and Lin strangled their fingers.

"I don't know. I don't care." She muttered, and Rane swallowed, tears welling again. This time, they did nothing to hold them back.

SIOCH WAS CARRYING an armful of blood-soaked bandages, light-headed. The scent of iron and copper in his nose, his eyes watered. They had been too late for so many.

Neither he, nor the sorceress, could have saved them. And he would never forget them, all of them, as long as he lived. Every face, still and glassy-eyed. The blood, black and red and blue and green, and the wounds and the...

He stopped himself, shaking his head to clear the cobwebs. Every nerve was strung high, so high that he didn't hear his sister screaming in his head.

When he finally did take it in, her cries, and her fear, and her pain, he nearly collapsed onto the mound of stained cloth.

Panicked, he reached out for the dark web-like expanse in his mind, plunging into it, and seeing through Lindara's eyes.

What he saw left him in ruins.

Coren.

Coren, engulfed in light. Coren, fighting a *dea*. And invincible force. Coren, barely fending off an attack. His cousin-brother.

He jerked away from Lin's consciousness, shutting away the dark web for minutes, trying to regain his bearings. *Coren, Coren, Coren...*

He blinked, rapidly, swiping away the tears, leaving a smudge of snow, melting on his pale brown skin.

He had to get up, to tell Theodosia that everything had happened. Everything. They had failed in their one task, they hadn't decided, so Coren had chosen for them. He had chosen a plan that, if it succeeded, would save Erathien. If it failed, he would die. He alone would take the blame.

ILLIRA WAS THERE, WATCHING. She was there, and then gone, to the makeshift medical relief centre that had sprung up in the woods.

The *Malefica* Theodosia binding scrapes, setting bones, easing pain, with the boy working with her. The pacifist, nauseated at the sight of blood, choosing to help save lives rather than take them.

She walked among them, gently easing the passage into the Void, her realm.

In a blink, she was back in the killing fields, watching, waiting. Soon enough. Soon enough. He had to succeed.

Had to. She would force him to stay here, in the realm of the living, until he did.

It was time. It was time.

The light around the godling flared brighter.

CV - The End

THIS TIME, COREN BARELY managed to escape the whining sting of the Lady Chaos' blade. Her smile had faded when she realised that he was going to be able to hold her off, if barely.

Her grace had leaned more towards a wild dance. She snarled at him, her black eyes gleaming -

No.

He felt his balance going.

No, no, no.

He tripped. He stumbled, exhausted, the light blinding and fuzzy, and he fell. Something beneath him cracked, and he sobbed. The bow. His bow. The quiver dug into his back.

Lady Chaos was on top of him in an instant, her blade at his throat. It was his dream, made real.

Her gaze was cold. The dream, the future-dream... That's what it had been. A prediction.

The sharp edge pressed into his neck. She was smiling now, the cold, familiar smile.

"You really think that you can beat me? One boy? With a fragment of power? Oh, child. You're sorely mistaken." She leaned in. "And you know what upsetting the balance, banishing my siblings, my daughter and I again would mean."

He lay there, prone, his gaze never leaving hers. His knives had fallen from his grip, and the fire was burning bright again, with nothing to distract him from it.

He could see himself reflected in her mirror-like eyes, and his own glowing golden ones, the aura around him, they terrified him. He didn't show it.

He smiled a bit. "I know. I cannot banish you. I cannot defeat you. Not alone." He fell silent again, waiting. Every muscle in his body was tense.

"You are nothing. You will be defeated, my daughter will take you." Her cold smile stretched wide. "It's over, so soon after it began."

His fingers scrabbled in the melting snow, the mud, the beaten, browned grass, searching. Praying to his patron, to any benevolent god listening, that Lady Chaos wouldn't notice. One knife. Anything.

His quiver lifted his shoulders, left his head hanging back, exposing his throat all the more.

The sword was cold, and it bobbed as he swallowed. He could feel himself dimming faster than before, the edges going black, dark and spotty.

"Only a god can defeat another god. You're nothing but a boy."

Only a god. Only a god, only a god.

He had to force his face to stay still, stony cold, instead of laughing the crazed, high laugh that wanted to worm it's way past his lips.

Coren had a fragment of a god inside of him. It was in his blood, glowing in the snow, lighting up the air around him. Chaos had to be blind not to see it coming.

He had control of the Veil. He knew what to do.

He searched for his knives, scrabbling, frantic now, and Chaos applied pressure. He could feel the sting as the razor-sharp steel drew drops of blood, red and gold and dark.

And one more puzzle piece clicked into place, somehow piercing the bleary fog that had enveloped his mind. The light, already bright enough to blind, had somehow grown brighter. It was leaching away his essence.

Coren's hand flew back, out of the mud, back over his shoulder, reaching back, and down, past the shattered wooden fragments of the bow he had spent hours whittling, until it touched the fletching of an arrow, just as broken as the bow.

The arrowhead was still as sharp as the day it had been forged.

He pretended that he had found nothing, his hand dropping down. He allowed his face to fall still, cold, closed. The picture of defeat. His heart was struggling, his veins burning.

Chaos, her void-like form wisping, applied a bit more pressure, and Coren's chest was heaving. She leaned in a bit more, and - there!

An opening. Under her sword arm, a straight path to the heart. It wouldn't kill her, but it would bring her very close, very quick.

He knew what to do with his gift now, as it trickled away.

One last prayer to his patron, to the goddess usually ever-present in his mind, and he locked eyes with the Nameless Goddess one more time. It had to be done, and gods, it was hard.

It was right.

Lady Chaos saw something there, in his eyes. A sudden burst of satisfaction beneath the pain and the struggle for breath, for life. It was too late to do anything.

In a jerky movement, the werecat boy surged up, the blade digging deep into his throat, sliding through skin and arteries and cartilage, and he was killing himself, and it hurt, every fibre in his being burned, and gods, he was finally at peace, finally knew what he wanted from life - But it was done.

The arrowhead was lodged deep in her chest, black streams pouring down from the wound, his fingers somehow still clasping the jagged piece of metal embedded there.

And he bunched up the Veil around him, gathering all of the filaments of his remaining power, somehow, incredibly, grasping the threads glaring, glittering in the air around him, and pushed them up his arm.

It was an explosion, focused, threading up his arm in a burst of power like nothing he had been able to channel before. The light left the air around him, and the force was enough to split the sky.

His breath rattled, wet dripping down, and his head fell back, white and black all he could see, afterimage from the glow seared into his retinas. He couldn't see what happened next. Any of it.

He heard a long, piercing, unearthly scream, maybe Lady Chaos, maybe he himself, and then... Everything muted, dulled. He couldn't breathe, was bleeding out, the blade had gone deep. His life force had been threaded with the fragment of Lady Kinaar's power. Most was gone now, channelled out. It had taken everything with it.

Everything was so quiet now. From far away he heard his name being called.

It was too late. So much pain had been endured, manifesting in scars, and he felt as if he had been burned from the inside out.

He couldn't hold on. He had done what he could. Everything finally, finally went dark.

CVI - After

LINDARA SCREAMED AS he fell. The sound was shrill and harsh, and Rane just hugged her close.

Both of them had known that this was coming. They had known that he would fall, somehow. There was no way that a mortal boy could stand against a goddess.

There was no way to see what was happening now. The light left searing afterimages, Chaos' shadowy form the sole dark point.

Rane had to look away, crying. They had known that he would fall. The power draining away would be enough. It was too soon.

A wail came from before them, and they forced themselves to face the glow, shoulders heaving. They had to watch. They had to know what happened, to be ready.

When the glow flared bright, and then was gone, there was a millisecond of stunned shock, and fear when they saw the tableaux before them. Coren on the ground, bleeding heavily, his arm raised to a wound that he had created, right where the Lady Chaos' heart beat.

And then the glow surged back, brighter than ever before, coming with a cracking sound like the sky splitting down the middle.

It was gone before they could take in what that meant.

The scream that followed raised the hair on Rane's head, and the concussive force of the blast nearly knocked them off their feet. Clasped fingers and boots dug deep into the icy soil were all that kept Lin and Rane from falling.

Then it was over. A crumpled form, dark and wisping, lay on the ground, still, but breathing. A boy lay metres away, not moving at all.

Lin screamed his name, but he didn't move. They were clustered around him in an instant, all of them, elves and werecats and Fae and drakons, allies, shaken and bloodied.

When it came down to it, no one cared about the threat, the goddess. They cared only for their friend, the brave one willing to give up everything.

It was Lady Sora who knelt in the mud, and lifted his wrist to check for a pulse.

As if the stillness and the blood were not signs enough.

She shook her head.

Everyone was crying, even the regal queen Rosana. Even sarcastic, cold Fyeren, his wings limp, his clothing already in shades of black, for mourning.

It was over. And they had paid a price.

NO ONE SAW DEATH, WHEN she came by. Coren never saw her lean over, and place the kiss, when it was his time, and no one was watching when Death stood over her mother, her tiny, child's form stiff with anger, her face twisted cruelly.

Blood seeped down from a shallow cut across her chest, mirroring Lady Chaos'. Balance had been restored. All the gods had finally been brought down, down to the same level, ready to rise again.

Death kicked the weak, bleeding form.

Mother. She snapped, and the elder goddess shifted, just barely.

Daughter. Help me. Please.

Lady Illira smiled darkly. *Why?*

I gave you everything! A kingdom. Power. Please, daughter.

The child goddess sneered. *You gave me power, only to take it when you needed it. You gave me a life, but not my own. One to serve you. One that you twisted and used when you saw fit. It's over, Mother. That boy finally brought you to your knees, and it is my time to end it.*

Illira spat into the snow. She leaned over, her expression cold.

You wronged me. You wronged so many. You are power hungry, jealous of the attention given to your siblings. You tried to take this land. You would have upset the balance all by yourself, by taking too much control.

Lady Death knelt in the snow. She took her mother's hand, and raised it, nearly to her lips. Her tiny fingers were dwarfed by her fallen mothers.

I will finally get what is mine.

She brushed a kiss across Lady Chaos' knuckles, and they both faded away, slipping into the deepest, densest part of the Veil.

CVII - One Last Wraith

MOMENTS BEFORE EVERYTHING ended, time dragging and overlapping, Sioch spotted Theodosia across the field of the injured and dead. He began to run out of the thicket, Lin's thoughts running through his mind in a torrent, their emotions blurring.

It was all coming to an end with this accursed golden glow, and he couldn't accept it.

He had to tell Theodosia. If anyone could do anything, it was she.

Sioch didn't see the Wraith looming just beyond his shoulder, just out of arm's reach. One last Wraith, sent into the woods purely to cause harm.

His gaze was fixed on the *malefica*, and he screamed her name. She whirled around, and her kaleidoscopic eyes widened. She saw what he could not.

He yelled out what had happened, his voice breaking, and her face paled even further, and she yelled out a warning, too late.

He turned, and saw the shadow-beast reaching for his shoulder. He tried to speed up, and more panic, if that was even possible, shot through his veins.

Something crackled across his skin, something like static, but he barely noticed it.

I am unarmed.

Maybe he would have made it. Maybe. If not for the battle between Coren and Lady Chaos, and it's disastrous end. If not for the taking of a pulse, and a quiet shake of the head.

Nearby, and still too far away, Lindara watched her cousin fall. Her panic leapt across the link between her and her *comitis*, and Sioch was hit with not only her pain, but his own, and he was crippled by it, falling to the ground, his outstretched hand not enough to brace the fall.

His palm stung, grating across the frozen crystals on the ground, and the breath was knocked out of him.

His vision blacked for a second, from the force of the fall, from the shock, and then the Wraith was upon him, and then...

There was a flare of bright green light that soon faded away. Probably Theodosia trying to help.

It wasn't enough. The Wraith was back before Sioch could stumble to his feet, and then.

Pain.

CVIII - Goddesses

LADY CHAOS HAD REGAINED some of her strength. She was struggling, weakly, dark ichor still seeping from the ugly wound in her chest.

Lady Illira held her fast. She was grown now, taking the form of a woman tall enough, strong enough, to subdue a goddess at full strength. Chaos seemed doll-like in her pale arms.

The Veil was soft and grey around them, a thick, foggy haze. Beyond it all was the Void, it's crumbled pillars and scarlet blooms imposed over a grey, snowy forest, in the most remote parts of the untravelled, unmapped Far Regions.

Death was standing where the Veil was at its densest, impossible to move by any mortal, be they ward, or merely witch. Shifting this part of the Veil was a struggle for even Kinaar.

It was easy for Lady Illira, Queen of the Dead, Mistress of the Void.

She could slip between worlds as easy as could be.

Death set her mother down, and the woman whimpered, her form wisping, becoming smaller. Soon enough, she was just a woman in a silver dress, her armour and weapons gone, the wound in her chest already staining the fine cloth.

Her pleading for mercy fell on deaf ears. Her daughter finally had her revenge.

The Veil began to roil around them, bubbling and twisting with the fluid movements of Lady Illira's hands.

She stepped away from her mother as a sphere began to form, dark and growing darker. Lady Chaos screamed as it tightened, until she could barely move. She could not bend it, her powers did not extend to this peopleless realm.

No mortal would ever aid her here, and Chaos had snapped the thread between herself and her daughter long ago.

Lady Chaos, the Nameless Goddess, would remain here, weak. She would heal. But it would be slow. And Illira would make sure that she never escaped again.

CIX - When Everything Is Over

MYR WAS BACK ON THE rock, beneath the snowy skies. Alone. No one would come for her this time.

Her hair had tumbled loose again, long dark brown locks falling over her shoulders, concealing the bloodstains.

Black and red and blue and green. Her victims', and her allies', and her own.

Her hand went to her side, and the scar again, her mind to Coren, and his sacrifice. Over. It was over. Her child would grow up in peacetime, thank the gods.

The North would have new contact with the other magickal races. There would be a new age of knowledge, travel, and health.

But they had paid a price.

RANE WAS SLUMPED AGAINST a tree, their head in their hands. They had stripped away their armour, their weapons, and left them lying in the snow.

Hardened leather, a battle axe, a broadsword, two poisoned knives.

The shock had worn off, giving way to loss and anger. It was over now. They had won.

Coren was dead. And so many others had fallen. Something had happened to Sioch, and Lindara had rushed off to find him. Myr was nowhere to be found. Fyeren was speaking to his people. *Regina* Rosana, the *Malefica* Theodosia and Lady Sora were preparing bodies for funerals, each in the way of their people.

And there Rane was, alone, under a tree.

It was over. And they were left alone against the world, yet again. Abandoned to the elements, to whatever wandered their way.

ROSANA BOUND THE EYES of yet another corpse with steady fingers. Too steady, almost. She had seen war before, in all its awful glory.

She had survived that war, and she had survived this one, if only just barely.

Steady, steady.

She drew the rough blanket back over the young man's chest, tucking it gently in at the chin - As if he had been her own child, whom she was tucking into bed.

Theodosia laid a hand on her friend's shoulder, and smiled sadly.

"So much loss. Lord Duman's name. Come on, Rosa. Let's go and lie down."

The queen shook off the gentle hand with sudden anger. "Despite what you and Lady Sora believe, I am not some weak-minded child! Please don't speak to me that way, I am perfectly capable."

Sora ducked in at just that moment, of course, and frowned. "My Lady, the *Malefica* Theodosia is just trying to help. She means no disrespect, nor do I."

The *regina* sighed. "Of course, of course. Apologies. My temper is not as stable as it should be." She tried for a smile, trying to suppress the boiling feelings in her chest.

It was this whole business. It reminded her too much of the last funeral she had attended, that was all. She was all right.

Lady Sora cast a wary, melancholy gaze at the rows of silent bodies. All were ready to pass into the Void in the way of their people. In the way of all the old peoples of Erathien.

Eyes bound in black linen, bodies covered by shrouds - beneath the cloth, they were dressed in their full battle armour. It was an old tradition, one that reached back to before the Fall of the Gods. One that Rosana had seen performed for too many people.

She looked down at her worn hands, the wedding band on her slim, dark finger, remembering a handsome, laughing face, sparkling dark eyes... The love of her life. Dead and gone now. Just like Coren. Just like all of them.

"Aleixei." Theodosia murmured, watching Rosana's fingers fiddle with the ring.

"Aleixei." The elven queen confirmed.

"Gods, is it truly over? We've lost so much." Sora whispered. "So many lives."

LIN WAS COMPLETELY numb, and gods, did she want a drink. She squeezed her brother's hand, wincing as a stray spark of green light jumped off his skin to shock her.

He was alive. Thank the gods, he was alive.

Theodosia had been able to kill the Wraith before it could strike a killing blow, but it had done a serious amount of damage to his face.

Lin's face crumbled as she looked at the bandages one more time. Her own cheeks prickled with a faint reflection of Sioch's pain.

He was alive.

She stared down at their clasped hands again, and nervously flicked the fingers of her free hand. Theodosia had said that the attack had unlocked something inside of him, something powerful. Magick. True magick, the kind that had been lost for years.

She closed her eyes, trying not to cry.

It was over, and everything was different. Everything had changed in a matter of minutes.

Coren was dead. Sioch was injured and magickal, and she was alone in a much too quiet tent.

CX - The Void

HE WAS COLD. HE FELT as if something were missing from him, some great piece.

He couldn't remember what.

He stood in the centre of a ruined temple, black marble columns reaching into the sky. The floor was buckled, deep cracks dividing great slabs of dark stone.

The roof that the pillars had once supported was lying in chunks all around him, leaving a clear view of the sky. It was starless and clear, the twin moons hanging heavy and full in the velvety dark.

He reached for something to say, but the words seemed out of reach. He was alone, and in a strange place. What was there to say?

He bit his lip, staring down at his boots. The leather was stained with something dark and dripping, seeping into the cracked floor, and reeking of iron and sulphur.

His stomach twisted, and he clenched his fists, scars standing out pale against his tanned skin.

He didn't remember where he had gotten the scars, the memories just out of reach, hiding somewhere, along with his words.

A voice rang out in greeting, startling him, and he spun, hands going for something at his waist - a reflex. Nothing was there. His back - Nothing but an empty quiver.

"Hello, werecat." The voice came again. It sent shivers down his spine. It wasn't one voice, really, but many, twining into one eerie tone.

He could have sworn he had heard a weaker, barely echoing version of this once before.

He just stood there, silent, watching as a little girl slipped out from behind a chunk of marble. Her skin was as pale as moonlight, her eyes and hair black as the surrounding night. She was barefoot, her slip just as pale as her skin.

"Welcome home." She said.

He was silent, unwilling to speak to her. He swallowed, and his throat twinged. Raising a hand, he felt a raised ridge of old scar tissue there, and frowned. That wasn't right.

"Ah, yes. Disorienting, is it not, first coming here." She gestured around, her many-toned voice strange. "You are in my kingdom, the Void. Welcome."

Finally, the words came, his voice creaking as if it had gone unused for a long, long time. "The Void. Death's kingdom."

"Yes."

"I - What..." He trailed off.

"You saved hundreds of lives, little werecat, you truly did. You made an immense sacrifice for the ones you held dear." The child - Lady Death - said softly.

I can't remember. Lady of Stars, why can't I remember?

This was so wrong. Unfamiliar scars, no memories, this strange, ethereal child. This was wrong. He couldn't be here.

Death froze suddenly, and whirled around, her voice ringing out much louder than should have been possible.

"The Veil does not reach here, Aunt. Let me see you." She snapped.

Backing up, the boy tripped over a crack in the floor, and fell down hard, blinking back a sudden prickle of tears. What in the hells?

"Kinaar! I know you are here!"

A sigh rang out through the crumbling temple, bored and disdainful. A woman, dressed in a gown of light and stars, her auburn hair tumbling down her back, stepped into view. A bow was clutched in one long-fingered hand, and her green eyes were distant.

"Hello, Niece."

"What do you want, Kinaar? He is mine." Death snapped, and in a blink, the child had grown to a tall woman, her slip now a fine, lacy gown, her hair reaching her waist, dark and floating.

"Yes." The new woman, Lady Kinaar, looked at him, and closed her eyes. "However, he gave you something. You finally have had your revenge, and the balance is in order. The others are waking, and we will be able to restore Erathien to its former glo-ry soon."

"You want him back." The Lady Death stated, and the boy shivered, confused.

"Yes."

"He is in my kingdom now. He is mine." Lady Death said petulantly.

"He was mine before he was yours, Illira. He gave you what you wanted. Allow me to have him back." Kinaar lifted her chin, staring down her niece.

For a second it seemed that maybe Lady Death would give in, but then something shifted in her expression, a dark realisa-tion creeping in. She set her jaw, and curled her lip. "Why? Why should I? My mother drained me and used me, but neither you, nor any of the others did anything to help. You allowed me to suffer, as long as you remained untouched. If you hadn't needed my help to imprison my mother, would you have ever reached out to me?"

Kinaar looked down. Maybe, just maybe, a flicker of shame danced across her face, but it was gone too soon to be able to tell. There was a long pause while Kinaar stared at the cracked marble floors. When she finally choked out the words, it sounded like a cat being strangled.

"I am sorry."

The boy was very much confused. Was he being bartered for by two goddesses?

No. This was ridiculous. All of it. He was dreaming, he had to be.

But then, why can I not remember who I am? Where I come from?

"You're *sorry*?" Lady Death sputtered.

"Yes. Truly. I am sorry, Illira. I... I didn't understand. I didn't realise..."

"You didn't *try* to understand, Aunt Kinaar." Death - Illira - snapped back, recovering quickly. "What, did it take me stealing away your pretty little toy to wake you up? Did it take you seeing my temple in ruins?"

Her layered, echoing, murmuring voice crumbled away, and unexpected tears glittered in the corners of her eyes.

"I was powerful once. I am regaining some power, yes. But look-" she gestured again, "Look at this. This cannot be rebuilt so fast. It is like Micha's wood. It must be regrown, slowly, slowly, with proper care, and time. And you allowed it to come to this. To this destruction."

Another pause. Wind swayed the scarlet heads of the poppies that grew all around the ruined temple.

Kinaar swiped at her emerald eyes. Her shoulders slumped as she looked around again.

It really could have been her. It could have been her strength that lay in shambles.

"I am so sorry, Niece. I truly, truly am." Kinaar dared to step forwards, and then Lady Illira was a child again, her black eyes huge in her delicate face. She turned away from her aunt, her bare toes digging into a crack in the marble underfoot.

"Illira. I swear. I swear it upon all that is under my control... I will not ever allow this to happen to you again." Lady Kinaar murmured.

The mistress of the Void glanced back at the boy, who shuddered under her glance.

"You are just saying this to get your boy back." She whispered. She didn't want to believe the promise, did she?

"I want him back. But... I never want anything like what happened out there to occur again. I never want to have to watch that. I never want to feel as helpless as you were. To watch my powers be used, feel a bit of me seeping away, to fight my own kindred." Lady Kinaar's pale brow furrowed, sadly.

"I never want to see any of my own so shattered and weak again."

Lady Death's face screwed up, teary.

These were gods? As emotional, as flawed as I, beneath their calm facades? The boy mulled the thoughts over. And then: *Oh, gods. They are still bartering for me.*

Illira's voice was nothing more than a wisp of a whisper. "You swear it?"

No hesitation from Lady Kinaar. Just: "I swear."
The bartering was done.

CXI - Vanished

LINDARA SCREAMED, HER hands balled into tight fists, her green eyes snapping with a cold fire.

All she had wanted to do was to say one last goodbye. One more time before he was lost, his name silent for six long moons.

A goodbye that would have to be said alone, because her twin was still recovering, and she was alone.

Lin whirled on the poor swarm of sprytes who happened to be hovering nearby, and immediately began yelling at them.

"Did you see anything? What in the hells happened?" Her voice fragmented. "What did you *do* to him?!"

The sprytes stared, their black eyes emotionless. One shrieked something in a high language that Lin couldn't understand, and she stamped her foot, screaming again before sinking to the ground.

One last goodbye, was that too much to ask?

The tent flap was pushed open, and the sprytes swarmed out, chittering what must have been curses. Rane swore, batting them away from their face, before taking in the sight.

"Lin?"

She didn't reply.

"May I sit?"

No response, so they just did, without asking again. Something was off, and it took Lin a moment to notice. Rane wasn't wearing their ever-present armour, nor any weapons.

Just their moonstone jewellery, and soft worn clothing, whose deep red dye matched their hair.

"What happened?" They asked quietly. They hadn't noticed. They hadn't noticed the empty cot, the coins and the bandages that had fallen to the ground, the -

A few stray tears crept down Lin's face, and she gestured blankly at it all.

Rane froze, shock and anger and a thousand other emotions warring behind their eyes as they tried to take it all in.

"Dear gods above, where - What? Oh my gods." The name was heavy, begging to be said, screamed, anything, but the rites forbade it.

"I know." Lin's lip quivered, and she screwed up her face to prevent herself from crying, but it was too late, too much, and she had cried in front of Rane before, but that was different, and
-

The tent flap swung open. Fyeren, surrounded by the damned sprytes. Everything, even his nails, his wings, his hair, were a deep black. Mourning.

He took in the scene, the empty cot, and a flurry of his own colourful oaths escaped him, before he whirled and spun out of the tent.

"Shit." Rane hissed. "Here comes the storm."

They were right.

Moments later, there was uproar, panic, fear. Leaders were shouting theories, throwing out anything that could explain the disappearance of a corpse.

It didn't take long before someone found the seal of Lady Ki-naar burned into the cloth, right where the boy's left hand had rested.

CXII - Return

THE DAY WAS CRISP AND cold, and soft snow was falling from iron clouds. The boy tilted his head back, enjoying the feeling.

He was sitting on a rune-covered rock, rising from the centre of a glassy smooth lake, ringed by low mountains. The whole place seemed eerily familiar, as if he had spent much time here, in another life. Everything was just... Blurry.

He reached for the name, this time refusing to let the details slip away from him.

Conpitum.

Crossroads.

With the name came a flood of images, laughing faces and waves, campfires and sunsets. So this place was... Home? Or at least very, very close.

He put his head between his knees, trying to weather the storm of memories, his palms pressed flat against the rough stone.

When he had finally caught his breath, he dared to look around. His eyes widened when he saw a glow beginning to solidify in the air, and he tensed his shoulders, bracing himself for more of... Whatever that had been...

The light continued to draw together, twisting and solidifying until it took a solid form.

It was the woman. The red-haired goddess from the Void. She stood before him, her bow in hand, and smiled. The gesture didn't reach her eyes.

"Hello, Coren."

"What -" Was all he could choke out, before the name - his name - brought another torrent of memories. Just his name, over and over, by so many voices. Whispered, shouted, cried and cursed.

"Just breathe, child. You're in the Cortach Rane, in the north of Erathien. You're alive."

Coren's shoulders shook, as more memories, memories of hunting in the deep woods, of people like him, their fangs and slit-pupiled eyes gleaming in a wintry half-light, washed over him.

When he had recovered enough, the goddess held out her free hand, and he accepted, his heavily scarred fingers trembling. A surge of power jolted through him at the touch, and he trembled at it - at it's familiarity.

A flashing, strobe light memory: A glow, bright and then brighter, of a shadowy menacing form, and pain coursing through his veins in place of blood.

His breath caught again, and the Lady Kinaar held him up.

"What happened to me?"

"Oh, Coren..." There was such a heavy sadness, or maybe something closer to regret, hanging on to her every word.

"Why can't I remember?" He pleaded, his voice rising and keening at the end.

The goddess bowed her head. "You did great things. You saved us all. But you paid the price."

It was a half answer at best, and he frowned, biting his lip. "What *happened*?"

CXIII - Uproar

IT WAS FYEREN WHO NOTICED the light on the horizon, snapping everyone out of the dazed reverie they were in. "Is that glowy light normal?"

"What?!" Rane spun, spotting the light instantly. It was late evening, it shouldn't have been there, but it was, and it was growing by the second.

They whirled around, yelling to Rosana, Sora, all of the curious people who had come to see Coren's empty cot, before grabbing Lin's hand. Her face was streaked with tears, as they were sure theirs was, but a new sort of emotion had crept into her eyes.

"It's coming from the *Conpitum*." She said.

"Hurry." They broke into a run, dragging Lin behind them.

COREN REELED, A HEADACHE pounding in his temples as Kinaar drew her fingers away from his forehead.

Images flashed across his vision, memories of everything coming rushing back. Swords and blood, messages and elves, storms and sacrifice. And he now understood who Kinaar was.

He stood shakily, bowing his head before his patron goddess, and extending the hand that had once borne her Seal. "My Lady Kinaar. I am sorry I -"

She held up a hand, staying him. "Coren. You don't need to apologise. You saved us, you are alive, and that is all that really matters, no?"

"Of course." He murmured, keeping his gaze firmly pinned on the rock beneath his feet. This was all so much to take in, everything was moving so fast...

"I have to go soon, child. I have just one thing to ask of you." Kinaar said, and Coren finally met her eyes. She smiled, and this time her eyes showed the tiniest hint that it was real. "I would like to be your patron again, if you would accept the burden. I understand if what happened -"

"Yes." The word slipped out before he had thought everything through.

Kinaar stared at him, perhaps shocked that he had said yes, perhaps only startled that he had dared to interrupt.

Closing his eyes, Coren slowly began to piece his thoughts together. "I accept, Lady Kinaar, especially if it means I can keep protecting the people I love."

The goddess smirked and took his left hand, running her fingers across his palm, the same motion that she had made in that dream, so long ago.

The pain was as searing as it had been that first time, and Coren dropped to his knees, stars dancing behind his eyes as his veins caught fire for what was hopefully the very last time.

When his vision cleared, Kinaar was gone, and there were hundreds of people gathered on the shores of the lake, shouting something that sounded a lot like his name.

Epilogue

COREN LAUGHED, THROWING a berry at Rane's head. They ducked out of the way, snatching Lin's hand and glaring at Coren.

"Love, defend my honour!"

"Pfft, defend yourself." Lin smirked, shoving them.

Coren cackled, leaning back on his hands, the cold of the melting snow biting through his gloves. Kinaar was quiet in his head, letting him be for a while.

So much had happened in the last five months.

With the war over, everyone had returned to their home-lands with heavy hearts, mourning the loss of siblings, parents, and friends. The North and South, it's people awoken from their magickal sleep, had staked out new boundaries, as the West and East were gone forever. The battlefield where so many had fallen would forever remain sacred land, unsettled.

Someone tapped his shoulder, and Coren looked up at Myr, who dropped her baby girl, Thris, in his lap. He grinned and bounced the baby on his knee. "Where's Lana, Aunt?"

"Oh she's bothering one of the other mothers." Myr rolled her eyes, tightening the gold net around her bun. "She's always worrying."

"Aw, you're both great moms, Chieftainess." Rane chimed in, their eyes gleaming "I think that Lin's going to be the mom we're going to have to worry about. She'll be giving the kid knives from day one."

Lin growled in response, blushing.

"Lindara, how's Sioch doing?" Myr broke in, cocking her head curiously.

"Oh, he's doing great! He and Theodosia are in Laeris, I think, letting the horses rest."

Coren's cousin had begun training with the *malefica* Theodosia as soon as his wounds had healed, as magick shouldn't ever be left to go wild. His eyes had sustained serious damage, leaving him nearly blind, but he was excelling as a healer, eagerly learning anything Theodosia could teach him. Now the two of them were off to anywhere there had been rumours of human mages, trying to resurrect the dying art.

He was about to tell Lin to say hello to See for him, when Kinaar's voice rang loud in his head, making him wince.

Coren. There's something I must discuss with you.

"Coren?" Rane asked, a worried look crossing their face.

"It's Kinaar, I'm fine, don't worry." He said softly, handing the baby back to her mother, and slipping away into the woods. His family watched him go, and it took all he had to ignore their concern.

"Kinaar?" He asked as he walked, the glow of the campfires fading behind him.

My siblings are waking. She said, and he frowned.

"I thought they had been awake?"

No, child, they just regained the strength to wake after we took down my sister. They were lingering, asleep, but now they're waking, and Nyx has taken a ward.

"All right." Coren took a seat on a fallen log, fingers straying to the heavy scar at his throat at the mention of the war. "I'm sorry, but are we really supposed to be getting involved?"

Kinaar sighed. *She made a mistake, Coren. Her ward is confused, and has somehow blocked Nyx from her mind. She's going rogue, and of course, Nyx called on me to fix her mistake.*

"We're supposed to be a clean up crew?" He asked incredulously, biting back a laugh. Gods, were these deities flawed, he could really see it now.

The burdens of the eldest sibling. Kinaar sighed again. *We leave tomorrow.*

"Kinaar!" Coren said. "*Tomorrow?*"

Yes.

"We're the only ones who can deal with this."

Afraid so. Be packed by dawn. And then the goddess was gone.

Coren sighed, closing his eyes. He still remembered the smell of dust and warm grasses, the sounds of wildlife and the clatter of human markets, and he really did miss it.

His family's worried faces flashed in his head, and he sighed. They worried, perhaps for good reason. Maybe it would help if he travelled for a while, proving that he was truly all right.

Besides, as much as he loved being at home, he was a ward, he was supposed to help people. The North was settled, so maybe it really was time to move on.

Either way, it wasn't like Kinaar was giving him much of a choice.

"Fine Kinaar. I'll be ready."

The world was entering a new age of magick and gods, and it seemed that Coren would be on the forefront yet again.

A Guide to the Characters

- *Asoban & Kelaban of the Burning City*

  ○ *{AH-soh-baan, KEH-lah-baan}*

  ○ Asoban and Kelaban are drakon guards, sisters who patrol the borders of the drakon lands. Asoban has scarlet scales, while her sister has white ones. Otherwise, they are indistinguishable from one another.

- *The Bandit King*

  ○ The thief who took control of the Painted City, a once-grand desert city. He is vicious and cruel, and often holds ring fights for his own entertainment.

- *The Bandit Prince*

  ○ Aralie {AIR-ah-lee}, often just called the Prince, is the daughter of the Bandit King. She has less of a temper than her father, but is just as skilled at what she does.

- *Chieftain Rane of the South*

  ○ *{Rain}*

  ○ The Chieftain of the South. They are the youngest Chieftain that the four werecat bands have ever seen, taking the title at the age of sixteen. Their Shifted form is that of a clouded leopard.

- *Chieftainess Myr of the North*

  ○ *{Muhr}*

  ○ The Chieftainess of the North, with a leopard Shifted form. She led the North through the last half of the Twenty-Years-War with the South, and is Mai and Khara's older sister.

- *Coren of the North*

  ○ *{Kohrenn}*

  ○ The chronically anxious hero of our story. A Northern werecat, who can Shift into a lion. He is the ward of the goddess Kinaar.

- *Corrinne of Eire*

  ○ *{Kohr-RIN-eh}*

  ○ A maid and messenger in the underground city of Eire.

- *Farse of Corinnestāt*

  ○ *{FAR-seh}*

  ○ A vampire, and one of the *Medice* Racha's adopted sons.

- *Fyeren of the Faerie Empire*

  ○ *{FEE-air-enn}*

  ○ The Faerie guide who brings Coren and Rane to the well-hidden heart of the Faerie Empire: The Nameless City.

- *Heor of Corinnestāt*

  ○ *{HAY-ohr}*

  ○ Racha's half-Faerie adopted son.

- Imperator *Kalai of the Faerie Empire*

  ○ *{KAH-lie}*

  ○ The emperor of the Faerie Empire. While initially friendly-seeming, fae are anything but.

- Imperator *Quai of the Faerie Empire*

  ○ *{qu-AYE}*

  ○ The long-deceased Faerie emperor during the first Great War, and an ally to Rosana.

- *Kalien of the North*

  ○ *(kah-LEE-ehn}*

  ○ Coren's deceased father.

- *Khara of the North*

  ○ *{KAH-rah}*

  ○ Coren's aunt, Lin and Sioch's mother, and sister to Mai and Myr. Sadly, she is murdered at the very beginning of our story.

- *King Arthur of Wierna*

  ○ *{AHR-thur, Vee-err-nah}*

  ○ A legendary human king who fought beside Rosana during the Great War.

- *King Soer of Eire*

  ○ *{SEW-heir)*

  ○ Rosana's mentor, and the king before her.

- *Kir of the South*

  ○ *{Keer, sharp}*

  ○ Rane's jealous older brother. A traitor and a liar, who gets what's coming to him, in the end.

- *Kortana of the North*

  ○ *{KOHR-tah-nah}*

○ The Head of the Guard in the North, and a Councillor. She carries a deep grudge against Myr, and the power that the Chieftainess has.

● *Lady Forartha of the Cortach Range*

○ *{Fohr-ARTH-ah}*

○ The ruler of the werecats from before the bands split, and an ally of Rosana's during the first Great War.

● *Lady Sora of the Elven Territories*

○ *{Sohr-ah}*

○ The heir to the elven throne, and a powerful *Elementa Incendi.*

● *Lana of the North*

○ *{Lah-NAH}*

○ Myr's pregnant wife, whose even temper often helps keep Myr in check.

● *Leon of Corinnestāt*

○ *{LEE-on}*

○ *Medice* Racha's only human child, and the youngest boy.

● *Lin of the North*

○ *{Lin, short and sharp}*

○ Coren's cousin, twin sister and *comitis* to Sioch. Her Shifted form, like her brother, is a lynx.

● *Lord Aleixei of Eire*

○ *{Ah-LEIKS-ei}*

○ Queen Rosana's deceased husband.

● *Lord Elija of Eire*

○ *{EE-lie-jah}*

○ The elven guide, messenger, and trader who saved Coren's life.

● *Mai of the North*

○ *{Mai, short and sharp}*

○ Coren's deceased mother. Sister to Myr and Khara.

● *The* Malefica *Theodosia of Laeris*

○ *{Thee-oh-DOH-jah}*

○ An ancient healer and sorceress. She was Rosana's greatest ally and best friend during the first great war, and the witch who sang the *cantamen,* banishing Lady Chaos.

- *The Medice Racha of Corinnestāt*

  ○ *{RAH-chah}*

  ○ The best doctor in Corinnestāt, and one of the last practitioners of magick in Erathien. She is the adoptive mother of four orphaned children, three of which are magickal.

- *Prince Zephran of the Drakon Lands*

  ○ *{ZEF-ren}*

  ○ The heir to the drakon throne.

- *Queen Rosana of the Elven Territories*

  ○ *{Roe-SAH-nah}*

  ○ The queen of the elves, and an *Elementa Terra.* She was the one to gather the people of Erathien, and lead the army during the first Great War.

- *Queen Wyeran of the Drakon Lands*

  ○ *{WEE-air-ahn}*

  ○ The queen of the drakons, and the drakon lands.

- *Sioch of the North*

○ *{SEE-o-ch}*

○ Coren's cousin, and twin brother and *comitis* to Lindara of the North. Like his sister, he can Shift into the form of a lynx.

● *Valeria of Corinnestāt*

○ *{Vah-LEHR-ee-ah}*

○ A medusa, and the *Medice* Racha's only daughter.

● *Wrisan of the Burning City*

○ *{WREE-sahn}*

○ Advisor to Queen Wyeran of the Burning City.

A Guide to the Locations

- The Cortach Range - *Mountains in the centre of Erathien, home to four werecat groups*

  ○ The *Conpitum: The Crossroads, the lake and stone at the centre of the Cortach Range*

  ○ The North: *The northern region of the mountains, home to the Northern Band, which has multiple camps scattered throughout it.*

  ○ The South: *The southern region, home to the Southern Clan*

- The Drakon Lands - *Grasslands, home to drakons, wyverns, and everything in between*

  ○ The Burning City: *A beautiful cave city, full of strange creatures, glowing plants, and deep treasure troves. It tunnels through a deep chasm, and is home to the drakon nobility*

- The Elven Territories - *Although the territory is named home of the elves, the deep woods are home to much more dangerous monsters*

○ Eire: *The underground city that spreads beneath the forest. Little is known about it, and even less about its inhabitants, who went to ground hundreds of years ago.*

○ The Great Road: *The only place aside from Eire itself where you will be safe from the beasts in the wood*

● The Faerie Empire - *No one who comes out of Faerie is ever the same. Be careful.*

○ The Lake of Glass: *Syrens dwell there.*

○ The Nameless City: *No one is able to reach the capital city of Faerie without knowing its true name, and so it has forever been closed to most, its secrets kept locked within its high walls.*

● The Human Kingdoms - *Compared to the stability of the magickal races, human kingdoms are unstable, ever changing. They are beautiful though, and blanket the majority of Erathien.*

○ Corrinestāt: *One of the largest human-built cities, the city-state is a bustling centre of trade. It is safe for most, and a popular stop for travellers.*

○ Laeris: *Although officially governed by humans, the true rulers of the city at the Fae. Situated directly on the border between the Human Kingdoms and the Faerie Empire, it's not safe to stay in Laeris for very long.*

○ The Painted City: *Once a great centre of research for human mages, it has fallen into disrepair as magick faded from Erathien. Now the only residents of the desert city are the members of a violent gang of thieves, and their many prisoners.*

A Guide to the Old Language

ERATHIEN IS A LAND of many languages and dialects. Magickal races, such as the werecats, the elves, and the High Fae, speak the Old Language, which contains many dialects, and is the language of magick. While most magickal beings learn to speak at least two dialects, as well as the Common Tongue, humans are rarely familiar with more than the Common Tongue, due to the complexity and variation in the Old Language.

- *Acclaro / Acclarare / Acclaratus*

  ○ Manifested, used in reference to Lady Chaos's Wraiths

- *Cantamen / cantaminis*

  ○ Song-spell

- *Comes / Comitis*

  ○ Comrade, companion / comrades, companions

  ○ A term used for two people who share a mental bond, allowing them to share thoughts, emotions, and sometimes (in rare cases) senses

- The *Conpitum*

○ The Crossroads

○ The lake at the centre of the Cortach Range

● *Dea/Deae*

○ Goddess/goddesses

● *Delustro*

○ Disenchant

● *Divus/divi*

○ God/gods

● *Elementa / Elementae*

○ Elementalist / elementalists

○ *Anima*

▪ Air

○ *Terra*

▪ Earth

○ *Incendi*

▪ Fire

○ *Aqua*

- Water

- The *Evanida*

  - The Vanishing

  - When an elementalist's, or a ward's, power consumes them

- *Fatum*

  - Fate

- *Honoris*

  - The seal of a god or goddess, placed upon their ward. The mark glows or burns when the ward calls upon their godly power.

- *Illusio / Illusionis*

  - Illusion / illusions

- *Imperator*

  - Emperor

- *Incantatio / incantationis*

  - Incantation, spell

- *Medice* (fem.) / *Medens* (masc./neut.)

○ Doctor, physician, healer

● *Magia / magiae*

○ Magick / magicks

● *Malefica (Fem.) / Maleficus (masc./neut.) / Malefi-cae (Plu.)*

○ A word with many definitions: Usually sorceress or witch, but sometimes used in reference to herbalists, and seers

● *Patroni*

○ Patron god or goddess

● *Pupillus*

○ Ward of a god or goddess

● *Regina (fem.) / Rex (masc./neut.)*

○ Queen / King

● The *Rica*

○ The Veil. The magickal in-between between our world and the Void.

● *Signo*

○ Mark. The spirals that mark an *Elementa*'s skin when they use their powers. They extend further across an elementalists skin the more of their power that they use.

● The *Vacivus*

○ The Void. Lady Illira's kingdom, home of souls after their bodies pass on.

● *Visus*

○ The Sight, ability to see into the Veil and the Void

Acknowledgements

I STARTED THIS BOOK when I was ten or eleven years old. The story is not the same as it first was, and my characters have aged and changed with me, but they never would have had the chance to evolve if not for my wonderful support system.

So a big thank you goes to my friends (online and off, but especially the folks of TUFN and BQ!) who have proofread and listened to me hash out plot details over and over again, and to my family members, who have always encouraged my imagination, and my book addiction.

I love you guys so much and I have no idea where I'd be today if not for you.

Extra-special thanks goes to my dad, and friends from the Alpha Writer's Workshop, who gave me all the information I needed on publishing, and what makes a story a *story*.

And finally, thank you to the readers! This story is very close to my heart, and I hope that you love it as much as I do.

(IF YOU STUCK AROUND all the way to the acknowledgements and/or noticed the haiku in the dedication you get bonus points -)

[1] Some Fae, most notably the High Faeries, use formal pronouns (fae/faer/faers), which are used until they give you their personal pronouns. It is considered severely disrespectful to do otherwise.

(This use of pronouns is similar to the German formal you of our world)

About the Author

It's a secret, sorry folks...

However, if you're very determined, you can find them @achaoticfaerie on Instagram and TikTok, or send them an email at aspenirelandwrites@gmail.com !